TRAPPED ON TALONQUE

BY
VERONICA SCOTT

To my daughters Valerie and Elizabeth, my brother David
and my best friend Daniel
To Debbie N, friend for life!

Acknowledgments

Michael R

Joyce L

Julie C and The E-book Formatting Fairies!

CHAPTER ONE

At least you're not dead. You can handle a headache, even one that feels like your brain is slowly beating itself to a pulp inside your skull.

A guard interrupted Nate's stern internal lecture, poking him with a razor-sharp, gleaming spear tip. A thin line of red blood trickled down Nate's arm, mingling with the dried remnants of similar "encouragements" suffered over the course of the five days since his ship crashed on this hellhole planet.

He checked his peripheral vision to make sure Haranda was limping along, managing to keep his balance on the road's uneven stone paving. The way their captors had them restrained—arms bound tightly behind their backs, short metal shackles on the ankles, a chafing leather collar with a thin chain linking each man to the next at the neck—made walking a challenge. There were more prisoners at the end of the chain, locals, a few injured much more grievously than any of the offworlders but able to walk.

Stripped of their uniforms and made to wear the short kilt like all the other prisoners, Nate and his men had varying degrees of sunburn to contend with, but no serious physical impairments.

Unexpectedly, their progress stopped, and Nate crowded the local in front of him, nearly falling. Both men cursed in their respective languages, jerking apart as far as the thin neck chain allowed.

"What the seven hells—"

"Look ahead," Thom Curran said behind him. "I guess we know where we're going now."

Nate stared. The road had been curving uphill for the past few hours. Now he stood in a spot where the pavement widened beyond its average span of twenty feet, becoming a circle. Sheer cliffs rose above and fell precipitously away below the round platform. Across a wide ravine lay more heights, the pale stones of the road ascending in lazy curves and disappearing at the top, guarded at the crest by pillars or statues too far away to make out in detail.

And to get across the ravine—a swaying nightmare of a rope bridge, easily three hundred feet long. The cables appeared to be a mix of wool and plant fiber, tightly woven into massive supports suspended from towering masonry structures on either side of the chasm. The guards snarled orders, shoving their prisoners to the side of the platform against the cliffs, ordering them to sit.

"Have to wait our turn, I guess," Thom said, rubbing one ankle as he and Nate watched the bridge sway and twist while five locals, each leading a blindfolded riding animal, worked their way carefully across the span in single file, coming from the other side.

"At least we can see the damn thing is sturdy enough to hold that bunch, so it ought to hold us." Nate craned awkwardly to check on Haranda once more. "Doing okay, kid?"

The young pilot trainee swallowed convulsively and nodded before averting his gaze. The death of the more senior pilot and the events since the crash had left him in a precarious mental state.

Grateful for the chance to rest, Nate shrugged and watched the slow progress of the group on the bridge. Their captors had set a rapid pace, as if afraid to miss a deadline for their arrival at the ultimate destination.

Number one rule in the Sectors Special Forces—don't get up, close and personal with the residents of an unknown planet prior to a full eval, linguistic analysis, detailed observation from orbit...yeah, he'd managed to break about every regulation. Nate suspected he and his two companions were going to pay for the lapses in the near future. The Lords of Space threw the dice for a man and then left him to play the game out on his own. No help was coming from the Sectors. The ship and its passengers had probably been written off as lost by now.

"Are my eyes giving out, or is the sky going a little darker all the sudden?" Thom's query broke into Nate's reverie.

Squinting against the glare of the too-hot primary sun, he said, "A triple eclipse?" He risked one more quick glance. Three moons of varying dimensions were slowly edging their way onto the big, glaring disk of this planet's oversize sun. Nate lowered his eyes, checking the reactions of the other prisoners and the guards, all of whom were exhibiting various signs of unease. Many were mouthing chants or prayers. The eclipse increased the agitation of the officer leading their group. He advanced to the lip of the bridge and yelled at the oncoming cavalry, unmistakably exhorting them to move faster.

The last of the five riders cleared the bridge and removed the blindfold on his animal. Remounting, the squad thundered past, heading in the direction Nate and his companions had come from, the shod hooves of the horselike animals throwing sparks from the flat paving stones.

"Chika, chika!" the guards shouted, prodding the prisoners to their feet and into a rough line.

"Chika. Yeah, right, whatever you say," Nate muttered as the guard walked past him.

"I sure miss the hypno briefing on the damn language." Thom echoed Nate's frustration. "Not that we're exactly on a mission, or that the Sectors has a translator for this gibber."

"I think I got 'chika' translated, after five days of them screaming it at us. Means *jump and don't wait to ask how high*." Nate scrambled to his feet along with the rest of the long column.

The prisoners were strung together in chains of eight. The two groups ahead of Nate's moved out, clearing the bridge and marching up the mountain as he set foot on the woven structure. He couldn't help but admire the ingenious way the bridge was constructed of dark blue and yellow ropes woven together and triple-knotted tightly at regular intervals. Narrow boards had been inserted crosswise through the bottom set of ropes, making it necessary to step carefully from one to the next. Nate wished his hands were free so he could grasp the waist-high side ropes for extra stability. He had no fear of heights, and as he came onto the bridge, he glanced down. So far below that it was nothing but a narrow, shiny ribbon, the inevitable river flowed, its roar faint at this height. At the pull from the chain at his collar as the men in front of him stepped onward, Nate lifted his gaze, watching his step on the uneven, shifting floorboards.

He heard snatches of low conversation between several of the men chained in front of him. Despite the fact he didn't understand more than a few words of the local language, Nate tensed. The tone of the hasty whispers suggested action about to take place.

Bad place to stage a rebellion.

The man at the head of his set of eight prisoners yelled a defiant oath or a curse and threw himself off the right side of the bridge, tilting effortlessly over the rope and falling, taking the next two men with him in the blink of an eye. Man number four, directly in front of Nate, evidently wasn't part of the suicide pact, or lost his nerve, because as the others fell, the prisoner tried to pull back, bracing himself against the guard ropes. The chains and gravity threatened to take Nate, Thom, Haranda and the last prisoner behind him to the bottom of the ravine as well.

The prisoner's neck snapped with an audible crack, echoing eerily across the ravine, and his lifeless body jackknifed over the ropes. The other two men who'd already fallen were choking as the deadweight of the original suicide jumper pulled the leather collars taut. The bridge tipped sideways under Nate's feet from the unbalanced load. The ropes creaked ominously. Thom braced on the bridge behind him, trying to keep his feet without strangling Nate. The guards were shouting, trying to work their way along the bridge to the spot where the suicide attempt erupted.

Suddenly, the dead prisoner's center of gravity altered imperceptibly in response to the motion of the swaying bodies below. He fell off the bridge in graceful slow motion. The neck chain whipped taut on Nate, cutting off his air. The thin chain snapped off the thicker loop fastened to the collar at the base of Nate's throat, flying hundreds of feet into the ravine with the four dead men. The jagged end of the chain cut the underside of Nate's chin as it whipped past him. He doubled over the rope side rail, its knots digging into his stomach muscles. He could feel the pressure on his neck from the chain binding him to the sergeant and was thankful for it, steadying him even as it threatened to choke off his air.

"Take it real slow," Thom said.

Nate straightened carefully and shuffled his feet on the floorboard, retreating until he stood in the middle of the bridge. His head spun from lack of oxygen, and his peripheral vision flickered.

The guards grabbed his arms, urging him forward. The men supported him the rest of the way across the bridge, Thom and the others remaining on the string dragged behind. Nate was allowed to collapse onto the paved circle platform on the other side, bringing the others to their knees as he did so.

He lay on his side, chest heaving as he struggled to draw enough air into his lungs and recover from the near miss. The remaining strings of prisoners came across the bridge without further incident and were led along the curving road. The entire train of prisoners disappeared from sight by the time the guards decided Nate must be recovered and yanked him to his feet. The officer in charge eyed Nate for a long moment, fingering the broken link on his collar thoughtfully. Then he spun on his heel, yelling the now familiar order to move out.

"Chika! Chika!"

Nate and his companions toiled up the curving road to the crest of the hill. As he passed between the guardian statues, Nate studied the one on his right. Standing double his height, it was a crude representation of a warrior. Nate realized the deity clutched a braided skein of scalps in each of its four hands, from which were suspended eight bleeding heads. Huge clawed feet trod on a carpet of bones and skulls.

"Huitlani." The prisoner at the end of their shortened chain gave a name to the horror. Nate turned his head and met the man's eyes. The captive, Atletl, spat at the statue and let loose a string of what sounded like curses as he walked between the statues. This defiance brought him harsh blows from the officer in charge, and Atletl fell silent under the onslaught.

The road widened substantially and became more crowded the closer the column came to the city on the plain beyond the ridge. Foot and vehicle traffic proceeded in both directions. The prisoners were kept to the edge of the pavement and given no chance to rest or slacken their pace.

"Always in a hurry on this damn planet, ain't they?" Thom made his complaint after a renewed burst of prodding from the soldiers.

"The eclipse is ending," Nate said, taking a rapid glance at the giant sun. "Too bad—my headache was doing better."

"Next time we evac a crashed ship on an uncharted world, I'll be sure to grab the headclear for you." Thom assumed a tone of mock deference.

"I'm surprised it's not prominently featured in the regs." Nate managed a tired grin. A good sign if Thom had enough energy left to joke.

There was a brief halt at the gate to the city, while the officer in charge held an animated discussion with the guards and then the squad was waved through, moving deeper into the city. The pace slowed, due to the throngs of people clogging the streets.

"We seem to be a curiosity." Nate watched how the crowds parted and people stared and muttered together as he and the others marched past.

The guards didn't appreciate their talking, jabbing at them with the butts of their spears, so Nate fell silent. A huge, walled compound appeared to be the destination, its guardstands adorned with green and black flags bearing a stylized bird of prey. The prisoners were marched along the base of the wall for a few hundred yards before coming to an open gate guarded by an alert cadre of warriors and two more horrific representations of Huitlani.

"Bad sign." Thom jerked his head sideways at the statue nearest him.

The guards hustled them into the compound, entering a narrow, whitewashed corridor beyond the gate.

Suddenly, Nate emerged from the confined space, stumbling into a brightly lit chamber. He stopped short, blinking furiously at the stark sunlight. Even in the late afternoon, this no-name planet's hot white star was too harsh once the multiple eclipse by the trio of moons concluded. The light made Nate's headache flare in a wave of hot pain across his forehead.

As he blinked, eyes watering, trying to adjust his eyesight, he realized he stood at the edge of a throng of what had to be the upper crust of this planet's society. Dressed more richly than anyone he'd seen so far, the crowd was a sea of color in jewel-tone robes. The men wore elaborate feather headdresses rising easily a yard into the air and heavy, broad gold and silver collars lavishly set with jewels. The women wore filmy, pastel robes and more gold and jewels, casting rainbows in the sun's glare. Drawing back as if afraid to touch the newcomers, the nobles whispered and pointed.

Hampered by the chains, Nate walked through the courtyard as best he could, ringed by the military escort, whose demeanor took on a certain strut of pride. Out of the glare of late afternoon sunlight at the far end of the room, Nate made out the details of a raised dais and several ornately carved thrones. Trained to observe details and build a strategic assessment, he tried to concentrate despite his raging headache and figure out what he might be dealing with here. Was there any possibility of escape or bettering the situation for his men and himself?

Too many guards, alert for a move from us.

He strove to relax his muscles, give off a nonthreatening air, hoping to lull the soldiers into overconfidence. Give Thom and him a fair chance and they'd put up a fight. The chain dragging at his ankles reminded him of the overwhelming odds.

The larger throne was occupied by a man with a truly awe-inspiring scarlet and black headdress that rose from a golden crown. Leaning forward as the prisoners came closer, this personage clutched a thick, golden staff, a carved bird of prey adorning the top. The man's face reminded Nate of the bird—cruel, harsh, deeply lined, with glittering black eyes. Jagged red scars ran across his forehead and left cheek.

The guards shoved Nate and the others to their knees, adding painful bruises to his already plentiful crop. A gruff command from the figure on the throne had the guards yanking Nate and his companions back to their feet.

Leaning on the staff, the official descended the three steps from the dais. Two women dressed in somber black robes followed him. Nate stood at attention while the noble and the women circled him and his men. Silently, the man studied the prisoners. Chattering between themselves excitedly, the women waved heavy feather fans. Each lady had ebony black hair slicked back in an elaborate chignon, a heavily painted face, glittering gems set at the ears and long diamond-crusted pendants between generous breasts. Heavy floral and spice perfume assaulted his nose as the pair examined him, making him long for a breath of fresh air.

A younger woman in translucent pale green and lavender robes stood off to the side, eyeing the prisoners curiously, but timidly, as if afraid to come any closer, or to interfere with the trio. Nate kept glancing at her because she was in such contrast to the other women. Her dress was encrusted with colored bead work in floral patterns, but at the hem was a swirling depiction of blue and scarlet serpents. Her brown hair hung loose, save for two dainty braids framing her face. She'd no jewelry, no feather fan or other accessories. Unaccountably, Nate had the feeling she was the only person in the room sympathetic to their plight.

But obviously powerless to help.

Dismissing the lady as a possible ally, he focused on the lively discussion off to the side.

The ruler snapped question after question at the officer who'd first captured them. Nate detected a family resemblance between the noble and the man he was grilling, but the man in charge didn't appear satisfied with any of the answers he received, kinsman or no. In five days and nights of captivity, Nate had picked up a smattering of the local language but not nearly enough to follow the rapid question-and-answer session.

A new woman arrived, emerging from the palace and walking to join the noble, placing her arm possessively around his waist. Head tilted imperiously, her white-painted lips set in a thin, straight line, she listened to the discussion in silence. Nate met her eyes briefly before she contemptuously tossed her head and centered her attention on the gesticulating officer. She took a few steps forward, one hand raised to silence the ongoing briefing. Standing in front of Nate, forcing the protesting officer to move aside, she cupped Nate's chin with one hand, nothing gentle about the gesture. Her long fingers were tipped like talons, with long, curved, purple-gray painted nails resting on his cheek with a clearly implied threat. He glared at her, attempting to communicate his defiance through his expression and stance. Still holding his chin, she asked the officer a question, which he hastily answered. The woman released Nate's chin but ran one hand through his hair, caressingly, down the back of his neck and onto his bare chest. Her touch burned his skin. He wondered if she had poison painted on her nails.

As if impatient with her inspection, the ruler fired a question at Nate in a dialect unlike anything he'd heard on this planet. Shaking his head, he said, "Sorry, not a language I speak."

There was an indrawn hiss of breath from those closest to the man in charge. He recoiled a few inches, wide-eyed, mouth open in excitement. *Fear. Why would anyone be afraid of us, especially chained the way we are? How do I use this?*

The woman stalked in a circle, studying Thom and Harada, peering closely at their faces. When she came to Atletl, she laughed, shaking her head. Taking the officer by the elbow, she engaged him in rapid conversation.

Atletl stood motionless, his demeanor proud. Obviously, he understood the discussion regarding their fate, but whether it was good or ill, he gave no sign. Nor did he speak.

Finally, the soldier grabbed Atletl's left arm and tugged the prisoner sideways a few steps, imploring the haughty noblewoman to examine him more closely. Nate tried to see what the item of interest might be. A tattoo on Atletl's well-muscled bicep in the shape of a small, stylized reptilian creature in blue and scarlet inks was the focus of attention. The symbol matched the decoration on the young priestess's dress. Rival deities perhaps?

"T'naritza," the officer said insistently, tapping one finger on the tattoo. He waved his other hand to take in Nate and his men, including them in this designation.

Elegant eyebrows raised, the woman nodded. She spoke to the man in charge, and the two of them paced hand in hand to the thrones, seating themselves. Chin resting on his fist, the ruler took a pinch of a pale green substance from a platter at his side and chewed lazily as he studied Nate, Haranda and Thom for a long moment. Raising the staff, the dignitary made a lazy circle in the air above his head, a gesture of dismissal accompanied by one curt syllable from fleshy lips. The crowd filed silently out of the courtyard.

"Wish I had a clue what they want from us," Nate said, more to break the uncanny silence than for any other reason.

"Maybe we don't really want to know." Thom straightened. "These primitive planets have pretty unpleasant ways of dealing with unexpected guests."

The black-clad ladies—the ones Nate thought of as birds of prey—conferred with the ruler. Face set in a disapproving frown, the lavender lady listened. After issuing a flurry of orders to the women, the queen gathered her skirts and departed. As she left, the noble rose, striding to the rear of the dais. He shoved aside the impressive black leather curtains, ruthlessly crumpling an embossed mountain scene, and disappeared. The guards pushed the prisoners to the rear of the dais and through the same curtains. Nate found himself in another narrow, whitewashed corridor. The guards administered rough encouragement to pick up the pace and follow the ruler more closely. The three women trailed along in the rear, the two in black whispering together unhappily.

This new corridor twisted and turned. After two moments or so, the procession branched off into a smaller side hall, dead-ending in a chamber lit by sluggishly burning torches.

"Must be deep inside the building by now," Haranda said. "We've been descending steadily since we left the main corridor. These walls are like geological layers, remnants of older and older buildings. Typical, to place new construction on top of the original structures. Like going back in time."

Thanks for the archaeological footnote, kid. Wish any of that analysis would help me figure out a way for us to escape. Nate blinked and focused on the wall in front of them. As his overworked pupils expanded in the soothing balm of relatively dim light and the throbbing pain in his head eased, he perceived the wall had an elaborate set of designs carved into it. The two women in black elbowed their way past the prisoners and guards and chanted a sonorous set of phrases over and over. The noble walked to the wall and began placing his hands on various portions of the carving in a highly stylized, ritualistic manner in time with the rise and fall of the chanting. Making a double fist, he pressed on a portion of the carving.

A chiming sound emanated from everywhere. A green glow shimmered over the whole party for a long moment. Fat snakes of pure light crawled over them all and winked out, reappearing elsewhere in the narrow space. The guards flinched apprehensively, although the ruler and all three women appeared comfortable with the phenomenon. *They've obviously done this before.* Nate blinked, flinching involuntarily as the green lights crawled over his face and scalp. He realized his headache was gone.

"What the—"

The carved white wall slid aside.

Under pressure from the guards, he went farther downward, through a narrow, sloping, nearly pitch-black corridor. Nate wished for more room to maneuver, sure he and Thom could take the local men with a small amount of luck, but no chance presented itself.

The narrow corridor opened into a bigger chamber, at first also only dimly lit, but Nate realized the light was increasing gradually, subtly. A smooth, darkly gleaming black stone wall faced them. About seven feet high and ten feet wide, it was translucent, but squint though he might, Nate couldn't make out what lay behind.

After clearing his throat, the ruler chanted three words, trying to artificially pitch his voice to an unnatural high note. When nothing happened, he and the two black-clad women exchanged resigned glances before he made another attempt, enunciating more clearly in an ear-splitting falsetto.

Nothing.

Wheeling to his right, the man grabbed the elbow of the young woman in lavender, shoving her to the front, inches from the wall blocking their way.

She licked her thin lips nervously and launched into a chant. The syllables sounded the same, but her voice gave them clarity and a musical pitch, showing how far off the mark the ruler's attempt must have been from the required tones.

The stone door vibrated, emitting a musical hum, and then the black stone barrier vanished as if it had never been there in all its tons.

Nate gasped at the sight before him.

He stood on the edge of a high-tech chamber out of place on a primitive world such as this one. Ringing the room were strange displays, blinking lights, roving green beams, unknown instruments. The sophistication of the technology was well beyond anything the Sectors had achieved, let alone the dwellers of this planet. Nate spared only a second to glance at these wonders. His attention was caught and held by what occupied the center of a large alcove directly across the room.

The cubicle was lined in shiny metallic material and from the floor rose a graceful pedestal of the same material, topped with a thin platform at waist level. Neatly arranged on a layer of dark purple padding lay a woman, apparently asleep. She certainly wasn't from this planet, nor any world known to Nate. This mysterious female had ivory skin with the palest of lavender undertones in her cheeks.

"I'll be moon-damned." Thom's attention was riveted on the sleeper as well. "An Ancient Observer?"

"Can't be—no one's ever found actual remains," Haranda said from the other side. "Although this room certainly suggests a high level of technology, it's not AO. Another sophisticated, highly advanced forerunner civilization. The galaxy is a big place after all." Roused from his state of funk, he studied the walls, apparently more interested in the devices and displays than in the woman. "I minored in AO studies at the Academy."

"I don't think she's a well-preserved corpse." Nate couldn't take his gaze from her, not even to watch what their captors were doing now. He took himself sharply to task for the lapse. *What if we've been brought here as a sacrifice?* He had to be mentally prepared to fight, not gawk at a pretty girl. But the next moment he found himself studying her again, unable to keep himself from indulging in another view.

The woman was tall, probably his equal in height, definitely humanoid. She lay pillowed on her own hair, a thick, sweeping fall of glorious blue mixed with amethyst purple, set here and there with twinkling jewels. From his location across the room, he couldn't see whether she was breathing, yet he had a definite sense of a living presence.

Her clothing was a simple, silvery white and lavender sheath, like finely woven metallic thread had been spun to make the dress. Thin jeweled straps held the garment at her shoulders. The finely pleated fabric clung to her curves sensuously. She lay on her back, arms stretched out a little on each side, her graceful, six-fingered hands spread open on the cushion. She wore no jewelry save for an elaborate bracelet on her left wrist, studded with colorful stones whose facets caught and amplified the lights in the main room.

Grimacing, the woman arched her spine as if in pain, moving her head on the pillow restlessly.

"What the—" Nate swiveled his head and saw the noble flipping small jeweled medallions set into one of the wall panels.

Apparently remaining unconscious, the woman struggled to raise her hands from the bedding, her face contorted. A harsh chiming emanated from the walls, as if warning against whatever procedure he'd initiated. Undeterred despite a second sirenlike sound joining the cacophony, the noble finished his task with a satisfied grunt. The black-clad priestesses seemed to want him to stop, one going so far as to touch his sleeve before being impatiently shaken off.

The lavender-clad lady cowered at the far wall, covering her ears and crouching pathetically.

Nate's head suddenly filled with fire, and then icy cold replaced the heat, a piercing pain shooting through his entire nervous system from the top of his brain, along his spine and out to peripheral nerve endings. He fell to his knees, dragging the other three prisoners with him, exclaiming curses in their surprise. Barely hanging on to consciousness, Nate fought the alternating hot and cold waves and the associated pain in his head. Dazzling streaks and multicolored pinwheels obscured his vision, staying even though he screwed his eyes tightly shut.

"Sicondame sliquon…" came a deep, female voice from all around them.

Nate raised his head, eyes tearing, staring at the woman on the table. *Is that her voice? How can she sound so calm under apparent torture?*

The alarms and klaxons abruptly shut off. Nate's ears rang with the aftereffects of the discordant noises.

Hands on his hips, the noble nodded and made a declaration to the priestesses in a tone conveying satisfaction.

Nate shook his head again as the guards impatiently yanked him to his feet. The soldiers tugged at him and the other three prisoners, indicating their time in the chamber of the sleeping lady was at an end. He twisted to catch one last glimpse of her in the gradually fading light.

She opened her eyes, looked directly at him, and in his head he heard two words. *I'm sorry.*

"She must have been lying there for centuries, maybe thousands of years, judging from the multiple layers of building remnants we passed through on our downward trek. You expect us to believe she spoke to you? And apologized in Basic?" Haranda's voice conveyed his skepticism. "Captain, whatever equipment was running in the room obviously affected you—"

"I know what I heard." Nate decided to ignore the edge of insubordination in the cadet pilot's voice in the interest of discussing the phenomenon. "The private communication was the same female voice speaking out loud in the room, so what I heard in my head had to be her."

"Maybe close to a language you were hypnotrained for on a past mission?" Thom asked. "I admit this local stuff don't activate any of my stored files."

Nate shook his head. "Basic. She spoke Basic to me. Now how could an alien woman entombed here all this time know Basic?"

Thom shrugged. "I got no answers. She's a mystery stashed in a puzzle box, but we don't exactly have the luxury of studying her. We gotta concentrate on our own problems. Better get some rest. No telling what new surprise they'll have for us in the morning. Are you going to finish your bowl of mush?"

"No, you're welcome to it." Nate pushed the offending red clay bowl along the stony floor to Thom, straining against the chains binding him to the wall. They were in a big room with enough space for fifty more captives without crowding. The only light came through widely spaced, narrow slits in the wall near the ceiling as the sun set.

Nate sighed and tried to get comfortable, leaning against the rough stone wall. At least his headache was gone, possibly cured by the restorative effect of the few crumbs of dinner, or the mildly alcoholic beverage served with it. Nate drank his fair share once he realized it was an intoxicant, however low a dose. Anything to ward off a rebound of the pounding in his head. Not to mention the excruciating pain of returning circulation in his arms once he'd been freed from the restrictive bindings and locked into a looser set of chains attached to the prison wall.

Battered and bruised, he drifted into a troubled sleep.

He stood wreathed in gray-green mists coiling around him like the ghosts of snakes before falling away to reveal the mysterious subterranean room deep under the palace. He faced the sleeping woman. Finding himself unrestrained, Nate descended the three stairs and walked across the chamber until he stubbed his toe against an invisible but potent barrier. Trying to reach through or past this obstacle, Nate saw his hands outlined in pale green light. He shoved harder. If he could just reach her, wake her, ask her a few pointed questions… As if sensing his efforts, she moved her head on the mattress and opened her eyes, revealing dark lavender irises flecked with gold.

"I *am* sorry," she said, clear as day, in Basic.

But no, Nate realized, he heard the words in his mind, not with his ears. Her lips moved, but not to shape the syllables he heard.

"Sarbordon thinks you and I are of the same people. Therefore, what he wants lies outside your power to provide," she said, as if the piece of confusing information would help him navigate the perilous situation.

"Why are you sorry?" Nate stayed with her first words to him. "You've done nothing to harm us."

"I pity anyone trapped here on this cursed planet. The king will sacrifice you to his hungry gods when you don't produce the miracles he expects. *Demands.* I—I didn't tell him the truth when he asked." Brow furrowed, she studied Nate's face. Biting her lower lip, she said, "Honesty on my part would have brought instant death for you. He believes you're my father's warriors, come to rescue me, so I agreed with his conclusion. I said you were also sent to retrieve certain possessions. He's desperate to acquire the marvels my father wielded. My deception may give you time, perhaps a chance to save yourselves." She studied him from head to toe, and her lips curved into a slight smile. "You have the attitude of a warrior, one able to survive. You must play the game." After a moment, she averted her gaze, but Nate still heard her next words. "Sarbordon will bring you here again if you earn the privilege. If you can survive to that point, I may have a plan, a chance for you to seize freedom. I can't promise."

He was woozy, possibly an aftereffect of the wine with dinner. Maybe the drink had been laced with a primitive drug. His powers of concentration were affected, and frustration with his uncharacteristic lack of focus built. "What's your name?"

This vision he was having was dangerously fascinating, and he wished it were real. No one had ever even seen a representation of a living Ancient Observer, much less conversed with one. He accepted Haranda's educated assessment that she wasn't a member of the mysterious race of galactic forerunners from a million years ago, but the way her chamber was encapsulated deep in the palace, as if the building had grown organically to house her, spoke of centuries, if not millennia, passing since she was placed in her high-tech prison. The equipment must have kept her alive, but why was she here in the first place?

The incongruity of trying to solve her puzzle while his life and the lives of his men hung in the balance made him shake his head. This was one hell of a dream, built on his fascination with her earlier in the day.

"We're not dreaming." Seizing on his unspoken thought, she denied his conclusion scornfully, staring at him with wide-eyed contempt. "I *dream* only of death. We're communicating. Perhaps your people are too primitive for the concept, fallen from the sky or not."

She was fading in front of his eyes, the edges of the scene going fuzzy and black. Nate focused on the pale oval of her face. "Tell me your name." He wanted the conversation to continue, intent on coaxing her to keep her eyes open. He feared when she slept, his dream would end.

"These fools call me T'naritza, the Sleeping Goddess." The woman's tone held disdain and dislike. "It will do—"

"Tell me your real name." If there was any chance this encounter was real, rather than a dream, he wanted to make a connection with her, convert her view of them from unfortunate beings to be pitied into allies. He'd clearly lost ground with her when he called their link a dream. She might represent a slim chance of escape. Apparently, she'd already interceded for them to a limited extent.

His use of his command voice to issue an order brought her back for a second from the brink of nodding off. Blinking, she focused on Nate's face. "What will my name do for you, unfortunate one?"

"We're both captives. We should be friends. Is a mere name so much to ask? I'm Nate Reilly."

There was silence while her eyelids flickered heavily, like those of a sleepy child. The curling lashes brushed her cheeks as her eyes closed, then opened briefly. She sighed. "Bithia. My name of birth is Bithia. But a name has no magic to help you—"

It was a whisper floating into his mind at the same instant the dream ended. Nate jerked upright, startled awake by the abrupt loss of the images beguiling him. Thom grunted, shifting uneasily on the rancid straw serving as bedding, but didn't waken. Haranda snored.

Eyes gleaming in the dark, Atletl watched him in the dim moonlight, a strangely satisfied expression on his face. He pointed at Nate and then indicated the tattoo on his arm. Nate recalled how fascinated the ruler and the women had been by the man's inked artwork earlier. "T'naritza," he said with a nod.

Nate settled against the wall, determined not to examine the recent dream too closely.

"Bithia," he murmured, pleased by the sound of her name. Assuming he'd experienced a form of actual mind-to-mind communication, then her instant decision to lie on their behalf had bought precious time, maybe even a chance to escape—Nate couldn't argue with her choice. Trying to think of how to leverage the tiny bits of information he now had, he fell asleep again.

CHAPTER TWO

In the morning, Nate roused from a deep, dreamless state when the guards crashed the door open. There were more soldiers this morning, lined up across the room, at ease against the opposite wall, not bothering the prisoners. The sweet-faced priestess with the braids came in, dressed today in pale green with touches of lavender at the collar and hem. Followed by two servants, she supervised the serving of hot, steaming mush into the four bowls. Each prisoner received a small cup of water, a hard roll and two pieces of fruit as well.

"Generous this morning, aren't they?" Thom sniffed at the steaming mush and made a face. "Hope we can eat this stuff."

"Scans showed this planet to be within the acceptable ranges." Haranda bit into a purple fruit dripping juice. "If the locals can eat it, we probably can too. Mmm, tangy."

"Food poisoning wouldn't be my preferred way off this rock." Nate searched for an unbruised section of the fruit on his tray. "Maja—thank you," he said to the priestess as she handed him a roll.

She inclined her head graciously and shyly, the two braids falling across her cheeks. She unleashed a breathless explanation, of which Nate understood only the word *T'naritza*.

"We've got to get up to speed on this language," he said, gazing speculatively at Atletl, who was flirtatiously exchanging words at great length with the lady until a guard intervened. "I'm thinking he's going to have to do emergency tutoring here."

"Didn't hear him volunteer." Thom took a heaping serving of mush. "Don't they have eggs on this damn planet? All those bird feathers yesterday, you'd think the cook would serve eggs."

Ignoring the banter over food, Nate said, "He's linked with us now, one way or the other. I'm hoping he's a smart enough guy to recognize the situation and want to be useful." He looked at his partially eaten piece of fruit and winced, setting the rough wooden plate aside. The idea of eating more overripe fruit made his stomach heave, but the hard roll and the cooked cereal went down well enough. He felt slightly hungover, but thankfully the headache was only a dull echo of yesterday's monster.

The guards were impatient, talking among themselves and checking fitfully on the prisoners' progress on their rations. The squad leader waited until Nate and his men had eaten most of their breakfast. Then he issued a flurry of orders resulting in the four men each being locked into a new set of chains that allowed more mobility than the ones they'd endured since falling into captivity. While the new shackles were a definite improvement in comfort over yesterday's, the design was secure against easy escape.

The priestess watched this with a faint air of sadness on her face. She was definitely not in accord with how the prisoners were being treated. Where exactly did she fit into the whole scheme of things? Could she be an ally? Seeing him watching her, she flashed him a quick smile and then left, taking her servants with her.

"Something's up," Nate said as he and his men were herded into the hall. "Maybe we have to start earning our keep today?"

"Where did our guardian priestess go?" Thom checked the corridor in both directions, but she and her two companions were gone from sight.

"Celixia." Atletl took Nate by surprise with his pronouncement. He made mock motions of braiding hair. "Celixia."

"Well, we're learning one thing at a time here—guess the good witch is Celixia," Thom said as he shuffled through the corridor next to Nate. "Wonder if he knows what she wants with us?"

"Maybe we'll find out," Nate said.

The next event on the agenda was an unchained, closely guarded plunge into a cold, communal bathing pool and a change of clothes. Their dusty, tattered blue kilts were taken away by a servant while they were toweling off. Another brought four identical piles of garments, placing a set at each prisoner's feet.

"Let's see what the fashionable prisoner wears to the palace. Thom held up a serviceable gray sleeveless tunic and a pair of loose pants, loincloth and sandals. "Oh man, harsh, like this stuff is made out of tree bark."

"Woven plant fibers most likely." Nate flipped his new shirt over, preparing to pull it over his head, and paused, fingering a large symbol painted on the front in glaring red pigment. "What do you imagine this stands for?"

"Not going to blend into the crowd with this, are we?" Thom plucked at the symbol on his. "Mine probably stands for extra-large." He winked.

"My guess is more along the lines of 'poor dumb fools too stupid not to get captured in the first five moments on the planet.'" Nate's reply was good-natured. Food, a bath and more favorable treatment gave him hope for opportunities to figure out an escape. Their captors might grow lax.

"All that in one symbol?" Thom asked. "Elegant language on this planet."

"Will you two shut up?" Haranda yelled at them. "Stop it. Who cares what the damn symbol means? Big tough Special Forces operators, cracking jokes all the time. Well, this isn't funny in any respect I can see—"

"You're way out of line," Thom said, moving closer to the cadet. "You think I'm getting on your nerves? You ain't seen anything yet. Keep bitching and moaning, flyboy. You and the late Jurgens got us into this damn mess in the first place."

Nate cut the sergeant off with a shake of his head. "I've had enough of your defeatist attitude," he said, admonishing the young pilot. "We aren't going to get out of this situation by giving up and making it easy on these people to slaughter us. You have to keep your spirits good and your eyes open. Be observant, watch for anything we can use, an edge, a way to get the better of—"

"So knowing the meaning of this one lousy symbol will set us free? I think the damn alien machinery in the basement played with your mind. Sir."

Nate and Thom exchanged glances. The stress of their captivity was adversely affecting Haranda, and his precarious mental state could endanger them all at a critical moment.

But before Nate could call Haranda to order again, he hung his head. "I'm sorry, sir, it's just I never expected anything like this to happen, not to me." His voice scaled higher on the last word, but Nate decided to ignore the hint of hysteria. He reached over and punched the younger man's shoulder.

"At least you got us to the surface in one piece. Stick with us, and we'll get you offworld again, I promise." Having donned the loincloth, Nate pulled on the loose pants, tied the rope belt and started working on the fastenings of the sandals.

"Yeah, been through worse any number of times," Thom chimed in, recognizing his cue, as Nate knew he would.

"This type of situation is the reason I didn't join the damn ground troops," Haranda said, kicking at his pile of clothing. "Survey duty was supposed to be easier—observe the planets, take measurements, stay out of trouble with locals."

"Don't believe what the recruiters tell you, son." While delivering the belated advice, Thom rolled his eyes at Nate.

Not too surprising to find Special Forces and Survey weren't on the same page. Are we ever? He and Thom would do everything in their power to bring Haranda through this catastrophic, unintended contact mission in one piece. "Better hurry getting dressed," he said to the pilot. "Before our minders get impatient."

The guards hadn't paid too much attention to all this byplay between the three Sectors soldiers while they were dressing. Haranda hastened to pull on his new clothes. Already done, Atletl leaned on the wall, arms folded, listening to Nate, Thom and Haranda. His attention flicked from face to face, as if trying to assess the men he'd been thrown together with, since he was apparently to live or die as they did.

The guards locked the chains onto each prisoner carefully, as if expecting resistance. Nate calculated the odds, given the large squad of soldiers surrounding them this morning, and decided this wasn't the time to make a break.

Nate and his men were escorted into the main corridor. Bearing to the right, the group made good time through endless hallways. He kept a mental map so he could find his way through these corridors if ever given a chance. The excursion took them a long way from the cellblock.

Emerging into blazing sunlight, he found himself at the top level of a huge natural amphitheater. The place was filling with chattering, excited people, although no one ventured into the area where the prisoners were directed to sit. Nate took his seat on a hard stone bench with an unobstructed view of a rectangular playing field. The walls were lined in smooth stone, red veined against dark green and black. There were five small openings in the wall opposite them, set in no obvious pattern, spaced about fifteen yards apart. One was low on the wall, three close to the top and the fifth at knee height at the other end. Nate judged the entire court was probably seventy yards long. He leaned over and found an identical set of openings in the wall below him.

Play the game, she said. Had Bithia meant a real game?

The crowd was restless. Occasionally, someone would cheer or chant, which would be taken up by others and then slowly die out.

Thom nudged Nate in the ribs. "Over there on the other side. Isn't that our pal from yesterday? The head honcho himself?"

"Sarbordon." Nate filled in the ruler's name from his dream. Ignoring Thom's puzzled glance, he stared across the sandy court at the ruler settling himself in the center of a royal enclosure that featured more elaborate seats. The noble raised his arms, and the crowd screamed approval.

"Guess we're in the cheap seats," Thom said as he surveyed their side of the court, where all the fans were dressed in clothing not much fancier than their own prison garb.

Haranda touched his arm. "These people are keeping us alive to make us watch games? What's your guess, sir?"

"No idea. Beats dying." Nate shrugged. "I hope we don't have to sit in this damn sun too long. Gives me one hell of a headache."

"There's our Celixia." Thom pointed across the playing field.

"Along with the bitch queen herself and her attendant birds of prey. I wish to hell I knew where we fit in, where this is going," Nate said. Annoyed at his lack of usable intel, he assessed Atletl, waving jauntily in an apparent attempt to get Celixia's attention. "I think he knows what's going on, but this language barrier between us is a definite issue."

"As long as he doesn't panic, I guess I won't worry either," Thom said.

"Good plan."

"Here come the players." Haranda gestured at the far end of the field below.

The ensuing game was exciting, engaging Nate's attention despite the circumstances. Opposing teams of four players each strove to capture a black leather ball as it shot at random, apparently, from one of the wall openings. The men fought to ram the sphere into one of the openings on the other side of the court. The other team did its best to steal the ball and inflict maximum damage on the other players in the process. Violence and aggression met with roaring approval from the crowd.

The game progressed rapidly, limited to three scores. Whenever one team or the other managed to get three balls into the wall despite the defenders' best efforts, the proceedings came to a halt. The winning team paraded around the court, arms held high, accepting the cheers of the crowd, eventually moving out of sight into the holding area under the amphitheater. The four members of the losing team were dragged to the middle of the sand and knelt in a line, facing the king and queen.

As the last man on the winning team left the arena, a complete hush fell over the crowd. A quartet of black-clad priestesses escorted by guards marched onto the court. Moving quickly, each woman looped a heavy golden chain over the head of an unresisting player before leading him out through a different exit. Servants carried anyone too injured to walk.

Groundskeepers emerged to rake the sand, hiding the bloodstains from the rough play of the previous round. The crowds fell to animated chatter and wagering, coins changing hands. Servants brought the nobility refreshments. Harsh-voiced vendors hawked food and drink on the commoners' side. At first nothing was offered to the prisoners, although their guards accepted free drinks from vendors willingly enough. Later in the afternoon, as the games continued, two servants appeared with flagons of watered wine. Nate recognized them as Celixia's assistants from earlier in the day when she'd brought them breakfast.

He took his flagon and tried to identify her in the glittering crowd of nobility across the way. Catching her eye, he rose, lifted the container as if to make a toast and then drank. She nodded her head slightly before one of the black-robed priestesses reprimanded her, gesticulating in the direction of the prisoners. The guards hastened to make Nate sit and took away his now empty mug.

"Doesn't bode well for the losers, you think?" Thom asked as the same grim ending repeated after each round.

Nate shook his head. "Our captor has to be showing this to us for a reason. Are you paying close attention? I'm watching for any kind of strategy at work, or is victory obtained primarily by brute force? I thought I noticed a pattern to the passing, especially when the red team was working their last ball."

"You think we're going to be the visiting team?"

Nate sighed and stretched as far as the chains allowed, settling on the bench with a satisfied chuckle as he realized the guards were getting nervous. "Not today, I hope. But why else drag us out here?"

"Reminds me of soccer, or Betyran tisba," Haranda said, clearly enjoying himself.

"You play?" Nate asked.

"Tisba. I was lead wing on the varsity team at the Star Guard Academy, two years running."

"Don't get cocky," Thom said. "I don't think you had the same kind of rules. The Sectors Star Guard generally doesn't want its recruits killing each other. These guys are out for blood."

The day stretched on. Nate watched four more matches, each as rapid and as brutally played as the first two. The final match was played late in the afternoon, and the team in red shirts and shorts was clearly the crowd favorite as the chanting rose to a high volume. "Do you think Kalgitr is the team name or the guy who scored the goal?"

"I'm guessing the man. He's a bruiser, all right."

Nate nodded. "Plays dirty too. I think he broke the other guy's arm."

"Win at all costs or die," Thom said. "Nice rules."

As expected, the red team won, and the leader strutted during his procession on the perimeter of the arena accepting the adulation of the audience.

"Full of himself," Nate said. "His squad must win all the time."

When the last set of losers was led away in the golden chains, the king rose and made a short speech to the attentive crowd, after which the populace filed out. With gestures, the guards ensured that Nate and his fellow captives waited until the arena was empty.

Then they were prodded to their feet and taken out the way they'd entered hours earlier, but not back to the cellblock. Instead, the three offworlders and Atletl were led to an upper balcony on the other side of the palace offering an unobstructed view of a huge public square. The population of the city appeared to have commuted to this area to wait for a follow-on event. A flat-topped, pyramidal dais dominated the area.

"There's the big guy again. What'd you call him? Sarbordon?" Thom pointed to a flurry of activity on the far side of the dais. "How do you know his name, by the way?"

"The lady told me in a dream."

Eyebrows raised, Thom eyed him suspiciously. "Right," he said, drawing the word out. "Had too much sun maybe? Too much local wine last night?"

Before Nate could explain, a fanfare, sounding as if it was blown on massive seashells and repeating three times, brought silence to the chattering crowd below. A parade entered the square from the south. The crowd parted silently to let them pass. In the lead came the musicians, now accompanied by drums and flutes, followed by at least thirty black-robed priestesses.

"No sign of Celixia," Nate said, scanning the length of the procession, oddly relieved she wasn't in attendance, given her apparent link to their fate.

"Aren't those the losing teams?" Haranda pointed to the rear of the long parade, only now coming into view. "I remember that team's green and blue uniforms for sure."

Nate had a sick feeling in the pit of his stomach.

Sarbordon and his consort walked onto the platform hand in hand. The ruler spoke briefly, after which she chanted for a short time, while the musicians accompanied her. Then the couple retreated to the side, and eight burly temple guards worked at a complicated set of wooden gears and levers set into the edges of the dais. While Nate watched, the stones in the center of the platform parted, sliding into recesses below the pavement. An opening thirty feet across had been created when the guards finally stopped working the mechanism. Leaning over, he caught a glimpse of murky water far below and movement as large, predatory creatures circled in anticipation.

"This isn't good," Thom said.

As Nate dreaded, the twenty-four men who'd played and lost earlier were brought to the dais, four at a time, and forced by grim-faced guards to leap or be shoved into the chasm. Terrible screams pierced the quiet as whatever aquatic creatures lurked went into a frenzy over the victims. One of the teams attempted to fight the guards, to no avail, although the prisoners did drag a terrified, cursing soldier into the well with them. Nate gritted his teeth, forcing himself to honor the brave men being slaughtered by watching their last moments and vowing to get revenge for all the wrongs done by the savage people holding him and his men captive.

Haranda retched up breakfast off to the side, while the guards pointed at him and snickered.

"Good thing we have the checkout code," Thom said in a low voice. "I don't want to be food for whatever lives in the well."

"If it comes to that." Nate had to admit he was glad to have the Mellurean mind implant buried in his subconscious, a code he could activate that would kill him between one heartbeat and the next. He checked on how the white-faced, trembling Haranda was doing. Only Special Forces operators were given the implants, because of the classified nature of their missions. "But he doesn't. We'll have to do our best to make sure the kid doesn't suffer."

The huge stone plates were being ratcheted shut again, sealing off the pit where the losing team members had been fed to the beasts. Nate risked a glance at the square below to find a drunken festival had begun, led with enthusiasm by the priestesses, who left their platform of death to mingle with the crowd. Of the royal couple there was no sign.

"Obviously, we have to win the damn game if we're forced to play," he said. "I didn't see any of the winners led to the slaughter, did you?"

"Didn't see them go free either." Thom's answer was pessimistic. "Maybe you live to play until you have a bad day, suppose?"

"I'll take a chance to play over an immediate trip to the well of horror," Nate said. "The lady told me we had to play the game, which at the time I interpreted to mean going along with whatever Sarbordon wanted, but now I get it."

"Some complicated dream you had."

Nate leaned close. "She said she had a plan if we survived to see her again."

Before Thom could reply, the guards took them into the palace, leaving them in a barracks-style room with actual beds boasting mattresses, hard pillows and a set of thin, striped blankets. Each man was secured to his bed by a long ankle chain before the guards left.

"Haranda, you okay?" Nate asked as the heavy door slammed shut.

The younger man collapsed onto his bed, shaking, arm across his eyes. The guards had carried him the last few yards into the room since he'd been trembling so badly. "Leave me alone." Rolling over, face to the wall, the pilot buried his face in the rough woolen blanket.

Nate figured he shouldn't push the cadet. *He's got to find his own way to come to grips with what we're facing.*

Aside from guards bringing a full dinner of overcooked meat, more hard rolls and stewed, repulsive-smelling red vegetables, they were left in peace. There was no sign of Celixia. The light faded from the barred windows set high on the wall, and the room became completely dark. Nate heard Thom snore fairly soon thereafter. Haranda hiccupped periodically before he sank into restless slumber. Whether Atletl slept or not, Nate couldn't say. Their teammate was one of those light, quiet sleepers.

Hoping to dream of Bithia again, and possibly learn more about the situation, including her role, Nate welcomed sleep. Tonight his dreams were nothing but nightmares where he fell into blood-red water filled with formless terrors.

He must have seen the game by now. Did he understand what I tried to tell him? Bithia "sat" with her knees pulled to her chin, leaning on the wall. Of course, she was perfectly well aware she was lying motionless on her cushions, held in place by the healing device, as she had been for eons. But at least her mind roamed free in this space she'd carved out over the centuries. A retreat for her consciousness when the machine's control slackened and she was released—or she escaped—from the unconscious state. Intriguing that she'd been able to pull him to her in the dreamspace the last time. He had a flare of psychic abilities but didn't appear to realize his capabilities, or control them, which was a pity. He'd be an even more formidable opponent.

This man, Nate, and his companions were clearly from offworld, which meant a high level of technology. *I must share more in common with them than with my captors.* Yet he was a prisoner too, his chains real while hers were invisible. Bithia pondered how a man like him could have been taken. Her own circumstances were unique. Perhaps he'd landed—or crashed—on Talonque and been ambushed by its still-primitive people. Spears and swords could be effective weapons in the right circumstances.

She shut her eyes and tried to recall his face with as much detail as possible. Having a new factor in the situation raised dangerous hopes, and she ought not to indulge herself. Temptation was too great, though. He was tall, well built, heavily muscled. His brown eyes had been intense in their focus on her, and his whole demeanor was that of a soldier, wary, ready to seize any chance, his thoughts a fierce and angry tapestry, yet with a keen intelligence at work. There was a sprawling, colorful bruise on his forehead and stubble on his chin. He was handsome to her eyes, in an unusual way. She ran her hands over her cheeks and chin. *I wonder how I appear to him?* Another of the humanoid peoples scattered through the galaxies. Who knew what their standards of attractiveness were?

The first few times she'd been awakened, to find none of her own people present, brought crushing disappointment. Now she no longer expected anything, grown numb to her abandonment. *Or so I tell myself.* Yet this last time, when she'd realized what—who—she was looking at, who Sarbordon had brought to her, the hope rose painfully in her heart. Could these beings, these strangers, be her way out of an unbearable life? *I'd gladly help them, and maybe they can assist me.*

The machine detected her level of consciousness and pushed firmly against her control. Sighing, Bithia released her hold on wakefulness and began the descent into oblivion. *Tonight brings no opportunity to speak to Nate. And I mustn't waste my hoarded store of power merely to think of him. By the time I wake again, he may be dead and gone to dust centuries in my past, like all the others.*

She allowed her restorative guardian to obliterate her awareness.

In the morning another substantial breakfast was delivered, supervised by Celixia, who chatted vivaciously with Atletl as much as the wary guards would permit. After the meal, Nate and his companions were taken in chains out of the palace and loaded into a cart drawn by four ponderous animals Atletl identified as bracalx. The cart was driven to a huge walled field outside the city walls on the western side. Dozens of men were there already, running drills, exercising and practicing the sport Nate had watched the day before. Guards were posted in large numbers, and the trainers on the various fields were armed with long whips applied freely when the men were displeased.

Under guard, Nate and his men waited next to the cart while the officer strode off toward the central building.

"Reminds me of the first day at boot camp," Nate said, watching men run laps while others practiced intricate footwork patterns.

"Except the drill instructors didn't have whips." Thom eyed the field. "Guards on the walls, guards on the perimeter of the area. Watching the prisoners like hawks. Not gonna be easy to break out of here."

"Yeah, our assessments match. We'll play along, see what happens, watch for opportunity."

Rather than offering any opportunities for escape, the succeeding days became a numbing cycle of eating, training, sleeping and linguistic sessions Nate instituted in the evenings after dinner. He and his men needed to understand what was being said in their presence, as well as learn as much about the culture as they could. Their teacher, Atletl, had a vested interest in making them a better team, since their fates were tied together. Nate and Thom had had many languages hypno implanted for previous missions, and the side effect was to greatly enhance their ability to learn new ones. Haranda approached the task like a college assignment, grimly determined not to be outshone.

Nate and Thom were in excellent physical condition. Special Forces operators trained hard at all times, and even after suffering minor injuries when their ship crashed and on the grueling trip from the mountains and their subsequent imprisonment, they hadn't lost their edge. Haranda didn't have their physical power, but he was young and wiry and quick to catch on to the nuances of the game their captors insisted they learn. Atletl had evidently been a high-ranking warrior of his own people and matched Nate's accomplishments easily on the endless drills.

"Don't these people have holidays? Or days off?" Thom asked one night, nursing a sore arm he'd sprained in the early days of training. It wasn't healing well at all due to the unrelenting pace of workouts. Celixia'd given him nasty-smelling green paste to rub into the muscles at night, which helped alleviate the discomfort, but what he really needed was to rest for a couple of days straight.

"Training stops only for the games," Atletl said. "Or for special blood sacrifices or feeding of the beasts in the well. Many of those who came in chains with us on the day the sun sickened as the moons wandered were doubtless killed at once to influence the gods to restore the sun."

No more wishing for time off. Nate asked a clarifying question about their future opponents. "So all these guys we're training with are prisoners? Captured in battle?"

"Mostly. A few are criminals or fell afoul of the priestesses in some manner and were condemned to the games. They take offense easily at any slight. These people use the games not only to provide worthy candidates for offerings to the god, but also to settle disputes and serve as omens."

"After what we saw today, when that poor bastard tried to escape, I'm convinced our best plan is to win the game," Nate said.

"He never had a chance," Thom agreed. "Even with a fight going on to distract the guards those five spears skewered him before he was halfway up the wall."

"The one who died was a prince of his tribe. The others were trying to help him by pretending to fight to distract the guards." Atletl's flat tone indicated he was unmoved by the man's fate. "The ploy failed."

"I could have done without the trainers giving all of us three lashes to underscore the message about not attempting or abetting escapes." Nate shifted carefully on his bunk. He'd be sleeping on his stomach for a few days.

"The trainers went easy on us because we belong to T'naritza," Atletl said. "We've been moved from the ranks of beginners and those who'll die easily. The fat, the weak, the stupid. You understand the rules of sapiche better now. Soon those in charge will expect us to play against more seasoned teams. You remember Kalgitr? The team leader at the end of the day? Men of his caliber and cunning."

"Which we're not ready for. You may be an excellent 'stealer,' and Haranda there is a genius at the damn game, but we haven't jelled as a team. We need more time." Nate was a strong shooter and blocker, as was Thom, but the four men had to play as one smooth unit, as if reading each other's minds, and they were nowhere near that high level yet. He and Thom operated instinctively together, the skill developed over years of training for and running Special Forces missions, but Atletl and Haranda were wild cards. Thom nodded at the pilot. "Seven hells, kid, you're so good even the guards pay you compliments."

"Reminds me of my days at the Academy." Haranda's voice was proud and a bit nostalgic. Nate was relieved to see the pilot's improved morale but concerned because men such as the thuggish Kalgitr played a brutal game, willing to disable or kill their opponents in order to win, and Haranda was clearly in a collegiate intramural mind-set. He and Thom could hold their own in such a game, calling on their hand-to-hand combat skills, but the cadet's training in martial arts had been minimal at best.

After ten days of drills and practices, the trainers ordered a scrimmage. Nate's team had to play a full game for the first time and in short order lost miserably, not making a single goal. Disgusted at the level of play, Atletl exhorted them constantly with what Nate guessed were choice curses.

"Can't blame the guy," he said to Thom in Basic while riding to the palace in the evening, chained in their cart. "We screw up and he dies with us."

"He'd better elevate our level of play to match his, then." Thom massaged his arm and shoulder. He scowled across the cart at Atletl, who rolled his eyes and pretended to be fascinated by the bracalx. "This is so crazy, you know?"

"It's a chance."

"Not much of one."

Nate couldn't argue.

But as they ate their dinner, sitting cross-legged on their beds, Atletl gave them their first piece of good news, which he'd been told by a trainer impressed with Haranda's skills. "If a team can win ten straight games, these superstitious people say the god has favored them. The lure of the accomplishment is why Kalgitr and his men don't care if they kill their opponents in the process of winning and why they play so rough even in our scrimmages—he wants all of us to be afraid of them. The entire team would be set free, rewarded with gold and wives and never have to play in the ball court again."

"I know which girl you'd have your eye on if we won ten times," Nate said. Atletl's fondness for flirting with Celixia every chance he got was a running joke among the team.

"You don't think winners have to choose one of the 'birds of prey,' do you?" Thom opened his eyes wide. "Those women are scary."

Nate laughed. "His heart is set on our guardian priestess, Celixia. Don't you pay attention to these things?"

"If he gets to pick Celixia, who's left for us?" Thom said.

Atletl took the teasing good-naturedly but shook his head. "Don't joke about the priestesses of Huitlani. They're married to the god. They may take lovers, but not mortal husbands. And the lovers don't live long, because Huitlani is a jealous god."

Haranda, apparently not interested in this topic, distracted Atletl, diagramming a new play with dishes and utensils and asking his opinion about how well it would work.

"What are the odds anyone has ever claimed this fabled 'win ten games, go free' reward?" Thom asked Nate off to the side as Haranda and Atletl talked ball-passing strategies.

"Kalgitr's sure trying. Did you see him snap that guy's arm today? If this pipe dream of winning ten and going free helps the kid cope with his constant state of funk, then I say let him believe," Nate said. "He's been much more stable since we got sentenced to training. And he's a natural at this damn game. Lucky for us."

Thom persisted with his pessimistic assessment. "Nobody can win ten straight. To win so many games would be like doing ten missions in a row behind the Mawreg lines and living to tell about it. Not gonna happen, not in this lifetime. If we're going to get out of here, it's going to have to be some other way."

"I know." Nate leaned back on his bed, trying to find a comfortable spot.

Lowering his voice even further, Thom asked, "Have you been able to contact the lady again?"

Nate shut his eyes. "No. I'm not sure what enabled the first dream. Maybe it was the fact I'd been in her presence the same day for a few moments. I've been trying, believe me."

Information from Bithia might be essential to their survival, but he had no idea how to force himself to dream a specific set of events, much less ensure he met her in the dream. He'd been hoping she'd reach out to him again, but as far as he could tell, she'd made no attempt. The small ration of wine in the evenings wasn't facilitating any dreams, if it ever had. He returned to their quarters so exhausted each night from the rigorous training that he'd fall asleep before he could try to reach her. Often he felt her presence as a light touch in his mind, almost the equivalent of glimpsing her from the corner of his eye, but she never responded to his questing thoughts.

Not tonight. I'm going to make this work tonight and come to you, lady.

Drawing on techniques he'd been shown once as a kid, he slowed his breathing and visualized himself walking through the tendrils of the strange fog toward the lights of her chamber. His mind kept trying to wander, full of worry over the intricacies of the life-or-death game he was learning, or making frustratingly inadequate plans for escape. He took a moment to refocus and shake off his worries. Drawing a deep breath, he counted to ten, closed his eyes and relaxed into the scene he was painting for himself. *Think of it as preparation for a mission and she's the objective.*

The military frame of reference helped.

He stood in the gray-green mists, a strong sense of pleased anticipation flickering through his consciousness when he realized he was going to see Bithia.

"Bithia?" Nate called her name as he stepped through the fog. There she was, lying on her immense high-tech couch, motionless save for slowly opening her lavender eyes. He walked across the chamber, the mist falling away, until the inexorable, invisible barrier guarding her halted his progress.

Eyes wide, she stared at him. "How did you get here? I didn't summon you, so maybe you're learning to use the psychic potential I sensed when we met." The furrows in her brow smoothed, and her lips curved in a wide smile. "I'm glad to see you, and it's pleasant to hear my birth name. I've missed the sound." For a moment she studied him from head to toe. "I'm surprised you remain alive. My congratulations."

"What's going on here? Why are you a prisoner of low-tech killers like these people?"

"I might ask you the same question! If your only wish is to remind me of my hopeless existence, always at their beck and call, then go away and let me sleep. Oblivion is my only escape until I can die, or force Sarbordon to kill me in his endless quest for answers and omens. There's nothing else for me." Expression annoyed, she closed her eyes.

Nate waited, expecting the dream encounter to end, as the first one had, once she shut her eyes. When it didn't, he realized she must still be conscious. *Hiding from me. But I need answers.* He studied the delicate planes of her face, finding her compellingly attractive. Her mere existence was intriguing. No matter how many worlds the Sectors explored, how many artifacts and abandoned installations the Archaeology Service dug through, no one had ever seen so much as a painting or a statue or a hologram of an Ancient Observer. The AO took great care to leave no representations of themselves, although many worlds had legends about them. He accepted Haranda's verdict that Bithia wasn't a member of the specific forerunner civilization that fascinated the Sectors, but he wondered if she was aware of them.

And what of her own people and their accomplishments? She was definitely from an era predating his own.

"You're still here—" Her surprised voice, with a hint of amusement, interrupted his ruminations. "Staring at me."

"I'm not leaving until I have to, until the encounter really ends. I'm not sure I could, even if I wanted to, since control of this process appears to rest for the most part with you. And you're the most beautiful woman I've ever seen on any world, well worth staring at." He couldn't believe he'd made such an inane remark. *Like an idiot cadet on his first date.* She had an unsettling effect on him, maybe because their minds were linked. He imagined what her skin felt like, how soft her hair might be—annoyed at himself, he wrested his imagination away from Bithia's form.

"Stubborn, I see, not to take my hint and withdraw," she said, the pleased expression on her face blunting any hint of criticism. "Actually, I'm glad you stayed. It's been so long since I had someone to talk with who was from offworld."

"How many years have you been—?"

"In this place? I've no way to know. Tell me, do you know of the Aralapanni? Or the Serennian?" The names she uttered were nothing he recognized, and even in a dream in which he shared a language with her, the syllables carried no meaning. Bithia watched him closely with those great, shadowed eyes and nodded. "You don't know these great peoples, do you? Not even legends to you? Then truly we must have passed from the galaxy, and all our knowledge with us. And this tale of Ancient Observers I pluck from your mind means nothing to me. Certainly not my people, nor any of the races I know."

Nate was frustrated by their lack of any common reference, aside from the planet upon which he now stood, equally alien and hostile to both of them. *Start there.* The current situation ought to provide enough of a foundation for them to relate to each other.

"I don't know how you got here, but our ship crashed," he said, leaning against the barrier and crossing his arms over his chest, settling in for a chat. "We were being chased by a Mawreg client race—enemies of our entire species. To escape we had to go into hyperdrive too close to a blue giant star, ended up out of control in this system and crashed." He touched his forehead where the last remnants of the bruise remained. "I was knocked out in the crash, and these thugs grabbed my men when they were crawling from the wreckage and dragging me to safety."

"Where did you crash? And who are these Mawreg?" Despite her prior claims to want nothing but untroubled sleep and oblivion, Bithia seized on new information with the hunger of a highly intelligent creature denied fresh mental stimulus for a long time. "Can you visualize one for me?"

He did, in automatic response to her question. The memory made him nauseated. How the Mawreg looked was wrong in all respects.

Bithia didn't react with instinctive repugnance to the Mawreg, at least as glimpsed in his hastily shut-off memory. "Hideous, yes, but unknown to me."

Nate had seen them up close, which few people ever survived, much less retained a hold on sanity, but that was in another life.

"Another life?" She plucked the phrase from his mind. "You believe in the recycling of the spirit through time?"

"No, you misunderstand me." He chuckled. *Have to get used to her ability to instantaneously read my private musings. Or develop a mental block to keep her out.* The second strategy didn't hold much appeal. He liked hearing her musical voice in his head. "I'm an officer in the Sectors Special Forces, usually working behind enemy lines to carry out assassinations, sabotage installations, accomplish military objectives. Another life than the one I'm leading here on this cursed planet. Here, I'm in training for the sapiche playoffs."

"I don't know this Mawreg. Fortunately for me, judging from what you say and remember of them." Bithia frowned. In the resulting "silence," Nate's irritation grew. She could pick any thought of his at will, but he could only "hear" what she chose to "say" to him. After a contemplative moment, she sighed. "I came to Talonque, this world, of my own choice with my father's expedition. He was an explorer of great renown among our people. He also wanted to help the people here learn and grow more civilized."

"We leave indigenous planetary populations alone, unless they've already reached a specific level of civilization," Nate said. "We learned the hard way a few too many times that it's no good to go in with what the Sectors can offer if you're dealing with people who haven't yet evolved technical sophistication. The population gets the wrong idea—"

"Think of you as gods?" Bithia asked wryly. "I believe we were learning the lesson. I can certainly testify to it now. A growing number of my people liked the idea."

"But not you?"

"No. Even before I was forced into this career as the all-knowing goddess T'naritza. Nor did my father approve of such a concept. But his associates Tedesk and Syrmir, well…" She fell silent. "But bringing the novelties of a new world home to my people engendered much profit and fame. My father wasn't immune to the lure of both but wouldn't dream of presenting himself as a god. The truth mutates unrecognizably over time, doesn't it?"

"What happened? Why did you get left here, in this way?" *How do you stay sane?* He guessed the machine kept her in a form of suspended animation or cryo sleep between summonses from those who worshipped her. He speculated that the device must have a beneficial effect on her mind, to keep her from overwhelming despair.

The dream ended before she could answer, much to his chagrin. The guards kicked his bed, ordering him and the others to rise for another endless day of drilling and scrimmage.

Thom gave him the eye as they ate breakfast mush and fruit. "You saw her?"

Nate kept his voice low as well. "Yeah, but the dream was too short to learn much. She's never heard of the AO or the Mawreg, and I've never heard of her people. She came on a scientific expedition, as near as I can figure out. I don't know how she got trapped."

"Nothing useful, then." Thom dropped his spoon into his empty bowl.

"Other than proving I can reconnect with her? No. I'll try again tonight."

CHAPTER THREE

The day's practice was especially intense as the trainers concentrated on passing and stealing drills, which were not Nate's best sapiche skills, to say the least. Exhausted, frustrated and in need of serious sleep as he rode to the city in the slow old cart, he was grateful for the twilight's soothing effect on his eyes. The only time of day the oversize sun didn't cause Nate vision problems.

Once they reached the palace and the cart was parked in the small courtyard adjoining their dormitory, two guards held Nate aside. The others were taken across the courtyard, while Nate stood and waited.

"What's with the change in routine?" he asked Murrax, the junior officer in charge of their daily transportation to and from practice.

"Queen Lolanta has sent for you."

"What the seven hells?" Thom tried to delay as he realized Nate wasn't going to the dormitory. He shouted across the courtyard, "What's going on?"

"Don't get yourself in trouble with these guys on my account. I'll be okay." Nate tried to express a calm assurance he was far from feeling. He watched his three teammates disappear into the building, not much liking the idea of being separated from his men. As the cart driver led the placid bracalx to the stable, Nate's three-man escort took him to the other side of the courtyard, entering a different corridor and leading him farther away from his comrades.

Nate deliberately sought the state of inner calm the Special Forces taught their highly lethal operatives to achieve under the most severe conditions. It was a patient watchfulness, hard edged with readiness to take instant action on any opportunity presenting itself—to escape, to wreak havoc and mayhem on the enemy, whatever the situation called for. Sarbordon and his people were capable of just about anything, in Nate's opinion. He had to keep his wits about him.

The nature of the hallways changed as he climbed flights of sweeping stairs, moving ever higher in the palace complex. The wall decor transitioned from dour gray stone to clean, whitewashed surfaces with elaborate, colorful frescoes. Certain themes repeated, all involving Huitlani. Scenes of the horrific deity with his priestesses, with captives, leading warriors into battle, trampling over the bodies of what Nate could only assume were previously vanquished people—the common theme was an emotion-battering stew of blood, death and destruction.

As he walked he studied the mural for clues about the people who held him prisoner, trying to imagine how the ruling dynasty could inspire loyalty and obedience, indeed, anything other than sheer terror and repugnance. The soldiers must have an ironclad assurance the military ranks would never be culled, never die at the priestesses' hands. The guards took him at last through a hall filled with small knots of chattering, laughing priestesses, all dressed in variations of basic black. They ranged in age from young girls to wizened old crones, but all displayed the same haughty manner. The sight of them made Nate's skin crawl, and his stomach turned. *Like being in the middle of a large flock of birds of prey. How could people who commit atrocities on a daily basis be so lighthearted?*

Murrax brought him to a halt in front of a double door. Two of the unusually tall and muscular temple guards stood on either side of the burnished wooden panels.

"We're expected," Murrax said, licking his lips nervously, addressing first one guard, then the other.

Not even loyal soldiers enjoy proximity to the priestesses. Nate wasn't the only one who didn't want to be here, surrounded by Huitlani's devoted servants.

One guard knocked lightly on the left door. It cracked open, and the man offered a rapid explanation to the priestess peering out at them. The woman nodded.

"She's waiting for this one. Bring him inside."

Nate did a quick scan of his surroundings as he stepped past the guards and into the room. A fountain played in the center of an intricately tiled floor. Off to the right side was a row of fanciful birdcages made from cunningly woven black twigs, sitting on an immense black wood table. The gaily colored avian residents of these cages flapped iridescent wings and chattered as he walked past. Across the room, beyond the fountain, was a low-slung, leather couch piled high with silver and black silk cushions. The walls were blessedly free of any decoration—no more gory frescoes to assault the mind.

The quick impression of his new surroundings was all Nate had time to absorb before the guards pushed him to his knees on a striped red rug. He didn't see any immediate menace. He waited, conserving his energy.

The sensual spice, smoke and floral perfume hit him as the queen sauntered into the room from the right. He swiveled his head to watch her warily. At first, she pretended to ignore his presence, standing idly and feeding small bits of bread to a particularly large green bird. It cooed at her and rubbed its head on her hand. The artificially sweet scene annoyed Nate.

He cleared his throat. "Does your adoring pet know what you do for a living? Does he suspect you're probably planning to have him for dinner?"

Unhurriedly, she fed the last of the bread to the bird, stroking its brilliantly crimson feather crest. Then, dusting crumbs from her hands, she pivoted gracefully.

Lolanta stood, hands on hips, staring at him. Her long, straight, ebony hair was held from her cruelly beautiful face by an elaborate gemmed clip. Her dress today was the usual black, a tightly woven skirt with a long slit and two small pieces of fabric that barely contained her ample breasts. This garment was held together by one continuous loop of embroidered black cord. Two intricate, crystal pendants hung from heavy gold chains at her neck, drawing the eye inexorably to her cleavage. Equally impressive gemmed earrings dangled from elongated earlobes to brush her shoulders. Heeled snakeskin sandals showed off her shapely feet. Her toenails were revoltingly long and curved, to Nate's eyes, and polished with the same gray purple lacquer as her talonlike fingernails.

A proud, confident woman used to getting her own way. He and the queen continued to regard each other for a long moment as if no one else existed in the room, locked in a silent battle of wills.

Then she raised her eyes from contemplation of Nate's face to direct a chilling look at Murrax. "Leave us," she commanded, waving the young officer and his men off duty with a careless flick of those talonlike nails.

Murrax unaccountably hesitated. "But the king commanded—"

"You question me in my own chambers?" Her voice was low, calm, with the lazy deceptiveness of a top predator luring the unwary into making a mistake. She tapped the bars of the birdcage, feeding one last tidbit from a bowl on the table to the favored pet. It cooed at her.

"Such impudence would be unthinkable," the nervous officer said. He swallowed hard, stared at the floor, even glanced at Nate as if for help, amazingly enough.

On your own here, buddy.

Murrax took a hesitant step toward the birdcages. "But I'm charged with keeping this prisoner closely held."

"Do you believe he can escape me? Or menace me? Think you so little of the powers I command?" Plainly, a trap lay in the simple questions.

Nate gave Murrax credit for not immediately agreeing to her demand contradicting his orders. The man wavered, clearly afraid of her, but equally reluctant to get crosswise with her husband's instructions.

Nate filed away for future use the information that Sarbordon and Lolanta apparently had separate, loyal cadres, and their aims conflicted on occasion. Maybe he could use the diverging goals as a wedge to achieve his own purposes.

"I want him in the red chair." Lolanta broke the impasse, gesturing at a pair of seats across the room. "I'll show you it's safe to leave him in my gentle care, and then you can go wait outside."

At Murrax's command, the two guards were all too pleased to haul Nate to his feet. With eager haste, they propelled him into the embrace of the wooden chair she'd indicated and hooked his chains onto protrusions designed for restraining prisoners. As the guards departed, Lolanta strolled across the floor. Pausing in front of Nate, she studied him from under heavily painted lids, her white-painted lips curved in a smile.

"I won't feed your heart to Huitlani this day, nor have you thrown in the sacred well for the beasts to eat. Do you think I conduct blood sacrifices in my own chambers?" She winked at him. "I only wish to talk today, to garner understanding." Lolanta paced away from the chair.

"Understand what?" Nate wanted her to stay where he could see her.

"What hold can a pitiful sleeping girl possibly have over such a warrior as yourself?" Lolanta moved into his limited field of vision. "I've been to the practice field and watched you play the game several times now. Fierce. Powerful. You're suited to a war god's service, which legend says her father is not. He prefers gifts of flowers and fruit. What kind of tribute is that for a god to sustain himself and his powers?" Scorn rippled in her voice. "No wonder the people who worshipped him were so easy to conquer."

"Her father has powers beyond what you can dream of." Nate concentrated hard, trying to hold his own in this bizarre conversation she was determined to have. After all, no one could contradict him, so he might as well slant the propaganda in his favor. "Her father doesn't want blood and the needless slaughter of good men."

Lolanta kicked the nearest stool closer to his chair and sat. "Sarbordon and I rule this nation equally under the law of Huitlani. I control the omens, the signs—Huitlani speaks to me and through me. My husband controls the armies, the temporal matters. So it has always been with our people. We have the required number of children together, strong heirs to succeed us both when the god decrees the time has come for us to step into the afterlife." She shook her head. "Yet he's been obsessed with your sleeping, ineffectual girl from the day we were first shown the secret by our parents. He seeks T'naritza's counsel. He dreams of acquiring the miracle-working artifacts her father controlled." She fell silent, brow furrowed, reviewing past insults, he surmised. "His father and grandfather before him were not so gullible. Those men had no need for consulting a sleeping girl. I wish I'd been partnered with their like!"

Nate saw no benefit in commenting on her assessment of people and events. Eventually, she'd get to the point.

Lolanta focused her attention on him again. Rising from the gaily colored hassock, she hooked her right hand under his chin, forcing him to look at her. "So, I must know—have you come to fulfill the prophecy?"

"Prophecy?"

"The legend states that one day her father will return for her, reunite with these people we've enslaved for many generations and lead them again. Are you here to prepare the way for his coming? To defeat Huitlani, to defeat us?" Lolanta's voice became shrill at the mere idea. She tightened her grip on Nate's chin. "Has Fr'taray sent you to carry out this destiny?"

"What does Sarbordon believe?"

"He vacillates." She sounded disparaging of her high-ranking mate. The priestess released Nate to pace. "Until the day you were dragged in, he was sure his destiny called for freeing her, mating with her to spawn a new race of demigods and take on the powers of Fr'taray for himself by so doing. His reading of the old tablets led him to that conclusion. The rare, triple eclipse reinforced those beliefs. But now he worries. In the morning he convinces himself you're from beyond the sky, a true warrior of her clan who must be reckoned with. At evening moonrise, he says you're nothing more than a man who sweats and bleeds, who can be killed without reprisal or consideration."

It was obvious to Nate that if Lolanta had been the decision maker, and if she'd known how to open the healing chamber, Bithia would have been sacrificed to Huitlani a long time ago, no questions asked. And he and his men would have met the same grim fate the day they arrived.

"T'naritza herself acknowledged us as her warriors," Nate reminded Lolanta. His private, worst fears about what a thin thread kept him and his men alive had been confirmed by her casual recitation of the king's dilemma.

Lolanta perched on the edge of the cushions on the chair across from his, restless, drumming her fingers on her thigh. "Either we wait for the outcome of the god's game to tell us how to deal with you, or perhaps you and I can arrive at an understanding. Compare our knowledge of what Fr'taray and Huitlani desire to achieve from this confrontation, use the information to our mutual benefit sooner."

"We must wait," Nate said, trying to buy time.

The priestess came out of her chair and paced across the chamber to the birdcages and back. Eventually, she faced Nate. "Every day our sworn enemies, the Githholz, invade more of our territory. Your fourth man is one of their high-ranking chiefs—I'm fully aware of his status. But for his tattoo, he'd have been given to the beasts in the well or sacrificed on an altar weeks ago. Keeping him alive is dangerous, gives the enemy hope." Her voice rose. "There's no time to waste on this affair of a stupid *game*. But I can't get my husband to see the urgency as I do." She pointed at Nate with one talon. "If you're proven mere mortal, or even if you are warriors from the sky, but Huitlani's team triumphs in the game, then we've frittered away precious time. My foolish mate is risking our kingdom on a hope of attaining powers and weapons that may be no more than smoke."

"What exactly do you want from me?"

She came closer. "Give me the secrets of Fr'taray. I'm sure my god would be lavish with rewards. *I* would certainly be most generous."

"I can't give you any secrets." All Nate wanted was distance from her. *The prison cell sounds damn fine as a place to be right now.* "You'll have to wait for the outcome of the game, just as your husband does. Send me to my cell. We're done talking."

The queen rocked on her heels, eyebrows rising to her hairline. "You dare to give me orders?"

"I don't think the king would appreciate your attempt to influence me to help you, instead of him, do you?"

"Issuing threats on top of orders? Truly you are a very confident man, or a very foolish one." She came to him, framing his face with her hands and leaning in until their eyes were only inches apart. "I'll enjoy sacrificing your heart to Huitlani after you lose the game. Death in the well is too simple for you." With that, she flounced out of the room, slamming the door behind her.

Murrax and his two men tiptoed into the chamber a few moments later, escorted Nate back to his cell and left.

"What in the seven hells happened to you?" Thom's voice was gruff.

"The high priestess wanted to know if we're working for a goddess." Nate laughed at the sheer absurdity of it all. "She didn't like my answers."

Nate walked through the swirling gray and lavender fog, calling Bithia's name softly. He desperately needed to talk to her.

"I'm here." The mist swirled away, and he saw her standing on the far bank of a small stream. Drifts of snow surrounded them both, and small chunks of ice floated by on the water. He could see her breath in the air when she spoke.

"We're in your dreamspace this time, warrior." Bithia's expression reflected surprise and amusement as she drew the heavy coat she wore closer around her. "A strange but beautiful place you choose. And so cold. Not anywhere on Talonque I recognize."

"We're on Taychelle's Planet, in the Sectors," he said, staring at the distinctive red woods surrounding them and the snowflakes drifting in eddies through the air. "A polar environment year-round, actually. I guess my subconscious has had enough of the heat on Talonque."

"I must thank you for your consideration, bringing me to a new environment and dreaming me a warm garment to wear as shield from the wind and the cold." She took a few steps, smiling. "Even in the deepest of my own dreams, I remain tethered to the healing couch, so how did you manage this?"

"I have no idea."

"Too bad." Bithia sighed as she sat on the edge of a crumbling, rust-colored tree stump. She caught a few errant flakes on her hand and watched them melt. "I was going to ask you to teach me the trick."

"But are you really here?" Nate didn't know if he could trust his own senses that the two of them were actually conversing. Was it a true meeting of their minds on another plane, or was the meeting a dream, taking place solely in his own mind? Was it wish fulfillment not only of his desire to escape the boiling heat, but also to spend time with her?

Drawing a design in the snow with her toe, Bithia glanced at him. "I perceive this as reality, you and me in the dreamspace, talking. But if it was a dream of your shaping, I'd reassure you, yes? How can we know?"

"I know." Nate strode into the stream, water splashing against his boots. He realized he wore his uniform, although even in a dream he couldn't get his hands on a weapon.

"What are you doing?" Bithia asked with a tinge of concern in her voice. "The creek water must be cold, considering the ice chunks."

"Testing a theory—"

Nate broke off as, at midstream, he ran into the ever-present barrier keeping them frustratingly apart. He stepped back a pace in the icy water and extended his hands straight out. The tiny green flickers of the healing machine's force field outlined his fingers. "I don't know whether to be happy we're actually together, or disappointed I can't reach you." He allowed his arms to fall to his sides and retraced his steps across the small stream, taking care not to slip on the treacherous rocks, grabbing a low-hanging branch to pull himself onto the bank. Dusting his hands off, he said, "So we know. Not exclusively my dream. You *are* here, because the damn barrier exists. I'd dream myself shattering it into a million pieces."

Bithia gazed at him quizzically over the blue fur collar of her coat. "Can't you be content that we have another chance to talk? There's so much I'd like to ask you."

"There's no time to waste." Nate debated what to ask her first. *Her safety matters above all else.* "Does Sarbordon know the secret to turning off the damn machine? Does anyone? Do you?"

"I know the procedure, of course. My father feared I'd disobey him and step from healing too soon in order to rejoin the expedition. I was upset to be left behind. So he disabled the internal control, else I would've been long gone before you ever arrived on this world. Why are you asking?"

"And the king? Does he know the secret?"

She looked away for a long moment, then brought her lavender eyes back to lock on to Nate's anxious face. "Yes. He knows."

"How—?"

"I can only tell you what I've been told. When his people conquered this peaceful nation, they tortured and killed the members of the Hialar Clan, trying to extort all the secrets of Fr'taray's powers and possessions and how I could be forced to prophesy, as the newcomers understood the situation. The deepest secret of the Hialar is how to release me, passed down to only a few in each succeeding generation of priests and priestesses, because without me at their command, the family would have no power. So the clan had no desire to let me escape."

She's bitter at the way the family exploited her, even after all these millennia. I sure don't blame her.

Bithia went on with her explanation. "Sarbordon's forefathers allowed the family to live, to 'serve' me as long as the clan obeyed the new rulers and woke me to prophesy on command. The newcomers found me useful to help keep the conquered people of the city of Nochen pacified. I'm viewed as a divine handmaiden to their own god, Huitlani. As soon as the current king came of age and was brought to see me for the first time, he became obsessed with me." She shook her head. "An ancient prophecy of their own people—"

"Yeah, I know. I hoped you hadn't heard about it."

"How do you—?"

"Lolanta had me brought to her room for a chat today."

"She hates me." Bithia shivered. "She's not entirely sane, I believe."

"You can say that again," Nate said. "How did these people learn the secret of the on/off switch?"

"As soon as the current king took the throne, he ordered Lolanta to sacrifice every single member of the Hialar family his soldiers could get their hands on. I've heard hints many in the extended clan may have escaped to the lands of the Githholz tribes. Those he did capture were killed, one at a time, in front of the others." Tears were slowly coursing down Bithia's cheeks. "I'm told the family went to their deaths proudly, in silence. But Celixia was only a little girl at the time, and all she understood was if she told the secret her grandfather had shared with her, she could save her mother."

"So she did."

"I don't blame her." Bithia wiped the tears from her cheeks. "If only I'd known what was going on, I'd gladly have given them the secret. So much pain, suffering...all because of me."

"Pretty standard approach for a conquering race to destroy or assimilate elements of the primary religion of the subjugated," Nate said. "Don't blame yourself. Atrocities would have happened whether there'd been a real person such as yourself at the heart of the Hialar Clan's beliefs, or a mythical god figure."

She clenched her jaw. "If I had a fraction of the powers the believers credit me with, all these people would be blasted and dead, the king dying first."

"Did he spare Celixia's mother?"

"I'm told he did. But he also took her as a concubine for a while, until she died suddenly. I wondered if she took her own life, or whether Lolanta had a hand in it. Either way, the mother taught Celixia the full duties of a 'priestess of T'naritza' before her death, and now she's the only one left of her entire family, in Nochen at least. The king is determined he'll awake the Sleeping Goddess, one way or the other, and so there'll be no further need for the Hialar Clan. He hesitates to take the final, irrevocable step of powering down the machine."

"Lolanta told me the same thing," he said. "By the way, Celixia's been watching out for my men and me, and I'm grateful."

"Celixia is a good person. Brave. She feeds information to the rebels outside the city, spies on the royal court, and no one ever suspects. To them, she's a child whose spirit the king broke long ago. To me, she's a valuable resource and has explained much, including the significance of this game. She seems to believe she and I are partners of a sort. I asked her to try to help you as much as she can, make sure you're fed properly, treated as well as can be under the circumstances. To make Sarbordon understand you have to be able to play a legitimate game of sapiche for the gods to manifest their will through the outcome." Bithia frowned. "Hardly an aptitude I desire, but after all these years, I usually know the right things to say. Celixia fills in the blanks where I've missed a nuance or a new development. Or where she has her own agenda. But I—we can't get overconfident."

"If he is so obsessed with you and has had the means to set you free all this time, to get at you, then why hasn't he?" Self-denial didn't align with the ruler's character as Nate had so far seen it displayed.

"Don't forget Lolanta."

"As if I could." He had no desire to think about the devious, cruel woman.

Bithia laughed at the face he made. "The warrior king and the priestess queen rule equally here. She speaks directly to Huitlani, after all. He doesn't. So the omens are never right for the ceremony her husband so desperately wants. The signs might have been favorable at the time of the triple eclipse. Even Lolanta couldn't deny or explain away the rarity and importance of such an unprecedented celestial event. Fortunately, your arrival at the same time sent everyone's attention in another direction as to how the ancient prophecy is to be fulfilled. The king's terrified of Lolanta, you know. Anyone with any sense is."

"He's the bigger menace to you right now." The idea of the ruler laying so much as one finger on Bithia made Nate ill and livid at the same time. "He thinks fathering a child with you will give him all the powers—"

"Attributed to my father and elevate Sarbordon to godhood," Bithia finished in a soft voice. "Yes, I know, Nate. When he forces Celixia to waken me and if Lolanta isn't present, he describes in graphic detail what he wants to do to me. It pleases him in a twisted way, just as it pleases him to inflict pain through improper manipulation of the device's neural controls. The phrase I find in your mind is he gets off on it."

"Twisted bastard."

"Using the neural controls is another trick the Hialar figured out over time and which Celixia's mother showed the king. The controls aren't meant as torture devices, but improperly applied, the effect is to cause me pain."

"I'll kill him." Nate made the vow with deadly sincerity, straight from the depths of his heart.

He opened his eyes as the door to the cell creaked open and the servants brought breakfast under Celixia's watchful supervision. Another day of the endless sapiche practice under the blistering sun lay ahead. Not surprising that he'd dreamed of Taychelle's Planet, perpetually covered in lovely, freezing snow. Nate knew his link to Bithia was gone until he endured another day. They communicated only at night, and then only if both were in the right phase of the sleep state. Last night's contact had been highly unusual, and again, he had no idea how to repeat it.

The next night, Nate dreamed again. This time, Bithia was awake, waiting for him, staring eagerly into the mist from her couch. "You're alive."

Nate took his usual place next to the invisible barrier separating them. "I don't know how much time either of us has, or how many chances we'll get to talk, but we can't afford to waste these opportunities. Much as I'd like to get to know you better, we have to prioritize getting out of this mess."

"I can't escape." The pleasure she had shown at his arrival dimmed, replaced by sad resignation. "If it were in my power to aid you, I would, but I'm helpless."

"Don't give up," Nate said. "There's always hope."

"Lecture me on hope after you've been confined as long as I have." Her retort was instant, a bitter tone underlying the words.

"I need facts. I know you said the device holds you, but why?" The questions had been gnawing at him ever since he had first seen her. He couldn't imagine why a member of a high-tech, powerful civilization had permitted herself to be so imprisoned. Unless her own people had left her here, which she'd hinted at in their last meeting.

She closed her eyes. He believed she wasn't shutting him out, but rather, examining her memories. "Since you're so fascinated, I'll tell you. This was my first trip with my father to the outworlds. I'd been training for years to earn a spot on an expedition. Competition is—was particularly fierce for my father's journeys. His workers split large profits and accumulated much prestige in our society. I earned my place on this team," she said, head held high with palpable pride, as if answering an old charge of favoritism. "The last thing my father would do was select a person based on anything other than talent and knowledge, although many whispered I was chosen only because I was his daughter."

"And the gossip bothered you?" Nate asked. "I understand. My father is a high-ranking war hero, and I caught grief at the Academyfor being his son and therefore allegedly having advantages. Not to mention a reputation to live up to. I joined the Special Forces instead, because he was Space Navy and I wanted to create my own name and record, not be seen as coasting by on his." He shut up, surprised by his willingness to talk with this woman about sensitive subjects. Was she exerting her influence on him? Or was he truly so at ease with her?

Bithia nodded slightly. "My father is—*was* a famous explorer, finder of new worlds. He imported many curiosities and new finds to the home worlds for the amusement of our jaded people."

"Amusement?" Nate caught her up on the surprising idea that her people invested in interstellar exploration for such a relatively frivolous purpose. "Your people traveled the stars for pleasure? Not to colonize?"

"Are things so grim, then, in your worlds?"

He considered her question for a moment, weighing the ever-present threat of the Mawreg attacks versus the peaceful life in a majority of the Sectors. He finally settled for, "It's complicated. We started out exploring for scientific knowledge and for raw materials to support our technology and to find more living space for our people." Thinking about how the people from his one small world of origin had spread, Nate smiled. "My branch of the human race tends to expand and multiply to fill the available planets. Then we met other spacefaring peoples, mostly humanoid but not all by any means, and the Sectors was created. Conditions were pretty peaceful for a long time, a few trade wars and border skirmishes. The Star Guard didn't have much to do in the way of waging interstellar, all-out wars until the Mawreg came out of nowhere."

"Being right out of school," she said when he paused, "I was the lowliest of assistants on this mission, but the others resented me, as I said, for being Fr'taray's daughter. I tried so hard, but my efforts, other than flying, were deemed incorrect or fell short. I even suspected one or more of the staff sneaking behind me and undoing what I did, you know? Because my efforts habitually came out so wrong. I had my suspicions, not that it matters now. Tedesk especially said I was hopeless and should be sent home with the supply ship." Bithia laughed. "And of us all, I'm the only one who stayed. Overstayed!"

"How—"

"I was careless where I sat one night after the evening meal. I was bitten by a tolokon, which is a fanged slitherer of this wretched world. Deathly poisonous to my people, although not to the locals. Residents of Talonque suffer only mild discomfort for a day. Beware of it—a nasty red and blue thing with a forked tail. At times, before the healing device corrects the dreamspace parameters, I have nightmares of being trapped in here with tolokon crawling all over my body." She shivered and went on with a wry laugh. "I've been told that through a strange misunderstanding these people now hold the tolokon sacred to me, a favorite totem of mine. If they only understood the truth."

Nate laughed outright, pausing to explain what was so funny when she frowned. "Our teammate Atletl owes his life to that misunderstanding. The priestesses only spared him the day we came to the city because he has a tolokon tattoo and was with us."

"As long as good came of the idea that I love the tolokon, then I'm happy. Don't ask me to admire the tattoo. I never want to see another tolokon—real or painted. But I digress. As I was explaining, one of the cursed things bit me, and the venom destroyed the tissues of my leg to the bone. The damage spread through my nerves and blood vessels into my core, so my father set me within this device of ours to be healed. A wise expedition leader brings healing modules, to be prepared for any eventuality."

"We have a similar device—well, the military does. Not generally available to the civilian population, because the elements needed to make it work are so rare. It's called a rejuve resonator. It can do pretty astonishing things, but it doesn't begin to compare to this setup." Nate gave the supporting apparatus an appreciative look.

"My father said that for a long time I was close to death, in a coma for several passages of the moons. Something happened with the mission during the last few days of my seclusion, but I don't know the details. I'd barely emerged from the coma and was too weak to be released from the healer unit when my father came with Tedesk to tell me he was going to our base camp to communicate with home on urgent matters. I begged them to take me—I couldn't bear to be left." She blushed and lowered her gaze. "I made a hideous scene. Father said no, it was too soon and I wouldn't survive without the continued emanations of the healer. The flesh of my leg was regenerating, growing new nerves and vessels. The process couldn't be interrupted. He left his number one local trainee in charge of me, a man named Hialar. Father expected to come back within a three-day span." She laughed again, bitterly. "Three million days and more, no doubt, have passed. It's certain we knew nothing of a people such as yours, and you've no knowledge of us, so what does that indicate?"

"The galaxy is a big place. It could mean we simply never crossed paths before."

She refused to be comforted. "You named me ancient the moment we first saw each other, before you'd been given any details. Don't try to deny it. You've seen installations like this, haven't you? Elsewhere in your area of the galaxy? Old and abandoned, as I am."

He nodded, hating to agree but unwilling to tell her less than the truth. "Yes. We've found installations estimated at over a million of our standard planetary years old and still working, just as this place does, keeping you alive. But never another survivor. Your technology doesn't match what we call the Ancient Observers. Your people are something else, unknown to me. Judging by the way the city and the palace have grown to enclose this place, my best guess is you've been here thousands of years. Haranda, my pilot, says if the weather and the geology were stable, a primitive society could remain fairly static for such an extended time frame. A highly motivated priesthood and a visible deity such as yourself could keep certain knowledge passing through succeeding generations, even if the truth at the bottom of the legends was lost." He'd discussed the issues with Haranda many an evening, striving to understand the mysteries surrounding Bithia's presence. "So this Hialar watched over you?"

"I suppose so." Her voice was flat. "The device put me into the healing deep sleep as Father and Tedesk walked out. When I next awakened, there was a stranger tending me. She said she was five times great-granddaughter to Hialar and serving as my chief priestess. I could barely understand the words she spoke, but I realized then how long it must have been already. She either would not or could not release me from the thrall of the healer. She wanted advice—what to do about an erupting volcano. As if I would know anything useful!"

Nate had the mental impression of her shaking her head in disbelief, although in reality she didn't move so much as an inch, the healing device maintaining its iron control over her body, even in dreamspace.

"I made up a plausible lie," she went on, "added practical suggestions for evacuation, and she forced me to the sleep again, which describes the routine going forward, and I had no way to tell how much time was passing, other than by the generations of the Hialar family. A complete stranger would waken me for questions, demands, omens. And each time the language grew more corrupted, harder to grasp."

"You never tried to win freedom again?"

"No one would listen. After the first few generations, the Hialar were terrified of me and understood all too well that their power as priests and rulers was tied to me lying here." She frowned. "Except once, a long time ago. There was a man—I could reach him mind to mind, as with you and I, but not nearly as well."

"What happened to him?" He realized with a keen sense of the absurd how ridiculous it was to be jealous of a long-dead priest.

"I don't know. I only met him three times. He was intrigued with me, excited by the idea of freeing a goddess to walk among mortals as his queen. I encouraged his enthusiasm. By then I was willing to pay any price to escape my prison. I'd rather live under primitive conditions with the people if I could be free of this chamber. Breathe fresh air on my own, walk, eat…" Her voice trailed off.

"Hey, I'm not here to judge you." He wished he could touch her hand, offer a gesture no matter how small to soothe her unhappiness.

"After the third time we talked, I never saw him again, and the next priestess claimed to know nothing of his fate, nor how much time had elapsed since he and I met." Tilting her head, she smiled at Nate. "We didn't dream together. You're the only person I've ever been able to communicate with in the dreamspace. I didn't even know it was possible until you came. And now I can't imagine not having your companionship this way."

Nate realized she'd picked up on his mild jealousy and was trying to give him reassurance.

Bithia continued with her story, going back to the issue of the constant changing of her attendants over time. "Eventually came the day I was summoned to waken by Sarbordon's great-great-grandfather, a captured Hialar priest in chains by his side. These new conquerors appear to me to be a cruel, sadistic people. Certainly, this present-day king enjoys making me suffer when he calls upon me."

Nate remembered how callously the ruler had manipulated the ancient controls, recklessly enough to spur the device to sound warnings. "We've seen pretty bad things done by the priestesses of Huitlani and him since we were taken prisoner," he agreed in a massive understatement, trying in particular to suppress the memory of the ceremony at the well in the square so she wouldn't acquire the disturbing images.

"This king wakens me more and more. He doesn't care that it hurts, or how I'm weakening. On occasion, the machine flickers and pauses, and I—I can't breathe. Now when I lie in the healing sleep, it fails to quiet my mind. I'm afraid." Tears leaked from her eyes, glittering in the jeweled lights of the chamber.

More helpless than he'd ever been in his entire life and caught on the other side of the invisible barrier, Nate was infuriated at his inability to offer more than words of comfort to the despairing Bithia. He slammed his fist into the faint green barrier out of sheer frustration, forgetting he shared a dream…

…and awoke in his prison bed, chained by the ankle. Thom, Haranda and Atletl were staring at him from their cots.

"Must have been one hell of a bad dream, man," Thom said. "You were yelling."

"Sorry. Must have been the damn stewed vegetables from dinner—they do a number on my system. Go back to sleep." Nate rolled away from their troubled regard and settled on the hard mattress to wait for dawn. There'd be no more dreams for him tonight, and there was a lot to think about.

CHAPTER FOUR

Eyes closed, Bithia sat with her arms around her knees, back to the wall, crunched in the tiny space she'd carved out away from the machine's control. She realized she was humming and that her spirits were curiously light.

"Foolish girl," she said under her breath. "You don't even know if he still lives. Hundreds of years may have passed since you dreamed with him." Shaking her hair loose, down on her shoulders, she ran her hand through the soft curls, plaiting tiny braids. This generation's king had been summoning her with increasing frequency as he became more worried about the invading Githholz. She laughed with little humor. *I hope my advice has brought his armies to grief. Why these people persist in believing I know anything about military strategy is beyond me. I'm a pilot, an explorer, a specialist in technology they'll never even dream of.* Mood darkening, she reminded herself the technology she knew was probably dead and gone, no matter what great accomplishments her people had achieved in the stars. *Nate knew nothing of us. Not even our name.*

As if thinking of him had summoned the man, she sensed his approach through the mists hiding her consciousness from the ever-watchful machine.

"Bithia?"

Her nerves sparked pleasurably, pulse beating faster at the sound of his voice, deep and resonant. "Here."

In the next moment, he walked into view, the mists swirling away from him as he reached the barrier. "How is it with you?"

"Much like any other moment of my existence," she said, refusing to admit how his arrival gladdened her heart. "And you?"

He ran his hand over the barrier, studying the green light outlining his fingertips. "More sapiche practice." He made a face. "Endless drills."

Laughing at his expression, she straightened. "You don't enjoy the freedom of the outdoors? I'd trade places, even for an hour. I'd gladly kick balls and run in circles, even in their miserably hot sun."

Nate said, "I'm sorry, I didn't mean to rub it in that you're stuck here."

She waved one hand. "No apologies needed. And your men are well? Your friend Thom and the others?"

"Yeah, my men are fine." He seemed to be assessing her, his gaze on her face as if cataloging the shadows under her eyes. "Has Sarbordon been bothering you?"

"Thankfully, not today. The machine stutters, and I've won a few moments to dream of whatever I choose." *No need to worry him with the other effects the machine's malfunctions have on me.* She wanted to be happy, to enjoy this encounter, not talk about failing tech neither of them could fix.

"And you picked me to dream about?" His voice was teasing, but his brown eyes were intense, focused on her. "I'm flattered."

Her breath caught. "You—you're the most novel thing in my environment currently."

"Novel?" He raised his eyebrows at her choice of words. "Not handsome, irresistible, clever, witty—aren't you the least bit worried my feelings might get hurt?"

Bithia laughed along with him. "All of the above? And welcome company."

"I thought I heard music," he said, sitting cross-legged at the edge of the barrier. "From you?"

Her cheeks grew warm, and she realized with surprise she was blushing. "I was humming one of my favorite songs."

"It was pretty." He whistled, trying to replicate the tune and failing miserably.

Giggling, she held her hands over her ears. "Stop or it won't be my favorite much longer. Here, listen." She licked her lips and sang a few bars softly, keeping time by tapping her fingers on the cushion where she sat.

He clapped lightly. "Beautiful, like you."

She blinked, and he detected a blush spreading over her cheeks. "Flatterer."

"If the truth is flattery, then so be it. I'll never lie to you."

There was silence between them for a few moments.

"What's the song about?" he asked. "I didn't understand the words."

"A man and a woman meeting for the first time in a lush garden, each knowing the other might be the answer their heart searches for." She leaned her head against the wall, which of course existed only in her dream, and sang the song again, making herself translate the lyrics for him as she did so.

"It might be about us," he said.

Startled, she glanced at him.

"We don't have a garden, of course, since neither of us seems able to conjure one up. You keep us meeting here in this barren room, and I managed an ice planet." Nate laughed. "At least I brought you a coat on that occasion."

"And I was grateful, even if it was one a former girlfriend of yours owned." Tilting her head, one eyebrow raised, she gave him an impish look.

"I tried to suppress the fact. She wasn't my girlfriend, just a woman I dated while I was on the planet. We had fun, no deep connection. I barely remember her, but I always loved that coat." He spread his hand on the barrier. "My attraction to her didn't come close to what I feel about you. All I want is to be able to touch you—"

Bithia drew away. "Don't. Please don't say these things to me."

"Why not? I mean them. I've never felt this attracted to any other woman, not once in my life. And I can't get closer than ten feet to you, even in my fucking dreams."

She closed her eyes.

"Tell me you don't have the same desire." His challenge was direct. "But remember that when we link like this, in your dream or mine, we both see into the soul of the other. I know you in a way I've never known any other person."

"When I go to sleep," she said, tears close to falling, "there's no assurance that I'll wake up again. And then if I do regain consciousness, I never know how much time has passed. I've already lost all the people I loved—my father, my friends—I can't bear to lose you too. I can't let myself care too much."

"Denial won't change the truth."

She shook her head, refusing to comment.

"I'm not trying to distress you. Have faith in me. I'm not planning to die on this fucking planet, and I refuse to let you die here either. Maybe I can't restore you to your own people or replace what you've lost, but I give you my word that you won't lose me."

"You can't guarantee such things." Now she did stare at him. "I wish you could."

"Either I'm waking, or you're going to sleep," he said. "I'm having a hard time remaining in the dreamspace. Promise me you won't give up. I want your word you'll try to hang on to hope."

She uncoiled and threw herself at the barrier, raising her hand to meet his, although the green light flared and she knew it was impossible to touch him or be touched. "I believe in you, Nate. Stay safe."

For the next week, Nate's main motivation to get through the day was to make it to the night, when he could hope to meet Bithia in the dreamspace. But night after night went by with no contact between them. His sleep was restless, disturbed by nightmares filled with blood and death. Each morning he awoke exhausted, disoriented and frustrated.

On the morning of the eighth day, Thom lectured him as the bouncing cart carried them to the practice facility. "Listen, you need to cool it with these dreams. Are you aware you're barely present during the waking hours? I think she's more real to you than the trouble we're in. You're not learning anything strategic, from what you've said, and we've got to concentrate on the here and now."

"I didn't realize I was allowing her to distract me so badly."

"I know, and your attitude scares me. I've never seen you so detached, so uninterested in what's going on. This is our only shot at any kind of a chance of surviving, and you're going to blow it for all of us." Thom leaned closer, as far as the chains allowed, and lowered his voice further. "Do whatever it takes to get through the damn nights, dream about your phantom lady, make love to her, for all I care, but shake it off while we're out there on the ball court during the days, you hear me?"

"Right." Nate shook his head, upset with himself as he realized his old friend was making an accurate statement. He walked through the days waiting and hoping to get to the hidden room in his dreams to see Bithia, to talk to her, to be with her.

"I didn't want to say anything, but I think it's gotten to the point where you're jeopardizing the mission, all of us, with your obsession." Thom's words were apologetic, but his tone of voice was definitely not. He was genuinely concerned. "She's like a drug to you."

"You're absolutely correct. Thanks." Nate nodded in acknowledgment of the rebuke. *Get a grip. Thom's right. I'm not learning anything helpful from her, much as I enjoy our conversations. She's a dangerous distraction.*

"We're dealing with life and death here, *our* lives, and Haranda's and even Atletl's, and you've clearly been prioritizing this alien woman's problems over ours. I'm not too sure she isn't deliberately influencing you to slack off—we don't really know her, and we have no idea what her agenda might be." Fists clenched, Thom wasn't ready to let go of the subject. "I'm sorry to be so blunt, you're my commanding officer and I'll follow your lead, but I have to trust your judgment. It's a two-way street with us, and what I see lately ain't encouraging."

Tamping down anger, Nate considered Thom's suggestion about Bithia's motives but dismissed his friend's concern on that issue. He and she didn't just talk, they met mind to mind, and he saw no deception in hers. But Thom was right that he'd allowed his growing attachment to Bithia to cloud his situational judgment. "You and I aren't just captain and sergeant. We're friends too, good enough friends for you to knock some sense into me when I need it, which I appreciate today," he said to Thom. "I trust Bithia. She hasn't asked me for anything or tried to influence me, but I'm in deep with her emotionally, and I've never tried to juggle a relationship and a mission before."

"Either break it off with her for now, or learn to compartmentalize a hell of a lot better," Thom said, jaw clenched. He took a deep breath. "At least remember we can't help her if we don't survive."

"Message received."

The morning passed with scrimmages against various teams. Behind by two goals, Nate's team was playing hard to keep the other team from getting their last, fatal point, when the blare of seashell trumpets brought action all over the field to an abrupt halt.

"What the—" Nate had just gotten the ball, fed to him by a rapid underhanded pass from Atletl. Taking no chances, he threw it neatly through the lower five hole to score before pivoting to see what the trumpets were blaring alarms for.

"The big guy," Thom said. "Coming this way. And the high priestess too. Watch yourselves."

The guards and trainers created a human wall between Nate's team and the other prisoners.

"Kneel to your betters, fools," the head trainer screamed at them, uncurling his whip and cracking it suggestively. "Bow your heads to the supreme one. Show proper respect to the high priestess."

Nate reluctantly knelt in the sand, followed a moment later by his three teammates. The king stood directly in front of him, placing his clenched fist under Nate's chin, forcing him to meet the ruler's gaze. "So you play sapiche now, more or less, eh?"

"We play," Nate said.

"She claims you're her father's warriors." Sarbordon's tone was mocking. He studied Nate's face for a moment, contempt plain in his eyes. "I can't believe this—you resemble the slaves who clean the stables more than you do the best players in Nochen." He laughed uproariously. Lolanta, her priestesses, the guards and trainers joined in the mirth.

Nate jerked his head free, rising from his knees. "What you believe doesn't matter. I'm the captain of T'naritza's guards, her father's warrior. I'm no more but certainly no less. Meet me under equal conditions, and I'll prove it." He reached out, too fast for any of the watchers to stop him, and tapped the scabbard at the other man's belt. "Or is your pretty knife only ceremonial?"

Murrax and another soldier grabbed Nate, shoving him back into the subservient position and keeping their hands on his shoulders.

The ruler stepped back a pace, shaken. He scowled. "We'll see the truth of this vainglorious boast. In one passage of the moons, the day of the games arrives again. You play for your lives and her life. Of late, I think her powers wane, her advice falters. She is of the Old Ones, and their pantheon has proven weak time and again. Have not my people defeated their armies in battle? Do I not sit on the Scaled Throne?" The ruler's voice had been rising with each statement. Now he paused and spoke directly to Nate. "I know the gods of my people desire me to feed her to their creatures of the well, to seal their rule over this nation and my place as their son, their equal. I'm the one born to fulfill the prophecies in all respects." Clearly savoring this vision, obviously not a new one to him, the king paced. "Only the timing is at issue, the most propitious moment to take—"

Nate reined in his temper with an effort and said nothing. He didn't like the mental pictures, particularly as they concerned Bithia, but at the moment there was no point in challenging the tyrant. Killing him, which Nate knew with certainty he could accomplish right now, wouldn't win freedom for his men or Bithia. The assassination would get Nate killed on the spot and doom the others.

The ruler eyed him speculatively, and when Nate failed to offer any rebuttal, he mused further. "I had thought perhaps this year, at the Festival of Tekal, to offer her heart to my gods. But I can't be sure. The omens speak with veiled direction." He shot a sidewise glance at Lolanta, who bowed her head, hiding secret amusement, Nate was positive. Clearing his throat, the ruler continued, "Therefore, the matter shall be settled in the traditional manner, by the victory or defeat on the field of honor in the games."

Since all eyes were now on Nate, the audience plainly waiting for him to respond, he launched into an uncomfortably flowery speech of his own. "The power of T'naritza doesn't wane. Your omens are false, your priestesses liars. My goddess stands beside us in spirit, and we will win." Nate injected confidence he didn't actually possess into his taunt. His makeshift team had improved their sapiche skills markedly in the past months, but were nowhere near as good as men who had played all their lives.

"We'll see." Seeming pleased that he'd goaded Nate into responding, he said, "I've selected Kalgitr and his team as your opponents. You know he's won nine games to date? The team currently most favored in the Huitlani's eyes. The omens agree. A game between the two teams will be a worthy test of the gods' powers—yours and mine."

A low murmur went through the crowd of assembled guards, trainers and prisoners. Kalgitr and his team had ruthlessly maimed and killed in their quest to survive and win the required number of matches. Unquestionably the top sapiche team on the planet, they stood one game away from freedom. It was also rumored that Lolanta had sent for the team leader to be brought to her chambers on more than one occasion, which gave him an extra swagger on the court.

"It doesn't matter who you send. We'll have the victory." Concealing his dismay at the odds, Nate maintained a nonchalant tone.

"As the gods will it." Sarbordon shrugged. "I doubt you'll be so calm when facing the great Kalgitr." Struck by an impulse, he wheeled to beckon the head trainer. "A scrimmage! I desire a scrimmage today between Kalgitr and these scum. Play to one point only. I don't want my team overly worked, though not much exertion will be required to score over these pitiful slaves. Arrange it immediately."

"Yes, my lord." The trainer bowed low before shouting orders as the royal couple and their entourage walked toward the exhibition court.

"What in the seven hells are you doing? What are you telling him? When did we enlist to serve a goddess?" Thom was incredulous. Atletl and Haranda gathered in close to hear. "Aren't we getting in deep here?"

Nate shook his head. "Going along with his theory. This is our chance, don't you see? If he thinks we're the soldiers of a goddess and we can win the damn game, then we're home free. Untouchable. And we won't have to play nine more matches first. It's perfect."

"But to beat Kalgitr?" Atletl questioned, his face set in grim lines. "Do you not watch when his team scrimmages? No one can beat Kalgitr."

"Maybe we haven't been playing this damn game all our lives like you, or Kalgitr, but we've gotten pretty decent at it," Nate said. "On any given day on any given planet, someone has to win and someone else has to lose, no matter the game. It might be Kalgitr's destiny to lose when we meet in the real arena. His luck has to run out eventually."

Atletl didn't appear to be convinced, but he didn't offer any further argument in the face of Nate's vehemence. He moved off after the beckoning trainers.

All too soon, Nate and his team stood at the center of the exhibition court, facing Kalgitr and his three oversize goons. The ball shot from the middle circle, and Thom fielded it, taking off immediately for the low five at the other end of the field, only to be tripped by Kalgitr's left defenseman, the ball coming loose as he fell. With supreme effort, Thom angled the black leather ball away from the enemy, and Atletl intercepted, passing off to Haranda. The game went back and forth, using the entire field. Haranda made the shot, banking it off the other side of the court and neatly into the right circle, which was a move he'd invented. The crowd of prisoners cheered themselves hoarse. The nobles were less amused, faces displaying shock. Nate, chest heaving from the exertion in the unrelenting heat, derived a savage pleasure from Sarbordon's reaction.

"It was a fluke, not a legal move." Kalgitr voiced his complaint loudly. "They cheat, Great Lord. Let us play another point and see who triumphs."

"You can't keep up with me," Haranda said, hands on his hips, laughing. "Admit it, I'm too fast for you, tub of vegetable curd."

"Stand down." Nate was concerned by Kalgitr's rising anger and embarrassment in front of his ruler. The other player's face was flushed with anger, and his fists were clenched. Nate had seen him explode in a rage more than once when mocked by a man he regarded as a lesser opponent.

"The teams will play to the second score." After a whispered conference with Lolanta, Sarbordon made the announcement with a wave of his hand.

The ball came whipping from the low five hole, taking all eight players by surprise, and the second round commenced. Kalgitr and his men obviously hadn't taken Nate's team seriously in the first round. Nate wished he could have kept their competitive advantage for the real showdown in the city arena. Now their opponents were on their mettle, embarrassed by the loss of the first point. Atletl collapsed in a heap as he collided with two of the bigger men from the other team. The ball shot straight up in the air. Haranda snagged it and faked Kalgitr out to send the sphere slamming home into the far left circle.

"Two!" The young pilot did a victory dance at the edge of the field, playing to the crowd of cheering prisoners.

Kalgitr pivoted and checked with the king, who nodded. A third ball flew into the court, and the battle was on in earnest. Once again, Atletl got the ball to Haranda, who was driving down the court when Kalgitr tackled him full body, shoving the slender offworlder into the stone wall headfirst. A sickening thud echoed through the enclosure. As the cheers died, Haranda slid to the sand on his stomach, head at an odd angle, the ball dribbling away from his outstretched hand.

The crowd was silent. Thom, who was closest, ran to kneel beside the fallen player, checking for a pulse. Kalgitr rolled away, rose to his feet and brushed sand from his shoulders like a man with no worldly cares.

Thom shook his head. "He's dead, broken neck."

Nate spun on his heel in the sand to glare at Kalgitr, who bared his teeth in a satisfied grin and spat in the direction of Haranda's body. "These men die like any other. They're nothing special."

Rising slowly, Thom laid a hand on Nate's arm. "Not now," he said quietly.

"There will be retribution, my word on it," Nate said to Kalgitr. He turned to the trainers who arrived to carry off Haranda's corpse, wanting to know what the staff intended to do with the unfortunate man. He had only a second of warning from Thom as Kalgitr launched himself across the space between them and tackled Nate, throwing him to the sand. Twisting free, regaining his feet and dancing away, Nate raised both hands to indicate he didn't want to fight. "You killed my man and I owe you retribution for the death, but let's settle this in the arena."

Apparently emboldened by Sarbordon and Lolanta's tacit approval of his actions, Kalgitr charged. Nate landed a punishing commando blow, flat-handed and deadly, at the base of Kalgitr's neck. Spinning in a blur, Nate finished with a roundhouse kick to the man's chin. The crack of Kalgitr's breaking neck was audible across the playing fields. As the bigger man fell bonelessly to the sand, Nate stood balanced on the balls of his feet, barely winded but on an adrenaline high.

Now the head trainer belatedly screamed at the guards. Sarbordon bellowed orders. Kalgitr's teammates ran for the safety of the viewing area, apparently fearing Nate might target them next. Five guards came at Nate, faces contorted in fear and anger, weapons ready, clearly intending to kill rather than recapture him in retribution for the death of the crowd favorite and reigning champion, never mind that Nate had acted in self-defense.

The fight was on.

With an efficient flurry of blows, Nate killed the first man to reach him. Snatching the dead guard's belt knife, Nate spun to defend himself from the next wave of attackers. Dividing his attention between the second and third assailants, Nate knocked one out and crippled the other before three more soldiers piled on, followed by others.

Dimly, Nate was aware of Thom wading into the fray at his side, killing two men, snapping the neck of the first and stabbing the second with a knife hastily grabbed from the belt of the first victim. He was strangling a third when four guards tackled him, pinning him to the sand on his back, spears at his throat.

"Don't kill him," Sarbordon screamed hoarsely. "He must stand his punishment as a lesson to all the others."

A moment later, Nate was overpowered by sheer force of numbers. He struggled in the grip of his captors, hardly hearing the strident commands.

The guards dragged him, fighting them every inch of the way, out of the arena to the punishment wall. Nate was a man possessed now, all the rage and frustration at their imprisonment and harsh treatment coming out. There was nothing to lose, no reason to pull the force of his blows. More than one guard went reeling away with a broken bone, but another always came to take his place. With great difficulty, six of them fastened Nate to the wall by the wrists, face to the stones. The guards stepped away, and the beating began, lash after lash of the head trainer's whip. There was no mercy, each new blow laying him open to the bone, until Sarbordon finally intervened. Nate was dimly aware of the activity around him.

"Enough," the ruler said. "Take him to his quarters. Celixia may treat the wounds tomorrow. For tonight, no man or woman is to raise a hand to help him, on pain of their own death. See if his precious goddess heals him. If he lives, then he'll face the test of the games. If he dies tonight, we have our answer as to the will of the gods. And his death will mean T'naritza is to be mine tomorrow to do with as I please."

"And this one?" Lolanta asked, pausing beside Thom, who had been forced to watch Nate's punishment from his knees, spears pressed to his chest and back to prevent any attempt at intervention. "What of him?"

The sergeant spat at her.

Eyeing Thom with contempt, her husband said, "If his captain dies, you may have this one for the altars with no further delay. And the other as well." He nodded at Atletl kneeling in the sand beside Thom. Atletl had been as stunned as the rest of the crowd at the eruption of deadly violence on the playing field. He had belatedly, willingly waded into the fray on Thom's side, but without the hand-to-hand combat skills of the two Special Forces commandos, Atletl had been easily subdued by the guards.

Without another word, or even a glance for his fallen favorite, the ruler swept away.

Dimly, Nate realized Lolanta paused a moment longer, staring at Thom. "You won't be so defiant once we have you in our tender care. Many of my priestesses have been eyeing you, red hair. The sisterhood will make special efforts to prolong your suffering on the altar, I guarantee it."

Thom suggested she commit an anatomical impossibility, which earned him a blow from Murrax that knocked him sideways into the sand. Lolanta laughed and strolled after her husband.

The guards unfastened the shackles on Nate's lacerated wrists and stepped aside as he crumpled to the sand, his legs refusing to bear his weight. One man motioned for Thom and Atletl to carry Nate to the cart for the ride to the palace and then, once there, to lug him to his bed in their quarters. His teammates laid Nate as gently as possible on his stomach. The guards gestured for them to move away to their own cots.

"Please, let me treat his wounds. He'll surely die," Thom pleaded with the guards, but mindful of their ruler's command, the men ignored everything the sergeant said. After securing the two men to their own beds, the soldiers left, the last man slamming the door violently.

"Your captain is a skilled and dangerous fighter," Atletl said. "To kill one such as Kalgitr barehanded in a fair fight! Not to mention the guards he bested. And you accounted for at least five more. I wouldn't have believed it possible had I not seen it."

"Wish I could share your enthusiasm. Kalgitr had it coming for sure, but what a hell of a way for a man like Nate to die. Just hope it goes quick for him and that he doesn't wake before it's over. For sure he ain't going to make it to the morning for Celixia to take care of."

"Not going to die," Nate said, jaw clenched. He wasn't sure the others heard him.

"If the captain dies, we won't see the setting sun ourselves tomorrow." Atletl's matter-of-fact prediction was grim.

"Nothing we can do right now," Thom answered. "What a fucking mess."

"Best to sleep now," Atletl advised. "Regain strength for whatever tomorrow brings us." He gathered his two thin blankets and rolled up in them, turning away from Thom.

Nate was caught in pain, in red-hot sheets and torrents of agony. He couldn't move, he couldn't think, he could hardly breathe. There was no escaping the web of suffering spreading from his ravaged back, enveloping his entire body. The other aches and injuries from the day's combat were lost in the flood of pain from the savage beating he had endured. The world consisted only of the pain and the heat, with a curious coldness creeping in at the edges as he lost more blood. He considered the checkout code but didn't reach for it in his mind. Not yet. He owed Thom his best effort to survive this. And then there was Bithia.

Nate?

A soft voice pushed aside the sheets of fire in his mind, if only for an instant.

Nate? What happened?

The voice whispered his name again, compelling, forcing its way into the whirl of his torment. He knew who called him, but he couldn't even breathe her name. Words were beyond him. Thoughts were mere fragments between the waves of pain.

A cool breeze fanned his skin, bringing a moment of blessed relief from the torment.

"Bithia," he whispered through bruised lips, trying to turn his head in the direction of the breeze before hot pain came flashing back.

What have those bastards done to you? Her voice in his head was tender, concerned, thick with unshed tears. He hoped she wasn't vulnerable to his agony.

"I killed a man. Several men. And I was punished." He was blunt, unapologetic, the mental reenactment of Kalgitr's death crossing his mind, overlaying the vision of poor young Haranda's murder at Kalgitr's hands, body left lying broken in the sand.

From Bithia there was surprise, revulsion, shock. A withdrawing, whether from the deed itself or from the intensity of the raw emotions in his mind, he couldn't tell.

"Kalgitr deserved it, believe me. The bastards all did." Even in his torment, Nate cared that she understood his choice. But what did she know about men who could kill? She was a peaceful researcher from an advanced civilization who'd probably never seen violence firsthand. What common ground could the two of them have, even if they could meet?

Nate sank into the awful fire and pain, reaching for the first symbols of the Mellurean checkout code. He was so tired, crippled by the pain. There was no reason, after all, to fight any longer. Thom would use his code tomorrow at the appropriate time, cheating the bloodthirsty rulers out of their anticipated revenge.

You're wrong. I do understand. I see in your mind how the one you call Kalgitr killed first, wantonly. That poor boy—

The cool breeze whispered across his back again, bringing fleeting relief.

Listen to me, you can't give in. You have to fight the pain, please. Hold on until morning, until Celixia can come with her healing potions and salves, I beg you.

"I can't. You have to let me go." He needed to warn her about Sarbordon's plans for tomorrow, but he couldn't even start the communication to send her. What could she do in her own defense anyway? He paused in his effort to summon the code. He couldn't abandon her. His death would lead directly to hers. She'd have no one to help her.

Come to me and I'll help.

"I'm too far gone. I can't free myself from the pain long enough to find the dreamspace, not even to see you one last time." Was she even there, or merely a hallucination, a harbinger of impending death? He couldn't summon the dream, couldn't picture her or the living tomb where she lay imprisoned. Not even to see her beautiful eyes one last time, he had no strength left.

Then I must come to you, no matter the cost. Grim determination edged with a hint of fear.

There was a gust of bitterly cold wind, sufficiently harsh and unexpected to rouse Nate. He opened his eyes with tremendous effort, using all the strength left in his abused body. Bithia stood beside his bed, tears tracking down her cheeks. She was there, yet not there, fading in and out of his vision, insubstantial but present. Accompanying her was a faint, abrasive humming sound, as if a piece of machinery was in the room, straining at a pace beyond its design tolerances.

"A moment only can I stay with you, a moment only can I share the powers of the healer with you. I pray it will be enough."

Nate attempted to raise one hand, to touch her at least once before he died. *Is that so much to ask, after all I've endured on this hellhole planet?*

The slightest motion of his arm pulled at the open wounds on his back, and the pain washed over him, sweeping him toward death's peaceful release like an outgoing tide.

"I won't let you go."

In his mind, a hand wiped away the half-completed checkout code symbols. Bone-chilling cold enveloped him from head to toe. He was wrapped in it, like a tightly wound shroud, helpless. Unbearable pain raced through his body, tearing an agonized cry from his throat, leaving his vocal cords bruised and lacerated. The sensation was as if each cell suddenly froze solid, rupturing its boundaries and then unfroze in the blink of an eye, reconstituting. Nate arched from the bed in a massive convulsion as a blinding green light exploded through the confines of the chamber, spreading like the corona of a massive star, ever outward from its center in Nate's body.

"I gave you all I had. Live, please live—" The voice, faint and fading, sounded like a prayer and was gone as the last of the green light fled.

Nate blinked. Thom and Atletl sat on their respective cots, faces rigid with fear and disbelief.

"The goddess was here. I saw her," Atletl said. "Truly you are lords of the sky, warriors of the god's house. Sarbordon was wrong, and the whole world shall know of it!"

Thom ignored his babbling teammate. "Nate, can you hear me?"

"Yeah." Even whispering hurt.

"What in the seven hells—did your AO lady pay us a visit? What did she do to you, man?"

"I think she—I think Bithia was able to reach out, along the link we have with each other." Nate lay still and concentrated on breathing, which was difficult but no longer brought the waves of fire and pain to his whole body. "Can you see my back?"

"My vision is screwed for the moment, pal. Not seeing much but flashes of green."

"Yeah, colored flares are pretty much all I can see too." Nate was pleased his voice sounded stronger this time.

"At least you can talk. Can you move?"

"The room is spinning like an out-of-control ship." He drew shallow breaths and kept his eyes closed. There wasn't any need for him to move anyway. Nowhere to go, nothing to do till morning, when there would be quite a surprising disappointment for the royal couple and their adherents.

Pleased by the victory, Nate grinned into his pillow as he drifted to sleep.

Was my sacrifice enough to save him?

Bithia lay on the purple cushions, weary in every fiber of mind and body. She'd no resistance to offer the healing machine, no strength to escape its control. As soon as the sensors detected her wakeful state, her guardian would promptly submerge her in sleep. Her hard-won mental niche to think and dream in was now gone. She'd used all the power she'd carefully saved over the millennia—once she'd realized the possibility of such hoarding—to go to Nate and deal with his wounds. *He'll never know what I did for him, but I don't regret my choice.* She wanted to weep with frustration, but the healing device kept the stasis locked tight. *I doubt if I have more centuries to build my power again, one tiny flare of energy at a time, certainly not to the point where I can escape…or die. The mechanism flutters and hesitates so much now, it must be failing. Or Sarbordon will come in here and turn it off and do all the things to me he salivates over. One way or the other, the end to this nightmare is coming.*

The familiar sound of the door opening on its rusty hinges woke him. The servants bringing the morning meal screamed and dropped the trays. Bowls shattered on the stone floor, cereal splattering in clumps all over the place.

"He lives! The goddess has healed him!" The older servant backed out of the room, pushing through the crowd of guards.

Nate sat up on his cot. "I must look pretty bad."

"Ready to feature in a horror trideo," Thom said. "How's your back?"

"Aches a little, but nothing like last night. I could use a shower for sure." Nate contorted his body, trying to peer over his own shoulder. "I wish the injuries were only cosmetic enhancement for mass entertainment." Blinking, he glanced at his wrists, first one and then the other. The joints were no longer open to the bone. Angry red circles like garish bracelets remained, new skin that had grown back overnight.

"A grid of thin red lines, but no open wounds," Thom said. "It's going to scar, no doubt."

"Beats dying." Nate stretched, cautiously at first and then more fully, as he found the skin and muscles of his back were for the most part restored to health. He pointed at the gawking, unsure guards lingering in the doorway, picking out the man in charge. "Murrax, go tell your leader I'm fine today, ready for practice. I'll lead my team to victory for T'naritza when the time comes. No problem."

Murrax, who'd barely escaped death at Nate's hands the day before, opened and closed his mouth like a fish, at a total loss for words. He'd apparently been expecting to lead a burial detail today, not going out to the training fields as if nothing had happened.

"I saw the goddess last night. Truly she protects them," Atletl said. "She came to him and touched him with her power."

Celixia shouldered past the guards with an unusual show of resolve, coming to examine Nate's wounds as Murrax ran to ensure the news reached Sarbordon's ears immediately. Nate obligingly rolled over onto his stomach so the young priestess could examine the healing scars. Her touch light, she said, "So she was able to reach out to you, warrior. You're fortunate."

A reserved tone in her voice caught his attention. He raised himself on one elbow and searched her face. "Fortunate? Odd choice of words for a priestess. Not blessed?"

Celixia leaned in close to his ear, so no one else could hear her. "She's no more goddess than I am, although she does have certain powers at her command."

"Yet you're loyal to her?" Nate probed this unexpected dose of reality. It could be a disaster if Bithia—and his men—lost Celixia's support.

"My family has always served her, and she serves us." Celixia straightened and pushed the braids from her face. "The goddess has demonstrated her power this day," she said, raising her voice for the benefit of the guards and cowering servants. "Her warrior is fit for the games. Clean up the mess you've made and bring fresh breakfast, idiots, so the team may prepare for the day's practice."

Surrounded by guards, the king himself arrived in short order. He stared at Nate from the safety of the door, frowning and unsure, obviously reluctant to believe the evidence of his own eyes, yet unable to deny a man who should have been dead ate his morning meal with gusto.

"When you're done admiring T'naritza's handiwork, I'd like to take a bath and go practice," Nate said, staring across the room at his enemy-in-chief. "And I'm going to need another man for the team. I'll select a player this morning, before scrimmage. Let the head trainer know, won't you?"

Sarbordon drew himself to his full height, frowning. Pointing a finger at Nate, he said, "Don't be so cocky. T'naritza may have been able to heal you this time, but I don't think you want to tempt me to administer this test again." Satisfied when Nate said nothing to refute the threat, the ruler waved a hand casually, as if nothing Nate did mattered to him. "Go to scrimmage, then, pick another man for your doomed team." His tone was magnanimous, nearly bored. "It doesn't matter; you'll lose on game day. The gods of my people are far stronger than your pitiful sleeping girl. She'll be Huitlani's meat soon enough." With that parting shot, he spun on his heel and left, guards racing in his wake.

Murrax and the men under his command were reluctant to touch Nate, so he and his teammates were allowed to go unchained. When the quartet arrived at the practice grounds, it was obvious that word of the miracle had preceded them. The head trainer stayed out of sight for the morning, then came and apologized to Nate for having beaten him nearly to death.

"I had no choice, you know," the trainer said in a whining tone, avoiding Nate's glance. He fidgeted and played with the strands of the whip at his belt. "You killed a man, and it's the law that you had to be punished."

Nate bounced the practice ball he was holding. "As you would have punished Kalgitr, of course, if he'd lived? Since he killed Haranda?"

The trainer took a step back, mouth falling open. "The situation was different. Your teammate died on the field of play."

"A fine distinction." Nate leaned over, the trainer backing farther out of reach, a muscle in his jaw twitching nervously. "Take my advice, little man, and stay away from me, stay away from my team, and don't bet against us on game day."

Nate and Thom laughed as the trainer scuttled away. Thom said, "Are you thinking to make a break for it, now they're scared of us and our goddess?"

"We can't." Nate's answer was unequivocal. "I owe her."

"I was afraid you'd say that." Thom didn't sound too surprised, nor was he protesting.

"Besides, if you pay close attention, our jailers aren't backing off." Nate evaluated the situation on the field, assessing the potential for escape, had he been so minded to make the attempt. "We'd be dead, spears sticking out of our backs like quillbeasts, if we made a move toward the walls." Nate nodded at the circle of guards on the perimeter of the practice field. "Between you and me, I think she exhausted her powers last night."

"How did she heal you? Any ideas? Can she help us get out of this damn place, you think?"

Nate shook his head. "No idea whatsoever. She and I have this weird mental link, an ability to communicate, and it's getting stronger the longer we're stuck here, but how she managed to save my life last night, I haven't a clue."

"I didn't have my hopes up. Considering she can't seem to set herself free, it'd be a stretch to think she could save us." Thom sounded calm as ever. "Or would want to."

"She's on our side, but there's only so much she can do, for herself or for us. From a few things she's said, I think she has a plan, but it all hinges on us winning the damn game."

"Well, then, we'd better make sure we do." Thom laughed. "No problem if we had a full roster. Let's go remind the weasel of a trainer that we need to conduct a draft today. Might be good if we can get Faric, the one from Atletl's village. We could probably trust him and he's played well in scrimmages against us."

Nate, Thom and Atletl selected their replacement player from a crowd of eager volunteers. Atletl basked in all the attention and the reflected glory of being associated with warriors of the goddess. He strutted proudly along the line of other prisoners and picked out eight possible candidates for Nate and Thom to evaluate, including Faric. Nate ordered the trainers to run a scrimmage, which he watched intently. At the end, he and his companions' choice was unanimous and Faric was assigned to them. A strapping warrior from the mountain foothills, he moved with deceptive speed and excelled at blocking opposing shots.

Nate expected to see Bithia in his dreams, if not that night, surely the next. Yet there was no contact. Try as he might, he couldn't reach out to her, detected no slightest touch of her thoughts. It worried him, but he didn't mention it to his teammates. Two weeks passed in a blur of hard practices and easy scrimmages, the other teams being reluctant to challenge men who had a deity backing them. There was no sign of the remnants of Kalgitr's team. Atletl managed to find out from one of the guards that their designated opponents had also selected a new fourth and were practicing in private on a separate field.

For days, Nate demanded to know what had been done with poor Haranda's body. Eventually, he and Thom were led to a graveyard behind the practice fields, where those who couldn't maintain the grueling pace of the training, or who died in "accidents" like Haranda's, were interred. There was no marker, no indication which rounded grave was the last resting place of the unfortunate young pilot. Nate and Thom observed a moment of silence, standing at the edge of the open field. Atletl stood at attention with them. Nate recited the short, standard Sectors prayer for the dead soldier, and there was nothing more to be done.

Two days before the games, the head trainer called for Nate.

"What colors do you wish to wear? What is your team to be called?"

Nate remembered what Bithia had said about the native reptile. "We're the Tolokon, which is her totem, done in the dark blue of the night sky mixed with the scarlet of the dawn from which she came." He frowned, and the man retreated a few steps. "Why are you bothering me with this trivia when surely you knew the answers?"

"Only to be entirely sure all is to your liking." The trainer was obsequious. Apparently, the man was now none too sure the outcome of the sacred game was going to fall on Huitlani's side.

"Ensure the uniforms are ready on game day, and until then stay out of my way." Nate was enjoying intimidating one of the people who held him prisoner.

On the day of the games, the team was awakened early by servants bearing a huge breakfast heavy on the carbohydrates. Celixia wasn't present this morning to oversee the meal. Nate decided not to worry over her absence. Now the fateful day was actually here he needed to concentrate on the game.

"Any sign from your lady?" Thom asked in a whisper as the team was escorted to the dressing room at the back of the palace arena.

"None. I figure if something were wrong with her, Sarbordon would have come to gloat. I'm trying not to think beyond this match this afternoon. I don't like our game being last."

"Plenty of time to get nervous, if we were the nervous types." Thom grinned wolfishly as he threw the practice ball high in the air and caught it. "Good thing we ain't. Here comes our fourth, Faric."

Nate didn't like the fact that Faric had been kept in the player barracks at the practice arena, rather than joining the three of them in the room at the palace, but no matter how hard he protested, the ruling stood. Faric wasn't known to be dedicated to the goddess and hence wasn't deemed worthy of special treatment.

At the start of the day, there were forty men gathered in the holding area, waiting their turn to play for the life-and-death stakes. Nate and his team stationed themselves against the far wall from the entrance to the court. He preferred a solid wall at his back, even this late in the proceedings. He didn't trust anyone, and Lolanta's threats lingered in his mind. Who in here might be willing to kill them at her behest, given the promise of escape from the altars she ruled? Nate didn't want to risk a knife in the back or a poisoned drink of water for himself or any man on his team.

"Stay loose, don't think too much," Nate advised his teammates, telling them to do the opposite of what he was planning to do himself. He'd take the burden of worrying for all of them, since he was the captain.

"Take a look at Kalgitr's team," Thom said.

"Where?"

"Over there." Thom pointed with his chin, and Nate swung around to find himself being glared at by the three men he remembered from the scrimmages, plus a fourth who stood slightly away from his teammates, looking unhappy to be involved.

"Their new guy doesn't seem to be with the program," Nate said to his team in a low voice. "That may be our edge. I don't think he's an eager volunteer."

"When we take the field, he'll want to live as much as any of us." Atletl's caution against overconfidence was delivered in a flat tone. "He'll play hard."

"Yes, but he isn't one of them," Nate said. "He's a draftee in a high-stakes grudge match. You and Faric played together in your own village, and you've been a member of our team since the beginning, so we have an advantage."

"I miss Haranda," Thom said suddenly. "Wish we could have saved the poor kid."

There was silence for a moment.

"All we can do for him now is win this damn thing," Nate said.

Nate heard cheers from the mouth of the arena and watched a team come swaggering in. One of the men was limping, but all four were elated by their victory and consequent escape for another month from a grisly death dealt by the creatures in the well.

The head trainer shouted for the next two teams to ready themselves.

"Going to be a long day." Nate sat on the sand, back to the reassuring wall. "Might as well rest while we can." He shut his eyes and tried sending a questing thought to Bithia. As in the past two weeks, there wasn't even a hint of communication. Resolutely, he shut away visions of her and made himself visualize play sets and strategies instead. *Have to get into the game now, before we hit the sand, or risk falling behind on the first ball while trying to loosen up.*

Eventually, there was only Kalgitr's team and Nate's left in the holding area. Both sets of players did stretches and simple warmups. There was no conversation exchanged.

Then the head trainer was standing in the middle of the room, waving his coiled whip at them all. "Take the field for your match! Get out there!"

He held Nate back for a moment as the others moved out onto the hot sands. "I bet on you, warrior. My whole savings. Lose and I'll kill you myself before the priestesses can sharpen their knives."

Nate jerked his elbow loose and glared, sending the man staggering back a step. "You already took your best shot at me, remember?"

The trainer paled and retreated into the waiting room.

Nate came into the glaring sun a few paces behind the rest. A low murmur rose from the crowd, unlike the raucous cheering usually accompanying the first appearance of a team. He revolved in a slow circle, his gaze sweeping the crowd, which shrank back almost as one, each person seeking to avoid eye contact, to escape being singled out. In the royal box, Lolanta waved insolently. Her husband glared at Nate with open hatred. Only Celixia, who'd been seated beside Lolanta, stood and cheered for them. Nate bowed low to her and then saluted crisply.

Celixia nodded her acknowledgment of his gesture and resumed her seat, fanning herself lazily, as if unconcerned about the possibility of the game going against her goddess.

Now Nate lined up with his three teammates, next to Thom, who glanced at him quizzically. "Okay?"

Punching his friend in the shoulder, he said, "Let's do it."

Sarbordon shouted from his royal box above the arena, and the first ball shot from the middle circle. Kalgitr's team got possession, the two blockers sending Atletl flying. The other team's shooter drove straight down the field and made the point in one easy motion.

Nate was livid. "All right, dammit, they got one. We can't give up any more. Faric, you were assigned to blocking him, remember? This is for real, people, not the damn scrimmage!"

Thom caught the next ball by reflex and passed off to Faric, who failed to redeem himself, losing the ball as he worked his way toward the goal. Atletl managed to steal it back as the opposing man was taking the shot, passed it across to Thom, who scored the point off the low five hole, right between the legs of a defender.

As the third ball emerged, Atletl tripped the man who'd tackled him earlier. The ball rolled free on the sand, and a mad pileup ensued, all eight men grabbing and kicking for possession. Nate came up with it and jerked free of the tangle of bodies. He took one step, hampered by an opposing player's arms locked around his lower legs, as a Kalgitr player made a desperate grab. Falling, Nate passed to Faric, praying the man had gotten over his earlier jitters. Instead, their new recruit fumbled the ball away, and only a lightning dive by Atletl saved the point. He flicked the ball off to bounce against the far wall and into Thom's sure hands. Thom again made the point.

"Two to one, not bad, but don't ease up!" Nate shouted above the roar of the crowd. "Thom, Atletl, try to stall them."

"What the seven hells? What are you going to do?" Thom yelled as Nate raced past him. "You're going the wrong direction!"

"Changing the damn game plan. Just hold them!" Nate charged Faric. "I think you're playing for the wrong team, you bastard. What did they offer you?"

The man shrank back until he stumbled against the painted wall of the court. "I play for you, warrior, for the goddess!"

"I don't think so."

Trying to sidle away, Faric mumbled, "They offered me life, win or lose."

As Faric broke away and ran toward the entrance to the holding area, Nate launched himself into the air and landed a knockout blow with his left foot, coming down neatly on the other side of the traitor as Faric slumped to the sand in an unconscious heap.

"Get over here and block, dammit!" Thom's desperate shout in Basic cut through the noise of the crowd.

Nate spun but was a few yards short of the action when the other team made their second point, going right through the overmatched Thom and Atletl.

"Are you out of your fucking mind?" Thom said in between breaths as he sprinted to the other end of the court, where the final, fatal ball flew out of a red-painted circle. "You cold-cocked our teammate?"

"He was a ringer. We're safer without the chance of him interfering. Now play!"

Outnumbered by one man, Nate and his team managed to get possession of the ball and move it upfield, passing and feinting. Nate directed his troops on the run. "Atletl, take it! We'll guard! Thom, anything goes. Gotta get this point!"

Atletl caught the pass out of sheer reflexive terror and ran toward the required spot to shoot for the designated circle. Thom and Nate made a stand to buy him time and keep the opposing players from outflanking them to tackle their smaller teammate. A disbelieving outcry from the crowd rose to the skies as Atletl slammed the ball in for the third and final score.

"All right!" Nate gathered his two teammates in a tight circle, slapping each man's palms in victory.

The black-robed priestesses came onto the sand to loop the losing team in the chains of death. Nate wheeled to stare at Sarbordon and an obviously enraged Lolanta. Celixia beamed.

"Your gods lost, admit it," he said, the taunt ringing out loud and clear as the crowd fell silent. "Our Lady T'naritza showed her power over Huitlani today. Now set us free."

The ruler glared at him. "Not so simple and easy, warrior. I admit you won the game. I keep my word—you'll live. But your goddess has something I want, and you're going to help me get it."

"What do you suppose he means?" Thom asked as the king left his box in the stands above them.

"I imagine we're going to find out soon," Nate told him. "Here come the guards. I bet we're going into the maze again, to her."

Thom shot him a speculative glance. "Which is fine with you, of course."

"I figure our best chance is to keep playing out this 'warriors of the goddess' act. We might get a break, an opportunity to escape. Remember she indicated she might have a plan."

"I'm with you," Thom said. "What about Atletl?"

"He comes with us," Nate said, both to Thom and to the guards surrounding them on the sand. "He's in the service of the goddess."

"True. She appeared to me, I serve her, she protects me," Atletl said grandly.

Murrax furrowed his brow for a moment, but apparently his orders were to get them into the palace to meet the impatient man in charge as quickly as possible, so he motioned for the three of them to follow him off the playing field.

"And this man?" The head trainer knelt by the unconscious Faric.

"He's a traitor. I don't care what you do with him," Nate said.

The rest of the guards fell into step with him, blocking any thought of escape for the moment. Escorted by the soldiers, he proceeded through the now deserted holding area and ascended the stairs leading into the palace.

CHAPTER FIVE

Nate observed Sarbordon and a pair of the black-robed priestesses waiting at the end of the corridor. There was no sign of Lolanta, whose absence made Nate glad. Celixia came out from behind the other two priestesses as the men walked up.

"Doesn't he have to preside over the hideous public ceremony in the square? At the well?" Thom said.

Nate shrugged. "Maybe Lolanta's handling the duties for both of them. I'd rather she was there than here. She's one scary lady."

He came to where the king waited, tapping one foot impatiently. The squad surrounding the team halted, Murrax and the guards saluting their ruler. Nate stood loosely, ready for action, secure in the knowledge that Thom had his six. Now that they'd won the sapiche game, he believed the balance of power had subtly shifted even further in his favor than it had after his miraculous recovery from the whipping. The team might still be prisoners, but their enemies were forced by their own belief system to view Nate and his men as backed by a higher power, making Nate a person to be seriously reckoned with.

Although he was concentrating on the king, Nate's peripheral vision was excellent. He was aware that the priestesses were examining him nervously, whispering behind their black feather fans. Their unhappy agitation at his state of health gave him satisfaction.

Celixia took a step away from the two Huitlani priestesses. She bowed her head to Nate. "Congratulations on your victory, warrior. The match was thrilling to watch."

"We go to see your goddess now," the ruler said. "She'll give me what I want today. You'll tell her to comply."

Raising a hand in warning, Nate shook his head. "I serve her. I don't command her."

"She promised that if you won the sapiche game, she'd request you to do my bidding. You'll tell her that you won, against all odds, I must say, including the deluded fellow on your own team. Where can he have gotten the idea that if your team was defeated due to subversive action on his part, he could avoid the altar?" Sarbordon's voice was lazy and richly ironic. One of the black-clad priestesses choked off a laugh and hid her face behind her fan.

"I wonder." Nate kept his tone equally dry. He and the ruler understood each other.

Eyeing him, Sarbordon evidently decided to let the subject drop. "Your win was decided among the respective gods we worship, and as a corollary to the unprecedented event, it's ordained that I am to have the sacred objects I've coveted for these many years. Come with me and let us set the events in motion without further delay."

The king strode down the long hall. Nate exchanged glances with Thom as he followed. Celixia fell in behind them, walking with Atletl. "This doesn't sound too good," Nate said to Thom. "What would she promise him we'd do? She never told me any details."

"At least you know she's alive," Thom said.

"Why she'd promise this bastard anything is beyond me."

Nate and his companions went through the long series of corridors, moving deeper beneath the palace, approaching the mysterious chamber where Bithia had lain imprisoned for millennia. Nate was determined to seize at least a quick word alone with Bithia before their enemy launched into his demands. As the group approached the white carved wall, Nate shoved past the two Huitlani priestesses, who recoiled at his touch. Grabbing Sarbordon's wrist, Nate prevented the ruler from activating the first symbol.

"I must speak with T'naritza privately first."

Eyes wide in shock, the ruler appeared ready to refuse.

Ignoring the guards, retaining his hold on the man's fleshy arm, Nate stared him down. "The goddess and I have matters to speak of which are not for the ears of others, not Celixia, not even yourself. Our discussion won't take long, but only when we've settled matters between ourselves can we give our attention to your demand."

The king sputtered, but Nate wouldn't let him get a word in edgewise.

"For weeks you haven't given me a chance to report her father's commands to her. The words of the gods aren't meant for others to hear." *Might as well go for broke and embellish the hell out of this lie.* "I'm but the vessel for her father Fr'taray's words. Anyone other than the lady herself hearing the private message will suffer instant, horrible death."

"And why would I believe ths is true?" The tone of the question was sharp, suspicious.

Nate kept a straight face and nodded with all the sincerity he could manage. "You've seen one example of my lady's powers when she reached forth to heal my wounds. Her father has a thousand times the powers she possesses. Don't tempt fate by overreaching in the moment."

The ruler swallowed hard, then again. He checked with Celixia for confirmation. Nate held his breath until the slender priestess nodded her concurrence with his demand for a private moment.

Sarbordon shook him off. "All right, but be quick." He waved one meaty finger in Nate's face. "No tricks, I warn you, or you and she will suffer, this I swear. We'll open this door, and you and Celixia may cross alone. She can sing the last barrier open for you. I'll allow the space of a few moments for this private communication you insist you must have."

"My sergeant stays here with you as hostage to my honor," Nate said, which appeared to mollify the king. Thom probably wasn't as happy about it, but made no comment.

Nate nodded to the priestesses. "Begin."

The women chanted as required, standing well back from the wall. As before, the ruler did his part, pressing all the required symbols but the final one, which he indicated Nate should do. Using his fists, he depressed the central symbol, and in a heartbeat he and Celixia were standing alone inside the next alcove, the fat green snakes of pure light crawling harmlessly over their bodies. Nate felt refreshed and restored, much as the lights had cured his headache the first time he'd been here. As he and Celixia emerged from their short walk through the sloping, darkened final corridor, he glanced at his scarred wrists. The effect of the healing green light was further dimming the raw, red marks left from the day of his beating.

Celixia shyly touched his left wrist. "You'll bear the scars, warrior, but as badges of honor."

"Badges I could have done without earning. Will you open this final door and let me have a few moments alone with her?" Nate nodded at the massive, translucent black slab barring their way.

She studied his face intently for a moment. "Sarbordon won't be patient for long, I warn you." Celixia chanted the three-word vocal key to the chamber, retreating as she did so.

Nate turned away from watching her to find the black door had already responded to her command by silently vanishing from view. He stepped across the threshold into the chamber where Bithia lay.

Strange to be walking where he'd been in dreams so many times over the past several arduous weeks. Nate descended the three stairs as he always did in the dreamspace and walked toward the silvery couch, the lights rising as he approached. Spreading his hand wide, he flattened his palm against the invisible barrier, staring at her.

"I'm here."

I know. She kept her eyes shut, but one elegant hand twitched slightly on the couch. *Meeting you again is a joy.*

"Thank you for saving my life the other night." Tongue-tied as he never was in their shared dreamspace, Nate berated himself for the inadequacy of his words considering she'd pulled him from the brink of death.

I had to save you—you've become dear to me, the only true friend I've known in all my time of imprisonment on this planet. I couldn't let you die without trying to prevent it. Of the two of us, I'm the one long past their time, the one who must die.

"Don't say that. We'll figure something out, I promise." Nate looked closely at her, realizing she was even more gaunt and drawn than when he'd first seen her. "Are you all right?"

I told you the device is not running properly.

Nate realized she'd mentioned that several times in the dreams, but he hadn't considered the ramifications, much less the potential physical effects on her.

I had to push the absolute limits of what's possible to come to you that night. But the sacrifice was worth it.

Nate closed his eyes for a moment in pain and frustration. There was so much he wanted to say, on so many topics, that he had no idea where to begin. Sarbordon would bull his way in any moment. The ruler's presence would end any chance to exchange plans or information. Torn between his personal craving to communicate with Bithia versus the immediate challenges facing them all if they were to survive, he had to prioritize this fleeting opportunity for the latter. The future would have to be dealt with another time. "We just won the sapiche game, and the king tells me you two have a side agreement about a task we're to do for him. Why should we do anything for him? What's going on?"

My father left a cache of supplies outside what was the city limit in my time. It's evidently well known as a shrine to this day. Sarbordon craves the contents, which he imagines to be weapons. He believes the treasures will give him victory over the enemies crowding his borders.

"Is he right? Are there weapons?" His fingers itched to hold an offensive weapon with real firepower.

Not as you are thinking. We didn't deal in such things.

"It's been a long time," he said with cautious understatement. "Do you think anything will be left intact?"

Our storehouses are equipped with a special form of stasis device to maintain the viability of everything within. Let me show you how to open the storehouse doors. Bithia appeared to understand how rushed they were.

He stood with his eyes closed, trying to quiet his own racing thoughts. A rapid series of symbols to be triggered, gemmed switches to be thrown in exacting sequence, flickered through his mind, leaving him dizzy. "How do I find this place?"

The king will take you. This is your chance to escape. My father never let his most trusted local aides inside the storehouse, not even Hialar.

Nate caught a backlash of bitterness in her memory of the assistant her father had trusted in all other ways and who had so betrayed her.

But Father knew someone might figure out the sequence for opening the cache by watching him. So he rigged a safeguard to render unconscious any locals who enter.

Clever. But he detected the flaw immediately. "How does his precaution help if it knocks Thom and me out?"

The sensor detects one particular set of subgenetic tertiary markers found only in residents of this planet. A side effect of being born under the radiation of the particular star. Do you want an astrophysics-based genetics lecture right now, or can I perhaps recite from the protective-devices manual at a later time?

Nate heard her amusement at his doubting caution.

You should be fine. The enemy will be completely at your mercy once you reach the warehouse level. They will sleep as long as they remain in my father's facility. Then you can escape the city, make your way to your own ship and depart from this planet to freedom in the stars. I leave the details to you, my fine warrior friend, but I know you'll manage. I'll miss you. Even in my sleep, I dream of you now.

Voices sounded in the small corridor beyond the chamber. Celixia's soprano tones rose above the general hum, protesting Sarbordon's move to join them, warning Nate to conclude his private chat. He kept his attention focused on Bithia. "I'm not leaving you."

You must, you have to. Panic suffused her tone. *You'll have only this one chance. Don't waste it.*

"I don't hear any words of the gods," the king called from what he'd evidently decided was a safe distance behind them. "I'm coming in, and you'll do my bidding, warrior. You've had long enough to talk to your goddess."

"Fortunately for you, we're finished," Nate said calmly. Stepping away from the barrier, he watched the ruler rush into the chamber. Catching a sideways glance from Thom, Nate made a subtle hand signal to show things were proceeding all right.

Sarbordon strode to the control panel on the far wall. Nate wasted no time in joining him there, clamping his hand over the ruler's fist. "Gently, we're going to do this gently. There's no need to be forceful with her today. She's eager to grant your wish, but neither she nor I want to endure the pain you inflicted on us both the last time. Got it?"

His enemy glared at him, but whatever he did to trigger the device this time was less physically stressful for Nate, so he hoped it was also easier for Bithia.

She opened her eyes and searched for Nate as soon as the device released part of its absolute control over her. Her gaze remained fixed on his face even as she spoke with the king.

"I've instructed my warrior to take you to my father's storehouse," Bithia told her enemy in the eerily amplified voice. "He's to make available all of its contents to you today before the sun sets."

Her voice in my head is lighter, more musical. Nate bit his lip. Now was emphatically not the time to let himself be distracted by thoughts of what he and Bithia shared.

"After you gain entry to the treasures of my father, Fr'taray, you must release my warriors to take passage in their sky chariot to his realm. This must also be done before dawn, or you'll suffer the consequences of my father's wrath."

"You'll stay?" Sarbordon fingered his belt knife.

"Now that she's proven her powers he wants to keep her," Nate whispered in disgust to Thom. The sergeant nodded, a grim set to his face.

"I shall stay," Bithia agreed, docile and submissive. "My warriors don't have orders to remove me from this place. I protect and serve you and your people. My duty remains unchanged."

Not if I have anything to say about it. Nate marveled at her ability to deal so calmly with her tormentor, but supposed after all the millennia of inadvertent captivity, Bithia had relinquished any hope of release from servitude as a prophetess. *She should trust me not to leave her behind.*

Nate picked up Bithia's cue about the timing. "You've heard T'naritza's decree. We're to go now, before nightfall. Are you ready?"

"We'll go at once." The ruler was excited, rubbing his hands together while he visualized the marvels soon to be within his grasp. Abruptly, he flicked the citrine- and amethyst-encrusted gold switch, plunging Bithia into sleep.

Nate lingered behind the others, gazing through the barrier. Gently, he set one hand on the invisible boundary between them, sending an emphatic message: *All I'm asking is for you to hang on. I'll return for you.*

Nate heard the faint whisper of her voice ordering him not to take chances, and then there was only silence in his mind.

Sarbordon couldn't stop talking as he led the way upward through the various corridors, away from the healing chamber. He alternated between speculating with the two priestesses as to the exact nature of the marvels he'd soon be cataloging, repeating snatches of old myths, and telling Nate his impressions of the strategy at various points during the sapiche game.

"Man would make a good play-by-play announcer for the All Sectors Games," Thom said as the ruler embarked on a long dissertation about how he'd handled the low five shot when he played sapiche as a boy. "He sure can talk."

Nate stayed focused on what lay ahead, even though he had as yet only the vague outline of a plan based on Bithia's quick briefing on the warehouse's self-defense setup. He relied on Thom to unquestioningly follow whatever lead he set. After all their years of working missions together, he and his partner didn't require much, if any, advance discussion. Atletl might be a help, might not. He certainly wouldn't work against them.

Sarbordon must have been confident of the outcome of his conversation with Bithia. As Nate followed the ruler out of the palace through yet another exit he'd never seen before, a fleet of chariots were waiting with impatient, high-spirited quadrupeds stamping and snorting in the traces.

"This pile of rock has more doors than a Deebian thousand-valve clam," Thom said, gazing behind him at the hulking palace. "I remember an old myth on Earth about the guy who invented the first blaster being afraid of the ghosts of all the people who were killed by it, so he kept building more and more additions onto his house."

"Why?"

"So the ghosts couldn't find him. Maybe the ruling family has the same kind of guilty conscience about all the people they've killed, so they keep adding doors and more doors to escape from the ghosts?"

"When we get home, you can apply for a job doing psych evals of new contact planets, okay? But right now—"

"You want to concentrate on the task at hand." Thom laughed. "Same old Nate, never change."

Sarbordon cut off the banter. "Warrior, you and the red-haired one will ride with me. Quickly now. The teams of kemat are fresh and pulling at the reins!"

The king opted to drive a chariot personally through the gathering gloom of sunset. Throngs of people, who were probably heading for the public square to attend the ritual of feeding the losing teams to the predators in the deep well and subsequent drunken orgy, scattered in the streets as the cavalcade thundered past. Nate peered through the choking dust clouds at the four chariots following theirs, carrying a complement of the black-robed priestesses, as well as soldiers. Atletl waved from the second chariot, squeezed in with Celixia and a guard.

Closing his eyes, Nate retraced the motions Bithia had implanted in his mind for opening the doors of this mysterious storage chamber. He wished this side trip wasn't necessary, but saw no other way to accomplish his twin mission objectives of freeing Bithia and escaping.

"Not too many Special Forces guys can say they found an AO-like treasure cache and then tamely handed it over to the locals to plunder," Thom said in wry Basic, leaning his head close to Nate's left ear. "You don't genuinely believe he'll keep his word and let us ride away into the night?"

Nate shook his head. "No chance. Not the way his mind works."

"So what's our play? I'd like to get back to the ship and lift out of here. Bithia's advice is right on target."

"Will the ship fly? It wasn't disabled in the crash?" Nate asked the crucial question he hadn't dared to explore since the moment he had regained full consciousness as a captive in chains. At the time he'd been focused on moment-to-moment survival. The condition of the spaceship was a moot point.

Thom fiddled with the leather straps on the chariot rail. "Not sure. Before we were captured, Haranda thought it would be fine. Needed time planetside for the AI to carry out adjusting and compensating, he said."

"This would be the late *cadet pilot* Haranda"—Nate laid extra emphasis on the title—"who was on his first real mission outside the home Sectors? He was sure, huh? What did you see?"

"I'm no flyboy," Thom said, raising one hand in protest. "There were a few singe marks on the hull, no obvious penetration of anything vital."

"Except we crashed. A crash usually indicates something about the condition of the ship."

"The AI was working after the crash, which is a good sign. Those courier ships are built tough. My guess is we're good to go."

"Not until we rescue the lady." Nate shook his head emphatically as Sarbordon whipped the kemat "horses" to greater effort. "We're not leaving her here." He didn't dare utter Bithia's name while standing elbow to elbow with his enemy in the chariot, even though the ruler was paying no attention to their whispered conversation. *I'm not taking any chances from here on out.*

"Your personal mission objective may not be possible," Thom said. "I'll back any play you make, but don't get your hopes too high is all I'm asking. So many things could go wrong. This ain't exactly been a smooth-running mission from day one. Even winning the sapiche game was damn ugly, what with Faric playing against us on our own team."

"I'm concentrating on this next task we've been set to accomplish and not thinking any further." Nate clenched his hand on the chariot's top rail as Sarbordon took a curve so fast the offside wheel left the ground for a moment. "None of this was in the orders of the day. Our original set of orders got rewritten when Jurgens panicked, decided to go into hyperspeed next to a blue giant and took us off all the known charts."

Thom cleared his throat. "Been meaning to talk to you about that."

"You saying it didn't happen that way? This planet sure doesn't match the description of the world where we were assigned to go Mawreg hunting."

"I think Haranda was at the helm when it happened."

Nate briefly considered the implications of who'd been piloting during the disastrous set of maneuvers. "Then Jurgens was an even bigger fool than I believed to let a fresh-out cadet fly us into the goddamn corridor," he said.

"Figured you'd want the report to be accurate," Thom answered.

"Seven hells, you know damn well if we ever get back to file a report, I'll make sure both Jurgens and Haranda come out heroes. Whatever happened and whichever one of them got us into this mess, both paid the dues."

Nate surveyed the rapidly darkening sky, scanning for the welcome stars. Inhaling a deep breath of the fresh air, he said, "Sure is good to be outside and not playing everlasting sapiche."

"Here I dreamed we'd make our fortunes by introducing sapiche in the Sectors when we get back. Create a league, the whole deal."

"Have to change the rules for the losers," Nate said. "I think we're almost there." He got a better grip on the chariot's rail as the team slowed to navigate a steep, winding paved grade. Sarbordon wielded his whip with abandon, apparently not willing to accept delays in reaching his long-sought treasure now that he had a proven messenger from the gods to unlock it for him. The health of his prized racing kemat was a secondary consideration tonight.

The road came to an end on the plateau. A miniature step pyramid stood at the far end, its contours softened by unimaginable passage of time since Bithia's father had constructed it. Vines, trees and other forms of nature's green demolition experts had done their best for uncounted centuries to insert roots between the tightly fitted blocks and pull the place apart.

The tired kemat brought the chariots to within a few yards of the structure before halting. After handing the reins to a spare driver, who came running from the tail of their caravan, the king strode eagerly to the pyramid. Nate and Thom matched him stride for stride on the well-worn path to the front of the structure. Nate noticed Celixia stayed close to Atletl. Murrax and the guards kept a wary eye on Nate and Thom, confirming his estimation of their basically unchanged status as prisoners.

The pyramid was constructed from massive blocks of local stone, in a style similar to what he'd seen in older portions of the palace and the sapiche stadium.

Thom whistled. "Look at the heaps of stuff on the stairs."

As Nate walked closer, he saw offerings ranging from simple candles to food, flowers, strings of cheap beads, toys, feathers and other small items piled along the steps of the structure.

"People still believe in the power of Fr'taray, I guess." Bending over, Thom picked up a small wooden carving of a tolokon sitting next to a lush but wilted bouquet. He examined the figurine and gently set it down. "Wonder what the person hoped for?"

"No telling." Nate shook his head, dismissing the subject as he surveyed what lay ahead of them.

At the top of five wide steps was a small, houselike structure that lacked windows. A single, elaborately carved and polished bronzelike metal door was set flush into the face of the building. Twice as tall as Nate, the panel was surprisingly narrow. Bright enamel in riotous colors outlined the symbols, undimmed by thousands of years of exposure to the planet's weather and the reverent touch of countless pilgrims and supplicants. The collection of symbols resembled those in Bithia's chamber and on the outer, whitewashed portal to her part of the labyrinth beneath the palace. Nate recognized quite a few, especially those painted at the edges of the portal.

Sarbordon coughed.

Nate found the ruler staring expectantly at him. He pointed at the door with his coiled whip. "It'll be dark soon, and the three moons don't rise early this night. I've no desire to conduct this entire operation by torchlight."

Nate nodded. Before he could go forward, Celixia worked her way through the small crowd to stand beside him. She pulled on his left arm. "I have to speak to you first."

"What's the delay now, priestess?" Sarbordon frowned. "Why couldn't you speak to him before this moment? And what must you tell him, eh?"

"We were in separate chariots by your order, my lord," Celixia answered mildly, her tone gentle and placating. Knowing how much the woman must hate him, Nate gave her high marks for self-control, as well as acting skills.

"What is it?" he asked, leading her away and wrapping her more closely in her elaborately beaded, lined cloak against the early night air as they strolled. Watched by the suspicious king and the hostile, nervous guards, Nate drew them to a standstill, using the pretext of gallantly fastening her cloak to turn his back to them all. Subtly, Thom shifted his stance, further blocking a clear view of Nate and Celixia.

"I know you plan to try to free her." Celixia's whisper was urgent. "There are things inside that I'll require to bring her safely out of her sleep."

"You can't go in there, not possible."

Taking him by surprise, she said dismissively, "I know. My family's hard-guarded knowledge makes the stuff of ordinary people's legends. I know the truths in the myths."

"We waste the light," Sarbordon called from behind them. "No more conversation."

Nate ignored the increasingly impatient ruler. "Tell me."

"All I know is the need for a red box. You must find it if you wish her to live."

"Why didn't she tell me this herself?"

"Perhaps she no longer believes anyone can rescue her. Maybe her father didn't bother to tell her the contents of the red box were necessary, since it was the task of the first Hialar to provide them."

"I'll add this box to my shopping list, I promise." Squeezing her arm gently, he escorted her to where Thom and the king lingered.

"What does she want?" demanded the latter.

"A particular trinket from the trove inside to wear to prove to her rival priestesses that Fr'taray's treasures do indeed wait within." Nate lied with a wink.

The ruler rubbed his chin and gnawed his fleshy lip for a moment before guffawing. "These petty jealousies between the factions never cease. I must select pieces for Lolanta as well, or I won't hear the end of it." He narrowed his eyes. "I get first claim on all items within this place of your god."

"Of course." Nate bowed, ignoring Thom rolling his eyes off to the side.

"Can we proceed?" Thom said.

"We've delayed long enough." Bounding up the five steps, the ruler swept everything out of his path that had been so carefully set in place by supplicants and pilgrims. The pitiful offerings fell in a jumbled, crashing mess to the base of the stairs. Celixia cried out against the sacrilege.

Resting a calming hand on her shoulder, Nate rebuked Sarbordon. "For one who came seeking the treasure of Fr'taray, a modicum of respect for what his worshipers left him would be advisable."

Even in the gathering gloom, he appreciated and took satisfaction from the way his enemy's face reddened. *He's probably never been spoken to like that. Better not get too carried away. Balance of power's on his side for a few more minutes.* "Step aside and give me room. It's my job to open this place, not yours."

Obviously reluctant but with as much dignity as he could command, Sarbordon descended, taking a childish swipe at one last stack of candles on the bottom stair, his glare challenging Nate and Celixia alike to protest. Neither did.

Picking his way among the wreckage of the offerings, Nate ascended until he reached the narrow step in front of the vast metal door. The portal was literally covered in symbols, many incised into the metal, others displayed on slightly upraised tabs or buttonlike devices. He closed his eyes to visualize the first symbol he had to find to trigger the opening sequence. When he opened his eyes again, it was as if Bithia stood there, guiding him straight to it, to his left, close to the threshold.

"Not an obvious spot for the door handle." Nate bent to press the tab. He swept his hands across the door, twisting a symbol there, depressing another next to it and finally, after hesitating a moment, brought his closed fist down with deceptive gentleness on one intricate turquoise, red and yellow whorl directly above his head.

The door slid smoothly into a hidden receptacle in the pyramid. Nate had to take a small, awkward hop back to keep his balance. *The panel must have curved into the roof somehow.* He extended his right arm to block the king's rush forward.

"We must go together. This is only the first step of gaining access to the treasures you seek," Nate said mildly. Searching for Atletl in the small crowd. Nate pointed at him. "Warrior, I charge you with the safety of the Lady's priestess. Stay with her and wait."

Their former teammate did a double take and exchanged a swift glance with Celixia, but saluted and drew her off to the side.

"Why may she not come?" Sarbordon was, as always, suspicious of anything he hadn't decreed.

"The secrets of Fr'taray are not for a woman's eyes, lord. Surely your reading of the old tablets has revealed this fact to you? And so they"—Nate gestured at the black-clad priestesses of Huitlani—"must remain outside as well." He hated to exclude them from whatever potential knockout effect had been set in place for curious locals, but he felt duty-bound to protect Celixia, which meant protecting the other priestesses too.

For the moment.

"The decree is as you say." The ruler shooed the disappointed women away. "If there are no further strictures or reasons for delay, let us proceed." The ruler's temper was plainly fraying at being so close to his heart's desire but endlessly sidetracked by his companions.

Nate, Sarbordon, Thom, their old jailer Murrax and two of the guards entered the small space revealed behind the door. The five charioteers and other soldiers waited outside. Celixia strolled to the side of the plateau with Atletl, and the last view Nate had of her, she was seated on a low bench beside a small tree, clearly resigned to wait as ordered. She and Atletl were engaged in a low-voiced conversation, laughing from time to time as if no slightest worries disturbed their mood.

As soon as six men were inside the pyramid's vestibule, Nate keyed a glowing red symbol embedded in solitary splendor on the far wall. The metal door slid shut, cutting off their access to the outer world, and the floor sank.

"What treachery is this?" The king drew his short sword, put his back to the wall and glared at Nate with escalating fury.

"My lord's treasury lies below the ground," Nate said as he leaned away from the sword, hoping his pronouncement was true. Bithia hadn't had time to tell him much more than the sequence for gaining entry. What was coming next was anyone's guess, other than the hoped-for unconscious state of the locals at some point. Nate was good at acting without advance planning when the situation called for it. His ability to react in a split second was one of the things making his Special Forces team so successful on missions behind enemy lines back in the Sectors—the Mawreg and their allies couldn't predict where Nate's team would be and what they'd do.

Drawing on a long-ago class in mythology, he embellished his lies as the platform continued its descent. "We stand on a device of magic that's taking us effortlessly and unharmed past the guardian demons and spirits of the underworld to the level where Fr'taray left his most-precious and sacred possessions."

"You'd better be speaking truth, or by Huitlani's Knife, you'll die." Sarbordon slammed his sword back into the scabbard, and the soldiers followed suit.

"Patience, sir," Thom said. "This magic is a common mode of transport for us, as common to us as your chariots are to you." To Nate, he added in Basic, "Not exactly a lie, right?"

The platform continued its stately descent, noiseless and smooth. The lighting gradually became brighter, emanating from the walls as it did in Bithia's chamber. With growing impatience, Nate waited for the device to render the uninvited unconscious. Was the mechanism going to discriminate successfully between him and Thom and the local men, the way Bithia told him it should? He was tense, ready to take action.

The platform came to a halt without so much as a bump.

Another bright metal door faced them. Nate stepped forward without hesitation and once again performed the sequence for opening closed doors. The panel slid upward, and light streamed in from the vast chamber revealed beyond.

In the space between one heartbeat and the next, the four Talonqueni crumpled bonelessly to the floor, falling with heavy thuds that echoed in the confined space.

Thom let out a gusty breath, obviously having held it in case a gas was being used, and both men laughed.

"Guess the old boy thought it would be fun to let the locals get to the edge of what they wanted to steal and then knock them flat," Thom said between chuckles. Kind of have to admire his sense of humor."

"Let's see what we have here." Nate took a step off the platform and through the open portal.

Thom hesitated. He craned his neck to peer up the long, featureless shaft to where a faint light indicated the entry door. "How do we keep the lift at this level? I don't want to be stuck in here until the ancient sky pilots return, which—based on all available evidence—will be never."

"Good point." Nate frowned. "Bithia didn't say anything about how this platform works." He scanned the walls and pointed with relief at a complex, glowing red emblem. "I think this is the control. Unless the platform is summoned from above, we should be fine. No one on the planet but Bithia knows how to get in here. Come on."

"Seemed worth mentioning." Thom strode resolutely through the opening and stopped beside Nate. "Little thing I learned the hard way in basic training—be sure to keep your exits open."

Nate didn't bother responding to this running joke between them, because he was staring around the chamber they'd strolled into.

A high-ceilinged room stretched in all directions as far as he could see with his enhanced night vision. The place was lit only in the immediate vicinity, although Nate felt sure the lighting would follow them as they moved farther into the storehouse. There was a definite pattern to how the ancient explorers had run their operation, which was reassuring under the current conditions.

"Old man Fr'taray was quite a packrat," Thom said, walking a few paces beyond where Nate stood. He did a slow three-sixty. "Or am I understating the situation?"

Containers vaguely resembling crates or barrels—objects with no human-equivalent name—were all piled in a messy heap of random stacks suggesting haste or panic, or both. It certainly wasn't the orderly warehouse Nate had visualized.

"Wonder what actually happened, what her father was called back for?" Nate said, surveying the mess. He squatted by the nearest object, which was an orange cylinder. He touched the symbol he now recognized as shorthand for "open." With a click, the container split neatly in two, spilling a dried substance onto the black stone floor.

"Food? Sample of the local spices?" Thom asked.

"Could be either or both. Or neither. We'll never know. You try one."

Thom eyed the assorted piles for a moment and plucked a tiny blue and green triangular object off of a perilously askew stack of squares and rectangles. He shook his selection slightly. "Good things come in small packages, as my gramma used to say. I push this, here?"

"Right—you got it."

"Hey, we're experts now." Thom laughed. "Oops—damn!" His container had held dark green liquid that now splashed onto his sandaled feet and the floor, creating a massive puddle. Thom tossed the partially deflated triangle back onto its former resting place and stepped gingerly away from the liquid. "As much fun as this is, now what?"

"You see anything like a red box, about, oh, this big?" Nate mimicked the size with his hands, much as Celixia had shown him.

"You've got to be kidding me. We're required to find one specific thing in all this mess?" Thom's laugh broke off abruptly as he took a closer look at Nate's expression. "Seriously? We need this box? For what?"

"Bithia didn't mention it, but Celixia was adamant that freeing her from the healing device requires the contents of a red box."

Hands on his hips, brow furrowed, Thom eyed the vast room with a noticeable lack of enthusiasm. "I'm game. We have time while old Sarbordon sleeps. Bithia said they'll be unconscious as long as they stay down here. For sure no one's going anywhere before we report back. Any ideas where you'd like to start? Hints from Celixia?"

Nate shook his head and considered the challenge. "This aisle runs straight through the room. Let's see if there are paths branching off. You watch to the right, and I'll take the left. If this red box is so damn important, maybe Fr'taray left it, I don't know, where somebody besides him could find it."

"If he left it here at all. Working off intel thousands of years old doesn't give me much confidence."

The two soldiers advanced straight into the room, back to back for defense, warily eyeing the treasure horde of the ancients. The illumination source followed them, as Nate had expected. He found it eerie and disconcerting to be in the center of one pool of light in a vast darkness. The exposure was counter to all his training, as well as his well-honed instincts for self-preservation.

The light in the lift shaft stayed on even as they got farther and farther away. A reassuring beacon.

"I feel like a goddamn target out here in this spotlight," Thom said after three or four moments of cautious pacing through the stockpile. "Like a pair of idiot cadets on their first war sim, walking right into an ambush."

"Let's finish the sweep and get the hell out of here. This is a waste of time, I'm afraid."

But after only another five yards, Thom came to an abrupt halt, staring off to the right. "Nate."

"What?" He pivoted and stopped, stunned by the sight that had caught Thom's attention.

There was a side corridor that had been hidden by the piles of containers until Thom drew even with it, the charred remains of a body, skeleton showing through ashy black layers of burnt clothing, lay on the cold stone floor.

"Well, I'll be moon-damned." Nate walked toward the remains.

"These crates and things have burn marks," Thom said, eyeing the black score marks. "Firefight?"

"Shows all the signs." Nate knelt by the body of the long-dead alien explorer. "Burnt to a crisp. No way to tell if the victim was male or female. From the size,

I'd guess male." He rocked back on his heels, scanning the area in frustrated bewilderment. "Damn, what happened here? She swore to me her team had no deadly weapons, or at least not the type I was visualizing, like our blasters."

Thom moved past him. "Maybe she didn't know," he said over his shoulder. "Command don't confide in the lower ranks, even if she was his daughter. Here's another guy." Thom was about ten yards deeper in the warehouse. "Shot in the back. At least he—it—is facedown, which tells a tale. And Nate—"

"What?"

"I see a red box."

Nate got to his feet and sprinted to join Thom. "Where?"

Thom pointed at the second corpse and the red box cradled in one arm, partially hidden underneath the body.

"I hate to have to tell her about this," Nate said. "I wish I knew who these people were. Not her father, I hope."

"Happened a *long* time ago." Thom's eyes narrowed. "Or did it? How are these bodies so well preserved?"

"This will be today's news for Bithia, I'm afraid. She told me this warehouse has a version of a stasis field that keeps the contents fresh. I guess the effect covers corpses to some degree too. I think it's safe to assume these bodies date back to her time or thereabouts. Help me get the box loose. At least we'll have it to show for this expedition."

Nate and Thom worked the singed but intact container out from under the person who'd died clutching it, whether to protect the contents or to steal them there was no way to know. The corpse further disintegrated, no matter how respectfully they tried to handle it. Nate set the box on top of a pile of flat square objects and wiped his hands on his sapiche uniform shirt. "Wish we had whatever weapon these beings used to kill each other. Wonder where those went? Sure would come in handy."

"Or what was used to murder them both," Thom said. "Can't rule out a multiple homicide scenario either." He stood up, a short, gleaming chain dangling from his hand. It was set with round multicolored gemstones in an intricate pattern. "ID, you think?"

"Might be. See if the other guy has one too, would you? Might have sentimental meaning to Bithia to have them."

Nate searched the immediate area again as Thom went to recheck the other body for possible ID. Nate bent to retrieve the red box Celixia had been so emphatic about. "Wait a minute," he said, hope rising. He set the box on the floor and shoved a pile of containers a few inches to the left. Something that gleamed red in the shadows had caught his eye as he bent over to get the box. Leaning closer, he saw a glowing symbol on the butt of an unmistakable hand weapon. Nate was sure his find was the dead explorer's gun or blaster, flung off the walkway as the person died.

"Help me with this. I think we got a possible weapon."

It took them ten minutes of moving items from stacks and repiling them in the aisle to be able to reach the object that had attracted Nate's eye. He scooped up the shiny one-piece device in his left hand and backed into the clear.

"Deadly weapon if I ever met one," Thom said as he examined their find in detail.

The grip fit neatly into Nate's right hand, the red symbol on the left side under his thumb. Nate said, "I'm itching to push the damn button. What do you think?"

"Just don't aim it at me." Thom grinned. "We got nothing to lose. We don't even know what this junk is."

"True." Nate took aim at a purple trapezoid resting on a pile about ten yards away and pushed the button.

The purple trapezoid ceased to exist, leaving a small pile of oily, congealed black ash in its place.

"Nasty but effective," Thom said. "We lucked onto the ancient blaster, which I hereby designate the Alien Mark One. Think there are any more conveniently lying around, waiting for us to find them?"

"Check in the vicinity of the first body." Nate carried the weapon in one hand and cradled the red box in the crook of his left arm as he walked toward the main aisle. "Wish this thing came with a holster."

"Never satisfied, are you?" Thom's voice was teasing. "Five minutes ago we were defenseless, now we've got the ultimate weapon in our possession, and you're complaining because it don't include accessories."

"Guess I did sound ungrateful."

They searched the area around the first corpse thoroughly but failed to find another weapon. Finally, Nate straightened and stretched, trying to ease sore muscles that were stiffening after the rigors of the sapiche game earlier in the day followed by the jarring chariot ride. His attention was caught by a container covered in symbols. "You see what I see?"

Thom swiveled his head in the direction Nate was indicating. "A whole box of these lethal beauties?"

Nate double-checked the red button on the blaster he'd found, then raised his eyes back to the box on top of the stack directly opposite him. *Same symbol.* It was even the identical blazing red color. "The Lords of Space are with us now. I think our luck has finally changed on this damn mission. Let's get to that box and find out if we're right."

Half an hour later, he was staring at an entire arsenal of the ancient weapons, complete with the desired belts and holsters.

"Mother lode!" Thom was happy.

"Maybe not," Nate said.

"What's wrong?"

"Not all of these have the red button glowing. Maybe they're not charged."

"Or the charge ran out? How much action are these babies good for?"

"No one alive on this planet can tell us, not even Bithia, I'm guessing." Nate tried one of the weapons whose button was dull, aiming at a pink circular barrel across the room at the edge of the light. Sure enough, pressing the "trigger" produced no result. He tossed the depleted weapon into the box with a spacer's curse. "Sort the good ones out, see what firepower we do have."

It took a depressingly short amount of time. From a cache of twenty, only three had the brightly glowing button. Several others had trigger symbols that only flickered. Nate set them firmly aside. "Not worth the trouble to carry. They'd probably fail us at the worst possible moment. "

"No sign of whatever recharges the action either." Thom checked through the pile one more time for anything he might have missed.

"We've spent enough time on this and had all the luck we're going to get, you agree?"

"I'm ready to get out of here." Thom latched the holster belt at his waist and adjusted the fit so the weapon was close at hand.

Nate handed Thom the other active weapon. "You take the extra, since I have to manage the red box."

He walked toward the elevator, Thom following close on his heels, staring around. He estimated they'd managed to do a cursory survey of perhaps one-tenth of the total floor space of the warehouse.

"What a waste. All these artifacts and one remaining survivor, no less, who could tell us what each and every thing is, or does, and we don't have the time to explore," Nate said as they headed for the platform. "I know of Sectors archaeologists who've made entire careers out of analysis on one shard of a broken symbol."

"Plenty of experts and treasure hunters would kill to be here, all right, genuine Ancient Observer installation or not. Place is old enough to be intriguing to those guys," Thom said cheerfully. "I'll kill to get out of here, if it's all the same to you."

"I'm with you all the way, my friend. Never was tempted to join the Archaeology Service, and I'm not enlisting now either."

"What are we going to do with the sleepers?" Thom asked as he stood at the lip of the elevator and watched the four men, all of whom lay as if dead. The sergeant hunkered down to rapidly check pulses. "Still breathing, more's the pity."

Nate considered his options. "Tempting as it might be to leave Sarbordon here to his proper fate, I can't do it. Can't leave even a sadistic bully like him to die of starvation in a coma."

"No argument from me. Did Bithia say how long the sleep effect lasts, once the locals are removed from the storehouse?"

Nate shook his head. "Never occurred to me to ask. I'm not sure I believed in the knockout device. We need to find something to tie them up with before we go back to the surface. The men waiting outside should be fairly easy to ambush. Certainly no one's expecting any trouble from us."

"We left two more guards, five drivers and the two priestesses up there." Thom reviewed the numbers rapidly. "Kinda heavy odds, even with these nice new toys we acquired. Atletl and Celixia are in an exposed position, situational awareness unknown but I'd bet they're engrossed in each other. Can't count on them to be combat ready." He frowned. "One soldier escapes and makes it back to the city to sound the alert, there goes our chance of reaching your lady."

"I don't disagree. Suggestions?"

"Go by yourself, tell them the big boss needs more help to collect all the goodies. We get as many of them down here as you can convince."

Nate considered. "So far I like it. What's the next play?"

"We dress ourselves like the guards, take a few choice parcels to the surface as lures for the priestesses and any other hangers-on. When they come to get a better look and are distracted, we overpower them. Tie up the whole bunch on the surface, then bring these guys up. I'm sure you're not planning on leaving anyone down here to starve to death while unconscious."

"Right, goes against the grain to do tat, even to a bastard like Sarbordon. Then I close the cache entryway, we steal a chariot, set the rest of the animals loose to delay pursuit and head back to the palace for Bithia." Nate nodded. "Efficient. Works for me. Excellent staff work, sergeant."

"I know you like the plan clearly laid out one step at a time."

Dragging the unconscious men off the platform took a few moments. Nate stepped inside the lift and paused, checking with Thom, already hard at work stripping the helmet and armor off the first guard. "You okay staying here?"

"Sure." The sergeant waved one arm at the storeroom. "Got all the comforts of home here. Someone's home anyway. Let's get this action under way."

Nate activated the symbol and counted slowly to himself as the platform ascended with stately grace. It took two full Terra standard minutes to reach the surface. He triggered the exterior door and found himself facing those left behind, crowded close to the step. The guards and charioteers fell back as Nate emerged onto the platform. Hands on sword, several men peered intently behind him, obviously surprised he was alone.

Good call on Thom's part for me to ascend by myself. If we'd both come without escort, the enemy would have been on the alert. Hopefully they won't recognize this alien device on my belt as a weapon. Shooting anyone was his last resort. He liked a fair fight, and the total destruction created by the sleek black Mark One blaster, as Thom had nicknamed the gun, was excessive against swords and belt knives.

"Sarbordon commanded me to fetch more help," Nate said immediately, not giving anyone time to ask awkward questions. He pointed at the guards. "You and you, now!" As the men stumbled to join him, Nate crooked a finger at the nearest driver. "You too."

"I need to stay with the animals." Another man retreated a few steps before Nate could tag him for the subterranean detail. "And guard the priestesses."

"Right, you two stay." Nate kept his tone amiable, not liking the slightly suspicious tone the man had. "Atletl!"

"Lord?" His teammate came front and center, pushing past the driver who'd been reluctant to accept Nate's orders.

"Be ready to depart when we return to the surface," Nate said, hoping Atletl would take the hint and be prepared for action next time the door opened.

"Wait." One of the Huitlani priestesses shook her head imperiously and made as if to step through the door.

"No females!" Nate slammed his hand on the activating symbol, and she barely avoided the instantaneously closing door.

He maintained an easy chatter during the descent, remarking about the magical, wondrous weapons and other things the king was now going to command. His nervous audience listened avidly, succumbing to the induced coma as suddenly as the first set of Talonqueni had when the door opened.

Nate gaped at Thom, now resplendent in the uniform of the palace guards, complete with green tunic, leather breastplate, short black-and-green-striped kilt, black cloak, sword and anachronistic blasters on both hips. "Nice feathers." Nate flicked the cluster of greenish-black chingaza plumage adorning the helmet.

Raising his bushy red eyebrows, Thom fingered his clothing and grimaced. "Good thing it's dark out, or I wouldn't fool anyone who took a second glance."

"Where's mine?"

"Right there." Thom pointed to a heap of clothes. "I've picked out a few sexy, colorful boxes and bins with unusual shapes for us to pile into the lift, guaranteed to distract even the damn priestesses for at least a moment."

"Good work. Drag my latest victims off the platform, would you, while I change? And then I'll help load the bait."

Nate stripped rapidly and donned his Talonque palace guard's uniform. "Bit breezy, this kilt thing."

"Wrap yourself in the cloak, plenty of fabric there, thank goodness."

Nate set the helmet on his head and fastened the chin straps. "Glad we serve in a modern military."

"Helmet buys us time, since it obscures the face, which is the only good thing I can say about it. Weighs too much, no real protection and screws up your peripheral vision."

Nate checked the small pile of items Thom had stacked on the platform, verifying the precious red box was off to the side where no one could grab it. He and Thom took their positions and made the slow ascent to carry out their ambush.

Although the strategy started well, the fight wasn't quite as smooth and simple as Nate hoped. When the door opened at his command, he and Thom carried the bait packages out, trying to keep their faces hidden from the waiting priestesses and drivers. The two women reached for the same glittering small box, each tugging on her side and berating the other loudly. The drivers stood by, trying not to laugh too obviously at the greedy spat. Nate and Thom descended the steps again, carrying a large box this time, and moved toward the group.

At a prearranged hand signal from Nate, they dropped the container, each targeting a different driver. Nate knocked his man out with a quick uppercut, but Thom's victim was only dazed. He staggered toward the chariots, Thom in hot pursuit.

The priestesses screamed, attacking Nate before he could move to help Thom subdue the fugitive. Atletl and Celixia launched themselves into the fray, Celixia grabbing one woman by her long, greasy braid and spinning her to the ground. Atletl clamped his hand around the upraised arm of the other, effectively preventing her from stabbing Nate in the back.

"Restrain them with these." Nate threw a handful of cloth strips to Atletl before he sprinted after Thom.

Thom and the driver were struggling at the horse line. As Nate got closer, Thom stabbed the driver in the neck, allowing him to collapse to the ground, spooking the nearest kemat.

Another chariot had arrived while Nate was below in the cache, and now the vehicle's driver whipped his team of kemat, trying to escape.

"Stop or die!" Nate yelled urgently.

The man redoubled his efforts.

Reluctantly, Nate raised his Mark One and fired.

The driver became a lump of steaming black bones covered in greasy ash, and the upper half of the chariot was burned away. The kemat on the traces screamed in panic, trying to drag the remnants of the vehicle. Nate slammed the weapon into the holster and ran to calm the animals without getting kicked or bitten. He released the simple mechanism holding the team to the chariot, wrestled the kemat to the line and knotted the reins securely.

Atletl and Celixia had finished binding the priestesses hand and foot and were now working on the man Nate had knocked out.

"Situation under control," Thom said. "Shall I let stampede the extra kemat?"

"Not yet. I don't think we have much time to waste, but we don't need stray horses, kemat, whatever these animals are, going back to the barn prematurely. Let's retrieve Sarbordon and his sleeping pals from the storeroom first."

"Good idea."

Thom and Nate walked across the rutted ground of the plateau to the base of the pyramid. Eyes wide, huge smile on her face, Celixia clutched the scorched red box. "You found it!"

Atletl eyed them cautiously. "Truly, now you wield the powers of the god. You blasted the driver and his chariot with a wave of the hand, and both were as nothing."

"Not a miracle, friend, merely a weapon. A potent weapon, I'll grant you." Nate showed Celixia and Atletl the Mark One. "We found these in Fr'taray's storehouse."

"One of the things the king sought most was the power to wield fire and death from a distance," Celixia said. "He was obsessed with obtaining that ability in particular."

"I thought all the legends about Fr'taray's people spoke of them as being peaceful?" Nate questioned the differing stories. "Bithia certainly didn't think her expedition had any weapons."

The priestess frowned and shook her head. "There were a few tales indicating otherwise, but the stories didn't come to us in the direct line of instruction from the first Hialar. I can't say how truthful any of it may be, after all these centuries."

"Does it matter?" Thom asked. "Let's get a move on. You have a sleeping beauty to rescue, yes?"

"What can I do to help?" Atletl was ready for action.

"Can you handle a chariot?" Nate asked.

"Of course. Why?"

"Pick two teams of kemat for us. Stampede the others. As soon as Thom and I bring the rest of the soldiers, drivers and Sarbordon from the storehouse, we'll be on our way to the palace to rescue Bithia."

"He isn't dead?" Eyebrows raised, Atletl sounded both surprised and disappointed.

"Sound asleep," Nate said. "Fr'taray left a safeguard in his warehouse. I could open the door for him, but neither he nor anyone else from this planet could ever step through to seize the prize."

"Ironic, ain't it?" Thom seemed amused by the concept. He pointed at their teammate. "If you're planning to come with us on the next adventure of the night, change into one of the guard uniforms. I stripped off a spare set for you, in case you planned on enlisting in the cause."

Frowning, Atletl drew himself to his full height. "I'm a warrior of my people, sworn to fight Sarbordon and the god he serves until my dying breath. Let there be no doubt."

Nate was amused by the way Celixia was lost in total admiration of the young warrior's eloquence, her brown eyes fixed on his handsome face, her lips parted slightly. Nate exchanged an amused glance with Thom and moved off to the pyramid to finish his set of tasks.

He was impatient to be gone, back to the palace and Bithia. Events were going his way now, but Nate didn't trust the good luck to last.

It never did, in his experience.

CHAPTER SIX

He commandeered only one chariot, because Atletl was the sole person with the ability to drive a team of nearly wild kemat. Nate and Thom had to admit their skills as drivers extended only to mechanical transportation. Nate didn't want to risk a first attempt at working with living propulsion units at night, driving down a steep grade in a wooden chariot. The extra transport wasn't needed, he decided.

The road descending from the plateau was deserted, and they made good time. Atletl had to lean on the primitive brakes to keep the chariot from overrunning the kemat on the final set of curves. Then he had to wait a few moments before inserting the vehicle into the traffic on the main thoroughfare into the city.

"What the seven hells is going on?" Nate watched people streaming in both directions on foot, on the backs of kemat, piled onto carts and in chariots. The moonlight dimmed and brightened as clouds scudded across the sky, but it was clear enough to see a massive and impromptu evacuation was occurring. "The city always this busy at night, Celixia?"

"Not at all. I can't imagine—"

A squadron of soldiers galloped by, going away from the palace at high speed. Nate and Thom ducked their heads as much as possible to hide their faces, but the troop seemed preoccupied with whatever urgent mission had sent them patrolling, which apparently didn't include searching for escaped prisoners.

"Something's certainly happening," Thom said, watching the riders gallop away.

"Nighttime sacrifices?" Nate asked.

"Not at this season." Celixia shook her head and examined the crowds, openmouthed.

"Whatever has the citizenry and the army distracted works in our favor," Nate said. He was optimistic about the whole plan, particularly with the alien weapons to back their play.

"We may have trouble getting through the gates to the palace compound." Thom's reminder impinged on Nate's good mood. "The city feels like a siege or attack is imminent. The guards may be extra alert tonight."

"The Githholz might be behind the upheaval," Celixia said. "I'd heard earlier today their army was on the march, but no one expected them to arrive in the lowlands much before the second spring planting."

Atletl laughed, even as he yanked the team to the side to avoid a lopsided cart with a broken wheel and the bundles of goods falling onto the road.

"Your foolish rulers consistently underestimate us—as if we couldn't fight our way to Nochen before the first planting."

"Sarbordon's troops captured you," she said. "Who was underestimating who?"

"An intervention of fate." Waving a hand to indicate he took no offense at her remark, Atletl was magnanimous. "Obviously, I was destined to play a part in all the miraculous events and the remaining efforts to free T'naritza."

"She prefers to go by her real name, if you don't mind." The time was right to set a few things straight. He didn't want Atletl working with them under false pretenses. Neither he nor Thom was going to claim shreds of divinity, not that he ever had, except for allowing their enemies to think they were warriors of Fr'taray. The locals had declared Bithia's father worthy to be a god, not Nate. He suspected Bithia would refuse to represent herself as a goddess once she was free of the device and her life no longer depended on the charade.

"Real name?" Atletl was puzzled. "Is she not the daughter of Fr'taray, then?"

"Yes, but her name is Bithia."

The Githholz warrior looked to Celixia, who nodded confirmation.

"Too much for me." Atletl flicked the ear of the left leader with the whip to keep the animal from veering to the side of the road as another troop of cavalry rode straight at them. "The games of the gods are above my head. I know my people fight to root out the evil worship of Huitlani. We despise all the blood and death and tribute he demands."

"We're on the same side," Nate said, watching these new mounted soldiers pass them by without pausing.

Atletl managed to keep his team trotting at a steady pace. Nate admired the man's skill and nerve and thanked the Lords of Space again for getting the warrior entangled in the enemy's net with him and Thom.

Once the soldiers left them in the dust and Atletl didn't have to devote his full attention to guiding the team, Nate continued the conversation. "Your people don't worship Fr'taray, then? Or T'naritza? But you have her totem tattooed on your arm—"

"My people worship the Seven Spirits of Talonque. T'naritza is one, certainly... She Who Sleeps. The tolokon has always been her totem. I was born at the foot of the mountain where she lived before she established her residence here in the heart of the city, so I wear her totem."

"Sounds to me like we've got conflicting myths here," Thom said in Basic. "Does it matter? Let her be who he thinks she is for him and herself for us. Let's get the hell out of here before Sarbordon works his way loose, or Lolanta goes searching for him."

"I'll have to ask Bithia to play along, or at least not be too hasty about renouncing her claim to the second name."

"We'll be at the palace in another moment or two," Atletl said, setting aside all the theological debate. "What should I say if the sentries stop us at the gates?"

"They won't." Celixia pointed at the banner whipping from a standard at the back of their chariot. "The king's personal flag. I made sure to fasten it on this chariot. The guards will bow and scrape and salute and ask no questions, I guarantee it."

"Hope you're right," Thom said without too much optimism.

The young priestess was soon proven correct in her prediction, whether because the mass confusion and chaos prevailing at the palace matched the panic in the rest of the sprawling city, or because she'd fastened the sovereign's ensign to the chariot. They were waved through the gate without a check. Celixia directed Atletl to drive them out of the central courtyard, indicating a narrow alley curving to the left.

"This leads to the private, royal courtyard," she said. "From there we can go directly through the throne room and through the passages to the Lady."

"Which leads to a question. How the seven hells are we getting out again, once we've rescued the damsel in distress?" Thom raised his eyebrows and glanced at Nate. "You planning to stroll through the palace with her in tow, climb into this chariot and drive away?"

"I've been puzzling over my options since we left the plateau." Nate patted the holster riding at his hip. "I'm strategizing on the fly here. We've got superior firepower now."

"Swords and knives will be effective enough for them if we get mobbed by a whole bunch of suicidal palace guards. Or even a pack of those fanatical priestesses. These Mark Ones apparently only work in single-shot mode. And we don't know how long the charges are good for." Thom seemed determined to make the worst possible case where the ancient weapons were concerned.

As Atletl drew the tired team to a halt in the small, deserted courtyard, he looked expectantly at Nate. "Orders, lord? Wait here, or go with you?"

"Celixia, any back doors out of Bithia's chamber?"

"I—I don't know. None were ever spoken of by the first Hialar."

Nate jumped from the chariot, scanning the empty courtyard, his Mark One at the ready, while Thom assisted Celixia to the pavement. Nate assessed the panting team of kemat, sweaty sides heaving, and shook his head. "I may not know much about livestock, but even I can see these animals are finished. If we separate, no subset of the four of us has the slightest idea where to rendezvous. We go in together, and we come out together. Agreed?"

Solemnly, his comrades nodded.

"The outcome can't be any other way," Atletl said. "This was destined from the beginning, when we first were joined in the slave chains. I who wear the Lady's totem, and you who are her warriors. Let's do this brave deed."

"Wrap your cloak over your arm so it covers your tattoo. No soldier of Sarbordon's is going to be wearing a tolokon. It'll attract attention we don't need," Nate said.

"Like we don't attract attention otherwise." Thom laughed. "My red hair is all the priestesses have talked about since we was captured, or so I'm told, and neither of us has the facial features to pass for Talonqueni, even in the dark."

"Celixia and Atletl will lead, we'll bring up the rear, keep our heads down, our helmets on and hope the dice continue to roll our way. We need to be quick about it." To Celixia, he said, "Take the most direct route you know. Avoid walking us through public spaces as much as possible. Thom's right—he and I don't blend in too well."

She nodded, hefting the weight of the red box, which Atletl had offered to carry for her, but she refused to be parted from it. Celixia set off toward the open portal of the palace, the men shortening their strides to keep pace with her. There was a hall leading from the open courtyard to the throne room. The side doors stayed obligingly closed as he marched past.

Fortunately, there was apparently no reason for other foot traffic in the royal corridor at this hour. The formal throne room was also deserted. For the most part, the chamber was in gloom, only a few sputtering torches along the walls providing illumination. Nate preferred things to be as murky as possible in case he ran into anyone who might issue a challenge. The four fugitives entered the long, rectangular chamber from the left side and veered left again to reach the throne dais and eventually pass through the leather curtains behind.

Nate climbed the steps and was even with the golden throne when a woman's peremptory voice called out from behind them. "What are you doing there, guardsmen?!"

For a second Nate thought it was Lolanta. He and Thom halted, keeping their cloaked backs to the woman. Moving into the pool of light provided by a torch, Celixia wheeled to confront the challenger.

"It is I, going to the Lady's chamber to commune with her."

"About what? Where's the king?"

"He remains at Fr'taray's treasure chamber. You'd scarcely credit the riches we unlocked there with the help of her father's warriors." Celixia stopped at the edge of the stairs, standing at Nate's elbow. He had his weapon out and ready, hidden under the edge of his heavy uniform cape. Thom was similarly prepared. "You should have seen Lileet and Uanna arguing over possession of certain of the boxes, Nanzin. It was positively comical. Lord Sarbordon had to intervene to remind them Lolanta will have first choice."

"First choice of what, girl? Jewels?" The other woman's voice sounded avid.

"Among other things. You'll see soon enough. I must be on my way because the king needs information from T'naritza, and you know how impatient he can be."

"Information the warriors of the goddess couldn't supply?" The woman behind them sounded surprised and a little suspicious. "Regarding what?"

Smart lady, not easy to lull her suspicions. From the increasing volume of the priestess's voice, Nate calculated Nanzin might be coming closer. He tensed, ready to spin and launch an attack, hoping to be able to capture or knock her out before she could scream, but willing to use the Mark One's destructive power if necessary to save the mission.

Celixia continued to handle the questions smoothly, however. "I can't discuss with you what must be asked of the Lady. Neither you nor Lolanta ever tell me what Huitlani's communications regard."

"True enough." A grudging response. "Be on your way. I'll report the progress to Lolanta meantime. She may want to go to the plateau with you, if so much of value is being found. The temple must have its fair share."

Celixia's voice was placating. "I'll send one of these guards to check with her when I'm ready to depart."

"See that you do."

Celixia spun on her heel and proceeded to the heavy leather curtains, which Atletl jumped to open for her. As Nate passed through the portal, he risked a quick peek over his shoulder. Tapping one foot on the mosaic floor, hands on her hips, the priestess gazed after them thoughtfully.

"Keep going, keep walking," Nate said in a whisper. "You handled the situation perfectly."

"I was scared." Celixia sounded pleased by his approval. "Nanzin is Lolanta's oldest daughter. Inquisitive and short-tempered, almost as bad as her mother."

"I'm not sure she bought the entire story," Thom said as he descended the first set of long stairs.

"She was standing there when we left the room, thinking hard from the looks of it. I'm sure she'll report what you said to Lolanta, but I'm not so sure she isn't going to add a few opinions of her own." Nate kept walking.

"All the more reason to hurry this rescue op along," Thom said.

After his group was safely inside the barrier of the whitewashed wall, Nate raised one hand, stopping his companions from moving to the next level. "When we get to the translucent wall, I'm going in alone."

"I'm the only one who knows how to release the Lady from her sleep." Celixia protested instantly, apparently territorial about her duties and prerogatives. "I must go with you."

"Bithia knows."

"She may not choose to tell you," the priestess said. "What then?"

Nate looked from face to face of his three allies. He saw understanding on Thom's face, puzzlement on Atletl's and dismay on Celixia's.

"This is between her and me." He directed his words at Celixia. "It has to be her choice what she wants to do."

"And if she chooses death? You said she's spoken of a death wish more than once." Thom's question was gentle. "You prepared to honor that request?" He removed his helmet, shook his head and brushed the too long red hair back from his face. "I know what you want, but are you prepared for the other choices she can make? High-stakes game, no guarantees. She might not want to run with us. We can't leave her here alive to suffer Sarbordon's vengeance."

Nate stared into his friend's serious face for a long moment, then nodded once. "You're not telling me anything I don't already know. I've considered all the possibilities. I've had too damn long to think."

"Not nearly as long as Bithia's had."

Nate acknowledged the point. "Whatever she requests of me, I'll take care of. Even if she prefers death to what I'm offering."

"All right, then." Thom moved aside. "We'll be waiting."

"If we're found out, you should have enough warning from the initiation of the white wall mechanism's activation to hustle down the stairs and through the translucent barrier." Nate regarded the deceptively solid wall behind them. It would yield easily to manipulation of just a few of the alien symbols. "Fortunately, only Celixia has the ability to reliably sing the final barrier open on the first try."

"We'll be fine." Thom gave Nate a good-natured shove in the direction of the stairs leading to the final barrier. "You're wasting time. Good luck to you, to both of you."

Nate swallowed hard, nodded again and descended the stairs two at a time. Celixia followed more cautiously.

Reaching the translucent barrier, she caught at Nate's sleeve. "I—I hardly know what to say to you. I realize you need no advice from me, no help, but I give you my blessing. As the keeper of the Lady's secrets, descendant of the first Hialar who took her into his charge directly from the hands of Fr'taray, I hereby relinquish the duty and responsibility to you." She set the red box on one of the steps and extended her hands to Nate, palms up.

He studied her serious face. Advancing a step, he covered her dainty fingers with his much larger digits. She clasped his fingers firmly, her small hands trembling against his callused palms. She raised their joined hands to her lips, kissing first one and then the other. "The duty is now yours, Nate Reilly." Releasing him, she smiled tremulously while tears rolled down her cheeks. "I never dreamed of handing over these responsibilities until I lay on my deathbed, and then it would have been to another of my own kin. Hard to accept this irrevocable alteration to tradition, I admit."

Nate was moved by her obviously strong, mixed emotions. "My fondest hope is the lady will need your help and companionship awhile longer. Thank you for all you've done for her and helping me survive."

She blushed. "I only did what must be done. Now I'll sing the portal open for you."

Nate was acutely conscious of time running out. Strange to contemplate that after Bithia had waited thousands of years, her time was now ticking away in rapid, measurable increments. His time had always been limited by the rules of a normal human life-span, so it was nearly impossible to grasp how long she'd been left to sleep, dream and think, time having been artificially suspended for her all these millennia.

The recent encounter in the halls above with the suspicious priestess, who was probably well on her way to Lolanta, was proof of how close to the edge of disaster they were both running now. And their friends and allies with them. He didn't want to be trapped here under the palace.

The portal disappeared in response to Celixia's chant of the alien voice-activation sequence.

He bounded down the three stairs. As he moved across the room, he took off the leather helmet with its towering crest of feathers, dropping it to the side where it rolled into the corner. He was bracing himself for the conversation he had to conduct with Bithia. The inexorable translucent green curtain of rippling light hung there, blocking his access to her. Nate advanced to the edge of the lights where the pressure against his chest was like running into a stone wall. *Like in our shared dreams.* He shook the memory off. *This time is reality, and my chance to free her only comes this once.*

"Bithia?" He whispered it aloud, the syllables echoing with an odd resonance. The light of the curtain danced, rippling in time with the syllables with a hypnotic effect. He blinked hard to focus.

"Nate?" His name, spoken aloud in a heartbreaking mixture of longing and sadness. She stirred slightly on the couch as a tear trickled from under the long lashes. *Free and gone.* Her beautiful voice sighed in his mind.

She appeared to be deep in machine-controlled sleep, barely at the edge of his ability to touch her consciousness. He had to pull her out of her solitary dream. It was imperative she realize he was physically present in the chamber with her. He needed her full attention before he could broach the subject of her freedom.

Nate scanned the symbols controlling her physical and mental condition, reaching to activate them before pulling his hand to his side. *No machine. Nothing artificial between us, ever again.* He'd reach her mind to mind, or not at all. Their bond was either a true connection to be trusted and relied upon, or it had never existed—a fiction created by the alien device.

This was the time to put everything to the test.

He placed both hands on the glimmering curtain. The massive energy of the device pulsed and flowed against his palms, unlike the way it behaved in the dreams. *Can I channel this power, use it to boost my signal?* Closing his eyes, he concentrated his will and desire on finding her wandering inner self. He visualized her as he wished he'd seen her more often in their shared dreams, walking freely through the swirling green and gray mists to meet him. Not immobile on the couch as she'd been in the majority of their encounters. He built the picture and held it, filling in the small details he so loved about her—

She was there, in the dreamspace, regarding him in shock and disbelief.

You were supposed to escape, not set foot in this damned place again.

Even in the signature, light musical tone he always heard in his mind, she sounded distressed, angry at him. Her lips moved as she switched to what passed for speech in their dream encounters. "Why are you here? Did Sarbordon bring you? Have we failed?"

Nate sensed terror rising in her and tried to inject calm and certainty into his own tone. "I'm not leaving while you're still held prisoner. We need to talk. You need to make a decision. Concentrate and come back from the dreamspace, come talk to me in the real world. Beat the fucking machine."

"You can't do anything for me beyond the happiness I took from our shared dreams these weeks. We've always known the limitations." Ignoring his plea, she sounded resigned.

"You're the only one on board with the idea of me leaving you behind. I've told you I won't go without you."

"All I wanted was to save your life, and now you're throwing it away," she said, voice choked as if she fought back tears. Nate couldn't get a word or thought in edgewise as she went on. "I never cared as much about anyone, not in all these long painful years, not since my father walked out of this same room. How dare you risk your safety for me? You must escape before anyone finds you here. They'll kill you in front of me, pleased to make me watch, unable to lift a finger to help you. If you care for me as you claim, please be sensible and go while there's time."

"*You* be sensible," he said. "Tell me how to set you free, and we'll get out of here together. I don't want to waste precious time any more than you do, but I'm not leaving you behind."

There was silence on the surface of their mental communication channel.

Nate heard her subliminally, so attuned had they become to each other in the last month. He opened his eyes for a moment, staring through the curtain at her. Seeing her pinned helplessly under the domination of the healing device pained him. It always did. He closed his eyes, re-establishing the mental link, deliberately changing the subject, but only temporarily. "Your plan worked as well as you hoped. It was terrific, in fact. Sarbordon and the others literally fell unconscious the moment we took them to the lower level of the storehouse. We ran off the kemat, brought him and his guards back above ground and left them outside the pyramid, tied up. The priestesses and chariot drivers too. How long will they sleep?"

"You didn't leave him underground to die, then?" Her question sounded relieved, pleased.

"I don't take lives in cold blood. We had this discussion, remember?" Nate shook his head. "When I killed Kalgitr, it was in self-defense." *In case she needed a reminder.* "Killing helpless, unconscious people is outside my code of ethics. Thom and I are soldiers, not murderers. Getting back to the real subject of our escape—we don't have much time, do we? Are they going to sleep for a million years the way you have?" He found the idea amusing, suitable payback for the ruler's cruelty toward her.

"Of course not." Bithia sounded annoyed that he could joke. "Since you brought them to the fresh air, the effect should wear off by morning, I imagine, at the outside. Abandon this absurd idea of freeing me. Save yourself and your friends."

"There were weapons, by the way." To avoid the confrontation over her refusal to discuss her own escape, Nate stalled for time. "I was glad to get my hands on those. Improves our odds."

"Weapons?" She was completely taken aback by the information. "You must be mistaken. Let me see."

He visualized himself holding the Mark One. He blocked the details of how the weapons had been found and of the bodies of her fellow explorers. Now was not the time to go into that subject.

He read the shock in her mind. "What would cause my father to provide these to the team? I didn't even know we had such a thing. Was there—was there any kind of a message or sign left for me?"

"Nothing recognizable." Nate maintained his mental block on the details of the ancient murder scene in the alien storehouse. "We searched in a grid pattern, as much as we had time for, but I imagine we wouldn't have known what we were scanning for unless it was obvious. We can't go back there. Too big a risk."

"At least we agree on one point," she said.

He got a mental image of her shaking her head and frowning as her voice continued. "There's something you aren't telling me."

He didn't confirm or deny her suspicion.

"It doesn't matter. Keep your secrets. Why am I wasting time?" Bithia was plainly irritated with herself. "You're distracting me. Please get out of here before you're trapped. Save yourself, with my blessing."

"Not without you." Nate made his voice as flat and uncompromising as he could. He spoke the declaration aloud and in his mind.

"You mustn't stay!"

"Neither can you. Sarbordon will kill you in the most painful, gruesome way he can devise when he gets back to the palace. We both know how he thinks. Having been thwarted of his desire for your father's possessions, he'll seek revenge on you. I know that for a fact, and so do you. I intend to see he never touches you."

"Stubborn—"

Nate spoke out loud again, for emphasis. "I'm not going anywhere without you. Or rather, without you making a choice, one way or the other."

"Choice?" She sounded taken aback, a little frightened.

Nate nodded, even though Bithia's eyes were closed. "I can't walk away and leave you here to suffer and die. Not an option."

"We waste too much time on this debate."

A crisp picture came into his head of patterns to the right and below the ones the ruler had traced on each of the earlier visits to the chamber. Opening his eyes, Nate walked to the engraved control panels. Extending his left hand, he touched the embossed dot marking the circuit's beginning.

Why do you wait? Set me free, as you promised. Bithia's voice was a soft whisper in his mind.

Nate watched the dot glow under his fingertip, pulsing green to black and back again. The hum from the device altered on a subliminal level, as if gathering power for the change in status. He shook his head and carefully lifted his finger away, afraid of triggering the system inadvertently.

"Bithia," he said, forcing himself to project patience he didn't feel. "I don't want to kill you. Don't lie to me. Don't make me your inadvertent assassin. You're not being fair to me, and you're dishonoring the trust we've shared until now." Nate sensed she was preparing to counter his argument. Now it was his turn not to allow her to get a thought in edgewise. "If death by healing device is your choice, I'll carry it out," he said, keeping himself under iron control, emotions locked, not sure he could bring himself to take the action required. "At least do me the courtesy of telling me that all you want from me is death. Don't you trust me? Does what we've shared time and again in the dreamspace mean so little? I hope I mean more to you than a means to commit suicide."

There was stubborn silence in his head again, with the sensation of her deep thinking simmering just out of his mental "hearing."

Nate spun slowly on his heel to face the shifting, glowing curtain and peer through it to her. "I'm right, aren't I?" he said out loud. "If I trace that circuit you showed me, you'll die, won't you? After all this time, all this waiting, what we've shared—you'd slip into death and leave me behind to mourn."

"How dare you sound critical of my choice? What do you know of the terrible, clawing loneliness I endure and could now end?"

He followed up on her angry question. "I can't presume to know exactly what you've been through. I didn't mean to sound as if I was judging you," he said. "I understand your grief, your loneliness for people and a way of life long gone."

"What have I to live on for?" Her bitter lament broke harshly across his mind, a physical pain in his head. "Why should you ask me to continue this existence? Why should I ask it of myself? To what conceivable end should I choose to go on, to live, when you can give me an easy death?"

Nate hesitated, reluctant to advance his one and only argument, afraid his heartfelt plea wasn't going to be enough to convince her. What if he failed to divert her from the direction her emotions—her fear—were plainly flowing? He'd never played a game where his personal stakes were so high, where he cared so much about one outcome and one only. His ability to be detached, not influenced on any personal level, was one of his strengths. He didn't allow people other than his own family and Thom to become close to him. To matter. The depth of his emotions now where Bithia was concerned was a fearsome vulnerability, terrifying in a way physical danger could never match.

After a moment, she spoke again, her mental tones flat. "I've been here for so long, locked in this living hell, beholden to whoever came in and traced the circuits, forced to answer their demands, their questions, knowing my answers would most likely mean death and destruction for people, no matter what I said. Making things up to save myself further pain, because I was afraid to suffer! I don't deserve to live—let me die." She wept, tears running down her pale cheeks, huge sobs shaking her body even under the iron control of the device. "My father never meant for all this to happen."

"I'm sure he didn't," Nate said. "He's not to blame for all the events since the day he left. And neither are you."

"I'm past my appointed time. At least peace waits for me on the other side of death. No one and nothing wait for me in life."

There was a heartbeat of total silence in the chamber.

"I wait for you." Nate wasn't sure he'd actually said the words. Her comment stung bitterly. Taking a deep breath, he forged ahead. "Live for me—live *with* me, in my world. You must know I've been waiting for you, living for you, since the first time my men and I were dragged in here and the king cranked this damn machine to high volume. He was torturing you and accidentally tormenting me, but at the same time linking us. You can't deny the emotions we shared, all those nights we exchanged thoughts. The connection was real, the link between us is real, this moment is real, dammit. You and I have a life to live together, if you find the resolve in your heart to trust me. Let me set you free."

"I trust you, but it's not possible," she said. "It can't be possible—"

"Why not? I don't know what had to happen to bring the two of us to this place, this time…but we're together. I have to believe it was meant." Nate closed his eyes and took a deep breath to steady his ragged nerves.

This conversation, this naked exposure of his emotions was the hardest thing he'd ever done, bar none, especially in the face of her denial of their bond. He never revealed this much of his personal side to anyone, not even to Thom, who was like a brother to him after all these years of camaraderie and shared danger. He'd rather face a whole nest of Mawreg barehanded than have to deal with this conversation, but the rest of his life, his happiness, depended on finishing what he'd launched into here. She was afraid, panicked. The idea of living without her scared *him*.

"Please, take the chance." He was afraid she was slipping away from him, and time was running out. Either she found the courage to let him power down the machine and free her, or he'd be discovered and killed. Or she'd die at his hand, by her own request, which he would honor. He'd sworn he would, and Nate never went back on his word. Killing her would be the worst thing he'd ever done in his entire life, and it would break him. He'd do it if death was all she'd accept from him. He realized he loved her enough to let her go, to smooth the way for her.

He tried one last time to reach the part of her inner self he was counting on to hold hope and a will to go on living. To want a future with him. "You saved my life when the guards whipped me to the edge of death, when all I wanted was to sink into the pain and die, remember? Now it's my turn to save you."

"What if I can't?"

"Can't what?" Her question confused him, and he puzzled over the non sequitur.

"Can't—live. What if, when you cut the power, I die anyway?" Her voice trembled and broke on the last two words like a frightened child's.

Nate fought his triumph at hearing her admit at least a possibility of leaving the chamber. *Everything I desire depends on choosing my next words carefully.* "I won't let myself believe even the remote possibility. The device has functioned since your father left you here to recuperate. When you've been awakened, you've been fine, right? Why would the mechanism fail its purpose now? Trust your father's technology. When I hit the off switch, you'll walk free, I swear."

"But the device no longer gives me the blessed sleep. I awaken on my own more and more often."

"Only since I came and we shared minds, shared the dreamspace, isn't that so?" Nate refused to yield on any point she tried to raise. He wanted fiercely to believe his own assurances, wanted the truth to be what he was saying to her. He tried to remember any report on ancient sites he'd ever scanned, how the devices and unknown machines continued to work long after their makers vanished from the star lanes. He strove to project his own knowledge to her as subliminal reassurance. "You and I are linked. I don't know why, I don't know how, and I don't care. For me, it's enough to know we are. I can't give you back the life you were originally destined to live with your own people, but I can offer you a fresh start, new possibilities, with me. Now tell me the right way to cut the power to this damn thing, and let's get out of here."

"I'm afraid." Her voice in his mind was low, trembling.

I know, sweetheart. He pressed his open hand against the green light barrier, wishing with all his heart he could touch her, hold her hand and give her reassurance.

"Life is about taking risks. You wouldn't have been here on this planet as an explorer alongside your father if your people weren't like mine. We never give up, not ever, not while there's breath in the body and action to be taken. I know you refused to admit defeat all these years, however long it may have been. You had hope, you wanted to live, admit it. Don't falter now, when we have the future together within reach."

"If only—" Her thought broke off abruptly.

Nate waited. Ultimately, this had to be her decision. He'd find the strength to abide by her choice, no matter what it cost him.

With a flash of insight, the right words came to him. "I swear I'll take care of you for the rest of our lives, if you want me. But if I'm wrong, and the worst does happen…" His voice shook at the sudden awful mental picture of her aging a millennium in a moment, but then he forced himself to shove the fear aside, to go on calmly. "You'll die in the arms of a man who loves you, not pinned to a goddamn table like a specimen in a lab. Nor on one of Huitlani's bloodstained altars with Lolanta's gloating face as the last thing you ever see."

Bithia was crying again. He felt like the lowest creature on the planet pushing her so hard, but there wasn't time for more prolonged contemplation of alternatives. If he left her behind in this chamber, alive under the device's spell, Sarbordon would cut the power and have his way, inflicting as much pain and suffering as he could. Not an option in Nate's mind.

He was well aware Bithia could see his mental pictures, because he wasn't shielding the potential sequence of events, ugly though it was.

Suddenly, so sharply it literally hurt his head and left an afterimage on his retinas, he had the vision of a different circuit. The implication was clear that if he traced the new set of symbols, Bithia would rise from the couch imprisoning her for countless centuries. The circuit was on the far side of the chamber. Nate spun, found the set of symbols and, without further hesitation, he did what needed to be done.

The hum in the chamber stopped.

The sudden silence was deafening.

Nate held his breath, afraid to look in those first heartbeats. Committing that one simple act terrified him more than anything he'd ever faced, even on his most dangerous missions. Taking a deep breath, he pivoted, crossed the floor to the couch, going past the boundary where the curtain of light had stopped him before.

"Bithia?"

Her chest was rising and falling slowly. She put one hand to her forehead, then the other, rubbing her temples. "Nate?" Her voice sounded rusty, hoarse, but with the same lilt her mental communications had contained.

"Right here." He couldn't keep the triumph out of his voice.

Bithia opened her eyes, focusing on him, lavender-blue pupils huge, expression bewildered, long lashes starred together from her recent tears. "You're real? Not a dream?"

"Here in the flesh. I told you it would be all right."

"I—I'm sorry I doubted you. Doubted us." She worked to sit, hands slipping on the slick surface of the cushions.

Suddenly feeling awkward, Nate reached to help her. She seemed to experience the same reserve, shrinking away from his touch, but then—after a long, tremulous breath—she reached out to him and he gathered her into a long embrace, holding her close. The contact was enough for now, giving comfort in this first moment of actually being together. Her body felt cold, hypothermic, but warmed gradually as she clung to him, absorbing his heat.

"You were frightened of the unknown. I understood." Nate leaned over to kiss her gently on the forehead. "Can you stand?" He kept one arm behind her back as a brace.

"Let's find out." Bithia gathered herself and swung her legs over the side of the couch. With Nate's strong arm to steady her, she straightened and swayed before flashing him a triumphant grin. The next moment, her knees buckled, and Nate caught her in his arms. He shifted to set her on the couch, and instantly she protested.

"No! I won't take the chance of being held by the device."

Moving away from the couch, holding her effortlessly in his arms, he said, "I understand your qualms. Let me carry you until you regain your strength."

"You can't carry me to the mountains."

"We can steal kemat, maybe from the royal stables. Have you ever ridden?"

"Once or twice, a long time ago."

Startled by the idea after all the emotional tension of a few moments ago, Nate realized she was teasing him. He laughed, and she joined in the mirth, together for the first time outside of a dream, her head resting on his shoulder. He was happy.

A moment later Thom clattered down the stairs and through the entryway, Atletl and Celixia right behind him. "Sorry to interrupt, but the alarm is up out there. All hell is breaking loose."

From her position safely in Nate's arms, Bithia studied the sergeant with interest. "This is your friend you told me about?"

"Sergeant Thom Curran at your service, ma'am." He snapped off a crisp salute. "My thanks for rescuing us in the first place. Now if we could get out of here…"

"The Lady must eat," Celixia said from behind Thom.

Nate set Bithia on her feet, keeping his arm around her waist for support. "We'll get her something, steal food from the marketplace—"

The priestess cut Nate off. "She must eat of the sacred food her father left and drink from the Two Wines."

"There isn't time—"

"Wait, I—I think she may be right," Bithia said slowly. "I have a memory of my father telling me Hialar would have things I'd need to ingest when I emerged from the device's care to stabilize my system."

"Does she have to eat it here, or can we do this on the go?" Thom asked, his patience apparently at the breaking point. "This ain't exactly the place for a picnic. The enemy is pounding on the damn door up there. If one of the priestesses can get the words and tone right, they'll be in here with us. Too close in here to use the Mark Ones. Don't think the lady and Celixia are going to do well in hand-to-hand combat. We need to try to find another exit, another tunnel, something."

"You're right." Nate looked over at Celixia. "We have to be guided by you. Does the red box hold what she needs? And can she eat it as we go?"

"My family kept its secrets well, despite the efforts of Sarbordon's people." Celixia was proud, triumphant even. "He believed he knew everything from poring over the ancient tablets. As if those contained all the knowledge of the Hialar."

"I grow light-headed, dizzy," Bithia said, her tone alarmed. She touched her forehead again and leaned more heavily on Nate's arm.

"Sit on the stair, and Celixia can fix you the required nutrients." Nate addressed his next remarks to the frowning, fidgeting Thom. "We have to strategize anyway. There's not any practical way we can fight our way out the front door. And we don't know if there's a back door."

Narrowing her eyes, Bithia squeezed his hand. "Of course there's another way out of the chamber."

Celixia opened the red box and handed Bithia a cylindrical container. The erstwhile goddess opened it with a fluid tap on the right side and drank it in one long swallow. "Marvelous to be able to eat and drink again. I can't tell you the pleasure of the simple act."

"Take it easy since it's been so long," Nate said as Celixia crumbled a dense breadlike substance packed with dried maroon-striped berries. "You don't want to overtax your digestive system all at once."

Bithia nodded, her mouth full of the bread. She reached for the second flagon of what Celixia had called the Two Wines and swallowed more slowly. "This room is only part of the installation we have here at Nochen. The panel there"—she nodded at the facing wall—"opens into the main research chamber, storerooms, private quarters. I can get my things, including clothing that's more appropriate." She frowned at her glimmering dress.

Nate realized she must be wearing a nightgown. She glared at him. Too late, he remembered Bithia could read any thought of his she chose, except for the ones behind the mental block he had on details of the storehouse excursion. He changed the subject from clothing to escape. "Can we get out of this complex? Into the city maybe? Or even better, into the open countryside?"

Bithia, chewing with gusto, nodded.

Into Nate's head came the sequence of the symbols to push to open the access to the rest of the installation. He located the correct portion of the display and keyed the circuit. Silently and efficiently, a panel slid back, revealing a lighted passageway beyond.

Intrigued to find out what lay ahead, Nate waited while Bithia finished her mouthful. Then she stood, a bit shakily, brushing crumbs from her clothing. Instantly, Nate was at her elbow, steadying her, earning himself a breathtaking smile.

"Well, boys and girls, shall we see more of the marvels of Fr'taray?" Thom asked. "Left to yourselves, you two would stand and make googly eyes at each other all day."

Nate escorted Bithia across the healing chamber and entered the passageway, the others close behind. The wall silently closed behind them, leaving no sign of their ever having been in the healing chamber, save for a few crumbs on the stair and two discarded containers.

The Sleeping Goddess of Nochen slept no more on her metallic couch.

CHAPTER SEVEN

As the wall panel slid closed behind him, Nate found himself in a brightly lit, featureless hallway ten yards in length. The floor sloped sharply upward. Bithia walked forward with confident eagerness, so he trailed her, senses alert for trouble of any kind. At the other end, the passage opened into a large room. Jaw dropping, hand on her chest over her heart, she stopped on the threshold. "This isn't right. Where are all the experiments? The supplies?"

"Place is a mess, all right, ma'am." Taking point, Thom stepped past her and Nate and moved into the center of the room, examining the disarray. "Kinda reminds me of the storehouse. Personnel cleared out of here in a hurry too."

The lab had been gutted, equipment and furnishings torn from their stands or wall fastenings. A few bulky pieces of unknown equipment sat askew on the floor. Several items appeared to be in the process of being disassembled, parts of all sizes and shapes spread on the floor, as if the technician stepped away in the middle of the task, expecting to resume later. One huge item hung suspended precariously from a nest of tubes and struts. Another tall set of shelves had been toppled to the floor, broken containers surrounded by ancient chemical stains etched onto the surface of the floor. Crates like those Nate had seen in the storehouse lay scattered here and there on the room's periphery, dozens of small flat items spilling from them, fanning across the cold black floor. Thom squatted to retrieve a handful of the tiny, colorful disks, letting them slip through his fingers back to the floor like glittering drops of water.

"Data records." Bithia's attention was drawn by the sound. "But those were the most precious thing to my father and his team. He'd never leave such things in disorder and upheaval. And why were people dismantling the lab? And so haphazardly?"

Nate hoped they weren't going to come upon more corpses. He didn't think Bithia was ready for murder mysteries involving people she knew. The destruction of the lab appeared to be upsetting her enough. "So this isn't the condition the room was in the last time you were here?"

"Not at all. If the staff was going to take the time to disassemble the fixtures and box the records, why didn't anyone come to the healing chamber and set me free? I was so close, one hall away. How could they have done all this work in here and not bothered to come for me?" Bithia's voice faltered. "What happened? To my father? Why was the work stopped before it was complete?"

Nate took her by the shoulders, turning her to face him. Her eyes glistened with unshed tears. "We'll probably never know. Maybe ignorance is for the best, all things considered. There must have been reasons, probably good ones, in their minds." He cut off her protest with a shake of the head. "I realize the concept's a hard thing for you to accept. I know the events happened just yesterday for you, or a few days ago in conscious time, but it's been thousands of years here. Even if we had the answers, knowledge wouldn't bring your father and your friends back. We have to concentrate on the here and now, and it's essential we escape the city without delay."

"I—I know you're right. It's hard to—to accept, to take it in." Bithia raised one hand to her eyes and dashed away the welling tears. "When I dreamed of leaving that cursed device, I visualized myself walking through the door and finding things as I left them. My father, my friends, the team I came here with—" Breaking off, she shut her eyes as if in pain. "I understood the impossibility of my dream, but the last thing I expected to find would be this mad chaos." She leaned against Nate, face set in a pained expression, and assessed the disorder surrounding her. "It's too chaotic to even know what to touch first to set things back to rights." She laughed ruefully, staring into Nate's face. "And there's no need for me to take on the task in any event. Of all the ridiculous things to think about, given our real problems—"

"Clothes, ma'am? I believe you wanted to change?" Thom said helpfully, as if a more mundane subject might ease the tension.

Bithia seemed grateful for the distraction. She regarded her beautiful, but inappropriate, lavender nightgown with disfavor, plucking at its pleats with her left hand.

"My private meditation compartment is across the lab and on the hall to the left. My clothes should be there. I don't want to be escaping across the length and breadth of Talonque in the nightgown I've worn for centuries. Come on." Bithia led the way, keeping one hand clasped in Nate's.

Atletl and Celixia trailed them, curious but apparently not impressed. This room held none of the flashy mysteries of the healing chamber, only piles of strange equipment and scattered bins and incomprehensible data records. A strong sense of complete and final abandonment hung in the lab. It was like a gigantic broken puzzle, missing pieces and impossible to reassemble. There was nothing there to hold any of them, save Bithia, and she was trying hard to focus on the actual needs of the moment. Through their link, Nate sensed her grief and anxiety under the relatively calm surface she was maintaining.

"Are you doing okay?" he asked, bending to speak privately to her. "You're favoring your right leg. Are you in pain?"

Bithia laughed ruefully. "Habit. My leg was so damaged by the tolokon venom before I went into the healing chamber that I could barely stand. I'm used to limping."

She keyed the open symbol to let them into the farthest left portal of four set into the opposite wall. The eexit led to another short corridor, lined on both sides with small rooms, like whitewashed monks' cells. The door to each was gaping open. As he passed, Nate could see all the rooms were empty and featureless, as if freshly constructed and yet to be used.

"Samia's, Tedesk's, Rebehr's—" As she walked, Bithia recited the litany of who'd claimed each room in her time.

"What was this area for?" Nate asked, trying to interrupt her stream of consciousness about her lost friends and colleagues. "Temporary quarters?"

"Yes, I think I told you our main base was in the mountains. This facility in Nochen was for field research, so we all had our own small space to keep a few things while we worked on assignment in the area. I could catch a nap between duties, meditate, be private with another person if I so desired. But I don't understand why my team's possessions are cleared out, as if everyone left had time to pack but didn't come release me." She walked faster, stopping in front of the only closed door.

Bithia freed her hand from Nate's and tapped a quick sequence of musical notes across one of the pearlescent disks on the massive bracelet circling her left wrist.

"What is that thing?" Nate asked. "I figured it for a piece of jewelry, but if you're using it to open doors, it must be more than a gaudy bauble."

"Much more than mere adornment." The mere suggestion seemed to strike Bithia as highly amusing. She extended her left hand to him so he could examine the device more closely. Thom leaned over Nate's shoulder to see better. Amused, Nate stifled a chuckle. His ever-practical friend had no interest in jewelry, but technology drew him like a moth to flame.

"It's a gilintrae," Bithia said. "We all have our own, of varying degrees of sophistication and usefulness. My father gave me this when I graduated from the final set of advanced classes required to be accredited for a field expedition. It's one of the best, much better than what I had to use as a student."

Gently, Nate manipulated her wrist to see all the detail. The face of the bracelet-like device was approximately three inches in diameter, he estimated, and covered with densely packed, miniature iridescent disks, like scales on a fantastic fish. There were three smaller dials at equidistant points on the main surface outlined with a thin rim of gold, each set with a different precious stone. A string of roughly one-carat diamonds outlined the edge of the face, nestled side by side in an unbroken string. A ring of even bigger diamonds, interspersed with gems he didn't recognize, was set into the heavy gold outer rim. On the left and right sides, sat three tiny sapphire-topped buttons, each a different geometric shape. The massive golden band holding the gilintrae snugly on her slender wrist was an interlocking series of flat plates, each inscribed with a different symbol.

"I'm impressed," Thom said. "Even if it doesn't do anything but open doors, the thing is amazing."

Bithia laughed again, gently untangling her hand from Nate's loose grip. "We use them for many purposes. I should have been able to open the healing chamber with it, but my father blocked the menu of commands, as I told you. I'd discovered the secret of stealing power from the healing device in dribs and drabs and stored my cache in the gilintrae, which is how I was able to use it to project myself to you the night you'd been beaten and help you, Nate," she said, giving her attention to the door of her assigned room. Quickly, she tapped a sequence, her fingernails flashing between the tiny disks on the face of the device and the large gems on the rim. After a moment, she frowned and tapped again. "It's not responding."

"Could your father have left the door locked?" A reasonable enough precaution for a devoted parent to take, in Nate's view.

Eyebrows raised, lips compressed, Bithia obviously didn't agree. "Against me? My own door? Why?" Her musical voice held a note of annoyance.

"None of this makes much sense. How could it after all these centuries? You want us to blast it open?" Nate unholstered his Mark One and pointed the weapon at the recalcitrant door.

She pushed the blaster aside. "No! From what you described about how the weapon works, my possessions would be destroyed along with the door. Let me try one more time."

The third time was the charm. The door slowly slid partially open. A blast of stale air gusted out, carrying dust and shreds of debris that could have been paper or fabric or some other perishable commodity. Nate grabbed Bithia and pulled her aside, out of the path of the mini storm. Thom threw himself to the far side of the open portal. Atletl and Celixia retreated toward the lab.

"This expedition to the Lady's private chambers is perilous," Atletl said. "Do we need to continue the quest?"

The inrush of air to the corridor stopped, leaving a pile of dusty gray debris piled untidily along the floor and into the open room opposite Bithia's. Nate held her back and peered into the chamber assigned to her. He shook his head. "I'm sorry, sweetheart, whatever your father left for you didn't stand the test of time."

"But if he went to the trouble to seal off the room, he should have applied a stasis lock to keep the contents of my room intact for me," she said. "To do otherwise makes no sense."

Nate didn't answer, choosing to silently stand aside and let her proceed. Bithia squeezed sideways through the stubborn portal and came to a standstill in the center of what had been her room. He prevented the others from following, blocking their view and shaking his head. "Leave her alone. Thom, see what's at the other end of this corridor."

After a few moments, Bithia left the room. Nate straightened from where he'd been leaning against the wall while she worked through her emotions about this new puzzle. He looked at her questioningly.

She tapped the gilintrae, closing the door to her chamber.

"You okay?"

She nodded, not glancing in his direction. With a visible effort, she straightened, squared her shoulders and then turned to Nate, summoning a smile that didn't reach her stunning lavender-blue eyes. "I'm fine. I have to take this"—she waved at the now shut door—"as fair warning not to expect anything. Nothing at all will be as I left it. Or as I believed conditions would be whenever I was finally set free. Certainly not like my foolish dreams of finding myself in my own time, with my own people."

"I'm sorry. Maybe we'll find something elsewhere in this complex that you can—"

Holding up one hand, she shook her head decisively. "I appreciate what you're trying to do for me, but I have to be in the present, not clinging to shreds of the past. You attempted to give me this advice in the healing chamber, but I didn't want to hear it. Now I see you were right."

He gathered her in for a hug, hoping the embrace would help. She was trembling and on the verge of hyperventilating. Her chaotic emotions roiled below the surface of their mental link, and Nate could only guess at the effort she was making to function. Offering what silent comfort he could, Nate stood with her in the circle of his arms for a moment.

Footsteps sounded at the far end of the hall. Thom was reporting back from his explorations of what lay beyond. Nate looked over Bithia's head, raising one eyebrow in silent question as Thom came closer.

He shook his head. "Another empty room. Even less debris, or junk or whatever, than back in the lab. Nothing usable."

"The room served as the hangar for our flyers, to commute back and forth to the main base on the mountain." Bithia's words were muffled as she rested her head on Nate's chest. "There's a tunnel to the surface."

"We need to go back to the lab, regroup and figure out our next move," Nate said.

A few moments later, the five were in a small cluster at one side of the ransacked lab, away from the doors as well as the entrance to the healing chamber. Nate and Thom gathered bins to use as seats, although Nate paced, not patient enough to sit. Thom chose to lean against the wall, arms folded.

"We have no food, no water, no transport," Nate said, "but we can get out of the city using the flyer access tunnel. Am I right?"

Bithia made as if to rise, drawing a protest from Celixia, who was busily working to arrange her incredibly long, thick hair into an arrangement more convenient than its present loose state. Properly chastened by her handmaiden, Bithia held her head rigid and answered Nate's question. "While reluctant to assume anything now, much less to promise, I think the tunnel should open for us."

"Unless whoever deactivated this place," Thom said, "decided to seal it off permanently."

"Where does this tunnel open on the surface?" Nate asked.

"We flew out of bluffs at the edge of the ocean." She used a meaningless unit of measure to describe how far away the exit point would be.

He shook his head. "How long to walk it? A day? Half a day?"

She had to mull over the question for a moment, apparently comparing her experience of racing through the tunnel in a flyer to the unknown concept of trudging the distance on foot. Estimating the relative times of the two modes of travel left her frowning. Finally, she shook her head, undoing Celixia's work and drawing another protest from the priestess. "Not nearly so far. Maybe the span of a morning."

"Could we descend to a beach, or climb to a cliff top, once we got there?" The last thing Nate wanted was to make the trip through the tunnel and find they were trapped and forced to retrace their journey. Once out of the palace complex at Nochen, he'd make every effort not to see the place ever again.

Bithia raised her elegant eyebrows. "I never considered making either attempt. I'm a pilot, not a mountain climber. I guess you could get to the beach."

Nate scrutinized Atletl and Celixia. "Either of you have any idea where this beach might be? Any legends or myths about it? Could we get inland to our ship, to where we were captured, from there?"

Atletl shook his head. "I'm from the mountain territories. I know nothing of the coastline."

"Celixia? I can tell you have an opinion," Nate said.

"There's a legend." She restored her hair-brushing tools to the small beaded green pouch at her belt, finally having done as much as possible to bring Bithia's hair under control.

Thom groaned. "Oh, great, another legend."

Nate frowned at him. "We've done okay using myths and legends as our source briefing on this damn planet so far."

"I'd just like, one time, to be dealing in hard facts. Is a map too much to ask for?"

"You require a map?" Bithia tapped one of the disks on the gilintrae. The room darkened a bit, causing her companions consternation.

"I'm not too keen on being stuck inside this abandoned facility in the dark," Thom said.

Gleaming like miniature jewels hanging from a black velvet backdrop suspended in the air, an apparition appeared. It floated about a yard in front of Bithia and five feet off the floor.

"The view of this planetary system as we came in from the outer reaches," she said. "The others laughed at me for capturing it in my personal library—arrival in new star systems was a familiar thing to them, but it was my first expedition and a special memory."

The depiction swirled and twisted dizzyingly. The three moons came from nowhere and rushed past, going over her shoulder. The scope narrowed to a three-dimensional view of the planet they were standing on, which rapidly enlarged and became a high-level view of a continent, the next moment shrinking too fast for the visual cortex nerves to take it all in, becoming a perfect representation of the city of Nochen—as it had been when Bithia last saw it.

"Definitely more than ornamental jewelry, or a remote control for opening and closing doors." Nate pointed at her bracelet. "We have devices able to do the same general kind of projection, but they're not as pretty."

"It also stores knowledge for retrieval." Bithia bit her lip and frowned. "It's hard to explain all the functions of the gilintrae properly. I'm not trying to withhold data from you. You don't have the words for all the capabilities."

"Guess we'll find out as we go along." Wondering how much capability the bracelet possessed, and how he could utilize it as an advantage in their escape, Nate walked to where the city hung, suspended in thin air. *Now's not the time to ask for a full demo, but at some point I'll need to know.* He motioned to Celixia to come examine it with him. "Can you expand the field of vision a bit, take in this coastline you referred to, where the tunnel exit is?"

Frowning, she clicked a nail lightly on the edge of her bracelet. The hologram expanded, now encompassing the coastal plain all the way from the city to the ocean's edge, extending east to the foothills, backstopped by an imposing range of mountain peaks.

"Hard to control the fine detail, I gather? And the only speed is fast-forward?" Nate shrugged. "Don't worry about it. This view will do for now." He transferred his attention to Thom. "Can you tell me where our ship is? I was out of it for the landing and the first day of captivity."

"No need to remind me. I basically had to carry you, convince those bastards with a lot of sign language and swearing not to kill you." Thom studied the terrain. Finally, he traced a finger across it, going from the large white dot representing the city on this level of detail, back across the river and into the foothills. "About here, I'd say. Remember it was a good five days' forced march, plus part of another day to reach the city after we got across the suspension bridge."

"On the scale shown here, a trip to the coast adds a day, maybe two, to backtrack, then," Nate calculated, eyeing the distances on the hologram.

Bithia came closer to the map her device had created. She poised one elegant finger above the loftiest mountain in the formidable range. "This peak is where my father has—had—our main facility." She focused on it like a starving person, eyes shining, despite her earlier brave words to Nate about not living in the past.

Atletl appeared astonished at her choice. "The mountain of the Sleeping Goddess, home of T'naritza. I was born in a village at its foot. Here." He showed them, a pleased smile lighting his face.

"A lot of coincidences. Not surprising the Nocheni were so ready to regard you as a goddess," Nate said to Bithia.

"I'm happy and relieved not to embody the exalted position any longer. Should we risk the tunnel?"

He considered. "Are there any other exits from this place, besides going back through the healing chamber?"

"Sarbordon, Lolanta and a whole crew of their nasty helpers are waiting," Thom said.

"Two exits exist." A quick tap from Bithia's fingers and the topographical map of the continent disappeared, to be replaced by the city again, an appealing collection of miniature buildings.

Celixia frowned as she scanned the new creation before her. "This doesn't show the sapiche arena. Nor the sacrifice platform of Huitlani or the wells. And the palace is much larger now."

"It's been a few thousand years," Nate said. "Change happens. Where did the other two exits take your people when they wanted out of the lab and into the field?"

"Here—"

"No good. The locals built their altars to Huitlani on that spot." Nate wasn't surprised. He hadn't had much hope about the other exits, but it was worth exploring all available options. "Figures. The ruling class appears to have perfected the art of assimilating elements of the religion or beliefs of the subjugated people. There must have been all kinds of legends about the location too."

"And the other back door?" Thom asked.

Bithia turned to him, eyebrows raised. "You won't like this one."

"Why not?"

"The main entrance to be used by the Nocheni who worked with us, or studied with us, was built into the east wing of the palace." She pointed with one graceful hand. "I know you don't want to try walking out there either. Am I right?"

Thom rolled his eyes and apparently lost interest in the whole discussion.

"Anyone could come and go in this complex?" Nate found the expedition leader's attitude surprisingly lax.

Bithia's response dispelled the image of the dangerously open facility he had been envisioning. "We controlled the entry, of course. No one was given the access tones and symbols, unlike the set Hialar was granted. Those worked for the healing chamber only. My father didn't want any Nocheni to wander freely in our labs and workspaces unescorted."

Celixia laughed with bitter amusement. "The entire portion of the building where you say your entry was located collapsed in the great quake of five thousand years ago. Many people died, including a significant number of my own ancestors. We almost lost the secrets of the Hialar forever as a result of the quake, but one of the keepers was rescued from under the edge of the rubble. She lived only until sundown the same day, but it was long enough to pass on most of her knowledge to two younger Hialar."

"And the palace wing?" Bithia inquired, not showing much interest in the fates of those who'd been keepers not only of their secrets, but of her person against her will. Nate noticed she was sensitive to any mention of the topic, whereas Celixia took understandable pride in the Hialar accomplishments. He hoped the relations between the two women would stay cordial, even with conditions radically altered. Hostility on Bithia's part to her former attendant could make escape through what was basically enemy territory a lot more difficult.

He needed Celixia's continued help, as well as Atletl's. The latter showed definite signs of interest in the priestess's future, which might influence any decision he made, should the two women come to a parting of the ways. The warrior enjoyed proclaiming himself to be a warrior of the goddess, but Nate wasn't sure Atletl's allegiance wouldn't shift as Bithia showed herself to be just as much a normal person as the rest of them. And then, in Nate's opinion, Atletl would be likely to side with Celixia.

This was yet another thing he needed to talk to Bithia about, if he ever got a private moment alone with her. Nate tuned in to what Celixia was telling the others.

"It was never rebuilt," she said about the palace wing. "Or the debris cleared away. The people believe the ground was cursed, and a great wall was built to contain the demons who caused the shaking. Even Sarbordon's ancestors chose not to venture there, although the conquerors occupied the rest of the palace and the city. When the ground shakes again, his people sacrifice a member of their own clan to Huitlani, preferably a young warrior."

"A famous legend," Atletl said with a grimace of distaste. "It is said the soldier becomes a demigod immediately upon death and does battle with the demons. If he wins this battle in the underground chambers, then Huitlani takes him into the hall of his special warriors. If the first sacrifice fails and is eaten by the demons instead, then another must be killed by the priestesses to commence the battle anew."

"At least the chosen one is a volunteer, one of their own." Anger laced Celixia's voice. "Unlike all the other demands of their god Huitlani, which can only be satisfied by the deaths of my people."

Nate shivered. Compared to the dry recitation of similar myths in long-ago classes at the Academy, this discussion was all too real. *I could give one hell of an expert guest lecture on the whole subject now.* For sure, nobody would drowse off during his depiction of the realities. "Back to what concerns us now, which is getting out of here. The flyer tunnel is the only choice. Fighting our way out of the healing chamber, through the palace and out of the city armed with nothing but three alien weapons, plus swords, is only going to happen in an adventure trideo."

"Agreed." Thom immediately backed his tactical assessment. "I'd say the tunnel is it. But is she"—nodding in Bithia's direction dubiously—"going to be strong enough for such a long walk so soon after leaving the chamber? Barefoot?"

"The tunnel floor is smooth enough to walk on without distress," Bithia said. "The walls are completely lined with black talmere—the same as this floor." She stamped with one slender foot. "As to my endurance, I can't say."

Nate realized he'd been ignoring an important aspect of their environment, taken for granted because it was a part of his own technology-driven world too. "What's providing the power for these lights and the healing chamber?"

"One of the first tasks on setting up a field expedition like this is to establish the pleikn generator in a special chamber of its own. At the end of this hall." She gestured at one of the doors they hadn't yet tried. "Why?"

"I want to see it," Nate said. "Gathering intel to support informed decision-making."

"I rank high enough to have access." Bithia held out her hand to him again, and together they walked carefully across the cluttered floor to the door she had indicated. From the corner of his eye, Nate watched the outdated vision of the city wink out.

Bithia had to let them through two large, heavy doors made of the translucent black talmere before reaching the power source.

It was like nothing he'd ever seen before. A thick panel of clear crystal blocked access to the actual chamber where the generator existed. "Clarified talmere." Bithia indicated the width with her outspread hands—about a yard, Nate judged.

A perfect globe of pure blue energy hung in the exact center of the forbidden inner room, painting its surroundings blue with reflected light. The miniature star of pure energy was nine feet in diameter. Revolving unceasingly in a counterclockwise direction, the light emitted a low-pitched hum. Tentacles of the blazing light reached out in a rhythmic pattern, touching square plates of glittering material inlaid deep into the walls at various points. A set of symbols was inscribed below each niche.

"The lab, the healing chamber, living quarters, the storehouse." Bithia pointed as she read them off, going across the room from left to right. "All powered from here. Don't stare at the pleikn too closely or for too long. It is best viewed through special visors, but the equipment isn't on the rack where it belongs."

"This unit doesn't power your father's mountain base?" Nate asked.

"The base has its own pleikn." Bithia sounded distracted, although she answered Nate's question readily enough. Despite the warning she'd just given, she watched the glowing blue energy provider, a frown on her face.

Nate eyed her, guessing from her expression that something wasn't right. "What's the matter?"

"See the surface ripples, and there, a flash of green—the light should only be pure blue, never the other colors."

"Which means what?" Thom asked. "There goes another ripple."

Sure enough, now Nate observed the subtle blurring and distortion passing through the blue globe, as if someone was vibrating a container full of water. The humming sounded off-key. The ragged undertone tore at his nerves. He seemed to be disgustingly attuned to the subliminal aural frequencies of working alien devices. *Damned inconvenient.*

The rippling effect slowly died away in the globe.

"It's going out of balance and needs correction." Bithia's pronouncement was unequivocal. "This must be why I was having recent problems with the healing machine. Any power surge or decline would affect the device. Over time, such problems would destroy the equipment." Rubbing her arms, she shivered. "And me."

"Do you know how to fix it?" Nate asked.

She shook her head. "It's rare for pleikn to fall from the self-sustaining state. It may have been established too hurriedly when we first arrived and not tuned properly to the underlying harmonics of the planet. My father wasn't happy with a number of things the advance logistics team had done in a rush, or omitted altogether. He was annoyed." Smiling at the memory, she shook her head slightly, as if to bring herself back to the present dilemma.

"What if it continues to fluctuate?"

She made a dramatic gesture with her hands. "It explodes. Eventually, not in the next few heartbeats." She stared at the chamber for a moment before activating readouts. "This unit, however, is extremely close to detonation. Checking the rate of the ripples and the intensity of the colors, maybe a few hours."

"How much territory does it take out? What happens?"

Bithia frowned over Nate's questions. She tapped the gilintrae to make the holographic view of the city reappear. "The blast would level everything from here"—she indicated a point about halfway to the coastline—"to just short of here." The last point was the river gorge where Nate and his comrades had crossed the perilous bridge. "No more city, only a flat plain of talmere. This is a small pleikn, you see. A large enough one could destroy an entire planet. But my people forbid the use of pleikn as weapons."

"Maybe not in your time," Nate said reluctantly, rubbing his jaw. "But Thom and I've seen planets left in the state you describe."

Thom obligingly rattled off a list. "Travas Three, Aldecr Seven. And a city on Flatira One. I guess we solved one mystery of the ages today. The Sectors would love a weapon with this capability. We can destroy a planet nowadays but not easily."

"There's no recorded history anywhere in our part of the galaxy as to why the people vanished or the civilizations were destroyed. We knew the how but not the why." Nate checked how Bithia was reacting to the information and wasn't surprised by the shock on her face. He drew her closer. "The death and destruction isn't your fault. You've no idea what may have driven your people to such lengths or even when it happened."

She buried her face in her hands for a moment, then threw her head back with a defiant toss of the braids Celixia had labored over. "I begin to see how living in your world is going to be a constant challenge. You speak so glibly of these ancient events, events which hadn't even happened at the time I was left here on Talonque. The concept of my people in an interstellar war, wielding our most powerful technology—why? Against who? Some of our own people? It's hard to process. I'm scared, not for myself, but for the people I loved. I know the events were thousands of years ago, but knowledge doesn't help me accept the truth. Do you understand?" She stared into his eyes, her hands locked on his biceps. "It's all too fresh to me still. What you discuss as irrevocably past is the future in a real sense to me." Bithia leaned her head on his shoulder, closing her eyes.

"I'm sorry," he said, putting his arms around her. "I'll try not to be so casual about these things, but they're facts of our existence in the galaxy, you know. Mysteries my people and others have long wanted to solve."

"Hadn't we better be getting out of here, if this thing is going to blow?" Thom asked.

"Is there any way to warn the populace?" Nate directed his question at Celixia and Atletl.

"Judging by the activity we saw as we came back to the palace, the city's being evacuated anyway," Thom said.

"Fear of the coming battle with my people." Atletl drew himself up taller, as if highly gratified by his own conclusion.

"What about radiation?" Nate asked.

Bithia wrinkled her brow. "Radiation?"

"Lingering ill effects in the area or carried on the winds that can kill people who were nowhere near the explosion," he explained. "On at least a couple of the worlds we were talking about, Survey teams measured radiation."

"No such other effects are present, to my knowledge. Nothing will ever grow in this place again, because the talmere bonds all the way to the core of the planet. Perhaps if my people or descendants of my people have turned—did turn—oh, these frames of temporal reference give me a headache!" Biting her lip, rubbing her temple, Bithia was exasperated. "It may be if researchers found a way to convert pleikn into a weapon, then the scientists also found a way to add this radiation, these lingering ill effects you speak of. I only know nothing relevant is discussed in the manuals I was taught from." She ran a hand along the controls. "I *can* tell you a pleikn that strobed even once the way this one does constantly must be disconnected and replaced by the specialists as soon as possible."

"We can't replace it," Nate said. "In the short time we've been standing here, it's strobed, or whatever you call it, at the rate of approximately once in three minutes. I bet it's been drifting out of balance for quite a long time."

"Probably. I know the healing chamber has been growing ever more problematic during the reigns of the last few rulers. I never dreamed the problem lay with the pleikn." Narrowing her eyes, Bithia assessed the power source again. "Close to the threshold for detonation, judging by the colors. Well before morning. About the time the three moons rise, assuming their cycle hasn't varied since last I saw them."

Thom did rapid calculations in his head. "Six Terra standard hours, give or take an hour."

"There's no alarm in this facility," Bithia said, referring to Nate's earlier question. "The pleikn was monitored. The proper personnel would have been notified via their gilintrae."

"We have no citywide alarm system," Celixia added. "A set of bells and trumpets to call people to sacrifice, but as I understand, what you desire is to set people fleeing, not drawing closer."

"Issue settled. Much as I'd prefer to warn the populace of the danger, we've got no way to accomplish it. I hope the mass evacuation in fear of the invasion will clear as many people as possible from the blast zone." Nate nodded. "Here's the plan for us. We check out the flyer tunnel and go like hell toward the coast exit. Sound good?"

There was no objection, not even from Bithia.

Once they were back in the lab, Nate paused. "Is there a tunnel from here to the storehouse, Bithia? Any chance of getting supplies? You could identify helpful or essential items."

She shook her head, obviously sorry to disappoint him. "No, my father desired the storehouse be an entirely separate facility, as was standard practice. We could check the food-preparation chamber and apparatus here in this complex—"

Nate had no desire to waste any more time. "Judging from the way this place was left, anything we'd find would be as unpreserved as the contents of your room. Good thing Celixia had us hunt for the red box, or you'd have been one hungry lady by now."

The priestess lifted her head, smiling in acknowledgment of his praise. "I was well taught in all the mysteries of T'naritza. My mother omitted nothing, not even details we never expected to need, such as the Two Wines."

Because the Hialar were never going to let her go.

"I appreciate the many services and favors you've done for me." To Nate's relief, Bithia seemed to feel she needed to give positive commentary on Celixia's attention to duty, although her tone was flat.

Without further discussion, Nate led his group from the cluttered lab, headed through the hallway splitting the living quarters and emerged in the large hangar space Thom had previously reconnoitered.

"The tunnel is across here." Bithia walked briskly across the bare floor.

"How many flyers did you have?" Nate asked.

"Three. Two were large, five-person models with room for cargo. The other was a single flyer with a capacity of two passengers and a small load of cargo. The flyers recharged from the pleikn while parked here or at the main facility in the mountain. See those large plates over there? Charging stations."

"No small pleikn for personal use?"

Bithia shook her head. "Below a certain size, it's too difficult to keep the pleikn skin from imploding. I think work was going forward on the concept at home, but it wasn't a subject of interest to me. My specialties lay in other areas." She stopped in midstep, pointing at an odd machine parked at one of the charging stations. "The tunnel runner, utilized to check the talmere coating in the tunnel because it was prone to cracking or crystallizing over time and needed repair."

"Are you thinking what I'm thinking?" Nate exchanged a glance with Thom, and both men changed course to examine the squat machine snugged close to a sparkly wall plate. The vehicle hummed, and an oval indicator on its front was cherry red.

"Can you drive this?" Nate made a rapid assessment of the runner's length. "At least nine feet long. We can all sit or stand along the chassis."

"Of course I can drive the runner. I can drive anything the expedition brought with it. This part here"—Bithia touched the bulky protuberance in the middle—"detaches. The device analyzes and automatically repairs the talmere as the runner glides along the tunnel. There's no reason why we couldn't drive the runner ourselves, if you're strong enough to remove the device."

"The lady issues a challenge." Thom laid aside his cloak and bent to examine the oddly shaped vehicle more closely. "How do you—"

She tapped the disk on her gilintrae, and a metallic snapping sound echoed in the hangar. "Now you can lift it free."

It took Nate, Thom and Atletl working together to budge the immensely heavy repair mechanism off its runner cart. Grunting and swearing in several languages, the men moved the unit far enough to the side to clear the runner's access to the tunnel and set it aside without much care for possible damage to either the controller or the hangar floor.

"All right," Nate said, examining a scrape on his arm from an inconveniently placed flange on the repair robo. "Let's get the tunnel open and we're out of here. At tunnel runner speed, whatever that may be. Propulsion of any type's got to beat walking."

Bithia activated the massive tunnel door with no problem, much to Nate's relief. Then she drove the tunnel runner away from its recharging stand and into the center of the tunnel, using a ramp built for the purpose. The vehicle moved with encouraging briskness for its size.

"Pick a comfortable spot on the runner, and let's roll," Nate said. "We need to be long gone before the pleikn blows."

"Should we close the tunnel door? In case something goes wrong and the pleikn doesn't wait to go nova?" Thom asked as he climbed aboard the tunnel runner.

Bithia shook her head. "The tunnel door, impressive as it appears, only provides mental comfort. If the pleikn explodes, the door won't repulse the effect for even a second. On the other hand, if we're caught in the blast radius, we'll die so rapidly there'll be no suffering."

"Nice to know." Thom didn't seem pleased with her assurance about how fast death would strike. "Leave the damn door open, then. One less thing to do before we get on with this plan."

"We need to go," Bithia said. "What if I'm wrong? What if this pleikn has been out of balance for so long the implosion sequence occurs faster than what's given in the manual?"

"Less time to get clear than we calculated," Nate said as the lights in the hangar blinked on and off. He jumped onto the runner next to her, clinging to a protuberance.

Bithia activated the mechanism, and the small vehicle rolled forward at a good pace, which she steadily increased.

The tunnel was completely dark, except for the pale glow coming from her gilintrae.

CHAPTER EIGHT

Humming as it proceeded, the tunnel runner took the fugitives away from the underground installation. It moved faster than Nate could have walked. Adding to his apprehension, there were several earthquakes, each tremor causing loud crackling sounds in the talmere walls, although no visible damage occurred.

"I've never been on a seismically active planet before. Or at least not when quakes were happening," Nate said.

"Remember I told you the pleikn is synced to the harmonics of the planet itself?" Bithia kept her attention on the controls. "Badly aligned in this case, which is probably why it went out of balance eventually." Brow furrowed, she grinned a bit crookedly. "I hope my father transmitted a negative report on the setup team. The company came highly recommended, but this installation job was certainly substandard."

Nate admired the way she was holding up, able to make jokes, despite finding herself displaced from her time and normal life. The necessity for action must have been helping her maintain self-control. He'd have to be extra observant once they had downtime, if the pace of events ever slackened.

"Why do I have a feeling it's going to be plenty spectacular when the pleikn blows, and I don't want to be anywhere in the vicinity?" he said after a particularly forceful quake pushed the runner off its straight course through the center of the tunnel. He raised his voice to be heard clearly over the slight humming of the propulsion unit and the breeze created by their progress.

"Sorry for the rough ride." Bithia stabbed repeatedly at the controlling symbols, first skewing them one way and then the other, working to keep the vehicle from plowing into the tunnel wall on either side. "The runner's guidance mechanism is confused by the conflicting signals caused by the quakes," she said. "The mechanism wasn't designed for such conditions."

Nate had an anxious eye on the red power indicator, glowing less fiercely now. He decided not to say anything that would alarm the others. Even if the tunnel runner eventually lost power, they'd gotten a respectable head start. He squeezed Bithia's shoulder gently to acknowledge her comment.

"We wanted to issue a warning," he said as the runner rolled forward. "Perhaps all these earthquakes will tempt a few more people to clear the area."

"Probably tempt Lolanta to sacrifice a few more too." Celixia's retort from her perch on the right side of the runner's long snout was heated. "Her death can't come too soon. I hate her even more than I loathe Sarbordon."

"This rapid travel in the dark is disorienting." Atletl covered his eyes with one hand and leaned over the hood of the runner as if he wished to lie flat. "I'm thankful we've had no food since before the sapiche matches."

"He's probably the first person on this planet to get vehicular motion sickness," Thom said in Basic, chuckling.

Nate's attention was to the front as he strained to focus on something looming ahead in the gloom. The dim light cast by Bithia's gilintrae showed the tunnel completely blocked by boulders and dirt.

"Brakes—stop this thing."

She fought the controls and managed to bring the runner to a shuddering, sideways halt, short of the debris.

Nate hopped off the tunnel runner, Thom behind him, and walked closer to the mass of rock filling the space from floor to ceiling. "Can you back the runner up a few feet, in case this caves in further with the next tremor?"

As she complied, Nate grimly contemplated the new obstacle. "Sabotage by parties unknown in Bithia's time? Or caused by the quakes today?"

"I don't know. No fresh dust in the air. Might have happened a long time ago—maybe during the great quake Celixia was telling us about. Impossible to tell. Damn!" Thom kicked a small rock out of the way. "Doesn't matter anyway. One hell of a lot of debris in front of us."

"What do we do now?" Atletl demanded, nervously checking the tunnel over his shoulder.

"How long have we been traveling?" Nate wanted to check her estimate of elapsed time with his own internal clock, which was usually pretty accurate on these things.

"More than three-quarters of the time I'd estimated to reach the coast," she answered after a quick peek at one of the tiny indicators on her bracelet.

"Time's running short. We have to dig," Nate said. "Lords of Space, I wish we had one of our Mark 27's. We could make short work of this mess by blasting a passage through the blockage."

"You think this'll do any good against rocks?" Thom drew his Mark One.

"Try it. Wait, all of you take shelter behind the tunnel runner in case the beam bounces back."

Dull gray flashes showed where the hits landed, the only observable outcome. Whatever the predominant mineral was in this area of Talonque provided an excellent blast shield against the ancient weapons. The rockfall remained intact after a short but sustained barrage.

Nate and Thom walked back to the edge of the debris field, agilely moving out of the way as a new quake sent a few rocks tumbling and rolling along the tunnel floor. "At least the debris appears loosely packed." Nate eyed the blockage as best he could in the dim light. "Maybe there's hope."

He scaled to the top of the rock pile, moving cautiously and stopping often as cascades of pebble-sized debris slipped out from under his feet. The process took ten minutes or so. "We're in luck. The rockfall doesn't go all the way to the roof of the tunnel. We can clear enough space to wriggle through to the other side. Thom, Atletl, let's get to work moving rock. Bithia, Celixia, stay back behind the runner."

"We can help," Bithia said. "I can throw rocks as well as any man."

"There isn't much room here, and you're barefoot. You've been doing your share, driving us to this point."

The three men worked feverishly in the gloom, trying to select and remove as many as possible of the critical rocks that held others in place. Nate's goal was to clear a passage for one person at a time to squeeze through.

"We're running short on time," Bithia said. "You've been working longer than you realize. How's it coming?"

Nate wiped a mixture of sweat and dust off his brow and squinted through the gloom, evaluating their progress. "The last boulder we dislodged was the final obstacle."

Nate sent Thom and Atletl to help Celixia and Bithia climb the pile of rocks, even more unstable now. When all five were perched at or near the top, he said, "I'm going through first. If I can fit, any of you can. If I get stuck, I can probably dig my way through. I'll yell as soon as I'm on the other side. Then come through one at a time as fast as you can. Thom, take rear guard."

Thom nodded. "Good luck."

Nate nodded and disappeared into the tunnel within a tunnel. Cursing occasionally as he had to scrabble and dig his way through new blockages, he kept moving except during the increasingly frequent tremors. Then he covered his head with his arms and tried not to think too much about the tons of dirt pushing on the ancient tunnel.

"Okay, I'm through," he said, raising his voice as he stood at the top of the debris on the other side of the rockfall. His voice echoed oddly, so he hoped the others were hearing him well enough. "It's about four yards of pretty nasty crawling, but there's room to maneuver. Bad on the knees, I warn you. Send the next person through."

Bithia came first, followed closely by Celixia and then Atletl. Nate ordered each one to be careful descending the unsteady slope to the tunnel floor. "As soon as you hit the talmere, run. Don't look back and don't wait for me. Thom and I'll be along."

A few moments later, the sergeant emerged from the makeshift tunnel, Nate grabbing his arm and helping to extricate him. "Where are the others?" Thom rose to his feet, dusting himself off.

"Sent them each running to the exit as soon as they came through. We must be out of time by now." Nate slid down the dirt and rocks, Thom right behind him, and sprinted along the tunnel after their companions. "Pray there isn't another blockage before the exit, because from the increasing frequency and intensity of the quakes, we don't have time to clear more rocks from the path. Bithia said we're substantially over the limit of time she expected already."

Nate skidded around a smooth, gentle curve in the corridor to find the women and Atletl standing in a pool of light from Bithia's gilintrae in front of a massive door like the one in the hangar bay.

"What's the holdup? Blow this thing," Nate said. "I ordered you not to wait for us."

"It won't open." Bithia's voice was taut with frustration.

"Not responding at all?" Nate said in disbelief. He came to a stop next to her, breathing hard, staring at the door with narrowed eyes.

"I don't believe it." Thom added a spacer's oath in Basic for emphasis, the tone leaving no doubt of his negative reaction to this new hurdle. "When do we get a goddamn break on this planet?"

Nate heard the grinding of whatever mechanism should be opening the portal. The door vibrated, straining upward a few inches, then thudded into its tracks. Another quake struck, this one violent enough to throw them all to the floor. Grabbing Bithia as he fell, cushioning her from impact with the floor, Nate was buffeted by massive seismic waves rolling through the ground under him. The sound—somewhere between a roar and a rumble—was deafening.

"I think the door's warped," Bithia said as soon as the rattling and rolling died away. Sitting up a bit drunkenly, she worked the dials of her gilintrae, stabbing at the jewels. "The mechanism tries to respond."

"We need something to wedge it open with. If we can get the door open far enough to slip underneath and make it to the outside, we'll be fine," Nate said.

"This door must weigh tons. We're not going to find anything in this tunnel strong enough to hold it," Thom protested. "Short of going back to the rockfall."

Another quake rattled through the tunnel. Nate heard a sharp crack behind him and then a roar as tons of rock fell through the tunnel sheathing. A rolling cloud of choking dust billowed around the curve. The door moved open farther and, as his hopes rose, stayed stubbornly in its new, slightly higher position. A cool, fresh breeze wafted into the tunnel from the small opening, creating an eddying backwash to the advancing dust cloud.

"The sea." Celixia drew in a deep breath of the tangy salt air. "We're so close. Can't you make the door move a little more, T'naritza?"

Bithia glared in her general direction but worked the controls again. The door mechanism emitted a metallic shriek as it attempted to obey her commands, struggling ponderously to rise a few more inches. All progress stopped with one final, ear-splitting complaint from the tortured metal.

"Not getting any better," Nate said. "We're going through now."

"What if it falls?" Celixia was wide-eyed and fearful.

"No time to worry, just go." Nate pushed her in the direction of the small opening that was their only chance at freedom and life.

"I'll go first." Atletl's voice was gentle, and he hugged Celixia reassuringly. Stepping past her, he wriggled through the opening as Nate and Thom pushed at his feet. Atletl's optimistic assessment of what lay ahead for them came from the safety of the outdoors. "There's a ledge out here, perhaps the size of a small table. It's unstable, crumbling at the edges, so step lightly."

Nate bent to shout through the opening. "How rough is the climb to the beach?"

"Not bad. There are a lot of vaiya vines growing from above." The answer was muffled by the door and the breeze.

"Vaiya?" Nate asked Celixia, raising his eyebrows.

"A tough, insidious plant growing wild. It spreads by sending out self-rooting runners."

"No time for botany lessons here," Thom said, impatience making his voice gruff. "Will it hold a man's weight?"

"Oh yes." She nodded confidently. "The roots go deep."

Satisfied, Nate yelled instructions to Atletl. "Celixia's coming through next. As soon as she's through, the two of you start down the cliff. Once you hit the beach, run like you've got Huitlani himself chasing you. Take your bearing to the left, away from the city. Celixia, come on." Nate held out his hand imperiously, and she stepped forward with reluctance, crying as she eyed the perilously suspended door.

"I'm afraid it'll fall on me." She gave Nate a piteous look, fear and apology mixed on her face. "I'll go last. Give me time to conquer my fear."

"Close your eyes, and we'll slide you through to Atletl. It'll take one second, the blink of an eye. It isn't going to close on you, I swear. Atletl won't let you fall either, once you're safely outside with him." Nate summoned all his dwindling reserves of patience for the panicked girl. "We'll make this quick. Thom and I aren't going before you and Bithia."

She swallowed hard and closed her eyes as commanded. Nate gestured to Thom and together they picked her up. He could feel her trembling as they slid her across the threshold of the tunnel. Atletl began pulling at her shoulders immediately.

"We go!" he yelled a moment later.

"Bithia, now," Nate said, extending his hand. "Wait for me on the ledge, and I'll help you down, but I want you out of here."

She kissed him on the cheek before going to her knees on the floor and wriggling carefully under the impending doom of the massive door. Her dirty and scratched feet cleared the threshold a second later. "All clear," she said. "Hurry, both of you."

"Thom, you next."

"Nate—"

"That's an order, Sergeant Curran. My turn to guard the rear."

Thom saluted and made his perilous but rapid journey out of the tunnel.

Nerves on edge as another small quake rattled through the tunnel, Nate wasted no time following his friend. He could hear the door straining above him, ratcheting an inch or two lower as he wriggled through, the sound raising his adrenaline. Bithia and Thom yanked him clear and steadied him while he found good footing on the narrow ledge outside. There was no sign of Atletl and Celixia.

Nate leaned over the edge, calculating the least-challenging descent. "Ever done any climbing?" he asked Bithia.

"Not a mountain climber, remember?" She shook her head, her face pale, loose strands of her hair whipping in the sea breeze. Her lavender eyes were huge in her face. She had one hand clenched on the exterior rim of the tunnel doorframe, her knuckles white.

"Thom, help me get her on my back. Lock your arms around my neck, your legs around my waist, and I'll carry you."

She didn't question his ability to accomplish the feat, nor did she hesitate as Thom boosted her into position. She clasped her arms on his shoulders as ordered, trying not to choke him. Nate waited until she'd locked her legs firmly at his waist, and then he took a careful step away from the door, assessing the effect of her added weight on his balance.

"If the height bothers you, don't look." Taking the thick vine Thom handed him, tugging on it violently to test its strength, Nate began a controlled but recklessly fast descent down the cliff. The sergeant paralleled their route, trying to go a little faster than Nate, watchful and ready to make a grab for them if Nate lost his footing, or if the vine gave way under their weight. Fortunately it wasn't a steep cliff, and the vaiya vines were not only abundant, the ropelike strands were as stout as Celixia had described.

Nate hit the beach, sliding the last yard in a landslide of pebbles and debris. Bithia slid off his body to the sand, landing ungracefully on her rear. Each man grabbed one of her slender hands, pulling her to her feet.

"Run for your life," Nate said, keeping his grip on her hand.

He took off, Thom and Bithia matching him stride for stride. Dimly, he made out Atletl in the slight early evening fog, carrying Celixia. Either her strength or her resolve must have finally given out. Bithia took a second to ruthlessly hike her lavender gown above her knees, tearing the delicate side seams in the process. She proved to be a fleet runner, her long legs flashing, keeping pace with Nate effortlessly as they fled.

Suddenly, a gigantic quake struck, its rolling motion throwing them to the somewhat forgiving surface of the damp beach.

A second sun, a blindingly blue one, rose inland over the city, or where the city had been. Nate fought the rolling motion of the ground to drag himself to Bithia. It was impossible to stand, a challenge to crawl, because the earth was shaking so violently. He threw himself over her, trying to shield her from whatever came next. Thom burrowed into the beach next to them, head buried in his arms.

A peculiarly small explosion sounded an odd note in the midst of the general chaos and uproar.

Despite the risk, Nate instinctively raised his head to see the massive door of the tunnel blasted off its tracks and out to sea. Right after it came a gush of pure blue fire blowing over the ocean like a blowtorch. He tried to flatten himself and Bithia even more securely into the beach as a roaring wind rose from nowhere and tore at them. The sound was incredible, a force unto itself, the sand particles stinging as the wind drove them. How long this lasted, he couldn't say. Eventually, the wind became a breeze and died away. All was quiet and serene again. One last quiver of the ground under him, and then it was still.

Nate realized he could hear the waves rolling in as the tide rose. He rolled into a sitting position, pulling at Bithia's shoulder. "You okay?"

She nodded a bit shakily and smoothed her hair away from her face, then reached to touch a bad scratch near his temple. "You?"

"I'm fine now." He bent to kiss her.

"I hate to interrupt," Thom said, "but I think Atletl is trying to get our attention."

"You okay?" Nate assessed his sergeant.

"Nice of you to ask—better late than never. I'm in one piece. Seven hells, did you see the tunnel torch? We barely got out of there in time."

"Not a moment to spare," Nate said as Bithia nodded.

Leaning on each other for support, the three of them got to their feet and started toward Atletl and Celixia.

Thom squinted out to sea. "Any danger of a tsunami, you think?"

"I hope not. The epicenter of the quake was pretty far inland. And shallow."

"I see a hut or dwelling of some sort," Atletl called as Nate came nearer. "I think it's deserted. We need a place to rest and shelter for the night, Captain. The priestess has a brave spirit but cannot go any farther."

As he walked over to the pair, Nate studied Celixia's drawn face and staring eyes, testimony to her exhausted condition. *Bithia's holding up better than she is.* He nodded. "I don't think any of us can go farther. Been a long, rough day, all right. Let's check this place out." He drew his alien weapon.

It took only a few moments to assure himself the small hut was empty, apparently abandoned for some time. Set well back from the high-tide line, the one-room cottage was sturdily constructed of tightly woven, dried plant material. A front porch showed evidence of serving as a kitchen in the past.

Holstering his weapon, Nate's gave a crisp assessment of priorities. "We have shelter for the night. Now we need fresh water, driftwood for a fire and something to cook. None of us are going to get much farther without eating. Water's a must."

"We need to do something about treating the cuts and bruises from climbing through the rockfall in the tunnel," Thom said. "We find water, I can at least clean the abrasions."

"There's a shelf stacked with sealed jars in the rear of the hut and a pile of finely woven blankets. Trade goods maybe. Too many for whoever could have lived here in this small place. Probably made their living fishing and crafting the blankets in the winter, when the ocean was too wild for lines. Evidently, whoever left this place did so in a hurry, abandoning their merchandise." Atletl's report was thorough.

"Or died perhaps." Celixia's verdict was grim. "There's an unfinished blanket on the floor by a chair, as if it was dropped in a hurry." She sank onto the edge of the wooden porch and rested her head on her knees, the thin braids falling loose about her hunched shoulders.

"Celixia, can you check out those sealed jars for us? You're more likely to recognize the contents, if by some miracle there's food or ingredients for anything vaguely edible." Nate squatted in front of her, his voice low and sympathetic as he tried to coax her into motion. "I know you're tired, but please do this one thing, and then we'll fix you a bed from the blankets, okay?" He tucked the braids behind her ears gently.

"I want to do my share," she said, her voice hardly even a whisper. "But I'm so exhausted." Turning her head on her knees to locate Atletl standing off to the side, she held out one hand in appeal. "Help me to my feet, and I'll go examine these mysterious jars."

The warrior grinned and came to lift her in one easy move. He carried her as the couple disappeared into the hut.

Nate moved on to the next set of orders. "Bithia, you and Thom are on driftwood duty. Stick together. Don't go too far along the beach, okay? I'm going to scout the general area, make sure we have the place to ourselves, see if I can locate a source of fresh water."

"Take this," Atletl said, reappearing on cue from the hut's interior and holding out two empty waterskins.

Nate looped the straps over his shoulder and moved into the scrubby dunes behind the hut.

Thom and Bithia had an easy time locating plenty of driftwood and soon had a fire blazing in the stone fire pit at the west end of the front porch. The sergeant used the trusty, age-old method of rubbing two sticks together to get the first spark after first teasing Bithia about the fact her magic bracelet could do so many things but was useless for a simple thing like starting a fire.

"Do you know how long it's been since my people needed open flame for anything? Your race must be far closer to the origin point of your species than mine." She was trying to tease him and was reassured by Thom's nod. He was Nate's best friend, nearly a brother, but a stranger to her. All she knew of him was what Nate had shared in their dreams together.

Thom fed the fire, but kept one piece of the driftwood aside, hefting it thoughtfully. Bithia followed his line of sight and found he was eyeing a flock of large, long-legged birds daintily feasting on small fish or other sea creatures in the shallows a few dozen yards away. The black-and-white-striped fishers had wickedly long, ivory-colored beaks, but hadn't shown any fear while she and Thom gathered driftwood. Nor had the birds made any threatening moves, even when he'd gotten close to a pair of juveniles straying from the main flock.

"The birds might be good eating, you think?" he asked. "Big enough to carry meat on those bones."

She didn't know what to say. "I've no idea. My people aren't accustomed to eating the flesh of other living creatures, although we have done so, at local feasts on this planet, for example." Biting her lip, she didn't say anything else. *I have to stop lecturing them about my civilization, which may not even exist anymore. I've got to fit into this world now.* Reality threatened to crash in on her, and her heart rate accelerated as her chest grew tight with anxiety. Instinctively, she reached for Nate with her mind and was reassured to find him still linked with her. She didn't try to talk to him, not knowing what he was doing at the moment, wary of distracting him, but sensing the warmth of their bond in her mind helped to calm her nerves.

"I'm going to go try my luck. Haven't hunted game since I was a boy, but something about the stomach being empty enough for the belly button to touch the backbone inspires a man to resurrect old skills." Thom eyed the piece of driftwood again, pulling out a belt knife. "Took this from the soldier whose uniform I'm wearing. This might make a good throwing stick, with judicious carving here and there. Well, guess I'll go find out in case Celixia doesn't come across anything edible in those dusty old jars. Keep the fire going, will you, ma'am?"

"Of course." She selected a small stick and placed it on the flames.

Thom gave her a salute and set off to hunt.

Pleased to have a moment to herself, Bithia leaned against the boulder behind her and stretched. The small luxury of being able to move freely after all those centuries of paralysis was intoxicating. Occasionally, a muscle or nerve cluster would refuse to do what she wanted, probably a residual effect of being held captive by the healer. She hoped the fleeting weakness would diminish over time. Taking a deep breath of the fresh sea air, she pondered the uncertain future. If she could get off Talonque and find the way to Nate's Sectors with him, she'd be fine. She was a member of a high tech society, after all. Surely she could fit in among his people. If she was doomed to remain on the planet, she had unwavering confidence in Nate to carve out a place for them to live. It wouldn't be anything like the life she'd dreamed of, so long ago now, but there would be Nate.

Ironic to find a companion soul where she'd never expected it, much less a man who was a warrior through and through. Bithia poked the fire a bit, reflecting on the men of her own society she'd been attracted to before. Nothing like Nate. She tried to imagine any of them enduring what he'd surmounted on Talonque, including convincing her to overcome her fears and grief and step into the world again at his side. Visualizing her favorite mental picture of Nate, the time they'd met in the dreamspace and spoken of songs and emotions, she felt herself smiling and relaxing.

When Nate retraced his path across the dunes in the darkening twilight, he found a satisfactorily domestic scene with two large plucked and dressed fowl being roasted on a spit across the fire pit. Thom tended the blaze, keeping it the right height to roast, not just sear, the birds. He was munching determinedly on dried fruit.

"Found this in one of the sealed jars," he said, holding up a handful.

Bithia sat, keeping Thom company, snacking on the stringy preserved fruit. She was amusing herself by making a fan with long lustrous feathers and a strip of cloth torn from her badly fraying gown. "See all these tiny, annoying red bugs? I think the cooking smell, or the dripping grease, attracts them. I hoped a fan might help keep the insects away." She smiled a bit ruefully. "High-tech as the gilintrae is, it can't repel a determined bug. The insects always win, don't they?"

"On every planet, universal law of nature. You made a lot of progress," Nate said as he unslung two bulging, dripping waterskins. "Nice clean spring water. Plenty more where this came from. In the morning I'll play guide to the pond, and the rest of you can take a dip, wash off some of the grime. I'm a new man, let me tell you."

"Any trouble?" Thom moved to make room for Nate to sit between him and Bithia. He took a water sack and offered it to Bithia first, then indulged in a long drink himself, belching contentedly. "Sorry. I needed something to wash down the fruit. I swear the cook preserved the seeds, the skin and the stem along with the good parts, and it all congealed to the density of a pebble." Moving a few feet away from the fire, he poured water over his head, vigorously rubbing his red hair and face to remove some of the accumulated grime and sweat.

"No trouble, no neighbors." Nate's report was succinct. He finished his own long drink. "There are flickering lights off in the distance, torches maybe, by the headland. Might be a fishing village. At least three miles. Mm, smells good. When do you figure it'll be done?" Nate reluctantly took a handful of the dried fruit Bithia offered him. The idea of roasted poultry was infinitely more inviting. His stomach growled.

"Couple hours. Have to get it thoroughly cooked to kill any parasites. There's dried fishmeal in the hut, but it's too salty. Maybe with the water you brought we can make soup to hold us off until the main course is done." Thom rotated the spit. "These birds are so fat they're self-basting. Should taste good."

"Where's Celixia? And Atletl?"

Thom jerked his head to indicate the hut. "She was totally worn out. Atletl said he'd sit with her since she was afraid to be left alone. Or so she said. Ask me, we have hot mutual attraction brewing there. Can't keep their hands off each other."

"Can't say I'm too surprised, the way those two have been eyeing each other since we first got to the city and met her. Aren't you tired?" Nate asked, studying Bithia warily.

She was his focus. Much as he'd grown to like Atletl and Celixia, the local couple could take care of themselves tonight. His primary worry was Bithia, her continuing good health, her mental state—in short, everything. She'd had to cope with so much since escaping the healing chamber, and Nate was expecting some knd of delayed reaction. He'd hated leaving her even for the short time required to carry out the necessary recon of the surrounding territory and to find water, but he'd known Thom would watch over her.

"I'm not too tired." She pulled the creamy white, fringed blanket she'd apparently taken from the hut more closely around her and leaned into Nate's embrace. After a moment, she made a little face of self-mockery. "Well, that's not strictly true. I'm afraid to let myself fall asleep ever again."

"Understandable after all those centuries of enforced sleep. Don't push it," he said. "When your body figures out you need to rest on your own now, you'll drowse off, I'm sure. Sit with me and enjoy the peace and quiet. We've earned a break for at least one night, although Thom and I'll stand watch. I'll be right here if you need me."

"What will we do next? In the morning? Strange to be talking like this again after so long, actually making plans. It feels a little frightening."

Nate gave her a hug.

"The lady has a good question. What are you planning for us to do tomorrow?" Thom characteristically brought the conversation back to the nuts and bolts of their continued escape.

Nate stared out to the sea, where the whitecaps of the incoming waves were visible in the gloom, marching to the beach in sets about six feet high. The sound of the water was rhythmic, soothing. A night bird warbled a few liquid notes as it skimmed along the sand close by them.

He took a deep breath. It was hard to force his tired mind to assemble the next set of moves. Relaxed for the first time since the sequence of events started light years away from Talonque, which eventually brought them crashing onto this damn planet, he craved freedom from responsibility. *Not home free yet, and you're in command. Everyone's depending on you to make it go right for them.* He sat straighter, squaring his shoulders as he took on the weight of the command duties he'd mentally set aside for an all too brief time.

"We can't stay here too long, idyllic though it's been so far. In the morning we'll check out what else is left in this hut and the outbuilding and junk pile in back. See if there's anything we can use. I want Atletl to take a trip to the fishing village, do some trading. We need sandals for Bithia, at a minimum, and local clothes for all of us would be nice. I don't want to march through the land resembling a deserter from Sarbordon's legions, you know?"

"We already got rid of those damn helmets. And I ditched the leather breastplate in the tunnel, which was another major improvement, let me tell you. The green uniform and black cloaks ain't too bad, if a man's gotta wear a kilt. I'm getting kinda fond of this cloak, actually. Got a nice weight to it. Pocket comes in handy," Thom said. "What are you thinking to use for trade goods? The blankets? Whoever lived here must have been pretty poor."

"Celixia took care of that," Nate said. He removed a green leather pouch from the pocket of his cloak. "She slipped me this as we were leaving the warehouse site."

"What's in it?" Bithia asked curiously.

"Coins. Gold, I believe. I have no idea how much they're worth, but Atletl should be able to stretch them while bargaining in the village. She said we'd need money to escape if I was successful in releasing you from the chamber."

"A woman who definitely plans ahead." Thom's voice held approval. "If she wasn't already spoken for, I might have to break my own rules about permanent involvements." He checked for Nate's reaction to this hoary old joke between them and guffawed.

Nate shook his head. "That'll be the day when you settle on one woman on any planet."

"After Atletl completes his trade duties, then what?" Bithia asked.

"We head inland, avoid trouble, try to locate our ship and hope like hell Haranda was right about it being spaceworthy."

"I don't want to think so far ahead tonight, if it's okay with you," Thom said. "Kinda had a full day and a half straight here. I like the idea of pretending to be on leave at some recreational beach somewhere in the Sectors. Tahumaroa Two maybe. Spent a good three weeks standard there once." Thom leaned against the hut and stretched. "I'm content with no worries, no schedule, nothing to do the rest of tonight but cook these fat birds and then eat, followed by a good night's sleep."

The three of them sat in companionable silence. Fat dripped from the roasting birds onto the fire with hissing sounds. A breeze sprang up, and the sound of the ocean came to them more clearly.

Nate realized from her soft, steady breathing that Bithia had fallen asleep despite her reluctance. He settled her more comfortably in the circle of his arms without waking her and looked across the fire to meet Thom's worried gaze.

"What are you going to do about her when we re-enter the Sectors? How we gonna protect her?"

"I won't be the first Special Forces guy to come home with the local girl who saved his life on-planet," Nate said. "The Sectors turns a blind eye to that kind of thing—you know the drill. I marry her, she becomes a citizen, I retire, we drop out of sight. Simple."

"Not simple." Thom's objection was immediate. "You know damn well when we do our mission debrief that there are going to be gaping holes—hell, monster black holes—in the story. How do we keep Command from realizing you're the first Special Forces guy to come home with an honest-to-goodness, living ancient alien citizen? I know she ain't actually AO, but she's from a time way before ours, with answers to a few mysteries." Thom frowned, apparently not liking where his thoughts took him next. "Sectors government is generally fair, but thinking the authorities'll leave her alone is a stretch. Let her vanish with you? Seven hells, it's technically against the law for a private citizen to own even one broken piece of an AO relic. And you want to marry a woman who *is* an AO, for all practical purposes? Have a normal life? Good luck, soldier! You may be able to shield the knowledge of who she truly is when Command debriefs you, but I ain't got your ability with mind blocks." His face bore a mournful expression. "I won't be able to stop myself from betraying you."

Unfazed, Nate sought to reassure his friend. "I know a guy who can help."

"Unless he's at the top of Sectors Command, or maybe the President of the Sectors Ruling Council, I don't see how." Thom shook his head dubiously. "This is serious stuff."

With a flash of gratitude, Nate realized the depth of Thom's genuine concern about Bithia's fate. So he opened up a little more. "When I was a kid, we moved constantly, lots of Sectors. My dad was a high-ranking officer, and my mother was in the diplomatic service. They were assigned to each new station as a team by the time I was born. We even got posted to Mellure once, for embassy duty."

Thom whistled softly. "Tough duty to pull. I'm fascinated, don't get me wrong, but I don't see what your childhood adventures have to do with us here on Talonque, nor with taking care of our lady there in the future." He scratched idly at a bug bite on his arm. Nate stayed silent, staring at the fire, not volunteering anything else. Thom asked another question. "The Mellureans don't let anyone set foot on their planet. Aren't the embassies all on a separate moon?"

Nate nodded. "The Mellureans don't mix much, and only on their own terms. There was a pair of brothers I spent a lot of time with—D'Aloun and David. David and I were the same age, both space mad to get into the Academy. His dad was Space Marines, going four generations back. So anyway, we three bonded tight, raised some hell in the outworlder colony on Mellure's moons. We were outsiders, no matter where we went in the Mellurean system, even at the school for embassy staffers' kids."

Thom added a few branches to the fire. "How does this help us protect Bithia from becoming government property and poked and prodded and forced to help solve AO riddles? I'm not following."

"My friends' mother was Sarinda Van Dorn Garcia, the First Mind of Mellure. Heard of her?"

"Who hasn't?" From his tone, Thom was impressed.

"Years ago she volunteered to join an Archaeology Service dig on Chichnir Six. Captain Tomas Garcia was in charge of the guard duty. The expedition got marooned during a Mawreg incursion of the Sector. Eventually, the group was rescued, along with Sarinda and Tomas's first son, D'Aloun Tuan."

"Wait a moment, I think I've heard about him, or rumors at least." Thom's hazel-green eyes got wide. He studied Bithia with new understanding.

"Right." Nate nodded, betting he knew what Thom was thinking. "D'Aloun's not actually their son. He's half AO, half genetic Chichnir Six. It was another ancient tech deal kind of like what happened to Bithia. I don't know all the details." Nate shrugged. "No one does outside his own family. But I do know D'Aloun is the only man in the Sectors legally allowed to collect as much AO stuff as he can get his hands on. He does special jobs for the government and has one hell of a lot of gravity, power and pull in the highest circles." Nate gently moved a strand of Bithia's heavy blue hair off her face. "He'll help us. His mother will help us."

"After all these years, you think Sarinda's going to remember you? No offense, but she's...a busy lady."

Nate watched the fire for a few moments, recalling old memories. Reflecting on the past wasn't usually in his character. Especially not in the middle of a mission with the outcome still in doubt. He continued with his story, for Thom's benefit, revealing something he'd never told anyone before. "Sarinda sent for me right before my father got his orders for the next assignment. Me alone. Not even my parents were included. I don't think my folks were ever aware she and I'd talked. Sarinda told me I had unusual abilities for a Terran-descent human, untapped potential at the genetic level, she called it, and if I wanted, she'd arrange for me to stay on Mellure with her family. She offered training for me in the human version of Mellurean mental powers."

Busy basting the birds, Thom whistled. "Unheard of to receive such an offer."

"At the grand age of fourteen Terra Standard years, the idea didn't appeal to me. Not at all, not for a second." Nate laughed at his younger self's brash refusal of, and total lack of appreciation for, what had been an unprecedented opportunity. "I was within a Terra Standard year of going into the Academy. It was all set. My father had pulled strings since I was conceived to be sure I had a place in the class of '03. *That* was what I wanted. So I thanked her politely, and the meeting was over. I don't think she was surprised either. But I've never forgotten her parting words to me."

"Which were? If it's not too much to ask?"

Nate closed his eyes, visualizing the kind, concerned face of Sarinda as she'd concluded their secret conversation so long ago. "The offer stands, Nathan Michael Reilly. When you're ready, find D'Aloun, and he'll bring you and those in your care to the sanctuary of Mellure." Quote finished, Nate opened his eyes to find Thom staring at him, eyes wide.

"She gave you a prophecy?"

"In a way." Nate nodded. "I never discussed it with D'Aloun. Actually, I don't think I've seen him since. David and I had a few classes together at the Academy, but we sure as hell didn't talk about his mother." Gazing at Bithia, he was stunned by an unaccustomed rush of tenderness in his customarily guarded warrior's heart.

"I figure those 'abilities,' as Sarinda termed them, or the genetic potential she told me I had, are what let me communicate with Bithia, made me so sensitive to the damn machine used to pressure her, to waken her in the healing chamber."

"I remember the first day we saw her. I thought you were going to die right in front of me when he activated the mechanism," Thom said. "Worse than a Mawreg neuron interrogator whip for you, but Haranda and I didn't suffer even a mild twinge."

"If our ship's in one piece, and if we can find our way to the Sectors, which are both big unknowns to me at the moment, then our first move is to get to D'Aloun. Before we report to Command. We get to him, and all three of us will be okay."

"All three of us?" Thom resumed his seat on the flat rock, leaning forward to rotate the roasting spit again. "Why should he—or his family—care about me? I'm not marrying an ancient alien."

"The authorities will want to know what you know about the AO now too. That's what Sarinda must have meant, about her offer extending to me and those in my care. I'm not leaving you out of this, not after all the years we've been watching each other's six." Nate stared at the foam-crested waves. "We're all brothers in the Teams but the two of us—you're the flesh-and-blood brother I never had. You're coming with me."

Thom made a show of turning the spit just so, apparently buying time to get control of his emotions. Finally, he said in a reasonably steady voice, "So we'll become high-priced government consultants, I guess, specializing in the interpretation of AO sites? Partner with your guy, D'Aloun. We'll have one hell of a trade secret—a competitive edge nobody but nobody can beat." Thom laughed, clearly relishing the idea. "Only I ain't getting rigged out in those Inner Sector cit suits—not this boy!"

"We won't ask you to. D'Al and I'll do the business stuff, and you can concentrate on the fieldwork." Nate changed the subject. "Those birds done yet? I'm starving, in case you haven't heard my stomach complaining."

Roused easily from her first real nap in millennia, Bithia was ready to share the delicious roasted birds once Thom proclaimed them done enough to eat. Nate woke Celixia and Atletl to dine also. Quite the cheerful group sat on the porch and in the soft sand, drinking pure spring water as if it were the finest wine and demolishing the greasy game birds like they were gourmet fare.

"Tomorrow I need you to reconnoiter the village at the headland," Nate said to Atletl. "Buy supplies, see what the news from Nochen is."

"And then?" Atletl inquired.

Nate stretched, strained muscles protesting at the expansive movement. *Everyone wants to know what I have planned next. Good thing for all of them I have plans.* "Much as I'd like to take a second day to rest at our charming beach hideaway, I think we'd better be on the move inland. The situation should be unsettled now with the capital city gone. The balance of power will be up for grabs, there'll be renegades from Sarbordon's army, bands of your people—"

"You envision chaos, in other words," Bithia said, head tilted.

He nodded. "I'm betting we can slip through the general disorder unnoticed if we keep a low profile. We need to make it to our ship and we can get out of here." Nate pointed one hand at Atletl, gnawing on one of the fat drumsticks. "I hope you and Celixia are willing to guide us inland to our ship. You know the terrain better than Thom or I do, which is to say not at all. I'm not sure how helpful Bithia's holo maps will be. Their detail was sketchy at the level we need for travel cross-country."

Atletl waved the drumstick in the air. "Am I not sworn to the service of the Lady? If playing guide is what she wishes of me, this I will do before I go in search of my own army."

"We may meet them on the way. Wouldn't surprise me," Nate said, hoping they didn't cross paths with any bodies of armed men, Githholz or otherwise. He was going to do his best to avoid such encounters at all costs. "Celixia, you on board for this?"

She frowned, daintily chewing and swallowing before meeting his eyes. "What else is there for me to do? My city's gone, my whole way of life—my reason for living, in fact. Now there's no Sleeping Goddess to be watched over and tended, my servitude is ended, but I've nowhere and no one to go to."

Atletl frowned, pulling her into his lap. "We settled your future earlier this night, priestess."

Blushing, toying nervously with her skirt, she eyed him sideways. "If you're sure—"

"It is clearly meant, possibly even foretold. You were the watcher over the Lady, and I'm one of her chosen warriors. How can you doubt we were destined to be together? Besides, we'll spread the true story of what happened to the evil city of Nochen, how the power of Fr'taray and T'naritza destroyed it in a single day." On that epic note, he took another bite of drumstick. "Our gods vanquished Huitlani at last and wiped his atrocities from the world."

Nate rolled his eyes as he and Thom exchanged grins. Even Bithia was hiding amusement. Their former teammate was as grandiose and self-assured as ever. None of the recent events had changed him in any respect. Celixia drank in his rhetoric as if she needed the supreme self-confidence Atletl displayed to bolster her own.

The meal, delicious as it was, settled in Nate's stomach heavily. It was the first substantial thing any of them except Bithia had consumed since before the sapiche games. As he finished the last scraps on his makeshift plate, he was yawning. Nate divided guard duty for the rest of the night between himself and Thom, ostensibly because Atletl was going to hike to the village in the morning. On general principle about who should handle high tech weaponry, he wasn't planning to relinquish one of the alien weapons to the Githholz soldier, and no one would be standing guard without one, end of discussion.

Atletl and Celixia retired to the interior of the hut, making only a polite, token protest about the generosity of having the indoor accommodation to themselves. Atletl unlooped the old, coarse quilt serving as a door, obtaining as much privacy as possible in such a flimsy dwelling.

Nate created a nest of blankets for himself and Bithia at one end of the porch. He sat wrapped in two of the thick coverings, braced against the wall, Bithia leaning against his chest. He held her safe. Slowly, his eyelids drifted downward, and he let himself float into an untroubled sleep for the first time since crash-landing on this planet.

Roused by a low rumble of faraway thunder, Nate woke to find Bithia gone. He struggled to his feet, fighting clear of the blankets, Mark One in his hand, trying to control his panic at finding her missing. Three steps took him to where Thom was standing guard.

"It's all right; she's at the edge of the water," he said as Nate came up beside him. "I'm keeping an eye on her, but she said she wanted to be alone for a while."

"How long?"

"Maybe an hour? You must have been exhausted to the bone not to wake when she got up. Guess you needed sleep."

"She's had all those centuries of it."

After holstering his weapon, Nate grabbed the white blanket Bithia favored as he left the porch. Barefoot, he walked in the moonlight to where she stood, inches above the waterline. An occasional wave washed gently over her feet. Fresh off the ocean, a breeze carried a hint of rain to come. It was a mellow night.

"You okay?" he asked in a low voice when he was about four paces away, not wanting to startle or scare her.

"Fine, glorious, ecstatic!" She threw her arms wide and did a graceful spin in the sand, braids twirling, then stopped and tipped her head, staring at the heavens. "Do you realize this is the first time I've been able to see the stars in thousands of years? Just deciding to stand and go for a walk—even under Thom's watchful eyes—was such a luxury."

Nate assessed the sky, now partially obscured by the clouds of the coming storm, and then her face, set in a more serious expression than her cheerful words implied. "But?" he prompted reluctantly.

"I don't recognize any of those constellations. The realization of how long I've been locked in stasis, asleep, and how much the universe must have changed terrifies me. When we were still within the confines of my father's research station, I pretended it hadn't been so long, hoped my own people might come back for me, you know? Or—be there, somewhere, waiting for me." Rubbing her arms, she said, "Do I sound crazy?"

"Not at all." Her meaning was clear to him, and he considered her attitude a normal response to the extreme situation. The human mind—and her people seemed to be another humanoid race like those unaccountably found throughout the Sectors—was tenacious about insulating itself from shock or trauma. At harboring hope against hope to keep people going. "Regrets?"

She looked him full in the face then, shaking her head emphatically. "None. I knew what I was doing. I made the right choice—I chose you and life." Reaching out with one hand, she drew him closer. "Being here, free to think and to be by myself without constraint, reinforces that knowledge. The old life is gone. I'll have a new life and I'll be fine. As long as you're there."

He heard the implied question in her tone. Squeezing her hand, he leaned over to give her a soft kiss on the cheek. "Always."

A genuine, confident smile was his reward. Bithia's eyes glowed with her happiness. "Which is why I decided the way I did."

"I think you have to expect to go through a mourning process," he said. "I'm no expert—when we get home to the Sectors, I know some people who might be able to help, good people we can trust, who won't raise an eyebrow over who you are or your story. You've lost so much, not only your father, but your whole civilization. How can you avoid suffering an emotional impact?"

She knelt in the sand for a moment, prying a colorful shell loose from a clump of drifted seaweed. "It actually happened long ago, while I slept." Rising with the delicate shell resting on her palm, she tilted her head, studying his face in the moonlight.

"Doesn't matter." He shook his head. "You told me yourself while you were in the healing device that you could avoid dealing with the realities. And for all practical purposes, it's only been a few days for you since you last were with your father and friends, no matter the real time elapsed. I get it."

"Being awakened as I was confuses things," she said. "The machine tried to suppress my emotions and fear each time I was summoned to prophesy and realized yet again how much time must be passing. But I have those memories. You can't imagine how it feels to wake, thinking you've only been asleep a few moments, and be confronted with people generations removed from the last person you spoke with." Bithia rubbed her temple. "It's disorienting, terrifying. And now I have to deal with all of it." She gestured at the starry sky. "I can't deny the truth."

"Don't try. I'll be more worried if you don't let yourself process your emotions and grieve your losses. Just know I'm here for you, anything you need, always available to listen. I'll do my damnedest to help."

He stood arm in arm with her for a few more moments, watching the waves roll gently in and wash the sand in retreat a moment later. The tide was ebbing. Miniature night birds ran along the edge of the foamy seawater, dipping their beaks gracefully in search of tiny, luminescent prey. The avian hunters ignored Nate and Bithia, pattering between their feet and going on, untroubled.

He came to a decision.

"Remember when you and I were debating, before you let me turn the device off, you asked me what I was keeping from you?"

She sighed heavily, not lifting her attention from the tiny birds darting in and out of the surf. "I knew there was something. Do I want to hear this?"

Knowing she'd let him keep silent if he so chose, he wasn't comfortable building mental blocks, having secrets from her. Their mind-to-mind link was a rare and precious aspect of the relationship he hoped he was building with her, so he felt compelled to be as open as possible. He spied a large, gnarly tree trunk washed up by a long-ago storm and smoothed by the successive pounding of waves until it resembled a fantastic architect's version of a bench. Taking Bithia by the hand, carrying the blanket across his other arm, Nate led her down the beach a few yards. He settled her on the broad tree trunk, wrapped the soft fabric more closely at her shoulders and sat beside her.

"Thank you." Bithia adjusted the blanket a bit and pulled her feet under her on the smooth surface of the driftwood bench. She gazed peacefully at the ocean again, content to wait to see if he decided to continue the conversation.

Hating to intrude on the serenity of the moment, but having decided to be honest with her, Nate launched into his revelation. "I believe there was at least one previous attempt to rescue you, but the effort met with disaster."

Waiting for the whole story, she maintained her silence.

"When Thom and I explored the storehouse, searching for the red box, we found it underneath a corpse. He'd been shot in the back—by one of the weapons we're using now, in fact. The person died shielding the all-important box."

She gasped, hand to her mouth, eyes widening in shock.

Nate continued the tale. "There were at least three people in the warehouse, because the apparent murderer of the first man was also killed with the same kind of weapon. Ambushed by someone else. And however many people there were, they had to be from offplanet, because no local can stay conscious in the warehouse. We found no sign of the third person, so he and his companions, if any, apparently got away."

"How long?"

He shook his head. "There was no way to know when these people made their incursion. I believe the group was from your home planet, because the weapons are inscribed with symbols matching ones I found in your father's warehouse."

"Why didn't you tell me sooner?" Her tone was less upset than he had feared, calmer and more detached.

"I was afraid if I told you in the healing chamber, you wouldn't want to deal with it. I was afraid you'd use their deaths as your final excuse to take the easy way out and choose death yourself." Nate kept his focus on her lavender-blue eyes, trying to make her understand. "I couldn't risk that, you know? Maybe the choice to withhold the information was selfish, but I wanted you to live. I—I was desperate for you to choose life over death, to stay with me. I couldn't see any compelling reason to discuss it with you then. Their visit and subsequent murders happened a long time ago."

"I know." She rubbed his arm reassuringly but asked in a steady voice, "Is there more?"

"Thom and I found what we think are identification bracelets on the corpses." He fished awkwardly, searching for the pocket sewn into his cloak. Biting off an oath as the two gem-encrusted bracelets stubbornly tangled themselves together in the folds of the pocket, Nate worked the bulky strands loose, ripping the seam in the process.

She studied his face for a moment before glancing at the bands clutched in his hand. "Was one of them my father?"

"I don't know. I can't read these symbols, remember?"

She took the chains from him and ran first one, then the other through her fingers, squinting to see them closely in the moonlight. "I don't recognize either of these names. These people weren't on our expedition, not anyone I ever met."

Except for the quiet hiss of the waves on the beach, there was silence for a long moment.

"The mystery deepens, and we may never know what happened," Nate said. He was tempted to shout out his relief that he hadn't just given Bithia proof of her father's death on Talonque. Obviously the man had passed away in some fashion and gone to dust millennia ago but to Bithia everything was just taking place now, as she heard about it for the first time. He didn't think she was ready to deal with specifics. "At least it wasn't your father."

"Which one was the man holding the red box?"

Nate took the two chains and eyed them for a moment. "This one, with the red and purple stones leading off." He handed them both to her again.

"I'll keep it and wear the links in honor of he who tried to rescue me, whatever his motives were and whoever he was. I choose to believe the intentions were good because it's a comforting thought." Setting the other bracelet on the flat tree trunk between them for a moment, she fastened the red and purple one around her right wrist with a quick motion of her graceful fingers, settling it right above her own. Then she took the second jeweled bracelet and extended her hand to Nate, the chain dangling and glinting in the moonlight. "Let Atletl use this in his bargaining tomorrow. Perhaps he can get us kemat to ride with such a treasure to offer in trade."

Nate set the rejected chain securely into his partially torn cloak pocket. "If you're sure—"

"I'm sure. Nate—"

"What?" He steeled himself to accept whatever reproaches or fury she felt the need to hurl at him. He probably deserved it. He fixed his gaze on a point far out at sea.

Bithia's voice was soft and gentle. "Thank you." Nate raised his head from his contemplation of the waves and met her eyes. She nodded in reassurance. "Thank you for not telling me while we were in Nochen, and thank you for telling me now. It helps to know I wasn't totally forgotten by my people, even if their rescue attempt went sadly awry. I—I'd like to be alone with my memories for a while. Do you mind if I stay out here by myself? I promise not to wander."

"Of course, whatever you want. Come to the hut if the mist turns to rain, or if lightning gets closer to shore, all right?"

"You'll worry over me the rest of our lives together, won't you?" she asked with a small laugh. "I know enough to come in out of the rain."

"Sorry," he apologized tersely.

Bithia laid a hand on his arm as he rose from their shared bench, preparing to hike to the hut. "I'll worry over you as well. I suspect a warrior like you will be in far more dangerous situations than I over the years ahead."

"We'll be together." He kissed her gently on the forehead. "Mutual worry—it's a deal. See you later, Sleeping Beauty."

Bithia did a double take. "What did you call me?"

"An old legend on my race's ancestral homeworld. We have our legends and myths too, you know. I'll tell you about it sometime." Smiling, he slogged through the sand, ready to accept the handoff of guard duty from Thom as the distant thunder rumbled again and the breeze strengthened.

Chapter Nine

Rain pattered on the beach and the hut for the rest of the night. Fortunately, the front porch area was sheltered by a roof of woven fronds, so Nate, Thom and Bithia stayed comfortable and dry. It was misting in the morning, but Atletl took off for the village cheerfully, right after breakfast of fish stew and dried fruit. Celixia accompanied him over Nate's initial protests. The less time spent on this expedition to town the better, and he didn't intend to create a situation where Atletl's desire for Celixia's company impeded the specific errands to be carried out.

"I'll raise less suspicion if I walk into town as a married man, bringing my wife to trade for new clothes," Atletl said.

"I'll do a better job at picking clothes and sandals for Bithia than he will." Giggling, Celixia poked Atletl in the ribs.

"All right." Nate threw up his hands in defeat. The two of them obviously wanted to spend the day by themselves and were prepared to go on presenting plausible excuses until he gave in. "Don't be gone too long and head back if anything doesn't feel right to you. I want kemat already broken to the saddle, but I don't want them enough to risk raising suspicions in town. So be discreet." He shook his finger at Celixia. "I'm counting on you to keep our friend here from talking too much to everyone he meets, okay?" Nate had one final instruction. "Do your best to make sure you're not followed. Don't lead anyone to us."

Atletl snapped a salute, as he'd seen Thom and Haranda do on occasion during their captivity together. "Yes, Captain. I'm a soldier and a seasoned veteran of assignments behind the lines. I've done undercover work in the land of the enemy before."

"And got caught," Celixia said drily.

"I was captured by overwhelming forces in an ambush situation, while commanding a patrol riding ahead of our main column." His correction was polite but firm. "I've never been close to detection when I was alone and spying behind enemy lines."

"Clearly, I'm sending the right man for the job," Nate said. *I don't have any choice, so it's a good thing Atletl has prior experience working undercover in enemy territory. I hope there isn't too much bullshit in this set of his stories.* "We'll be waiting. Good luck."

Flanked by Thom and Bithia, Nate watched from the porch until their local allies were lost in the morning mists on the beach.

"I actually want an armored ground transport or a damn flyer," Nate said, only partly in jest, as Atletl and Celixia disappeared from view over the horizon. "Or a Special Forces extraction team—forget kemat! But I figure even an intrepid trader like our pal there claims to be can't find me those items on this planet. So we're stuck to asking for what we can get."

The two men shared a rueful laugh.

"What are our plans for the day after we ransack the place again for hidden treasures?" Bithia asked cheerfully.

"Take a hike to the freshwater pond I found last night, take a swim. Be nice to thoroughly rinse off the grime from the sapiche game and the tunnel." Nate grinned, reflecting on everything he and his companions had endured since dawn broke on the day of the games. "I only took a quick dip last night. The water wasn't too cold," he said to Bithia, who looked dubious about his suggestion. "Maybe fed by hot springs. Thom and I promise to give you privacy."

"Oh, for sure." The sergeant blushed to the roots of his red hair.

"There might be fish," Nate said. "Did you see anything we could use to try and catch a few?"

"All kinds of junk out there we couldn't examine in the dark. I'll go check." Thom headed for the rear of the hut.

"Watch for tolokon." Bithia gave her warning with a serious undertone and a furrowed brow. "The slitherers hide in places such as the pile of discards. We no longer have the healing chamber to save anyone who gets bitten. I'm not special to the wretched species, no matter what these people insist. The creatures wouldn't hesitate to bite me again, let alone you."

"I'll be extra careful." Thom drew his Mark One and trudged behind the hut. Nate heard him whistling as he explored the one small outbuilding and the sprawling junk pile next to it.

Bithia sat on the porch edge and fumbled with her hair, which was escaping in spots from the arrangement of braids Celixia created the day before. Nate stood a few paces away, watching the ocean and the birds, lost in his own thoughts, not paying much attention to what she was doing.

"Do you think you could help me?" Bithia asked finally, apparently frustrated by the tight weaving the other girl had done.

Nate was sure he'd heard wrong. "You want me to help with your hair?"

Blinking at his surprise, Bithia bit her lip, stifling a chuckle. "I need assistance loosening the strands from the braid. If we're going swimming later, I want to wash my hair, or at least rinse it out. I prefer to wear it loose on my shoulders. It was nice of Celixia to style it, to make things easier when we were escaping the city, as she said, but I don't need it braided today. I rarely wore it this way before, and the crown of braids is too much weight on my head."

Nate came to the porch and sat behind her. He had started unraveling the one thick braid hanging over Bithia's spine when Thom came around the end of the cottage, still whistling.

"Found some good stuff." He held out a fishing pole in one hand and clutched the rim of an oddly shaped basket in the other. Gesturing with the basket, he said,

"I'm guessing this is the local equivalent of a net. If you don't mind, I'm going ahead to the pond, try my luck at catching a few fish for lunch."

"Sure, go on without us," Nate said. "I can see we're going to be here awhile, trying to undo Celixia's handiwork on Bithia's hair. Walk straight north from the house, through the dunes, and as soon as the sand ends, there's the pond. You can't miss it. We'll join you soon."

"Fine by me. No rush. I think we'll probably have all day by the time Atletl and Celixia hike into town, do the shopping and get back out here. Even if they buy kemat with the bracelet, bargaining takes a long, long time on these pretech worlds. In my experience, all the parties involved enjoy the process too much. See you later." Shouldering the pole and swinging the basket jauntily, Thom departed. Nate heard his whistling fade in the distance as the sergeant ascended the dunes, heading for the pond and the fish he hoped were waiting.

Nate concentrated on his unaccustomed task. "Your hair is so soft. I was sure it would be."

Stretching like a cat, she turned to give him a flirtatious glance, although her words were prosaic. "It's so beautiful here and peaceful. I feel as if all the problems and troubles are behind some invisible barrier, kept away from us, by the ocean maybe, you think?"

"Like the barrier in the healing chamber kept everyone away from you?" Nate said. "Even in my own damn dreams I couldn't touch you."

She was silent, gazing out to sea. He'd worked the thick braid loose and was now unraveling the crown of smaller braids, one at a time. Her lavender-blue hair was lustrous and shining in the morning sun, revealing itself to be composed of many variations on the two basic hues.

A man could be content here, for a while anyway. Raising his eyes from Bithia's hair for a moment, he watched the ocean. He'd get impatient soon enough, but right now, it was like being on a well-deserved leave.

Bithia's voice jarred him out of his reverie.

"So you did wish to touch me? In the dreams?"

"Of course." He answered without thinking, then felt his face redden. He was glad she had her back to him. "I wished I could get close enough to offer comfort, human contact. I hated to see you, paralyzed and helpless on the damn, cold couch." *Truth, but not the whole truth.*

"Oh."

There was silence. Nate couldn't decide if he'd answered her question the way she expected. *I'm so ham-handed at expressing my emotions—I probably disappointed her.* Not knowing what to say next, he finished the unbraiding and combed out the inevitable snarls with his hands, gently stroking through her hair like a ten-fingered comb, pausing from time to time to massage the back of her neck and head. All the while, he racked his brain for a way to start their conversation over again, to tell her what was in his heart where she was concerned. The last thing Nate wanted was to say something dumb or awkward. So he said nothing. He checked their mental link, glowing in the corner of his mind in the way he was now accustomed to. *So we're okay.*

Conversation with her—about anything—had been so damn easy in the dreamspace. Nate wished he could re-create the seamless state of rapport right now.

"The massage is soothing," she murmured, leaning against his chest, which effectively stopped him from doing the very thing she'd just said she enjoyed. He drew her close, and they sat, companionably leaning on each other.

"You know, I can't read them all."

Confused by the non sequitur, he asked, "Read all what?"

"Your thoughts. I can't read them all. I know my ability worries you. I know you don't like to let anyone see what you're thinking, or the depth of your emotions. Not Thom, not even me." She faced him, her hair swinging softly around them both like a silken blanket. "I wish I understood what's in your past making all the self-protection so essential. Maybe someday you'll tell me. But it shouldn't worry you so. There's nothing to fear from either of us, you know. I think the sergeant would gladly die for you—I read immense loyalty in him."

"I'm not afraid." His instant denial cut across her words about Thom. "I'm not used to talking about things. Feelings. It's hard for me to do. Most of the time I manage to get along fine without having to talk about it."

"But in the healing chamber you expressed—"

"The hardest thing I've ever done," he said honestly. "I never said things like that to anyone before, not ever."

She rested her hand on his cheek. "I'm touched."

He knew her well enough by now to hear in her voice how genuinely pleased she was. The idea warmed his heart, but immediately he worried about disappointing her in the future. "Don't expect self-revelation from me daily. I'm trying hard here, and I can't promise any more," he said a bit harshly.

"I can only read the surface of what you think," she went on, determined to reassure him about their mental link. "You have many barriers and blocks in your mind. I can't go there, can't see what you think behind them without your permission. Nor would I try, but I do sense them there."

"Was there someone on your expedition, or at home maybe—someone waiting for you?" He'd speculated during the long months of captivity.

Now she was startled and sat up, turning to kneel before him as he unlocked his arms in automatic response to her movement. Resting her hands on his shoulders lightly, she looked him in the eyes. "No. I was too focused on my schooling, on being accredited for fieldwork, to be seriously involved with anyone. There were certainly interesting people in my life, but I assumed there'd be time for pursuing the happiness of a lifemate later. Why do you ask?"

Uncomfortable as always with conducting a conversation that revealed his innermost emotions, he refused to meet her eyes. "I wondered."

"And you? Is there someone waiting for you in your Sectors, as you call them?" It seemed she'd been as curious about that subject when it came to his life. "Am I displacing someone who thinks she has your heart?"

"No."

"I'd be sorry for her," Bithia said, "but I wouldn't step aside. You mean too much to me, our link is too tight."

"What I do for a living is dangerous. The Special Forces has a high mortality rate. I couldn't ask anyone I cared about to sit and wait while I was on a mission, and then maybe I'd never come back, you know? A lot of Team guys wait until retirement to get serious about anyone."

"Was there ever someone who tempted you to change your mind?" Eyes narrowed, brow wrinkled, her face was set in serious lines.

Nate lowered his own eyes, toying with a long curl of her hair, twining it between his fingers. "Not until I met you," he said finally, meeting her steady gaze.

Bithia raised a gentle hand to his cheek, lifted her chin and parted her lips, extending an unmistakable invitation. Without thinking about it at all, with no hesitation, because the time and the place were right, and this was the woman he loved with all his closely guarded heart, Nate leaned forward and kissed her.

She smelled like fresh air and flowers and some exotic spice he couldn't name. She placed her arms around his neck as he licked her lips, seeking entry. She parted for him, her tongue testing his tentatively at first, then drawing him farther into her warm mouth, adjusting her position to more effectively stroke and suck. His arousal hardened to steel as she shifted on his lap, her bottom pressing on him. He raised one hand to cup her breast through the thin fabric of the ancient nightgown, finding her nipple pebbled and hard under his thumb.

So we're more alike than we are different. As she spoke mind to mind, Bithia rolled her hips on his cock. She reached between their bodies with one hand, massaging him through the kilt before sliding her hand upward on his thigh, under the fabric, gripping him through the thin cotton loincloth.

"Too many clothes," she said aloud, breaking off the kiss. She climbed off his lap and reached for his hand. "I'll never forget the first time I saw you in the chamber, half naked, in chains, full of anger, ready to seize any opportunity to fight for your life. Dangerous was the word that came to my mind. Then our minds linked, and I felt it here as well." She laid a hand on the vee between her hips.

In response to her tug on his hand, Nate rose. "Here?" he said, pulling her gown up to run his hand between her thighs and stroke his fingers through the soft curls and velvet skin, wet with desire for him. "Would this be the spot?" He inserted first one finger and then a second, massaging the delicate tissues and nerve endings.

Bithia threw her head back, eyes closed. "The exact spot. You'll have me screaming in a moment. It's been so long since I—I experienced these sensations."

"There's no rush. We have all day." He withdrew his hand and picked her up, hands under the soft curves of her butt.

"I'm the one who's been waiting thousands of years for you to arrive and set me free," she said with a smile, wrapping her legs around his waist. "I say enough anticipation." She captured his mouth, tongue darting between his lips and exploring him boldly.

He had to brace himself against the cottage wall as the embrace continued. His cock tented his kilt, aching to plunge into her. Breathing hard, he finished the kiss. "Shall we take this inside?"

Bithia kissed his neck, alternating between featherlight caresses and tiny nibbles. She took his earlobe delicately between her teeth and murmured her pleasure. "What about Thom?"

"He's a smart guy. He knows his job is to stay at the fishing hole until he sees us again." Making sure he had his balance under control, if not his raging hard-on, Nate carried her into the cabin, setting her on her feet inside the threshold. Atletl and Celixia had left the place neat, all the blankets folded away on the makeshift shelves. He grabbed the entire stack and spread them on the floor as there was no bed or even a thin mattress. Bithia helped him.

"Not exactly where I'd have chosen for our first time together," he said apologetically, reaching for her.

She drew his tunic off over his head, tossing it aside. "The important thing is us, together, not the surroundings. Someday I'm sure we'll have the opportunity for the flowers and silk sheets I see in your mind. Although I enjoy the mental pictures." Head tilted, she batted her eyelashes at him, smiling. "You have quite the imagination."

"I'm not usually a romantic guy," he said, struggling with the kilt, impatient to be free of the clothing. "You have that effect on me, though, and I like it."

Bithia ran her hand over his bare front, tracing his abs, moving her hand higher, pausing to tease his nipple for a moment. She frowned at his various scars. "Let me see your back."

He hesitated. "It's not pretty."

She walked behind him, running her hand over the tattoo on his bicep and across his shoulder, maintaining contact. There was a gasp of indrawn breath, and he felt her lips brushing softly over the network of scarred, ravaged skin. "I'm so sorry I couldn't do a better job of healing you."

"Hey." Turning, he clasped her hand, drawing her into his arms. "I'm fine. I wouldn't be here if not for you, so I can stand the scars if you can."

Her eyes shimmered in the dim interior of the cottage. "Do they hurt?"

"Not much, not enough to interfere with what I have in mind for today." Nate nipped at her lips. "Help me with this?" He tugged at his loincloth, wanting her hands on his body.

She obliged, taking her time undoing the knot, treating the task as foreplay, caressing his balls through the cotton before unwinding the fabric. She stepped out of reach as his cock jutted proudly. Head to one side, she surveyed him from head to toe, smiling.

"Is admire all you're planning to do?" he teased. "I'd like the same privilege, please." He tugged at her nightgown. Obligingly, she raised her arms, and he pulled the garment over her head, placing it to the side, then removed the single sheer undergarment. She was breathtakingly beautiful, her skin smooth, lavender darkening to purple on her sides, between her legs, her nipples... Bithia cupped her own breasts for a moment, displaying them for his admiration. He placed his hands over hers, pushing the soft globes together, enjoying the feel of her ample charms overflowing his hands. Bending his head, he kissed the top of each breast and then sought her lips. She tasted of the berries they'd had for breakfast, sweet and tart all mixed together, and perfect.

Locked in an embrace, they sank onto the piled blankets together. Bithia lay on her back to give Nate full access, and he caressed first one breast, then the other, relishing the lushness of her body underneath his. He kissed his way down her soft stomach before sliding one hand between her legs, finding her aroused and ready for him. Again, he inserted two fingers into her warmth and stroked, massaging the places where her reactions to his efforts indicated the most pleasure. Adding pressure to his hand with her own, Bithia moaned and arched, gripping him tightly to her as she climaxed.

After the tremors of her orgasm subsided, he moved to cover her, the tip of his erection pressing against her soft folds. Nate guided himself inside, going slowly to allow her to adjust to him, biting his lip in an effort not to come too soon. She was tight and hot, and he'd never experienced anything so good. The urge to plunge into her and thrust with all his power was nearly irresistible, but he held himself in check. He didn't want to rush this initial experience with her, and he very much wanted her to have all the pleasure he could provide, which required him to be patient.

Bithia adjusted her position on the blankets, holding him locked to her body. She moved her hips, increasing the exquisite pressure on his erection, and he had to stop, holding himself motionless. "I'm too close," he said in a whisper.

"As am I," she said, nibbling his earlobe. "Let this first time be a whirlwind, and we can take our pleasure more slowly the second time."

Freed from the need for rigid self-control, Nate drove deeper. Bithia met him move for move, her body welcoming his until he was convinced they were one person, moving in unison, the ecstasy building higher and higher between them until he lost himself in an intense and all-consuming release. He heard her saying his name, and in his mind there was a burst of beautiful lights and colors and sounds as she went rigid, locked on him in her own climax.

They lay together for a few moments in silence, breathing hard. Bithia trailed her hand over his back, gently caressing the scars before stroking his butt. "You have amazing strength, my warrior."

"Just as well the machine kept a barrier between us before," he said, rolling to the side. "We'd have shorted it out, if we'd done that in the dreamspace."

She laughed.

It was late afternoon. Nate, Thom and Bithia had finished dining on fried fish that was caught in the pond. Thom had the small lake all to himself for quite a long time. The sergeant made no comment whatsoever when Nate and Bithia eventually strolled through the grassy dunes, hand in hand. He'd merely shown them his excellent catch and boasted about his rediscovered skills as a fisherman.

They'd enjoyed a swim in the refreshing waters of the clear pond. Bithia was familiar with the concept and was a strong swimmer. Unembarrassed, she swam in her undergarment, having rinsed out her nightgown and spread it to dry on a nearby bush. Thom resolutely kept his eyes anywhere but in Bithia's direction until she was dressed. He concentrated on gutting and cleaning the fish with his Talonqueni army knife while Nate and Bithia swam together. Later the three of them had gone to the cabin to cook the fish, of which there were now only spiny remnants.

Nate suddenly moved to douse the fire.

"Someone's riding this way on the beach from the headland," he said, pointing for the benefit of his less-farsighted companions. "I hope it's Atletl and Celixia, but we can't take chances. We'll take cover in the dunes behind the hut until we're sure."

A tense half hour ensued before it became apparent that Atletl and Celixia were inbound from a successful shopping expedition. Each was riding a kemat, with three others trotting obediently on a lead from Atletl's saddle. One of the spare animals was loaded with baskets and sacks.

"So Bithia's jewelry and your coins were highly useful at the market, I gather," Nate said to Celixia with admiration.

"Indeed," Atletl agreed. "I'm an excellent bargainer, of course."

"Any trouble?"

Atletl shook his head. "None at all. Help us unload the kemat, and then we can talk."

As the men worked together to shift the baskets and sacks from the patient quadrupeds, Atletl told them that the lights Nate had glimpsed at the headland the night before were the outskirts of Poqueteele, a well-known deep-sea harbor city. The main part of the city was hidden from view beyond the curving coastline.

"Our ending up here is excellent, because people are constantly coming and going, and a pair of strangers doesn't excite as much interest as we might have caused in a true fishing village."

"A deep-water port?" Nate was surprised. "This country has trading partners?"

Atletl and Celixia nodded. "Oh yes," the priestess said. "There are several powerful countries across the ocean whose rulers don't fear Sarbordon. There is Inshpan, for example, from whom we get wondrous fabrics for gowns." She dimpled at Bithia and said teasingly, "None of which could we trade for today, my lady, due to your captain's harsh order we must go dressed as peasants."

Bithia ran one hand over her lavender nightgown, now much torn. "I can't feel too badly about not wearing something fabulous. I'll be happy to have a pair of sandals and a decent skirt and tunic, I assure you. I certainly would have worn something more durable into the healing chamber, had I any idea of what I'd be doing when I walked out."

"Looks fine to me," Nate murmured in her ear.

"I traded for something else I think you'll like." Celixia went to her dappled brown and gray kemat. She unfastened a small sack from behind the simple saddle.

There was a constant, faint air of tension between the two women, Nate noticed, as he had yesterday in the lab complex. On an intellectual level, he was sure Bithia realized she couldn't blame Celixia for what her ancestors had done in terms of keeping Bithia imprisoned and forced to serve as an oracle. On the other hand, Celixia was the only visible clan member left. He admired the effort

Bithia exerted not to be rude to Celixia, but the situation had to be stressful for both on some level.

"What is it?" Nate caught a whiff of a warm, spicy smell that set his mouth watering.

Bithia's face lit up as the aroma wafted to her also. "Six-spice cakes? Don't tease—tell me you got those?"

Celixia nodded, apparently pleased with her find and their reactions to it. She handed the sack to Bithia, saying, "There's a family legend about the original Hialar's wife—"

"Frantlia." Bithia nodded and named the woman, a faraway expression on her face.

"Yes, she supposedly baked a batch of these for you to eat after you'd consumed the contents of the red box. It was meant to celebrate your leaving the healing chamber, only of course, well..." Celixia fumbled to a halt and reddened.

"Only I didn't get out in time to eat them." Bithia finished the story in a neutral tone. "These are delicious—I can't thank you enough. You must all share with me."

"The cakes are baked for the Festival of T'naritza once a year in my village," Atletl said with a mouthful of one of the pastries.

"Aren't these good?" Bithia shamelessly took her third one from Celixia's seemingly bottomless sack.

"Much better than petrified dried fruit," Nate said somewhat absently.

"What's the matter?" Sensitive as always to his mood, Bithia frowned.

Shaking his head, not ready to explain himself yet, he took another six-spice cake and peppered Atletl with new questions. "Does Poqueteele have altars to Huitlani? Are there priestesses there?"

Sobering, the Githholz warrior nodded. "Yes, but the people of Poqueteele worship the Fourth Spirit, which is the sea, the dominant goddess of the coast region. Sarbordon's ancestors didn't dare tamper with the sea when they conquered the nation. Poqueteeli are an independent people, even in the old times under the previous rulers. The new rulers needed the trade, the fisheries, the shipbuilders too much to risk alienating the people by demanding human sacrifices."

"We told anyone who asked a fine tale of arriving fresh off a boat from the southern islands," Celixia said, "therefore ignorant of recent events. My invention of our origins also explained his terrible accent." She playfully dug Atletl in the ribs.

"People were only too happy to tell us the news." Laughing, Atletl dodged her elbow.

"Did you get wild rumors?" Nate asked. "Or pretty close to the truth?"

"A mixture of both. The city's packed with refugees, the majority having left Nochen long before it blew. For the most part, people have the story right—T'naritza's warriors won the sapiche game and freed the Lady—"

"And she called down the wrath of her father on the city and wiped it out in a single day." Celixia bowed to Bithia.

"Do the people think she—and we—traveled home to the sky?" Thom sounded hopeful.

Frowning, Atletl and Celixia exchanged glances. The priestess shook her head. "Some say she walks the land, seeking out the followers of Huitlani and taking vengeance on them."

Bithia's jaw dropped. "Why would people think I'd do such a thing?"

Nate rested a hand on her shoulder as he leaned past her to get another delicious spice cake. "Wouldn't surprise me if a few old scores are being settled these days and conveniently laid at your door. Not much we can do about the situation, I'm afraid."

While Bithia contemplated the events, chewing in silence, Celixia recounted more market gossip. "Others think she fled to her father's realm and took her warriors with her. I heard at least five variations on each version of the story. Many are fearful of what she may do next, which is a sad thing."

"Not if it scares the Huitlani worshippers into keeping a low profile." Thom snorted. "A little fear is probably a good thing."

"I don't want either our enemies or any would-be friends to search for us," Nate said, licking icing from his fingers. "You didn't say anything about Bithia? Or about having been in Nochen before it blew?"

"No. We stuck to our story of being simple south island immigrants come to establish ourselves on the mainland after finding the wreckage of a storm-driven Inshpan ship on our beach. The lie was to explain the rich treasures we had to trade." Nate nodded approvingly at the details Atletl had embroidered into the tale he and Celixia had told in town. "Now is not the time to draw attention to ourselves," Atletl stated the obvious, but with more forbearance and modesty than Nate would have expected of his grandiose recruit. "The city's under the control of Sarbordon's governor and his troops, although I heard a lot of restless talk in the streets. We may have cut off the head of the empire by destroying Nochen, but it'll take time for the rest of the body to die. Each governor will try to hold what he or she now has—they'll fight. Sporadic revolts will break out, and my people, the Githholz, will continue our invasion of the areas we covet."

"Speaking of the king, any word about him? Or Lolanta's fate?" Nate broke ruthlessly into what he could tell would be a lengthy recitation of the potential future triumphs of the Githholz.

"It's unknown where either was at the time of the great explosion."

"So one or both may be alive." Nate shook his head. "Not good."

"And really pissed off," Thom said.

"Did you see any priestesses?" The feral women worried Nate more than temporal forces. If the king was indeed dead, buried under the talmere, none of his surviving generals was likely to care about hunting for an elusive goddess. Each would be scrambling to seize as much territory and power for themselves as they could get, not seeking the kind of trouble Bithia unleashed on Nochen. But the priestesses were another story. If the entire order accepted the dogma Lolanta had explained to him in her chambers, the religious zealots would see recapturing and sacrificing T'naritza and her warriors as the solution to the current problems of the Huitlani faithful.

Atletl chased an errant crumb, intent on enjoying every bite of the treat. "I didn't see any priestesses," he said with obvious relief.

Celixia sighed. "I saw two of them watching me while I bartered in the clothing stalls. I didn't recognize them, nor did they give any sign of knowing who I was. Not all the priestesses trained at Nochen, so there's a good chance these women wouldn't realize who I was. In any case, I finished my trading and left immediately. I didn't see them, or any others, again the whole time. I watched carefully."

"What next?" Bithia asked. "Do we leave today?"

Nate stared out to sea, assessing how much time until sunset. With great reluctance he said, "None of us knows this territory well enough to ride at night. We may as well have another good dinner, a solid night's sleep and be on our way at first light."

"We can pretty much ride straight inland for two days and then connect with the great road bisecting the plains running to the mountains." Atletl drew a crude map in the sand beside the porch. "Easy to blend in with other refugees. Celixia and I bought serviceable but humble clothing, as you requested."

"Riding kemat will mark us as unusual," Celixia said. "Kemat are usually the property of the nobility, the priestesses and the military. The common people either walk or have bracalx to pull their carts, but those beasts are never ridden by anyone save small children."

"We'll stay off the road as much as possible and go as fast as we can." Nate was adamant about his plan. "Having kemat is worth the time we'll gain versus the risk of attracting too much attention."

"Small problem," Thom said. "I can't ride. Don't think I ever saw a horse outside of data records and one school field trip to the Sector's zoological preserve when I was a kid."

"Lack of experience could be a problem," Atletl agreed, glancing from one man to the other. "Kemat are highly intelligent, spirited animals who can sense an untrained rider and try to take advantage. Captain, what about you?"

"We had one short course at the Academyon the ancient art of horseback riding. Horses are our equivalent of kemat," Nate explained in a rapid aside to the Talonqueni, who was visibly puzzled over the Basic word. "The class was a long time ago, I wasn't good at it, and I have to admit traveling via anything without a propulsion unit isn't my first choice, but I'm sure I can remember enough fundamentals to deal with kemat."

"Teach you officer types a lot of useless, archaic trivia, don't they?" Thom's tone was teasing.

"From time to time on pretech worlds, guys have run into this kind of situation, which is why the Academy teaches otherwise outdated skills to the cadets. We'll have to get in a riding lesson before dark. I need to refresh my muscle memory."

"Since we're not departing tonight, and I *can* ride—I told you in the healing chamber, remember?" Bithia dealt with Nate's obvious skepticism in short order. "Hialar's sons taught me to ride, and I'm sure the concept has remained the same. I'm anxious to see what Celixia bought for me to wear." She brushed a few errant crumbs from her lap. "Can we go inside the hut now and see your selections?"

"I hope you'll be satisfied with what I found." Celixia lowered her voice, glancing at Nate. "I think the captain will be pleased."

Although delighted by Bithia's blush, Nate judged it wiser not to call attention to Celixia's comment. The two women linked arms companionably and prepared to step inside the hut to do wardrobe planning in private.

"Be glad you're practicing riding on a soft, sandy beach." Bithia laughed at the expression on Nate's face, and then she and Celixia went about their business.

It was drizzling and foggy again in the morning when they left their cozily shabby cottage, riding north across the dunes. Curiously reluctant to abandon his first safe, peaceful haven on this planet, Nate forced himself to order the departure rather than linger for another day.

The five rode hard for the first day, managing to stay off the roads as much as possible. Nate tried to move as fast as he could without overtaxing the kemat.

The party traveled unobserved for the most part, other than confounding a few refugees, who gawked as the five of them thundered past on their high-spirited quadrupeds.

Nate remembered the fundamentals of riding in short order. Thom amazed himself by being a total natural at it. He hadn't fallen even once while he was learning. The sergeant and his chosen mount had bonded almost telepathically, as demonstrated by the way man and animal worked together with a minimum of spoken commands. Nate found it fascinating to watch Thom with his kemat. It was a whole new side to the sergeant's personality. Thom was going to be genuinely sorry to leave the kemat behind when they finally lifted off from Talonque. Well, maybe if the AO exploration business he'd proposed in all seriousness made substantial credits, Thom could buy himself a stable of the equivalent horses someday.

The first night Nate selected a campsite in a forest clearing. He allowed only a small fire for fear of attracting attention, and his companions turned in after a sparse dinner of dried fruit and other journey fare that did not require cooking. Nate and Thom split the guard duty as usual.

The next afternoon Nate was at the head of the small column of riders, trotting down a deserted stretch of road, when suddenly he heard screams and raucous laughter from ahead.

He reined in, rising in the stirrups and motioned the others to halt.

"Thom and I'll ride ahead and check this out. Atletl, keep the ladies safely hidden in the copse of trees until I give the all clear."

Thom and Nate dismounted, handing off their reins to Atletl. Drawing their alien weapons, the two operators worked their way through the brush and under-growth along the stone road until they were within fifty yards of the ambush that had overtaken a hapless family party traveling ahead of them.

Two small handcarts were standing in the middle of the road, the sacks containing a family's pitiful possessions open to the wind. Clothes and other items were strewn about on the pavement. A bracalx stood in its traces in front of a cargo wagon, chewing cud, placid, oblivious to the blood pooling around its hooves from the man lying dead on the road close by. Two other men in rough peasant garb knelt side by side on the road, facing the forest beyond, hands bound behind their backs. The captives were closely guarded by four soldiers in royal uniforms. Several small children huddled close by the bound men, crying and wailing.

Three more guards, one wearing an officer's insignia, were manhandling two women, dragging them toward the grassy area underneath the trees.

Nate swore a spacer's oath under his breath. "I sure as hell can't walk away from these poor people."

"Agreed." Thom shook his head. "What's the plan?"

"I wish we had a way to measure how much charge these Mark Ones have left." Nate examined his weapon. The red indicator symbol glowed as fiercely as when he'd found it in the warehouse. "The officer first, then his men. I've got them. You take the joker to the left of the captives, the one who kicked the little kid." Nate frowned. "Hopefully, shooting him will spook the others into moving away from the prisoners and you can get a clear shot on them too."

"Call it."

"Give me two minutes to get into range of my targets."

Thom nodded. Nate moved soundlessly past the oblivious guards standing by the wagons, settling into a position close enough to be deadly even with his weapon's not too generous range. The officer was laughing uproariously at something one of his men, holding the older woman, said. Drawing a bead on him, Nate finished the countdown in his head. He fired, and Thom went into action, the sound of his weapon like a deadly echo.

The first few soldiers were easy to kill, caught completely unawares. Then one man remaining by the tree grabbed the younger woman and, using her as a shield, attempted to escape into the woods. Nate broke cover, pursuing them at a run. The soldier was hampered not only by his struggling captive, but also by the older woman, who clung to his legs. He slapped the woman on the ground, knocking her away, while retaining his hold on the younger woman. Nate circled in closer and closer. He made a fast visual check of the victim on the ground as he passed, relieved to see she was alive, if woozy. Finally, the enemy, panicked by Nate's relentlessly silent advance, threw the woman in Nate's direction and bolted. Nate caught the falling woman with one arm while blasting the soldier in his tracks, leaving a congealed pile of oily, steaming black ash.

Nate tried to help the woman regain her feet, but she shrank away from him, sinking bonelessly to the ground. The other woman rushed to hug her, nearly bowling her over again. The pair of them watched him warily, faces white, eyes wide.

"You're the warriors of the Lady, aren't you?" said the elder in a trembling voice.

Nate holstered his weapon and ignored her question. "We heard your cries for help, ma'am. Let me assist you in rejoining your people."

She took his outstretched hand and rose to her feet, trying to keep as far away from him as she could while not completely losing contact. The second woman stood as well, clinging to her companion, never taking her eyes off Nate.

Thom was untying the two bound men as Nate and the women walked to the carts. The children flocked to the older woman, sobbing and clinging to her muddy skirts. She leaned over, trying to comfort them all at once. The younger woman picked up a toddler in either arm and whispered soothingly to them. Nate helped Thom undo the last of the ropes.

At the unmistakable sound of approaching cavalry, Nate pivoted and took a defensive posture, drawing his weapon, ready for a new battle. Atletl and the two women rode into view, leading the other kemat.

"Dammit, I told you to stay put until I gave the all clear." Nate jammed his Mark One into its holster. "What the seven hells possessed you to disobey my direct order?"

"The Lady said it was all right to join you now." Atletl merely shrugged as Nate glared at him.

Nate debated what to say to the people he and Thom had rescued and found them all, from oldest to youngest, staring at Bithia. Even with her fantastic purple hair covered by the hood of her cape, it was obvious she wasn't a native of Talonque.

Slowly, as if in a trance, the refugees sank to their knees on the road, the adults pulling the puzzled children with them.

Bithia and Nate exchanged glances, the former probably well aware he wasn't pleased to have their identities revealed, even to harmless refugees stranded in the middle of nowhere. She threw back her hood anyway, permitting her glorious, otherworldly hair to fall free. The breeze lifted a few strands gently. Nate heard the Talonqueni family members muttering in awe, convinced they were in the presence of the fabled T'naritza.

"I'm pleased my warriors assisted you this day," she told the elderly man. Nodding at the corpse beside the bracalx, she went on, "I regret we weren't in time to save everyone."

"We're blessed by your intervention, Lady. Even though I lost my son this day, to see you with my own eyes—" The elder drew himself up with an audible crack of his ancient spine. "My grandchildren saved from the altars of Huitlani—I can't find proper words to thank you, to praise you."

Bithia shook her head emphatically. "No praise or thanks is necessary. My warriors did what was required."

"What is your will for us?" the older woman asked. "Are we to follow you?"

Good thing Bithia served as an oracle and unwilling figure of worship for so many centuries. Nate wouldn't have known what to say. Probably all the wrong, clumsy things in his eagerness to be gone, unencumbered by extra responsibilities.

Bithia inclined her head graciously to the woman. "Go your own way quickly, with my blessings. I'm fated to travel alone with my warriors and my priestess. None other can share my road, for I journey to my father's home."

The Talonqueni were obviously disappointed not to be asked to join her, but Nate was relieved. The idea of shepherding anyone else to some indeterminate, safe destination on the planet appalled him. Had Bithia invited the family to travel under her protection, the goddess and her warrior would have had serious words on the spot. He felt guilty he hadn't trusted her judgment to override her compassionate instincts.

Apparently, Bithia sensed the family's disappointment also. She gave commands designed to turn their thoughts in other directions than the dubious, forbidden glory of riding with her. "You must bear witness at every opportunity about the fate befalling those who serve the evil god, whose name I shall not honor by speaking it. Tell the people of this world to reject the evil path and follow one shining with light, valuing all lives. You've seen this lesson today—you can speak of it with authority. Your children and grandchildren must carry the message onward through time, even as the Hialar were entrusted with my father's messages before, in Nochen-that-was. You shall now carry my proclamation. How is your clan called?"

The old man bowed. "You do us tremendous honor, Lady. My name is Rek Narixtlal."

She extended her left arm, bedecked as always with the gilintrae, in a graceful motion. The sleeve of her riding cloak slipped to her elbow, revealing the full magnificence of the gemmed, golden braceletlike device. The adults in the Narixtlal family gasped and gawked.

Nate noticed the gilintrae was glowing in the harsh daylight, a rainbow of lights traveling counterclockwise in the air above the ring of jewels on the outer circumference of the bracelet.

"I choose you, the Narixtlal, to be the messengers of T'naritza, now and for all time," Bithia said with suitable gravity.

In response to some signal from her, the circle of rainbow lights lifted away from the gilintrae and flashed across the open space. The illumination settled on the old man's head, gleaming brightly for no more than ten seconds before blazing like flames and winking out. The aged patriarch was so moved, he practically fainted. His remaining sons had to hold him on his feet.

"We've heard how you unleashed the blue fire on Nochen and destroyed the city in one afternoon," said the younger woman. "I wish I could have beheld the glorious sight. I lost two brothers and a sister to the altars and the well in past years. The priestesses came time and again for more innocents to sacrifice."

"No more slaughter of innocent humans," Bithia said sternly. "Rooting out the remnants of the evil will take time and many good people such as yourselves working together."

"Time to go," Nate said as Thom rode up, leading his kemat. Taking the reins, Nate swung into the saddle and wheeled his restless mount in the direction they were heading. "Good luck to you on the rest of your journey." He kicked the animal into a trot and left, trusting his people to follow obediently and promptly, which they did.

He knew the refugees watched them until the road finally took a gentle curve to avoid a rocky outcrop, obscuring them from view.

Bithia spurred her mount to draw alongside his. "Are you angry with me?"

"I'm not sorry Thom and I intervened. I'd have preferred the family not see you. I don't want word to spread that T'naritza is riding in the countryside anointing messengers, in case Sarbordon or Lolanta are still alive. You must be number one on their list of people to hunt and either recapture or kill."

"You don't think the enemy'll be too scared of her powers to want to mess with her again after she destroyed Nochen?" Thom asked.

Nate shook his head. "Remember, I had an uncomfortable interview with Lolanta, whose view of reality was seriously askew. If she survived the blast, she's going to be thinking about revenge and blood sacrifices to rebuild Huitlani's power. She's a true believer."

"I agree." Celixia, who'd listened intently, nodded. "Lolanta has powers of persuasion beyond the blatantly obvious. She can influence others to follow her, to do her bidding and believe as she does. I've seen her at work enough times, in Nochen. Her royal husband depended on her abilities heavily."

"We'll have to stay out of her path. Hell, we don't even know if she made it out of Nochen." Thom injected a cheerful note into the discussion. "What are we worrying about here?"

"We need to be even more circumspect from here on out. I wish we didn't have to keep to the damn road." Nate checked with Atletl. "Are you sure there's no alternative route to our ship?"

The Githholz shook his head in regretful denial. "Your ship crashed in the meadows of the lower Golhant Plateau. There is only the one scalable path to the top of the plateau, and this road paved the trail many centuries ago. Hundreds of men died under the overeers' whips to grade the incline enough to make it easily passable for trade. No other approach to the plateau from the south exists, unless you wish to assault the cliffs themselves, which no man has ever done."

"And which we aren't going to do," Bithia declared in a tone brooking absolutely no argument. "I could hang on long enough to sort of slide down the cliff at the beach, but I could never manage to climb the sheer face of the plateau."

"You know the area?" Nate was surprised.

She nodded. "It's a major feature of this part of the continent. My father's crew mapped it all, remember?"

He shook his head. "Sorry, sometimes I forget you were a member of a scientific expedition. I'll take your word for it that we're stuck with the damn road. How many days' ride to get to the top of the plateau, and how far is the ship from there? Can we at least leave the confines and perils of the road and go cross-country to the ship once we're on the plateau?"

"Yes." Atletl's confirmation eased Nate's fears about possible ambush and the danger of their recapture by enemy forces. "We'll be on the road for the rest of today and part of tomorrow, probably until past the midday sun. There's a village at the foot of the incline. I am assuming you'll want to be unobserved as much as possible, which means waiting until nightfall tomorrow to make a detour?"

Nate nodded emphatically.

"It takes about half a day—or night—to reach the top of the plateau on foot, so we'll probably make better time with the kemat, although they'll need to be rested often. You crashed to the west." Atletl paused, face set in a frown as he spoke of the past. "Your ship flashed overhead, accompanied by deafening thunder, spewing flames in the sky. The officer in charge of the prisoners, Salinaxt, was the king's cousin. He was determined to investigate where you landed, in case it was something to do with Fr'taray's return. He was well versed in the family mysteries."

"He stood third or fourth in line for the throne," Celixia said. "So he'd been shown the secret chamber of the Sleeping Goddess and was educated on all the prophecies. He was rumored to have fathered at least one of Lolanta's sons."

"Salinaxt had us camp for the better part of a day while he took a party of warriors and marched due west to your crash site. When they brought the three of you to the camp, none of us could believe our eyes. At first we expected you to destroy the enemy, setting us all free. But then you behaved like mere men, no different from the rest of us, especially since you submitted to the chains and beatings, as helpless to resist as we were. But I was positive, even then, that this must be part of a grand, complicated plan on the part of Fr'taray to test how things were on Talonque since he left."

"The situation was complicated," Nate said. "Not sure there was a plan."

Thom took a drink from his waterskin. "Poor Haranda. He was so damn scared until we started playing sapiche, and then he believed he'd found the way out. At least he died happy and full of hope."

"May the Lords of Space keep him," Nate said somberly.

He rode in silence for a few moments, thinking about the young cadet's fate at the hands of Kalgitr. Then he sent Thom out to ride advance scout, picking up the pace, concentrating on the journey north.

Two days later, when he should have been flush with confidence, Nate had an unexplainable back-of-the-neck premonition that all was not well. He couldn't pinpoint any one thing causing his unease. They'd ridden past the village guarding the base of the long, exposed stretch of road climbing the plateau without trouble. As Atletl had suggested, they bypassed the bustling crossroads in the dead of night, the hooves of their mounts deadened with cloth so as not to alert anyone. By dawn, even after allowing their kemat frequent rest stops on the steep grade, they'd ridden into the grasslands atop the plateau. Nate set a fast pace, and the other four kept up without complaint.

The attack came when he least expected it, as the party, with him in the rear, crossed the plains toward a shallow river, heading for the cover of the dense forest on the far bank. Suddenly, a spear whistled past his left side, splashing into the river ahead. Even as Nate checked his six, his kemat screamed, crashing heavily under a fresh assault of short spears.

In retrospect, and while blaming himself bitterly, Nate had to accept he'd let his guard down slightly, riding so close to the sanctuary of their ship. Atletl's estimate had been perhaps another half a day of riding.

Tangled in the stirrups, Nate was stunned by the fall, his foot trapped under the dying animal. Drawing the alien weapon, he craned his head to shout orders across the stream at the others. "Ride, dammit, we can't let them get their hands on Bithia again."

A yelling pack of black-clad temple guards raced along the riverbank, coming from the cover of an outcropping of boulders at the stream's bend a few hundred yards away. Four men on kemat led the attack.

Atletl wasted no time in grabbing the reins of Celixia's mount and galloped west, disappearing into the depths of the forest.

Bithia screamed Nate's name from across the river. Standing in her stirrups, she fought for control of her panicked kemat. "I refuse to leave you."

Thom hesitated, drawing his weapon. He forced his mount into the stream, despite the hail of spears and the oncoming men. "I'll be right there." He fired a bolt past Nate, taking out one advancing kemat and rider, then made as if to jump from his saddle. "Swing up behind me."

"No time, I'm stuck—get her out of here!" Nate swatted at Thom's kemat savagely as it approached, startling it into a rearing jump in the other direction. As he scrambled onto the opposite bank, Thom slapped the rump of Bithia's mount, sending her in a headlong gallop in the direction Atletl and Celixia had gone seconds before.

"Keep going!" Nate yelled. He fought clear from his dying kemat and managed to squeeze off two shots on the run, burning one mounted guard and one foot soldier before he heard a buzzing sound. Checking the weapon's indicator light with a swift glance, he found the symbol flickering. Cursing, he threw the weapon into the river and slogged on, making a valiant, if futile, attempt to save himself by reaching the far bank and then sprinting for the cover of the trees.

A well-thrown club struck him in the temple as two cavalrymen thundered past him and across the river. Losing consciousness, slipping into the cold river, Nate hoped Thom and Bithia had gotten enough of a head start to escape.

More cold water thrown at him brought him to consciousness. Cursing, Nate tried to sit, but two spearpoints stabbed into his chest, convincing him resistance wasn't going to gain him any advantage. He lay on the muddy riverbank, glaring at a ring of soldiers.

"Wise," came the hated voice of Lolanta. "You're of no use to me dead. Not yet." She lingered over the last word, taunting him. "But I'll order them to kill you, if you resist."

The guards hauled him to his feet to face the waiting priestess.

"Do what you want with me, but you'll never get your filthy hands on her again," Nate spat.

"I wouldn't be too sure. Even if my mounted guardsmen don't capture her outright, there may be other ways." Lolanta nodded with apparent satisfaction. The richly embroidered hood of her black cape fell onto her shoulders. Nate stifled an exclamation. Lolanta hadn't escaped the destruction of Nochen unscathed. The left side of her head was bald, flame-red, misshapen, scarred, the hair having fallen out in clumps. Lesions and patches of necrotizing skin attested to the radioactive nature of the burns. Her left eye was ghastly white, blinking furiously and independently of its twin, and tearing.

Lolanta flinched only slightly at Nate's appalled reaction. "Your goddess did her best to kill me and failed." Running a gloved hand over her head, she said,

"My beauty will be fully restored by Huitlani once I make the proper sacrifices. If I bathe my wounds in T'naritza's blood, the evil will be undone."

Nate knew this woman was mad enough to expect such a thing to work. He prayed Bithia and Thom could reach the safety of their ship with their head start. Maybe Thom's Mark One held more charge than his.

"Bind him securely, but don't harm him." Lolanta tugged at her hood to hide the deformities. "Lash him to a kemat and let us be on our way." Turning to Nate, she said with contempt, "It was obvious you'd try to reach the place where you first came to Talonque. I'd no need to follow your travels, although my spies brought me word of your deeds, your progress. I came straight to the plateau, laid my ambush in the best spot, and you rode into the trap."

"The only one you caught was me, so you failed in your main purpose."

She didn't seem distressed by that. "We'll see. This game is far from finished."

"Where's Sarbordon?" Nate asked as the guards tied his hands securely behind his back.

"I assume he died in the greater death of Nochen." Lolanta didn't evidence any distress, much less grief, over the probable fate of her co-ruler. "The last time I saw him, he was lying on her silver couch, slashing the mattress with his belt knife, sobbing and raging against you for freeing her. Taking her away from him. I assume he was still there when her father's powers blasted the entire city to nothing."

"How did you escape?"

Lolanta laughed. "Huitlani watches over me. I didn't resign *my* allegiance to him in wonderment over a useless sleeping girl. I'd gone to oversee the sacrifices at the great altar near the bridge. When the earthquakes became numerous, I understood the tremors were a sign from Huitlani, so I gathered my company and fled. I wasn't quite quick enough, as you observed from your perusal of my face, but yet I live. And all shall be restored to me, as I've prophesied, once the right offerings of human hearts are made."

She walked away from Nate as the guards threw him to the ground to bind his legs. Watching to see what she was going to do next, Nate was puzzled to see the priestess take a few steps into the cold river, oblivious to the water lapping at her knees, drenching the hem of her garment. Raising her voice and speaking forcefully in the direction of the opposite shore, she called out, "There's an ancient temple nearby, on the edge of the plateau itself. My people constructed it when we first came from the mountains to begin our conquest of Talonque. It is the sacred spot where we beseeched Huitlani to grant us the power of life and death over this land. I've reconsecrated the altar in the last two days with fresh blood, new hearts. Huitlani is pleased and awaiting more offerings. At sunset, your captain dies there."

The guards dragged Nate toward a waiting kemat.

He tried to concentrate on reaching Bithia, mind to mind. He tried sending a thought one more time, wishing he'd taken the Mellurean training so long ago. *Don't listen to her. Don't do anything foolish like trying to rescue me. It's a trap.* He injected as much strength into the mental sending as he could, but received no response, no flicker of acknowledgment. The tiny flame emblematic of their link burned in his mind as always, but Bithia made no reply.

Lolanta mounted her own, sleek black kemat, and the mixed column of cavalry and foot soldiers moved out. The animal carrying Nate was placed in the middle of the column to foil any attempt at rescue. He made his peace with fate. There was no way Thom could rescue him, not with only one weapon. Nate allowed himself to hope Bithia was safe and wouldn't risk herself to come after him.

But he didn't really believe it.

CHAPTER TEN

Nate was dizzy from being carried head down, draped over a kemat like an oversized sack of grain. When the column finally reached their destination at the temple, a laughing guard tipped him headfirst off the kemat. Somersaulting helplessly, Nate slammed onto his back on the hard ground. Blinking to clear his head, Nate found himself at the foot of a massive, crumbling statue, one of a pair guarding the stairs to the top of the temple. Badly weathered and defaced though the idol was, Nate could make out the uniquely horrific features of Huitlani.

One of the guards slashed the ropes at his ankles. Other men hauled him to his feet.

"Climb the sacred stairs under your own power," said the guard on his left. "We've better things to do than carry you."

This pyramid was smaller than the one at Nochen, but it was a long slog to the top. He couldn't see much point in resisting, so he climbed as he'd been ordered. Lolanta rushed up the stairs to join him, grabbing his arm to steady herself.

There was something ancient and evil, not quite human, about Lolanta, even before her face had been marked by the radiation. "This place will have to do for tonight's ceremony," she said. "We've much rebuilding to do, since the shrines in the capital were destroyed by you and your Sleeping Goddess."

She continued climbing the broad flight of easy stairs with him, chatting away the whole time. The guards followed a stair or two behind, keeping a watchful eye on Nate.

"The Githholz no doubt are destroying or defiling any other places of our worship their soldiers find," Lolanta told him at one point with barely suppressed fury.

As if it's my fault.

"My network of priestesses tell me the enemy advance through the lowlands, welcomed by the peasants, and those fools, the city governors, are doing nothing to work together and fight the enemy. Too concerned with their own holdings to care about the greater sway of the empire we once ruled. Huitlani will gladly drink your blood and eat your heart, warrior, wherever he can get it—old temple, bare field, anyplace properly consecrated with the rituals. Your part in bringing this ruin crashing upon all our heads must be punished. He'll reward me well for killing you."

"Your day is done, and so is Huitlani's. Killing me isn't going to do anything but temporarily satisfy your twisted urge for revenge." Nate considered throwing himself backward, taking her with him in a deadly fall from the top of the stairs.

As if reading his mind, Lolanta disengaged her arm from his and stepped away. Instantly, one of the massive temple guards took her place, his grip on Nate implacable. The brief chance, if ever it had existed, to escape death on the altar by a suicidal plunge off the pyramid was gone.

"Huitlani told me what must occur in order for him to re-establish rule over this world." Lolanta's voice held contempt for Nate's predictions. "Your death is the first, essential step in that process. I follow the god's plan."

He studied her for a moment. "Why do you find it so necessary to argue with me, then? I think you don't genuinely believe your own words. I think you're questioning your faith and whether your god has deserted you forever."

Lolanta slapped him, rocking him in the hold of the temple guards. "Take him away. Put him in the holding cell until sunset, and then we'll have his heart."

"Do my words come too close to the truth for comfort?"

She turned, standing so she could gaze over the flatlands far below the plateau.

The guards dragged Nate across the smooth surface at the top of the pyramid, past more crumbling columnar statues of the god and moss-covered altar stones. His captors took him into the small temple at the far side of the sacrificial platform. The temple interior was basically a wide hallway with four small rooms opening off the passage, obviously abandoned for centuries. There were cracks in the roof, permitting shafts of waning sunlight in here and there, illuminating faded, flaking frescoes. Windblown debris and dead leaves crackled under his feet. Scurrying away, small creatures squeaked or hissed. One of the guards kicked futilely at an escaping rodent with a curse. Nate was escorted to the last room on the left and chained to the wall in a dank cell. The guards left him there in the near dark, slamming the rotting wooden door shut with a hollow thud.

A few minutes later, the cell door reopened. Nate tensed, thinking the guards couldn't be coming for him so soon. It was only late to midafternoon by his reckoning, and the giant sun of this planet made an unusually slow traverse of the sky.

Lolanta entered the cell, unaccompanied. She set the small torch she was carrying into a convenient holder beside the door. Then she stood for a long moment, staring across the width of the cell at Nate, her expression unreadable.

"What the seven hells do you want now?" *Can't she leave me alone until the appointed hour? Give a man a chance to make peace with his own deity?*

"Once in Nochen, in better times, I offered you a bargain, warrior, and you refused it. I've come to speak of possibilities again."

"I don't know how to make it any more plain. I despise you and everything you stand for. I'd kill you where you stand right now, my word on it, if I wasn't cuffed to the wall. You and I could never be on the same side of anything. We have no common ground. There are no possibilities where we are concerned."

"Don't be so sure, or so rash." She came closer until she stood in front of him. He tried not to pay attention to the ravaged side of her face, focusing instead on her normal eye. The intense perfume she wore washed over his senses in a cloying wave, overwhelming the stench of the mildew and mold on the surrounding stone walls.

"I've considered what you said to me just now on the stairs," she said. "Most of it was pure blasphemy, but perhaps there was some sense to a part of it. Perhaps it's not your death Huitlani demands of me today. Perhaps your heart is meant to serve in another fashion."

Nate maintained a stubborn silence.

"My husband is dead. I need a strong warrior to rule with me, to lead the armies to recapture what we've lost."

"You've got to be kidding." Even in these extreme circumstances, Nate laughed at the unthinkable suggestion. "You and I don't fight for the same side, lady." *How many times do I have to tell her the obvious truth before she leaves me alone?*

"But we could. Don't be so stubborn. I like strength in a man, but you carry it to the extreme." She touched his cheek in a grotesquely intimate gesture. "We could do much together, I'm sure."

Nate jerked his head away from her touch, from those clawed nails. "Leave me the hell alone."

She stepped away from him, eye glinting with fury. Lolanta fussed with the silky hood of her cape so the damaged side of her face was shielded from view.

Nate took a deep breath. "I'm sorry for you," he said, looking her right in the eyes, so she couldn't mistake his meaning. "Killing me isn't going to do you any good." He studied her averted face. "You're after revenge, pure and simple. You want T'naritza and me to pay, to suffer for ending your days of bloody glory. Admit it. Don't keep dressing it up, or trying to excuse your actions with these absurd claims about my death restoring the city of Nochen or anything else. You don't really believe what you're spouting, do you?"

Lolanta studied him for a long moment. "You know nothing of Huitlani and his powers." She tried to smile, working hard to regain her usual icy demeanor. "I might admit some of my actions are personal. But whatever I do also serves the greater purposes of Huitlani, even your death on my altar."

"You're in for a lot of disappointment."

"Perhaps your death alone won't suffice. You probably speak truth." Lolanta inclined her head in graceful acknowledgment of a point to Nate. "But you forget your value as the means to a more important end—the capture and sacrifice of T'naritza. Perhaps you do love that pitiful girl. We'll see how much she cares about you. I know your companions are nearby. Will they abandon you? At sunset, I'll make her my offer from the temple steps—her life for yours. Care to wager what happens?" Laughing, she swept from the cell, forgetting to take the torch in her triumphant mood.

Nate contemplated his options after she left. There was no way he was going to get free. The shackles were rusty and covered in green mold, but still stronger than he could pull open. He hoped Thom and Bithia had ridden on, per his emphatic orders. Knowing them, that was a thin hope indeed. Thom had never abandoned him in any tight situation before, nor would Nate have let his friend die on the altar, were the positions reversed, without expending every effort to save him. And Bithia, having put herself at risk before to save his life, was hardly going to stand by idly while Thom launched a rescue attempt. But how could the three of them hope to beat Lolanta, who had at least fifteen men at her command, as well as the high ground?

Something slid across his left foot, rasping over his skin. Glancing down, he discovered a scarlet and blue tolokon coiled next to him in the gloom. Its colors were iridescent and unmistakable even in the shadows of the cell. The reptile raised its head, studying him for a long moment before uncoiling and slithering out of sight through a large crack. Nate let out the breath he'd been holding. He wasn't a big believer in omens, but it was uncanny to see his first tolokon now after hearing about them for all these months. *Getting a little space happy.* He leaned his head against the clammy stone wall and closed his eyes.

Eventually, two guards arrived to take him for the sacrifice. Before unlocking him from the tight restraints, one of the men tipped a black bowl to his lips, trying to force Nate to drink the fluid sloshing within. He spat out the few sickly sweet drops leaking past his compressed lips but knew he'd swallowed some. "What the seven hells is that?"

The guard with the bowl clutched in one meaty paw stared at him, a sympathetic expression on his broad face. "You should drink the offering of Lolanta, warrior. A potion to take fear from a man's heart. She does you great favor to provide this."

And dull my reflexes so I can't put up a fight. "I've told the bitch before not to do me any favors. I'm not afraid."

"You will be," the other guard said with a leer.

There was no more discussion, and the guard didn't offer the contents of the bowl again. The men released him from the wall shackles and held him tightly by the arms, forcing him to walk into the corridor where Lolanta waited, decked out in what remained of her full priestess regalia. The effect should have been pitiful, but instead there was an aura of demented magnificence.

"Halt, I wish a few final words."

"He refused the quiloe wine, my lady."

"The more fool you," Lolanta told Nate, good eye narrowed, other eye twitching as she studied him. "I warned you this won't be an easy or quick death."

"Get on with what you have to do. Stop making threats." Nate was contemptuous.

Be ready. Bithia's voice was clear in his head. *Thom says delay her. We're nearly there.*

The signal I've been waiting for. Nate wrenched his arm free from the guard on the left, grabbing the bowl and smashing it into the face of the man on the right. As the soldier collapsed, Nate kicked the legs out from under his first captor and attempted to grab Lolanta. More soldiers arrived from farther back in the hallway and piled on as the priestess screamed and retreated.

Determined not to make it easy for them, trying to buy the time Thom needed, Nate resisted being dragged onto the platform with all his power. The enemy had the advantage of sheer muscle mass, but he'd nothing to lose now, no slightest compunction about killing, while they were under stringent orders from Lolanta to get him chained on the altar alive. Nate managed to get free for an instant, knocking one guard out cold with a well-placed jab to the throat and breaking another's knee with a savage martial arts kick. More of the hulking men joined in the fray. Working together, the pack of burly guards got him onto the black stone altar on his back, but not before Nate sent a third soldier reeling, his eye socket split by a well-placed kick.

He battled as the guards closed heavy shackles over his ankles and wrists, nearly getting free again, adrenaline lending him strength. Eventually, Nate was pinned, unable to move more than an inch in any direction.

Lolanta strolled to his side once the guards stepped away. Standing beside the waist-high altar, she toyed with the cuff at his ankle and laughed. "What a pity to waste such a man, but sacrifice is your choice, warrior. Too late to change your mind now."

He spat in her face. "Go to hell."

Wiping her cheek with the corner of her cloak, she said, "Now I'll make this ceremony as drawn-out as I can, to savor each moment of your pain, this I promise. The quiloe wine would have helped you to endure the ordeal, and I intended to be more merciful, but your actions of resistance anger me, and the gods."

She took a thin knife, like an old-fashioned scalpel, with poison or more drugs smeared on the blade, from a tray of instruments held out by a priestess. This handmaiden's left arm hung limp, most of her hair missing, revealing a shiny swath of burned skin. She coughed heavily, shaking the tray she was balancing.

Lolanta's priestesses aren't going to outlive me by much. They're all in varying stages of radiation sickness.

The queen chanted, the syllables discordant, ominous.

He closed his eyes and sent an urgent message. *Now would be good. I'm strapped down and she has a knife.*

Lolanta cut a shallow slash in his neck with the blade. Warm blood flowed immediately.

Opening his eyes in pain, Nate watched her catch his blood in a translucent-green stone cup. She sprinkled a pale powder into the goblet and drank the hideous concoction in one long gulp.Lolanta hurled the vessel against the side of the altar near his head and uttered what sounded like curses. Jagged fragments of the broken pottery struck his chest and face, leaving small cuts here and there. Reeling unsteadily, she grabbed a heavier knife from the instrument tray and placed her other clawed hand on his breastbone. Biting her lip as she concentrated, she cut his shirt open from collar to hem, leaving his chest bare. Nate stared unflinchingly into her eyes. Her one pupil was huge, dilated, probably from the drug she'd taken with his blood. Lolanta opened her mouth to taunt him again, but an imperious command from Bithia rang across the platform.

"Stop this hideous travesty at once. Touch him with that knife and you die."

"You wish to say something, T'naritza?" She lifted her deformed left hand from his skin and carefully laid the heavy, curved, black stone knife on the tray.

Bithia's beautiful tones carried well in the clear night air. "Let him go, Lolanta. I won't allow you to sacrifice my man to your evil, false god."

"And why not?" the priestess asked, tilting her head to the side and raising her eyebrows. She pivoted to face Bithia. "He bleeds as easily as any other man. I've proven his vulnerability. His heart will surely be as pleasing to Huitlani as any other warrior's. There must be an offering tonight. It's the eve of the red moons, you know."

Nate realized Bithia stood on the altar platform, glancing at him quickly to reassure herself he lived before she locked eyes with Lolanta.

"There'll be a death as tradition demands—your life will be forfeit tonight for all your crimes," Bithia said.

Nate realized she wasn't holding a weapon. *How could Thom let her walk up here unarmed? Where the hell is he?*

Ambushing her guards at the perimeter of the temple. Stop distracting me.

Totally focused on Lolanta, Bithia didn't even glance at him.

Two of the uninjured guards from the squad assigned to bring Nate to the altar had been circling ever closer as the women talked. Now the pair of thugs made their move, seizing Bithia, holding her tightly by the arms. Nate fought the chains holding him in place and cursed.

Bithia seemed unconcerned by her capture, or by their rough handling. "Think carefully about what you do here. Release me, leave this place now and you can live," she said to the men.

"Empty threats from one worshipped with the paltry gifts of flowers and candles. Let me deal with your lover, and then you can take his place." Lolanta glanced at the tray held by the trembling, coughing acolyte. The high priestess took her curved knife again, caressing its carved handle. "We waste too much time. Now that you're here, as I knew you would be, foolish T'naritza, we can get on with the death of this man before the moons reach their zenith."

"I don't think so."

Nate blinked. Either he was hallucinating, or a green nimbus was slowly surrounding Bithia, glowing much like the curtain in the healing device had done. Flares of green light mixed with red sparks spurted off into the fading late afternoon sunlight. Her luxurious mane of blue and lavender hair spread out in the air like the corona of a miniature sun. The burly men who'd been so triumphant at capturing her moments ago, now dropped their hold on her as if her bare skin had scorched their hands.

Perhaps it did. Who knows what this unexpected power of Bithia's can do?

Screaming in pain and fear, the guards shook their hands, now blackening and withering, and retreated, stumbling and falling across each other as whatever power Bithia wielded took lethal effect. Nate heard panicky yelling as the remaining participants attempted to flee before Bithia attacked them.

Clutching the knife in her fist, Lolanta whirled, raising her arm to deliver the stroke that would kill Nate.

Bithia snapped out her left arm, the one ringed by her gilintrae, fingers open, palm up. A sizzling bolt of the green and red light flew from her fingertips to engulf Lolanta before she could complete the motion.

Nate focused on the queen's distorted face. She dropped the knife onto the altar beside Nate, striking him a glancing blow in the side. Reeling, Lolanta staggered under the assault of whatever weapon Bithia had launched at her. She fell to her knees, yelling curses, writhing in the grip of the unearthly flames. A small explosion scattered sparks in the twilight, and the fire died sluggishly, leaving an oily black residue on the altar platform and no other sign that Lolanta ever existed.

Bithia rushed to the altar, taking a moment to reassure herself Nate was unharmed for the most part, before trying to locate the release mechanism for the shackles.

Thom came rushing across the platform as the shackles fell open with a snap. Nate struggled to rise with their assistance.

"Report?" he said as he gained his feet.

"The other priestesses fled. I let them go—they appear to be dying," Thom said. "Took me so long to get here because I was picking off Lolanta's guards stationed at the base of the temple, the ones lying in wait to ambush us again. Got a bit complicated, but we're good."

"You're in no condition to ride, and it's getting dark fast," Bithia said to Nate. "We'll have to shelter here tonight."

"Not here. I want to leave this damned place."

"There ain't exactly any good choices," Thom said. "We don't know this territory, and she's right—you can't sit a kemat tonight. Seven hells, give yourself a night to recover."

"We'll be gone at first light—be sensible," Bithia said as they made their way toward the temple entrance.

"Hold up, let me do a recon." Weapon in hand, Thom moved ahead to ensure no one was left hiding in the structure.

"There was something on the knife blade, some kind of drug. Making me lightheaded." Nate leaned on Bithia, unable to keep walking without Thom's strength to support him. "No more argument from me." He accepted the plain fact that he had no strength for descending the temple stairs, much less staying in the saddle while in search of a more congenial campsite for the night.

"Not a pleasant place, but empty," Thom reported, positioning Nate's arm on his shoulder so they could continue into the temple.

Together, Bithia and Thom got Nate to the open space inside the entrance, retrieving the torch from what had been his cell. After helping him recline on Thom's cloak, Bithia cleaned the neck wound as best she could with water from a well at the rear of the building, binding it and the slash in his side with strips from her skirt. "I've done as much as I can for now." Bithia sat with Nate's head in her lap, gently running her hand through his hair.

"Didn't I tell you to ride on and leave me?"

Not at all abashed, she smiled, shaking her head. "And you believed your best friend and I would of course do this foolish thing? Abandon you to Lolanta's knives merely because you ordered us?"

"The worst moment of my life was when I realized you were standing there on the platform and I couldn't do anything—not one damn thing—to help you."

"I know. I had several of the worst moments of my life tonight too. But now we're past it, and she'll never trouble us again."

"How did you work that? With the gilintrae? I thought it wasn't a weapon."

"You must be recovering fast if you're thinking about the technology again," she said. "You and Thom, so interested in everything my people developed and used." Relenting a bit, she added, "I enabled a last-resort, self-defense capability, draining nearly all the remaining power to inflict the burns on the men holding me and cast the bolt at her." She raised her wrist, and Nate realized the gemstones along the rim of the massive bracelet were barely flickering.

He touched the now lifeless jewels, then looked into her face. "I'm sorry."

She shrugged. "Don't be. I'd rather have your life. Besides, a low level of power remains. I won't lose any stored data."

"You strong enough for company?" Thom asked. "Friendlies?"

"Why?"

"Atletl and Celixia are climbing the temple stairs, backed by a squad of soldiers coming this way."

"A little late, but I appreciate the gesture of support." Nate gathered his energy to rise.

Bithia protested. "You're still woozy."

Gently but firmly, he removed her restraining hand and worked his way to his feet, leaning heavily on the wall. Thom watched, ready to step forward and help if needed. Fighting vertigo but on his feet, Nate said, "I want you to be the goddess one more time. I want you to be majorly impressive here, like you were on the road with those refugees we saved. Have you got enough power left to dazzle them?"

Eyes wide, she retreated a step, rubbing the gilintrae. "What do you mean? Why must I play the T'naritza role for Atletl and Celixia? Our allies know the truth about T'naritza."

"Atletl's soldiers don't. We owe it to him and Celixia to reinforce what they've undoubtedly told the Githholz leaders—you're the goddess, Huitlani is finished and Atletl played a major role in the victory. Part of my goal is to leave this planet with a chance to grow in a more civilized direction after we go." Nate finished with gritted teeth, nausea racking his gut.

"This kinda plays hell with the Sectors cultural noninterference regs, don't it?" Thom asked as an afterthought.

"Objection?"

"No." The answer was prompt, crisp and cheerful. "I like the idea. Probably ought to leave it out of the report, though."

"Reporting is the least of my worries at the moment, but thanks for the reminder." Nate laughed.

"I see." Bithia studied her plain blue dress. "I'm lacking in grandeur at the moment, but I can coax perhaps one more effect from the gilintrae's reserves."

"Good." He turned to Thom. "Tell them we're coming out to address the troops."

He saluted and left the room.

"All right, then." Nate took Bithia by the hand as if they were going to dance. "Ready, T'naritza? One last performance?"

She motioned for Nate to precede her through the short corridor. A faint green glow enveloped her, not as spectacular as the killing nimbus she'd deployed against Lolanta, but probably effective enough for this occasion, especially in the twilight.

Githholz soldiers now crowded the altar platform, and more were gathered on the steps.

As Nate and Lolanta emerged from the temple, Atletl held a curved sword aloft and waved it. "Silence for the words of the goddess."

The buzz of conversation died away. Nate and Thom stood at attention beside the entrance to the temple. Nate kept one hand unobtrusively braced on the doorframe to steady himself against the waves of vertigo. Bithia came out onto the single step, glowing pale green, her long hair spread out in the air as if it had life of its own. Green and red sparks pulsed into the gathering darkness from the tips of her hair.

"We've fought a great battle here today, my warriors and I, and defeated not only the evil priestess Lolanta, but the greater evil she served." Bithia's voice was sonorous and sounded amplified to Nate.

More gilintrae tricks.

"My warriors and I carried out my father's command and destroyed Nochen, where the Sarbordoni Clan and their evil gods held sway. We were assisted by my priestess and sister of the heart, Celixia." She gestured at the priestess, who came forward to clasp her hand, the green glow reaching out to surround her for a moment. The two women exchanged a few words, Celixia nodding rapidly. Bithia gave her attention to Atletl next. "We relied on the strong arm and courageous heart of Atletl, Warrior of the Tolokon Totem, proud representative of the Githholz, whose sacred mission is to now bring peace and harmony to this troubled land."

Atletl puffed up with visible pride as the crowd cheered for him, yelling his name and their approval of Bithia's pronouncements.

She motioned for silence, obtaining it instantly, the crowd clearly in her sway. "I reward you for your service by giving you the hand of my sister Celixia in marriage."

Bithia winked at Atletl as she said this.

"I'm honored, my Lady. I'll honor, love and treasure her all my life."

"Come and receive your bride." Bithia made a sweeping gesture, summoning the warrior to her side.

Atletl strode forward with his customary swagger. Bithia took his outstretched hand and placed Celixia's firmly in it. "What I have joined, let no person on Talonque dare to part."

Atletl faced the crowd, showing off a beaming Celixia, twirling her as if dancing, and again there was great cheering and yelling.

Bithia raised her hand for silence one final time. "My warriors and I shelter here tonight, with your army as my honor guard. You must be gone before dawn to begin your tasks in the lowlands. My warriors and I will depart this place as well, to seek our path home to my father. Let this be a night of celebration!"

On that note, Bithia swept into the temple, leaving the throngs cheering and a wild party breaking out.

Nate studied the happy crowd of Githholz before he followed Thom inside the temple.

I hope they won't be too drunk and hungover to march tomorrow, but that's Atletl's problem, not mine.

Shaking, Bithia leaned against the wall. "I'll never act as the goddess again. Standing in front of a crowd and proclaiming grandiose things terrifies me." Putting her forehead against the cool stones, she said, "Although I was happy to officially unite our friends. Celixia told me she wanted to marry Atletl, so I thought I'd try to give her as much status as I could."

Nate strode to her and took her in his arms, kissing her forehead. "Well done. If Atletl and Celixia can't build a better Talonque together, there's nothing more we can do for them. Are you all right?"

She nodded wordlessly. "I found it a lot easier to prophesy from the safe confines of the healing chamber, when I didn't know the people I was talking about and didn't much care what happened."

"We're done with Talonque's problems. Time to concentrate on getting ourselves home." He stroked her soft hair and held her close. Thom discreetly withdrew to the entrance of the temple and left them alone.

Atletl and Celixia came to the temple later, bringing dinner. The five sat beside a small fire in the temple's main chamber and shared a final, companionable evening together. When the meal ended, Nate studied his friends' faces and raised the crude mug holding his wine. "In the land of my people, we propose a toast, or a blessing maybe you'd call it, at the end of a meal like this one."

His comrades raised their mugs.

"To good friends, safe journeys and happiness. To us!" Nate and Thom touched cups, and then the others joined in, finally drinking the wine with laughter and light hearts.

Atletl rose from his seat by the fire, drawing Celixia with him. "We'll take our leave now, my Lady, warriors. Rest assured we'll be gone at first light."

They all rose. Nate shook Atletl's hand. "Giving you my thanks is inadequate. We couldn't have survived this without your help."

"It's been my honor to serve with you."

Then the Talonqueni left the temple, and Nate, Thom and Bithia were alone. "No more nation building for us," Nate said. "Tomorrow we go find our ship and we're out of here. Simple."

"We hope," Thom responded somberly.

"I guess we'll see tomorrow."

CHAPTER ELEVEN

In the morning, Nate woke with an abrupt start, coming straight from a dream re-creating the events of yesterday, only with Huitlani wielding the sacrificial knife over an altar where Bithia lay helpless. Heart pounding, he sat and reassured himself she slept beside him, safe and whole. Nate regarded the gloomy walls of the temple hallway where they'd camped for the night and frowned.

"Maybe Lolanta brought evil with her, but there sure as hell is something nasty about this place." The unnaturally vivid quality of the dream convinced him it hadn't come from his subconscious alone. This was, after all, the most ancient place of Huitlani's on this side of the continent.

Nate pulled the blanket over Bithia's shoulders. She murmured in her sleep and rolled toward him. Glad to know bad dreams weren't disturbing her slumber, he joined Thom, who'd volunteered to take the remaining nightwatch so Nate could sleep. The sergeant sat at the entrance to the temple. In the gray dawn, Nate could make out a small bouquet of flowers on the top step across the sacrificial platform, left there for Bithia by some well-wisher.

"Are the Githholz gone?"

"Atletl got them moving out about an hour ago," Thom said. "Guess he was a high-ranking officer or a prince after all."

"Lucky for us he got assigned to our slave chain," Nate said with a grin. "Shall I wake the lady and see what the day brings us, now that we're done mixing in the politics and religion of this world?"

"No arguments from me."

After a hasty breakfast, Nate set a course due north. They rode three of the four kemat Atletl left tethered for them at the foot of the temple stairs and led a fourth loaded with gear. By midmorning, they reached the river where the ambush had taken place.

Nate surveyed the area as he called a temporary halt to let the kemat drink. "I have to say Lolanta picked a good spot for her attack. Those boulders over there are the first real cover I've seen on this plateau. If we'd gotten into the dense woods over there, she never could have been sure of catching us."

"I figure she waited to spring the trap until you were on this side alone because she knew damn well the rest of us would come for you," Thom said.

"She was counting on your return." Nate scowled at Bithia. "Nearly worked too. Close call for all of us."

Another hour's ride brought them to the edge of the forested segment of the plateau. He trotted into a long meadow. Reining in, Nate stared at a huge furrow plowed into the soft soil by the crash-landing Sectors ship months ago. The sides of the rut were easily nine feet high, the burned vegetation not yet growing back.

Nate gave a low whistle. "Not a good sign."

"Not at all," Thom agreed, shaking his head, brow furrowed. "Think maybe Haranda lied to us about the condition of the ship?"

"Or didn't know. He was only a cadet after all." Nate stood in the stirrups, trying to see how far to the west the scar in the plateau extended before twitching the reins to direct his kemat to follow it.

"I don't understand," Bithia said as the kemat trotted over the meadow. "Your ship created this wound in the ground?"

Nate grimaced. "Yes."

"Surely this much destruction means a pretty uncontrolled crash. You expect to find the ship in flyable condition?"

"Not so much anymore," Nate said, not taking his eyes off the wall of scorched earth.

"I understand your emotions, having felt similarly myself when I walked into the abandoned laboratories at Nochen."

Half an hour later, they came upon the ship, nose buried in a mound of the rich, soft soil.

"No, no, no," Thom said, pointing at the blackened stern of the courier vessel. "The ship was in better shape when we landed, I swear. Even though I was kinda busy, I would have seen this much damage, I think."

"A smoldering fire in the engines maybe?" Nate spurred his reluctant kemat forward.

He rode past the grave Haranda and Thom had been digging when captured. Nate reined in. "At least the enemy respected our dead, however they treated us," he said with some surprise, gazing at the neatly mounded, undisturbed resting place of Jurgens, their pilot who'd died of an apparent heart attack during or moments prior to the crash landing. "Lords of Space, watch over him. And Haranda." Nate saluted and rode on.

Thom saluted the grave and followed Nate.

Bithia came silently after them. By the time she rode up to the midsection of the ship, both men had dismounted and were securing their kemat to the branches of a small, uprooted tree. Nate helped her from the saddle for the sheer pleasure of having her in his arms, not because she required his assistance, and then Thom led her mount to graze with the others.

"Now what?" Bithia asked curiously, eyeing the ship as she walked along the side. "This craft bears no resemblance to anything my people flew."

"We try to get access." Nate flipped open a small panel near the door and keyed in a sequence on the touch pad. He listened intently, waiting for the ship's artificial intelligence to respond. Nothing happened. Nate and Thom exchanged grim looks.

"Locked?" Bithia inquired.

"At least Haranda took a few precautions before leaving the ship," Nate answered, frowning. "Only he and Jurgens had the combination to their own ship. Of course, at any Sectors base, there'd be a number of people with the code who could get access—maintenance crew and the like. As a member of the Special Forces, I have an override code that the ship—any Sectors ship—ought to respond to."

"*Ought to* is the operative phrase," Thom said. "Want me to try the dorsal manual escape hatch?"

"Let me key this in one more time. Ah, there she goes." Nate pulled Bithia aside as a doorway neatly snicked open right in front of them. A narrow ramp unfolded, the end sinking into the soft earth.

Cautiously, Nate, followed by Thom and Bithia, stepped aboard the vessel. As soon as all three were inside, he retracted the gangway.

As the ship noiselessly sealed itself against intruders, he unclenched his jaw. "Safe for the first time on this damn planet."

"What a relief." Thom sagged against the slightly curved, opaquely gleaming corridor wall panel. "First order of business?"

Nate headed toward the bow of the ship. "Talk to the AI, find out what the hell shape she's in."

"I remember you saying something about wanting a shot of headclear, oh, about ten thousand times since we was captured," Thom said. "Want me to go aft and get the medkit?"

Nate stopped and swung around in the narrow passageway. "For the first time since I can remember, I don't have a headache. But get the kit anyway. We can work on these bruises and cuts Lolanta left me with." He held out a hand to Bithia. "Come with me?"

"Gladly. It's fascinating to see you and Thom in your proper element. A little unsettling."

"How so?" asked Nate as he led her past a series of tightly closed portals.

"I understood you are from a spacefaring race, like mine, but since I've only seen you in Nochen, dressed as slaves or sapiche players, or as Sarbordon's guards"—she chuckled—"I've had occasional trouble actually believing your technological prowess."

"You'll believe it even more easily when I get my hands on a proper uniform and get cleaned up. Here we are, the flight deck." Again, Nate provided his override code. This time, the door responded promptly, permitting them access to the control chamber where the main AI interface resided.

The flight deck of a small ship like this one was designed to be efficient in an extremely cramped area. Two seats with consoles were located all the way forward, large viewscreens above and to the sides, and a spare seat, with no console but a smaller viewscreen, was at the rear. Nate motioned Bithia to that one.

"I'll see what's to be done here."

He sank into the black leather pilot's seat and flexed his fingers a moment before sending them dancing across the console, typing in his code, then his ID, followed by a string of commands.

Bithia chose not to sit as suggested, but to lean over his chair. "You're a soldier and a pilot? You received a high degree of cross-training."

"I'm a pilot, more or less. Definitely less, if you ask anyone in the Space Navy. Have to admit I couldn't pilot anything much bigger than this, or maybe a starfighter, but I'm checked out on the basics for a ship this size. Sometimes we fly ourselves in and out of a mission location, depending on the conditions, what Sector it's in, what the job is, etcetera. This was kind of a luxury, being flown back to base. Some luxury." Nate shook his head. "Would have been better to have flown myself. Couldn't have done a worse job than poor Jurgens and Haranda. I've got the AI online now. I'd better concentrate."

Their technology fascinated Bithia, just as hers had entranced them, so she stayed where she was, but didn't try to engage Nate in conversation again.

The door slid open behind them, and Thom came in, carrying a small kitbag. Out of the corner of his eye, Nate saw his friend gaze at Bithia in silent enquiry. She shrugged and spread her hands.

"What's the prognosis?" Thom sank into the chair Bithia had declined.

Nate spun his chair to face them both. *No use in delaying the bad news.* "We're not getting out of here."

"Slagged?" Thom asked.

Nate nodded.

"What is slagged?" Bithia studied his face and then checked Thom's reaction. "Something bad obviously."

"We have strict rules about not leaving artifacts, much less a whole ship, intact on a world like Talonque, or when the enemy is present," Nate said. "The engines of this ship were badly damaged by a blast from a Mawreg client race's cruiser, which is why we entered hyperspace too close to a blue giant star and ended the journey here, wherever we are, off the Sector charts altogether." He looked at Thom. "From what the AI tells me, we were fortunate that Jurgens—or Haranda, if he was at the controls—panicked and hit the overdrive too close to the star. Otherwise, we weren't going anywhere. The engines were dying. We must have barely made it through the atmosphere. I'm not surprised Jurgens had a heart attack. I accessed his personnel jacket while I waited for the AI to finish its eval of the ship conditions. Oddly enough, Jurgens was an inner Sector ferry pilot for high-ranking hotshots his entire career prior to this last posting in the Outer Rim."

"So the blue star's fields gave the dying engines a boost?"

"Right. When the AI didn't get any further commands from authorized sources for a prescribed length of time, it slagged—destroyed—the engines, knowing they were unusable. There's a small, separate power source for keeping the life support going, the AI itself, essential services. Unless someone tries to access the ship who isn't authorized or who doesn't have an override code, the power lasts years," Nate said to Bithia.

"How long does this separate power source last?"

"Nothing like the length of time your installations stay functional, running unattended." Nate laughed. "We can't stay here in any case. This ship is in a totally exposed position."

Eyebrows raised, Bithia rapped her knuckle on the hull.

"No weapons," Nate said. "This was strictly a fast courier job not meant to take offensive action. The weight was reduced and the speed increased for atmospheric flight by not mounting any weapons, not even a small blast cannon. We couldn't defend ourselves effectively. No one could break in, not with the armament on this planet, but we'd be stuck. Run out of food and water eventually and starve to death."

"I see. Not a very inviting picture of your world so far, all this talk of weapons and enemies and death."

Somewhat irritated by what he heard as criticism, Nate said, "We didn't set out to make life about war. We expanded into what became the Sectors, making peaceful contacts and treaties with the other sentients. Trade alliances, you name it. And then the Mawreg hit, like a barrage of black holes through a crowded planetary system. And it's been war for sheer survival ever since, wherever the enemy and their allies make an incursion. And if the Mawreg ever do penetrate this system, by chance or on our trail, the ship'll draw them in immediately. We'll have to trigger the final self-destruct. Can't take any chances."

"Can we at least wait until tomorrow?" Thom said reasonably. "I've been dreaming about a shower and a decent meal all day. Well, hell, for months actually, but especially today, knowing we'd be at the ship. I'll grant you the bunks in this thing don't compare to a real planetside bed, but we ain't exactly had any of those either since we left here. It'd be nice to sleep one night without being on guard, in chains, crawled over by vermin—"

Nate laughed. "We'll stay tonight. The Mawreg probably aren't anywhere near this side of the galaxy, much less this system. One more night won't hurt. Gotta admit I'd like a real shower and food myself, even ship food."

"I know something else you'll want," Thom said, opening the kitbag and reaching inside.

He flourished a lethal, burnished black Mark 27 blaster.

"How many do we have?" Nate eagerly took the one Thom had brought for him, inspecting it and checking the counter on the grip. "Fully charged. We can protect ourselves a whole lot better on this crazy planet now."

"Three more in the weapons locker, with extra charges," Thom said, his voice conveying deep satisfaction about going properly armed from now on.

"Are these weapons so much better than the ones you found in the warehouse?" Bithia asked, leaning over to see the Mark 27.

"With yours, we could only render living creatures and their immediate surroundings into piles of ash. Kind of frustrating, to say the least. You can use Mark 27s as a blaster or to stun someone or something. They're pinpoint accurate, or can be set for wide spray. The Mark 27 has a longer range. The charge supports extended use—"

"I guess your people are more effective at designing lethal weapons. Perhaps mine were better at peaceful things."

He left the pilot's chair, setting aside the blaster, and gave her a quick hug. "I'm sure all civilizations have their good points and their flaws."

"Excepting the Mawreg," Thom said, index finger raised to emphasize his point. "Only bad with them—flawed, as you called it, from start to finish of their evolution."

Bithia leaned into Nate's embrace. "What now?"

"Lady gets first dibs on the shower," Thom said. "In the meantime, I'll work on organizing dinner." He pointed at Nate. "At some point I should check on your injuries from yesterday."

"Does this vessel have a name?" Bithia asked as Nate preceded her from the control chamber. "We named our ships."

"We do too," Nate assured her. "This is the *Murphy*, named for a Special Forces hero from our original home planet."

"A pleasing sound. Show me this shower you speak of. And then I'm hungry. I have all those years in the healing chamber to make up for."

Laughing, they retraced their previous path through the ship, Nate escorting Bithia to the small quarters area.

Bithia rejoined them later, dressed in a fresh blue tunic embroidered with fanciful lavender and green flowers. Her leggings matched the green of the flowers, with a hint of lavender threads in the weaving of the fabric. The outfit was from her pack, the lady having declined to wear a Sectors uniform, no matter how practical it might be. Her masses of hair were held away from her face by two black enamel clips set with small emeralds. "Celixia did an excellent job of trading during her day at the markets of Poqueteele."

She kept Thom company in the tiny galley while he prepared dinner and Nate took his shower.

A revived, refreshed Nate appeared in the combination galley and dining area as Thom and Bithia finished setting out the last dishes.

Thom whistled. "Spit and polish, man. Recruiting poster!"

Nate took a mock swing at his friend, who ducked easily out of the way. "Feels good to have the right uniform on again."

Bithia stared at him, a little shy of this crisp stranger in the formfitting black and silver uniform, black space boots, the Mark 27 riding at his hip in its battered holster, his thick chestnut hair now cropped short.

"You look so different," she murmured as he sat next to her. She touched his neatly trimmed beard. "I'm glad you kept this."

"Same old Nate," he said cheerfully, taking her hand and kissing it. "Less dust and dirt, certainly less hair, but same guy. Okay?"

"Of course." She studied Thom, raising one hand to finger his red hair. "Are you going to change as much?"

He blushed. "Well, ma'am, depends what you mean by change. I guess so. I mean, no one wears their hair as long in the forces as the guys on this planet. And Nate's right, our own uniform works for me better than this kilt and cloak costume."

"Let's eat," Nate interrupted. "You fixed six weeks' worth of rations."

"If we're going to slag the ship tomorrow or the day after, figured we might as well enjoy ourselves while we can. Most of this stuff can't be carried on the trail, since there's no way to reconstitute it." Thom passed a heaping plate of biscuits to Bithia. "Try these, ma'am. Not as good as those six-spice cake things, but probably better with beef and gravy. As reconstituted by the AI, of course."

"It is all fine," she said. "Except for those, whatever they are." Brow furrowed, she pushed away a plate of green beans. "Nasty. I can't believe you're going to eat such a repulsive dish."

"When you're through insulting our vegetables," Nate said, "we'd better discuss what to do next. I hadn't planned beyond getting to this ship."

"Ever since we was captured, the only thing I could think of was getting here and taking off in triumph, leaving Sarbordon and Lolanta and all of them in our back flash," Thom agreed around a mouthful of beef and gravy. "And then somehow finding our way to the Sectors." He took a long swallow of his drink and laughed ruefully as he set the glass on the table. "I worried about the astronavigation issues, not whether the damn ship would fly in the first place. I mean, Haranda was so positive."

"I have a proposal." Bithia spoke into the silence, toying with her plate. "Something I've been thinking about since we escaped the city."

"And?" Fork in midair, bite of steak forgotten, Nate eyed her.

"My father's main base was in the mountains. Since you say we can't stay on this ship, and I must admit it would be cramped and confining, could we not journey north? If the facility is even partly intact, we'd have a good base of operations."

Nate was interested, but his enthusiasm was tempered by a healthy skepticism. "How far north are we talking about? What if the facility was gutted, like the lab in Nochen? Why would someone go to so much effort in Nochen if they weren't going to be as thorough at the main site?"

"But the warehouse survived intact." Bithia had her counterargument ready. "Maybe the cleanup crew—whoever they were—didn't have as much leisure for disassembly of facilities as you believe. The three of us are technology-based people." She waved her hand at the galley fixtures. "High technology! I don't think either of you relish the idea of going to the lowlands and joining Atletl's army, or becoming farmers here on the plateau. Do you? What other career can we have in this place? Try to reinvent some hybrid of our own level of civilization with virtually nothing?"

Nate laid his eating utensils next to his plate and took a long drink of juice. Without looking at her, he said, "I want to be sure why we'd do that. If you're asking us to travel there in case your father left you some kind of message or—"

"No." She shook her head with a flash of anger. "I told you on the beach I'd finally, fully accepted my past life is over. Vanished. I wouldn't ask you and Thom to go with me to the main facility if my only reason was such a forlorn hope." She took his hand, waiting for him to meet her eyes. "We built a huge facility. The workers were obviously in a hurry at Nochen since the contents of the warehouse were left untouched. There may be all kinds of things left at the mountain base. Even if we decide for whatever reason not to live there, we can equip ourselves much better for life on Talonque on our own terms, more in the style I think we are all used to, comfortable with." She reached for her gilintrae, then stopped. "I forgot, nearly out of power. I'd show you the location on the holo map, but the base is built inside the crater of an extinct volcano."

"T'naritza, the Sleeping Goddess, I know." Nate grinned. "I've heard the story of the volcanic mountain where she was supposedly born more than once. Your father having built his base there undoubtedly contributed to you being seen as the goddess, you know."

Wrinkling her brow in a frown, she didn't deign to comment. "We ride north for a few days along the great road to the farthest village, and then it's a day's climb to the destination we seek. It'll be hard, but not impossible. And worth it if we find what I hope may be left there to salvage."

Raising an eyebrow, Nate checked with Thom. "You up for this?"

"Got nothing better to do, and the potential rewards outweigh the effort. I don't like the idea of going south again, I gotta tell you. Not if there are other options. So, sure, why not take a chance on exploring for alien treasures?"

Nate turned to Bithia. "You're positive the base is going to be accessible from ground level? What if your gilintrae doesn't have enough power to open the flyer tunnel door? Or if the last people to leave sealed it when they departed?"

"My father established a spot where the local leaders could come and meet with him. It was the farthest the villagers were willing to climb on the mountain due to superstitions about not waking the goddess. I walked there with him several times. He enjoyed learning the local legends, collecting the songs—novelty was all part of what drew him to explore new worlds, not solely motivated by the scientific rewards and the profits from importing exotic luxury goods. There's an access door beside the flyer tunnel we used for these walks down the mountain. With your weapons, I'm sure we can force our way in should I be unable to activate the controls."

"Sounds like you have it pretty well planned out." *She must have dreamed many times about doing this during all those years she was held captive in Nochen.* "All right, here's to successful mountain climbing."

Thom and Bithia raised their glasses and drank to his toast cheerfully.

Nate had to admit he relished having a purpose, even if it had nothing to do with getting them home. He'd been more depressed than he wanted to admit to either Thom or Bithia when he realized the *Murphy* wouldn't be leaving Talonque. He'd never had a fixed home in the Sectors, unlike some guys, but anywhere there was more home than Talonque could ever be. A man couldn't ask for better companions to be marooned for life with than Bithia and Thom, but it would have been so much more ideal to be in the Sectors, whether working at the consulting business he and Thom had planned, or doing something else. Bithia's proposal for their next course of action was inviting and felt right to pursue.

He finished his dinner with renewed appetite.

After the meal, he and Thom went to work sorting through the contents of the ship, setting aside whatever might be useful in their new life among the planet-bound. They left anything impractical for living planetside or too bulky to be transported on kemat.

"Not too much we want to take," Nate said, eyeing the pile of items on the galley table. "Weapons, meds, change of uniform, a few personal items from our own kits, not too much in the way of food or drink. We'll pack this in the saddle bags at first light, slag the ship and be on our way. No reason to linger."

"Will the kemat be all right out there tonight, you think?" Thom asked, raising an eyebrow at Bithia. "Any large natural predators? I can set the sonic perimeters if need be."

"Might be a good idea anyway," Nate said. "Let us all get a good night's sleep, which is something hard to come by on this planet, I've found. I don't want to leave a warm bunk in the middle of the night to go tangle with a mountain lion or whatever the local variation is."

"Consider it done." Thom rose from the bench.

"I'll do it. You were on guard all last night. Go grab your shower, and then why don't you hit the rack?"

"You sure?" Plainly tempted, Thom hesitated.

"You must be the most exhausted of us all," Bithia said. "You stood guard all night and rode all day. I can help with sorting."

"No more argument from this boy, then. See you in the morning." Thom yawned and left the galley, heading aft.

Nate and Bithia took a few more moments, organizing the supplies. Then they too left the galley and strolled to the front of the ship. Bithia watched while Nate instructed the AI to activate the sonic perimeter thirty yards out.

"Does this AI remember the way home to your Sectors?"

He laced his fingers behind his head and leaned back in the pilot's chair. "It has the coordinates of the blue giant where we first veered off course. It probably has the sequence of the hyperspace nexi we passed through on our wild ride here, despite how fast it all happened. And it contains all the star maps for the Sectors, which is one reason we have to slag any permanently disabled ship. Can't risk the Mawreg getting their multieyes on the classified data. So in summary, yes, the AI remembers how to get us home. But without a ship, what good does the navigation data do?"

She tapped the gilintrae on her arm. "The idea of allowing such irreplaceable information to be destroyed when there may be a way to save it bothers me. Let me see if my device can communicate with yours and capture the data."

"Didn't you say your fancy bracelet was out of power?" But Nate rose from the chair to let her take his place. Fine with him if she wanted to make an attempt and interesting to see if her technology could cross the gap between ancient alien and Sectors AI techniques.

Bithia sat gracefully, studying the console for a long moment, passing her hand an inch or two above the surface of the board. "This AI is a mind, is it not?"

"Not exactly. In the big ships, like the *Andromeda* battle cruiser, the AI is a fully conscious, registered sentient. But on little vessels like this, there's only a rudimentary, partial system. A brain stem, you might say, keeping the vital functions of the ship going, but not capable of the complex processing that the big systems—or the human brain—carry out. Doesn't have those modules."

"A helpful explanation, thank you." Closing her eyes, she began to hum, almost inaudibly, holding a steady note that extended on and on, as if she no longer needed to breathe. A faint vibration rippled through his own mind, an oddly off-balance sensation, as if he were about to slip sideways into a whirlpool. He shook his head to dispel it, not wanting to be drawn into whatever she was doing with the AI. *There are some disadvantages to these hidden abilities of mine.* The note she hummed affected him once more. The vertigo was more pronounced, and he regretted the big dinner he'd eaten.

Not wanting to disturb her, but curious to check the gilintrae, which she held parallel to the console, Nate leaned over her shoulder. A line of single, fat green motes of light looped from the jeweled cuff and to the console and back.

"Whatever," Nate said to himself and retreated to the rear observer's chair to wait for the end of this experiment. The beds on the *Murphy* were narrow, but if Bithia was in the mood to be creative, he had some ideas for whiling away the night in an interesting fashion in the privacy of the pilot's cabin.

He fought someone, striking out as if he was drunk or waking from a deep sleep. Nate tried to land a blow, but his opponent dodged, calling his name and swearing. "In the name of the seven hells, snap out of it, Nate, wake up!"

Thom shook him roughly again as Nate stared around the cockpit, staggering under his friend's violent treatment. Raising one hand, he said, "I'm okay, I'm awake, thanks."

Releasing his tight grip on Nate's shirt, Thom retreated a step. "What happened in here? I was afraid I'd never get you conscious again. Had me worried."

Bithia slept, snoring slightly, head on the control console.

Nate frowned, concerned at the depth of her slumber despite all the noise he and Thom had made right next to her. He stepped to the pilot's chair and laid a hand on her shoulder, giving her a gentle shake. No response.

"Bithia, time to rise and shine," he said, shaking her harder. He flashed a quick glance at Thom, whose expression was concerned and grim. Nate carefully raised her head from the control console, bracing her neck and shoulders with his arm. She was breathing, he reassured himself, and she had a pulse, though slow and intermittent.

The gilintrae showed no signs of activity.

Closing his eyes for a moment, he searched for their link and found only glowing embers where usually the flame burned steady.

Swearing, Nate plucked her from the chair. "Get the medkit on the double and meet me in the sleeping quarters. I think we need a strong stimulant. She's way under. I shouldn't have let her try her crazy idea, and I shouldn't have gone to sleep myself."

"Try what?" Thom followed on Nate's heels down the main corridor. "What was she doing at the controls?"

"Trying to communicate directly with the AI. I know it sounds crazy, but she was determined to save the trip data for us so we could find our way home someday. I didn't see any harm in it, but whatever she did had a hypnotizing effect on me. Get the medkit."

Her attempts at communication with the AI had lulled him to sleep, and he'd been on the periphery of whatever mental sweep she'd conducted. The effects on Bithia herself must have been tenfold what hit him.

Alarmed, Nate moved faster, being careful not to bump Bithia's head as he maneuvered through the tight spaces of the courier ship. As Nate laid her gently on the pilot's bunk, Thom hastened into the tiny cabin, juggling an armful of medical supplies.

He knelt beside the bunk and spread the contents of the medkit on the deck to decide what inject to try. "We don't know if she can tolerate our medications," Thom said. "This could be a real mistake. You sure you don't want to wait awhile, see if she sleeps it off?"

Nate took Bithia's pulse again, holding her left wrist firmly. He shook his head. "Even slower than before. We can't wait. What you got?"

Thom narrowed his choice to two injects, laying them side by side on the bed. He tapped the first one with his right index finger. "Adrenephix. Strongest thing in the medkit." Frowning, he touched the other. "And this is the finest quality, genetically derived neurocrysmeth that credits can buy on the black market—found this in Jurgens' kit yesterday."

"The idiot was mainlining starspeed? He was asking for a fucking heart attack."
Nate whistled. "All his flight pay must have been going into keeping the illegal
cylinder filled."

"And then some," Thom agreed. "But it's a thousand times more potent
than adrenephix."

"We don't need her addicted to that shit." Nate studied Bithia's beautiful face,
and his heart thumped painfully.

"But we do need her to wake up, and this is the stuff to do it. One dose isn't
necessarily addictive, and I have the right injects to administer a narco blocker as
soon as she regains consciousness, before the high kicks in completely. No high,
no addiction."

"Some other time I'll ask how you know all this," Nate said, remembering
Thom originally hailed from a rough Inner Sector planet. "For now I'm nothing
but grateful. Do it."

"You sure?" Thom held the chosen inject, ready to apply it to Bithia's arm.
Nate took Bithia's hand and nodded. Muttering a prayer to the Lords of Space
under his breath, Thom administered the full dose of the highly illegal upper. He
rubbed the site of the inject and sat on his heels. "The reaction may be violent."

"If it works."

"Unless her physiology is totally different from ours, which I doubt, the drug
will work. See her fingers twitching? The starspeed's hitting her central nervous
system about now."

Drawing a huge, gasping breath, Bithia sat bolt upright, shaking uncontrollably,
staring at them with wide-open eyes, apparently not recognizing either man. She
tried to scramble off the bunk. Nate grabbed her and didn't let go, no matter how
she struggled and fought, not even when she clamped her teeth into his shoulder.

"Hurry with the blocker, will you? I don't want to hurt her, and I can't risk
knocking her out again."

"Superhuman strength in short bursts is one of the side effects." Thom worked
frantically to mix the contents of three injects into one, hardly an authorized

procedure. He improvised, without spilling too much of the medications, which would have rendered his antidote too weak to do the job. Finally, he came up with the inject, dodging a flying kick from Bithia's left foot, and slammed the inject into her shoulder. "Sorry, lady, this'll hurt like hell and leave a bruise on your pretty arm, but I gotta do it."

Bithia stiffened from head to toe, sighed deeply and collapsed into Nate's arms, eyes shut. He took a deep breath. "Tell me we're not back to where we started."

"She's fine," Thom said. "Steady breathing. Take her pulse, see for yourself."

"Faster than normal, but definitely better than before. What next?"

"She'll regain consciousness in a moment or two, and she won't remember anything, but she's going to ache all over, with a hell of a headache in particular. She can't have headclear or any other drug for twenty-four hours. Her muscles may spasm off and on for a few hours. She'll definitely have the shakes. Fresh air would be good. We're going to have to stay here another day because she won't be capable of riding."

"I don't care as long as she's going to be all right. It's not as if we have any deadlines now. Not expected to be anywhere at all, in fact, much less at a certain time." Nate leaned close to Bithia, who opened her eyes as predicted, but with great difficulty. "Are you all right, sweetheart? Head hurt?"

"Yes." Wide-eyed, hands going to her stomach, she moaned. "What happened? Why are we in here? I'm going to be sick—"

Thom shoved a small basin under her chin, taking it away again when the episode had passed. "Be a good idea to carry her outside. The fresh air will do her good."

"Am I sick?" she asked as Nate lifted her from the bunk and headed into the corridor. "Why do I feel so wretched?"

"You wanted to communicate with the AI, remember?" Nate said as he awkwardly hit the controls to open the ship's door and lower the gangplank. "You put yourself into some kind of a trance in the process." He carried her down the ramp with great care and set her on the velvet-soft grass in the shade of the ship.

"Sent me to sleep too, but Thom was able to wake me. I nearly took his head off before I regained full consciousness. You were under too deep. We had to give you a drug to shock your system into reviving. Scared me to death."

"Any better, ma'am?" Thom asked as he came out of the ship carrying a couple of blankets from their saddlebags, including her favorite white one from the beach house. He was also balancing a steaming mug.

"The air out here is settling my stomach, but my head hurts so much."

"Drink this." Thom handed her the mug, which she immediately tried to thrust back at him, her face screwed up in a grimace of total repulsion. "I know you think your stomach won't handle it, but trust me, this is the best thing. Hold your breath and get the stuff into your gut somehow."

She gave him a piteous look for a moment, but Thom was unrelenting, pushing the mug toward her lips. She did as ordered and dropped the mug into the grass before reclining with a moan. "The liquid helps, thank you."

Working rapidly, Nate and Thom constructed a small shelter for her out of the blankets and alternated sitting with her throughout the day. Thom plied her with fluids of various types and seemed satisfied by her progress as the day wore on. She had a few attacks of violent shaking, as he'd predicted she might, but Nate wrapped her tightly in the soft blanket and held her until the episodes passed. The one thing he wouldn't allow her was a nap. She complained less and less of the headache and declared she felt quite well as the sun set.

"No solid food until morning. I'll give you headclear then, if the headache returns," Thom said. "It shouldn't, but these things can surprise you."

"I never expected to miss the damn healing chamber." Nate gathered blankets, preparing to move inside the ship for the night. "Sure would have helped today, though."

Bithia drained the latest mug of recommended fluids and handed it to Thom with a flourish. She shook her head. "I wouldn't trade my father's impersonal machine for the devoted care Thom gave me. And you."

"You're right, you—and I—owe your recovery to Thom. One more in a long string of things I owe him. This one is the most important, old friend." Nate clapped his embarrassed sergeant on the shoulder. "I'll always be in your debt."

"It evens out pretty fairly over the years," Thom said. "I'm glad I had the right drugs to work with. Adrenephix wouldn't have done it for her. She was too far under by the time I got to you guys this morning. Wouldn't have been a pretty story without a starspeed inject. Guess we owe Jurgens."

"I bet he got transferred out to the Far Sectors this late in his career because somebody wanted him and his addiction away from the high-rankers he ferried from base to base."

Nate took the folded blanket from Bithia and gave her a hand as she rose from the ground. "As for you, you're not setting foot in the *Murphy*'s control chamber again, nor getting anywhere close to an AI interface port. I don't care if you got the flight data or not, coming so close to losing you wasn't worth the risk. We can stay on Talonque forever before I'll let you take such a chance again."

"I've no desire to repeat this experience, I assure you. I think I did get the information we were after. I have a dim recall of success. But, as you say, we're not likely to have the chance to use whatever I saved."

"Talonqueni immigrants." Thom assumed an air of good cheer. "I'm getting real used to the idea."

"Sure you are," Nate said as he bounded up the gangplank into the *Murphy*. "Reveling in it like the rest of us, I bet."

The ship's portal closed on the sound of their laughter.

CHAPTER TWELVE

After setting the controls for self-destruct and complying with every last word of Sectors ship-abandonment regulations, Nate and Thom stood and watched the ship melt in upon itself. They remained, stoically observing, until the *Murphy* was nothing but a pool of molten metal, seeping into the ground below. Bithia said she found it too depressing to watch the entire sad process. She'd taken herself off to sit in the shade of a small tree and wait until her companions felt free to leave. When the last of the ship's material disappeared below the surface, Nate gave the order to saddle the kemat and ride away.

Nate was relieved to leave the area of the ship, abandoning his hope to get home as well. They rode all day without seeing anyone or anything, not even wildlife. The first night on the trail he'd selected a peaceful spot beside the upper tributary of the river for a camp, fished for dinner and slept soundly. The next morning they'd boldly taken to the great road, galloping past the few other travelers with impunity. The only people they met were Githholz stragglers or small-time trading caravans, all going southward. No one else appeared to be interested in heading to the mountains.

"It's partly the season," Bithia said. "The trading time is over, and winter will soon be upon us. The winters in the foothills and mountains are particularly fierce. Only the hardy people who actually live in these parts will stay over winter."

"Great, and we're heading straight into this bad weather?" Nate asked, remembering too late her penchant for leaving out little details, as she called them, here and there. "What if we can't winter over in your father's base? Or decide we don't want to?"

"It'll only take a few days to get there and find out," Bithia said confidently. "If we find living there is impossible, we can be safely on our way to the plateau or even all the way to the south before the winter gales develop."

"I don't know, maybe a trip to that southern island Atletl and Celixia claimed to be from, back at Poqueteele, might not be such a bad idea if we're going to be marooned on this planet." Thom's voice held genuine longing. "At least it'd be warm and we could fish."

So he and his two companions had ridden and debated their range of future choices, companionably, not too worried about anything but beating the first storms of winter. It was good to have a new purpose to replace all the planning and hopes he'd centered on the *Murphy*, although Nate was concerned about what to plan for after the excursion to the mountain facility was concluded. He worried about Bithia's reaction once she'd explored the last possible link to her father and her home. Her reassurances about not pinning too much hope on finding the main base operational sounded convincing, but he had his doubts.

As they traveled, the road rose imperceptibly until the track suddenly veered east to parallel the foothills. Bithia directed their small party to a narrow one-lane trail branching away from the main road and winding into the foothills, serving as the main passage through the mountains to the lands beyond. There'd been a town, which had taken them a day to cautiously detour around. Nate had no desire to set foot in such a large place, or attract attention, which would have been inevitable.

After two more days of slow going into the foothills and then the mountains themselves, leaving the road and detouring onto an even narrower, more winding trail, he'd made the decision to abandon the kemat, which were showing signs of respiratory distress. Nate traded them to a delighted subsistence farmer, whose family grew a few vegetables and tended a herd of sheeplike creatures at high elevation. The farmer gave them food and a single beast of burden, which was sufficient to carry their combined, pared-down possessions.

"He thinks we're fools, lowland idiots, trading four kemat for this homely old creature and some food," Bithia told Nate as they trudged away from the farm the next morning, working their way along the narrow, steep mountain road.

"I don't care what he thinks," Nate said. "And I don't like this damn, what do you call it? Yallurt? Acts like the classic description of a stubborn terran mule I once read about. Now I understand the concept vividly."

"Yes, but the beast is so strong." Bithia laughed, watching him and Thom trying to inspire the sturdy creature to proceed up the trail. "And basically sweet-natured."

"Sweet to you maybe, ma'am," Thom said in disgust as the yallurt finally condescended to trot a few yards. "It don't like me, and the feeling is definitely mutual. This animal ain't gonna replace the kemat in my affections."

"You don't appear to have any instinctive link with yallurt, the way you did with the noble kemat."

They made pretty good time in the mountains once Thom figured out the trick of encouraging the yallurt with handfuls of sweet grass. Nate thought it was a good thing they were hiking, since the trek gave them time to acclimatize to the ever-increasing altitude and resulting decrease in oxygen.

Nate heard music long before they came upon the village tucked into a bend in the mountain trail. The remote pocket of civilization was a small hamlet consisting of perhaps two dozen houses and outbuildings. The mountain trail became an unpaved street, leading to the heart of the village. The men pulled the hoods of their capes more firmly over their heads to shadow their faces.

Perhaps this high in the mountains, the people won't have heard anything about us. Nate needed a good night's rest and decent food before attempting the final ascent to Fr'taray's main facility. Bithia and Thom weren't in any better shape.

He got the impression the entire population of the town was gathered for a feast or a party or whatever the festive occasion was. The three weary travelers and their single pack animal stood on the edge of the small square and watched the dancers, unnoticed at first. Then people began to stare, nudging each other and whispering. Finally, the musicians fell silent in a discordant ending to what had been a rollicking dance tune. Everyone in the square stood and gaped at the trio of new arrivals.

"Please, we don't mean to disturb you." Bithia's voice carried effortlessly across the plaza. "We've come a long, hard way from the lowlands on a pilgrimage to T'naritza's mountain. We only wish to buy some food."

"And perhaps a room, shelter for the night," Nate said. "We can pay."

People glanced uneasily at each other for a moment. Finally, an elderly man in a wildly colorful overshirt and loose pants woven from black, orange and bright turquoise threads stepped forward. The villagers parted silently to make way for him. He made a welcoming gesture with his hands and bowed. "I am Hatur, First Elder of Shalonn. We're celebrating the wedding of my granddaughter tonight." He waved a hand at a young woman standing arm in arm with her new husband in the center of the now motionless dancers. "While it is much past the customary season for pilgrims, guests are always welcome at a wedding feast, as you surely must know, even in the lowlands. Please, come and join me. Speak no more of money—you'll be my personal guests."

"I appreciate your welcome and your kindness." Bithia stepped gracefully through the plaza beside Hatur, Nate and Thom silently following. She made quick work of introductions, adding, "Our good wishes to the newlywed couple."

Hatur summoned one of his grandsons to take charge of the pack animal, and it was led away, complaining but docile.

Not sure he liked the crowd's reserved demeanor, Nate decided to follow Bithia's lead. He made sure she was comfortably seated at the long table, in the place of honor next to Hatur, and had a glass of the local wine and a plate of steaming meat, vegetables and bread. He and Thom took positions behind her chair, alert but not overly so. The Mark 27 riding at his hip was a constant reassurance these days. Despite not encountering any trouble since leaving the ship hundreds of miles away, Nate was wary.

Nate watched serving girls place plates and wine in front of Bithia. He reached around her to snare a choice bit of crispy roasted meat. Bithia unhooked the clasp of her black cloak and removed it. A small sigh escaped the crowd as her long, flowing blue and purple hair was revealed in the torchlight and the delicate planes of her face came more clearly into view.

Hatur kept his composure admirably. Nate pushed his own hood back, Thom following suit a moment later. He bet Thom was the only redheaded person of either sex on the entire planet. His own chestnut-brown hair didn't blend in too well with the glossy black predominant hair color, but it was sure a lot less noticeable than Thom's or Bithia's.

Hatur harangued the musicians, who were gaping at Bithia from their platform off to the side of the head table, instruments forgotten. "Why aren't you playing? Haven't I paid you and fed you well enough, and yes, given you wine, lazy ones? We must dance, and my clumsy friends and neighbors can't do the steps without your noise!"

A ripple of laughter greeted his sally. The five musicians launched into a new tune, more or less together, and slowly the crowd resumed the evening's program of dancing and dining. Conscious of a great many sidelong glances in their direction, Nate regretted not discussing with Bithia in advance how they should present themselves in the village.

He leaned down to speak to her. "These people have to know who you are. Or who you're supposed to be."

"Yes," she agreed absently. "What does it matter now? Sarbordon and Lolanta are dead. We've nothing more to fear from them or any of their people. Why don't you and Thom relax and have something to eat?"

"Later."

The bride and groom danced to the table and paused. "We're honored you chose to bless us with your presence, great lady," the bride said, eyes demurely lowered. "Won't you join us in the dancing?"

Bithia cast an appealing look at Nate, who kept his countenance unreadable. He'd done any number of things for her on this planet, but dancing wasn't going to be one of them. "I'm afraid we don't know the steps, but thank you," she told the girl.

"The next dance is only for the women, and all present must dance or bad luck follows."

"I'll be pleased to dance in the circle. Thank you."

Nate helped her get out of her chair and handed her gallantly onto the dancing floor. Immediately surrounded by a laughing, happy circle of women and girls, Bithia whirled away into a rollicking circle dance weaving like a tolokon through every inch of the village square. Nate and Thom watched her obvious enjoyment.

Thom leaned over to tell Nate defiantly, "All I can say is there'd better not be a dance for the men, or I'm out of here."

"You and me both. Local customs be damned."

"You mean they didn't teach you to dance at that fancy school?"

"Let's say I paid more attention to the sword-fighting lessons."

The music changed tempo, and suddenly the men and boys of the village were moving into the square, each seeking his choice of partner and separating her from the hand-linked chain of revelers.

"I don't like this," Nate said.

Bithia continued dancing, hand in hand with some young girls now, but she seemed nervous as the men surged into the area.

Nate vaulted the table and moved quickly to her side. Smoothly, he took her hand from the youngest girl and swept them both out of the dance, saying, "I can't choose between you, ladies, so you'll both have to be my partner for the evening, agreed?"

"Thank you," Bithia said a bit breathlessly.

The young girl stared at him with awestruck dark eyes. "Are you serious?"

"Absolutely, my lady. What's your name?"

"Sharla," she confided, suddenly shy. But then she perked up, head high, making sure all her friends observed how the Lady's warrior had chosen her. Nate judged she was about six. He'd only taken her hand and twirled her a time or two to smooth over his abrupt extraction of Bithia from the dance, but now he decided to play out the game. She was pretty, with long, shiny black hair falling in ringlets. Her dress was a riotous mixture of oranges, pinks and turquoise, and her small feet were shod in soft pink woven slippers.

When Nate got both ladies to the table, Thom had two chairs waiting. Bithia and Sharla sat, and Nate sat beside them. A plate was brought for him, and he made a game of feeding his new lady whichever tidbits she wanted from the feast.

She told him all about her friends and her pets and generally chattered away in the open manner of small children the galaxywide. Nate listened and asked questions when necessary, and finally she drifted off to sleep against his shoulder.

"I'm impressed," Bithia told him. "You were good with her."

"I have friends with kids at home," he said, gently handing Sharla off to an old woman who came to claim her. The little girl didn't even stir from her dreams.

"My granddaughter will be full of herself for the entire cold season now, warrior," said Hatur, leaning across Bithia to address Nate.

"I hope I haven't gotten myself handfasted or anything, sir," he said with a laugh. "She surely is cute."

"The favorite of this old heart certainly," the elderly headman agreed. "The bride and groom will be retiring soon, accompanied by their more raucous friends, and then we old ones can decently seek our beds. May I offer you the hospitality of my own house, great lady?"

"I'd be honored, sir, as long as it doesn't create any hardship for you?"

"The headman's house is the largest in the village, and since my last child has married away from my household today, I've more room than I need. Let me escort you."

"But Thom—my other warrior—hasn't eaten."

"I've been sneaking bits here and there," Thom said.

Nate knew they were both eager to get out of this public place without further delay.

"In the morning after breakfast, I can escort you to the Place of Meditation on the mountain's flank," Hatur said graciously as they strolled across the now nearly empty plaza.

"Thanks just the same, but we can find it ourselves," Nate said. "We'll be leaving before dawn on our pilgrimage up the mountain, sir, so we'll try not to disturb you as we go."

Hatur seemed puzzled and a little hurt, but didn't press the point. Indeed the most imposing in the village, his house boasted two stories, although the second floor was more of a low-ceilinged loft than an actual set of full-sized rooms. He led them up the narrow stairs to the loft and left them to sort out the sleeping arrangements. He popped up the ladder one more time to inform them he'd leave a tray of fruits and breads for their breakfast.

Bithia thanked him excessively as Hatur appeared to expect, and then they finally had peace and quiet. Even the shouts of the last, drunken revelers died away in the square as the party completely wound down and the musicians packed their instruments and sought their own beds.

At this altitude, especially after a full day of climbing, it didn't take long to fall asleep. Thom took the first watch of the night, and Nate traded off with him a few hours later. Bithia slumbered peacefully in one low bed, covered warmly with quilts and furs. Thom curled on the other bed, the one Nate had just vacated, too short and too narrow for a full-grown man, and did his best to get comfortable. Soon he too slept, as evidenced by his low snoring, as his arms and legs draped off the bed, a man too tired to care about comfort.

Nate stared out the single window, which provided an excellent view of the mountain trail. Prepared for an uneventful watch, he did a double take when he noticed a line of torches coming into view on the farthest curve, wavering along the trail. *Someone's in a hell of a hurry to get to this outpost if they're climbing at night.* Nate woke Thom quietly. "Trouble. Big party coming up the trail."

"At this hour?" Thom moved quickly to the window, drawing his Mark 27, while Nate woke Bithia.

"Time to evac," Nate said, watching the lights move closer. The torchlit procession hit the last set of curves and would soon be at the edge of town. "This loft have a back door?"

"Why are you so sure this is something to do with us?" Bithia asked sleepily, stifling a yawn. "I'm reluctant to leave the warmth of the bed."

"You told us no one comes here at this season, not without a damn good reason. Too much coincidence for me." Nate ruthlessly flipped the quilts to the floor and drew her to her feet, wrapping her cloak around her shoulders. "We need to move."

"No other exit," Thom reported.

"We'll have to make time out the front and hope for the best. Come on."

Nate led them quietly down the stairs. Despite their attempt at stealth, Hatur and his grandson met them at the front door, the headman wrapping himself in a quilted red and orange robe. He nodded as he realized his guests were awake and dressed, ready for departure.

"Someone is coming, great lady," the headman said.

"We know. The newcomers could mean trouble for her, so we need to get her out of here. Is there someplace we can hide in the village, sir?" Nate asked.

Rubbing his chin, Hatur pondered the question. The boy tugged at his sleeve. "I can take them to the stable's basement, Grandda, but we have to hurry."

"Excellent, go there. Daven will guide you. Quickly!"

The boy led them outside and in a crouching run to the stable behind. The yallurt continued to munch hay, snuffling a welcome as Nate hastened past. Daven kicked aside bins, and the men shifted a few bales of hay to reveal a trapdoor in the floor.

"I'll let you out as soon as the visitors leave the village, or as soon as we find out there's no menace." The boy whirled and was gone at a run.

Raising the heavy wooden door, Nate eyed the unappealing, dark stairs leading to the cellar. Bithia touched his arm. "You said we must hide, so why the hesitation?"

He stepped back and studied the hayloft before glancing at Thom. "You thinking what I'm thinking?"

"Hell, yes, always take the high ground."

Nate spotted a crude ladder fastened to one wall by the yallurt's stall. He unhooked the ladder and assisted Bithia in climbing its rickety steps to the loft. Thom followed her. Nate restored the ladder to the wall and then jumped, Thom catching his hands. The sergeant hauled him the rest of the way into the loft.

"Window over here, Nate." Thom quietly opened a set of shutters on the barn's rear wall.

"Can we get out?"

"Nice handy tree right there." Thom pointed at the large tree growing close to the building. The branches rubbed the stable walls in spots. "We can get out of here and fade into the hills."

"You first, and I'll hand Bithia out to you."

Thom holstered his weapon and clambered through the open window, stepping cautiously out onto a massive tree branch.

"Why are we doing this?" Bithia asked as she prepared to follow Thom. "Don't you trust these people?"

Nate shook his head. "I don't trust any situation I can't control on this damn planet. I'm not staying in some cellar, or even in this loft, in a building where I'm expected to be. Just a precaution. No more talking, we need to move. Be careful out there."

She swayed on the slick surface of the tree branch, but Thom quickly lowered her to the ground. He jumped after her, and they moved off, efficiently taking advantage of the shadows, Nate coming right behind them. They worked their way behind the neighboring houses, none of which had windows facing in this direction, and took a spot four houses away from Hatur's stable, hidden behind a wooden fence, peering through the uneven slats to watch what transpired.

The torch-bearing party came into the central square of the town and spread out into a loose circle, the soldiers' demeanors on the aimless side, as they were trying to decide what to do next. One man pounded on the door of the headman's house. The loud knocking reverberated like thunder in the early morning air.

The door opened slightly, and Hatur peered out sleepily. Suddenly, the old headman was seized and dragged from his house into the square. As the party of newcomers regrouped, the torchlight fell squarely on the face of a man standing behind the others.

"Sarbordon!" Bithia gasped, doing a double take as the dawn light revealed the newcomer's identity. Hand at her mouth, she shrank from the fence. "It's really him!"

"Son of a bitch, you're right." Nate confirmed their enemy's identity with his enhanced night vision. "He must have left Nochen right after discovering you were gone. And he sure as hell understood where to come searching for you."

"There's one of the damn priestesses," Thom said.

"Shh, I want to hear what he's saying."

Fortunately, sound carried well in the still morning air. Sarbordon, surrounded by one priestess and a squad of ten soldiers, harangued Hatur and the few towns-people brave enough, or foolhardy enough, to come outside. The former ruler demanded to know if T'naritza or her warriors had been seen in vicinity.

"I'm the headman of this town and the voice who speaks to the goddess," Hatur informed the disheveled noble. Even in torchlight, the deposed ruler's appearance was haggard, as if he hadn't slept or eaten properly in a long time. "The Lady hasn't walked abroad in the land since well before the time of your forefathers, sir."

"But she was seen with two of her warriors farther down the mountain trail a few days ago. She has to have come here." The dethroned king's tone grew more angry and strident. "There's nowhere else for her to go, fool. Don't lie to me."

"No one calling herself T'naritza has walked in this village in at least ten generations. Behind me you see her mountain," Hatur informed his unwelcome guest with a sweeping gesture at the looming peak. "You must seek her there, at her home. Maybe she'll speak to you. Maybe she won't. It shall be as the goddess wills it. Does she regard you with favor?" Hatur peered closely at Sarbordon's face.

"I can ensure her favor. Or her cooperation at least." The former ruler laughed shrilly. Bithia leaned on Nate, hiding her face in the curve of his shoulder. He gave her a quick, reassuring squeeze as the former king ranted on. "I know all about your rituals, old man, and how you communicate with the goddess, how you call her forth. I've read the old tablets. We'll take the children and you. My priestess will conduct the ceremony herself, perform the sacrificial rite." The woman in black, who looked oddly familiar to Nate, nodded and smiled. On her, the expression was feral, like a predator scenting helpless prey. Something about this priestess was eerily reminiscent of Lolanta. The comparison turned Nate's stomach.

"We don't sacrifice to T'naritza," Hatur protested in confusion. "The chosen children drink of the sacred herb wine and dream, and the goddess speaks to the dreamers in the dream. But the ceremony is only done at the solstice, and this is months past then."

"You speak of old ways, inefficient ways, foolish man. Warm beating hearts and blood call gods," Sarbordon said. "If she speaks only to children, then so be it." He grabbed Hatur by the robe with both hands and threw him to the ground. "Tie him up. Search the village and make sure she's not here. Bring me all the children!"

"What is he doing? Is he mad?" Bithia lifted her head from Nate's shoulder and stared across the square. "What does he want the children for?"

Nate closed his eyes for a moment, knowing the answer to that. He opened his eyes a breath later and looked at Thom, who nodded, obviously thinking the same thing. "Gonna get ugly."

"Can't you do something with these terrible weapons of yours?" Distressed as the ramifications of the talk about the children sank in, Bithia had a tight grip on Nate's arm. "We have to help these people. It's our fault the village is in this trouble."

"Thom and I'll do what we can, but now is not the time. No one's in direct jeopardy right at this moment. Too many innocent people are in the way for us to launch an attack. There's no guarantee we can get Sarbordon from this distance. We might have to hunt him house to house in a firefight, destroy the whole place. You don't want that. Trust us, okay?" Nate was in combat mode, cold and emotionless.

Recoiling at his unusual tone, Bithia started to say something, but then bit her lip and nodded reluctantly. "Waging war lies outside my area of expertise. I trust your judgment."

The rest of the villagers were appearing in the square, herded by the soldiers at sword and spearpoint. The house-to-house search was cursory, and the guards never made any move in the direction of the backyard fence where Nate and his companions hid. From their halfhearted attitude, he surmised the lowland men were less than fully engaged in this personal mission of their ruler's. He wondered if he could play on their reluctance to his advantage.

The children clung to their parents, terrified by this unprecedented event. Some wailed. The former king and the priestess walked along the line of villagers, examining the children one by one, pulling out a small boy, then another, then two girls who appeared to be twins. Their last selection was Sharla, the little girl who'd been Nate's dinner partner the night before.

Nate, Thom and Bithia watched this winnowing process silently, tight-lipped. As the black-clad woman went in and out of the torchlight, Nate studied her face, trying to figure out where he recognized her from. "Got it," he said. "She's Lolanta's daughter, Nanzin."

"The one who nearly caught us in the throne room in Nochen?" Thom squinted to view the woman better.

"The same. Remember what Celixia said about her? She was almost worse than her mother? I'm ready to believe it," Nate said. "No mercy."

The priestess took charge of the children, looping a length of cord lightly around each tot's chubby wrists and herding them away from their families and onto the trail leading to the mountain. Two of the guards accompanied her.

The small crowd of villagers standing sullenly behind the ring of spears was silent now.

Sarbordon yanked Hatur to his feet and pushed him toward the trailhead. The lowland ruler harangued the crowd of villagers as his soldiers moved out. "No one is to follow or interfere, do you understand me? All I want is to speak to the goddess. She and I have unfinished business. Then we'll release your children and the old man after they've called her for me. Everything will be fine."

"Hand over their bodies, he means," Nate said. "We've got to get to the Place of Meditation Hatur mentioned before the enemy does, if possible."

"He's leaving a rearguard to block the trail," Thom pointed out. "Can't go openly without a fight. The sound will warn the enemy we're coming. We need the element of surprise."

"Do you know any alternative routes to the spot?" Nate asked Bithia.

"I only walked down from the facility above," she said. "I've never seen it from this side."

"All right, you two wait here. I'm going to find Daven. I don't see him in the crowd, so he's probably at the stable trying to find us. Maybe he knows a shortcut."

Nate rolled over and got to his feet in a low crouch, working his way along the concealing fence line and disappearing behind the nearest house. A few minutes later, Nate shepherded a nervous Daven with him. "The boy says there's a quicker, more direct way to this place where Sarbordon's going. He and some of his friends used to sneak up there to spy on the ceremonies, since none of them were selected to be the dreamers themselves. Let's move it."

"Wait." Bithia took the boy's hand in her own. "I'm sorry we've brought this trouble to your village. We never meant to be the cause of any harm, least of all to Hatur and the children. My warriors and I will rescue your people if you can help us now."

Daven swallowed hard. Nate could see him shaking. "We're a peaceful town, Lady. We know nothing of weapons, of soldiers. We grow the mountain klixen for their wool, shear it and dye it, and then make blankets to sell to the lowlander traders. No one ever attacked us. All we know how to fight is the mountain predators trying to steal our klixen. They"—he nodded at the cowering villagers across the way—"are too scared to resist, even when the children are in danger."

"And you?" Nate asked.

The boy raised his chin defiantly. "Sharla is my sister, Hatur my grandfather. The twins are my cousins. I can't stand by and do nothing. I don't trust the false words of the lowlander. Maybe he'll keep his word, but I gazed into the eyes of the woman, the eyes of a killer." He shuddered. Nate could relate to the boy's emotions, having been up close and personal too many times himself with the deadly priestesses of Huitlani. "I'll help in any way I can."

"Good lad." Nate patted him on the shoulder. "Now about this shortcut—"

The trail was nearly vertical. Nate was glad he'd had days of mountain-hiking conditioning already, or he might not have made it in time to have a chance at stopping the enemy's plans.

He clambered the last few yards to the small plateau designated as the Place of Meditation and found it deserted. A small, round, windowless stone hut sat midway across the open area.

Nate halted the others below the lip of the plateau, assessing the situation. Convinced they'd arrived first, he nodded to Thom. "Go for it. I'll cover you."

Thom, Daven and Bithia ran for the hut. Nate took off as soon as the last of them ducked inside, Thom covering him from the shelter of the doorway. Nate could hear the crying of the children as the captives and their guards approached slowly on the winding, ceremonial trail.

Nate leaned against the stone wall of the hut, regulating his breathing after the sprint at this altitude. "What do your people use this hut for?"

"When there's need to speak to the goddess, the selected children come here with Hatur and the other wisemen. The children are given the herbs and the wine and left to dream overnight, while the elders keep watch outside the hut. In the morning, the dreamers reveal their dreams to Hatur at dawn to interpret. It is said in the old days, the goddess would descend the mountain and speak to the headman herself, but now she only comes in the dreams." He stared at Bithia, as if realizing for the first time who she actually must be.

"Plan?" Thom asked. "Not much time here."

"I'm sorry, but it all depends on you," Nate said, addressing Bithia. "When the others get here, I need you to go out to Sarbordon, talk to him. Try to get the children away from that damn priestess with the itchy knife hand if you can. But the most important thing is, you have to lure him in here. Then I'm going to kill him. It's obvious this world will never be safe or at peace while he lives. And neither will we."

She regarded him gravely, her lavender-blue eyes serious and calm. "I understand. I need no further explanation." She leaned over and kissed him full on the lips with infinite tenderness. "Lolanta died by my hand. Sarbordon will die by yours. We'll be equally avenged for the wrongs done in my name, for the evil done to you and Thom and Haranda, and so many others."

"I love you," he answered, not caring that they had an audience. He was grateful for her serene acceptance of what must happen. "If there was any other option, I'd never risk you within reach of the bastard."

I love you as well, my warrior. "But there *is* no other choice, not if we're going to save the innocent lives," she said.

"He's here," Thom said in a low hiss.

The plateau was relatively small, maybe twenty yards across, jutting from the face of the mountain as if soldered onto the peak in the long-ago past. There was a straight drop-off down the mountain in most directions, except the way Nate had arrived, the way the ceremonial trail ran and in a third spot where a faint trail traced its way toward the summit many thousands of feet above.

As the enemy and their prisoners came into view, the elderly headman was laboring to breathe. Hatur fell to his knees as two soldiers shoved him onto the plateau. The priestess came behind with her string of potential victims. The ex-king and four other soldiers brought up the rear.

Disgust in every line of her face, Nanzin clutched her fur-lined, ebony cloak against the brisk wind. "What a pathetic shrine! So fitting for the powerless old gods. There isn't even an altar."

"I told you we don't sacrifice to the goddess." Hatur pleaded with the woman from his knees. "She won't come, no matter what you do. She manifests only in the dreams of the children after they take the sacred wine. We have none at this season—it isn't the solstice—so the little ones can't dream for you. Please, let the children go."

Nanzin laughed, sounding eerily like her mother. A chill ran down Nate's spine as he shoved away an unwanted flashback to Lolanta's ravaged face looming above him, knife ready to carve out his heart.

"I can manage without this wine you prattle of, without even a proper altar for that matter. Never fear, old man. And if my offerings don't motivate your goddess, spilt blood certainly appeases Huitlani. He'll force your goddess to appear."

"I've heard more than enough," Nate said. "Let's stop this before she gets really wound up. You ready?"

Bithia nodded, showing no trace of fear or nerves as she set aside her cloak and smoothed her tunic. Taking a deep breath, smiling fleetingly at Nate as she walked by him, Bithia stepped onto the plateau.

"I'm here, at your command. No need to talk of killing or sacrifice."

"T'naritza!" Sarbordon seemed transfixed by the sight of his obsession. He rubbed a shaking hand over his face, blinking as if she might disappear as quickly as she'd arrived. "You're here."

Smiling, she nodded. "You knew I would be, didn't you? You've passed the gods' test, and now you may claim the prize."

"Test? Prize?"

"Man doesn't think well on his feet, does he?" Thom muttered.

Patiently, Bithia led him through the logic of his "accomplishments."

"You survived the destruction my father visited on Nochen. You found me, fulfilling all the prophecies, so I'm yours to command."

"Grab her, and let's be gone," the priestess said.

"This is none of your concern." Contempt laced Bithia's voice. "This is between the great king and myself." She walked closer to him, swaying her hips seductively.

Nate's hand tightened on his blaster.

The lowland ruler appeared to be regaining mastery of his emotions. Nate counted on the man's belief in his own destiny as the progenitor of a new race of demigods. Licking his chapped lips, Sarbordon took a deep breath, eyeing her hungrily. "You know what I want of you, T'naritza. I told you enough times in Nochen, in the chamber when we were alone. Are you prepared to submit?"

"I must," she said, feigning surprise at the question. "You won the challenge of the gods. But the first time must be here, in this sacred place."

Uncertain, he evaluated the wind-swept plateau.

Bithia took his hand and gazed coyly into his eyes. "Not outside in the cold wind, my lord. Come to the privacy of my chamber in the meditation hut. I've prepared a wondrous place of magic for us to lie together."

He locked one thick hand in a choking grip at her neck. He shook his other hand loose from hers and grabbed her by the hair, yanking her close. "If this is a trick—"

"No trick," she answered calmly, despite his hold on her. "I've always been yours to command, even in Nochen. Remember? Nothing has changed. You can…fully command me now, here. In all ways. Nothing keeps us apart, save your own delays."

"Wait here," Sarbordon said over his shoulder to the guards.

Nanzin's protest was immediate. "But the sacrifices."

"No innocent blood must be shed in this place," Bithia said. "Send the children and the old man away. The hostages have served their purpose."

Frowning, the ruler addressed his priestess. "On no account are you to commence your rituals, do you hear me? Not until or unless I give the command personally."

She glared equally at him and at Bithia, apparently not liking being deprived of her prey, even momentarily. "What of her warriors? Why don't you ask her where the men are?"

"Damn," Nate and Thom swore in unison.

"Your mother killed them both," Bithia told Nanzin, eyes narrowed, her voice believably trembling like she was a woman in total anguish. "She spilled their blood on the altar, gave their hearts to Huitlani. I was too late to save them, but I killed her myself in revenge when I realized what she'd done. You wanted to be High Priestess of Huitlani? The title is all yours now."

Sarbordon and Nanzin recoiled in the face of Bithia's intensity, her palpable grief and fury. Nate admired her acting ability.

"The people at the farm said two men accompanied T'naritza." From the timid tone of Nanzin's reminder, she feared being struck with whatever power Bithia had used against Lolanta, but she was also unwilling to let go of her suspicions entirely.

"Men of my village." Hatur spoke, panting between words. "Sent for by the Lady when she decided to come home at long last. Daven and Harit, my grandsons. They're below, in the village. You can ask them yourselves whether they accompanied the Lady."

"We're wasting time," Bithia said, softening her voice and running her hand through Sarbordon's hair, smoothing the coarse strands from his face. "I've waited for so long for a man such as you to fulfill the prophecies." She took a step toward the hut.

He yanked her back by the neck. "No tricks, I warn you!"

Bithia tenderly caressed his cheek with her fingertips.

Knuckles white as he clutched his blaster, Nate ground his teeth.

"You've won, great king. There'll be no more resistance from me or my father's forces."

The ruler allowed Bithia to lead him across the plateau in the direction of the hut, her arm intimately placed at his waist. Nanzin glowered but subsided, going to stand by the guards. The children clustered beside Hatur, who murmured comforting words.

Bithia entered the hut first, by a step. Thom grabbed her forcibly away from Sarbordon and Nate shot at the ruler, intending to kill him out of sight of those on the plateau. Warned at the last second by some instinct, or inadvertent tensing in Bithia's frame, the dethroned king hesitated just enough so the bolt from Nate's blaster struck him a glancing blow on the right arm. Cursing, he retreated before Nate could get off a second shot. Blaster in hand, Nate chased the injured man, but his quarry was waiting as he exited the hut and launched himself at Nate's back, knife clenched in his good hand, trying to slash Nate across the throat. The two men fell onto the plateau, locked in combat.

Thom exited the hut door, blaster blazing, mowing down the row of Sarbordon's guards.

Nanzin flung herself at the children and snatched Sharla, using the girl as a shield.

"You won't kill her to get at me, will you?" she taunted Thom. "We have a standoff, yes?"

Dropping the blaster, Nate grabbed Sarbordon's knife hand and broke his grip on the weapon, elbowing his enemy in his unprotected rib cage and throwing him to the ground. Sarbordon kicked him in the left knee and rolled away, scrabbling to his feet as Nate retreated a step. He knew the despot had been schooled by hard years fighting battles all over lower Talonque, taking captives for the altars and defending his borders against the Githholz and others. Gossip in the sapiche training camp had said he'd survived more than one assassination attempt. He had his own well-honed skills. Nate wasn't allowing himself to underestimate this opponent, or his hatred for the man to cloud his judgment.

Nate and his opponent circled each other silently for a moment, then went at each other in another flurry of blows launched, parried, delivered with punishing force, twisting and turning on the plateau. Sarbordon tried to maneuver to where he could make a grab for a weapon, and Nate was determined to keep him from doing so.

Nate got in under the enemy's guard and snapped his neck with one well-aimed blow. The ruler was dead before he hit the ground.

Shifting his focus to his next challenge, Nate eyed Nanzin. "Put the child down."

Lolanta's daughter shook her head wordlessly, Sharla locked in her arms, and stepped backward.

Nate walked toward the pair. The priestess retreated farther.

"It's going to be all right," Nate told the girl quietly. "I won't let her hurt you, I promise."

Sharla took a deep, gulping breath, focused on his face and nodded. "You're my warrior."

Nanzin stopped at the plateau's crumbling edge, teetering over the abyss. Eyes wide and desperate, she glanced over her shoulder for a moment.

Taking advantage of her distraction, Nate lunged, ripping Sharla from Nanzin's grasp with enough force to tear the child's nightgown. The priestess, still clutching the torn fragment of fabric, plunged into the abyss. He heard her screaming as she fell, until the sound abruptly cut off.

Carrying Sharla carefully, Nate walked to Hatur. Daven had untied the children's wrists from the long cord and then had freed his grandfather. Nate kissed the child on the forehead. "I admire your bravery."

Hatur shrank away even as he took Sharla from Nate. "I've never witnessed such things as the battle you fought." He looked past Nate. "What is your will now, Goddess?"

"I defer to you," she said to Nate, coming to stand next to him.

Nate addressed his remarks to Thom. "Go offer the guards he left in the village a deal—surrender their weapons and leave the area, or the goddess will smite them. Judging by their sloppy discipline and how reluctantly the men took their orders, I expect the troopers'll be only too happy to escape. I don't want to shed any more blood today." Nate addressed that last remark to Bithia as if they were the only two people on the plateau. Then he flicked his gaze to Thom. "Bring our gear, and we'll be on our way. Sarbordon got in one good blow to my left knee. I can't make it up and down either trail to the village again, not if I'm also going to climb to Fr'taray's place today. While you're gone, I'll be figuring out some kind of knee brace."

Thom touched Bithia's elbow and nodded at Hatur, Daven and the children. "You'd best say something to them, ma'am, while I carry out my orders."

"Yes, of course." Bithia surveyed the plateau sadly and then addressed Hatur as Thom sprinted past them, taking the shortcut to the village. "I am sorry this place of peace has been desecrated by blood and death," Bithia said, her voice low and regretful. "My warriors and I won't be seen here again, once we've cleared the village of the other soldiers."

"Where will you go?" Daven asked.

"To my father's home on the mountain. I give you my blessings, if you'll accept them."

Hatur nodded, his dignity coming back slowly, his breathing easier. "Of course, Lady. You've done us no wrong, you and your warriors. I'll see the plateau is reconsecrated at the proper time, after you've gone. We'll give these men a proper burial also, whatever their sins were in life. We've been honored by your visit and your help in this dire situation. Our best wishes go with you." He gathered the children. "Come, little ones, let's get you to your parents, who must be anxious about you."

Bithia watched the group straggle off the plateau, following the easier ceremonial trail. Sharla lingered, with Daven waiting to escort her. Staring at Bithia, the child wasn't the least bit intimidated, only concerned for Nate. "Will my warrior be all right? Will you take care of him? He's courageous and strong."

"Yes, he is. I'll watch over him for you, all right?"

"Forever? You promise?" Brow furrowed, Sharla seemed serious beyond her years as she extracted the pledge.

"Yes, forever." Bithia treated the request with equal gravity.

Sharla ran to give her a hug and then skipped to take Daven's hand. He nodded at Bithia, and then they too were gone, leaving Nate and Bithia alone.

She tugged at his hand. "Come inside the hut and let me help you with your knee. I don't have any power left in the gilintrae, but at least I can provide moral support."

"When Thom gets here with our supplies, there'll be some painkillers in the medkit," Nate said. "Which will also help."

"Can you climb?" she asked, brow furrowed. "How badly did he injure you?"

"Let's find out. But we can't stay here—it's too exposed. I'm confident I can manage the trail, not too much farther, right?"

Staring at the mountain, Bithia nodded. "I can't believe how close I am after all this time."

CHAPTER THIRTEEN

The wind howled between the crags and crevasses as the afternoon progressed.

"Snow coming soon," Thom said, pausing in the middle of the trail and checking the gray skies to the west.

"We're nearly there," Bithia promised, glancing at the sergeant, who'd been trudging directly behind her on the narrow trail. "My father and I never took more than an hour as you measure your time to hike to the facility from the meditation place. Of course, we didn't make the trek in winter."

"Or with a bad knee," Nate said, leaning on the stick he'd fashioned into a cane. "I think I see our destination about a hundred yards ahead." He pointed up the mountain flank. "Looks like a flyer tunnel door to me. I'm sure glad we didn't have to climb all the way to the crater itself." He studied her face for a moment, trying to evaluate how tired she might be. "Should we take a break for a moment and rest? There's time. It isn't going to start snowing right now."

She laughed. "Get me this close to the place I've longed to be for countless centuries and then ask me if I want to rest? I can't believe you even suggested such a thing." She pushed past him on the trail and forged ahead.

"She'll wear herself out," Nate said to Thom as he climbed after her.

"No harm in a bit of overexertion as long as we can shelter inside this base for the night," Thom said reasonably. "Only a problem if we was planning to climb down the mountain today. How's the knee?"

"Doing all right. Nothing's broken. I managed to roll with the force. Come on, she's getting too far ahead of us, and she's not thinking about climbing safety today."

Nate finally caught up to Bithia when she stopped on a small ledge jutting out about two yards below the familiar massive flyer tunnel hatch. True to her promise, a small, one-person-sized door was set into the mountain below and to the right of the flyer entrance. The far side of the ledge, which in her time had provided easy access by foot, had crumbled away over the eons. This condition made progress tricky, requiring them to swing over to the smaller entry. Clambering inside once the door opened would be yet another challenge. Nate eyed the distances and the condition of the ledge and figured he and Thom could manage it and get her safely across too.

"Does this door respond to manual controls or only the gilintrae?" he asked, working the pack he'd been carrying off his shoulders and preparing himself for the next brief, but dangerous, stage of their journey.

A vivid set of symbols flashed into his head, taking him by surprise.

"It's faster than explaining out loud," she said, sinking onto a handy rock, apparently willing at last to rest.

"All right, no problem. I got out of the habit of receiving data directly. I can't see any other choice here but for one of us to crawl over and key in the symbols. I'll go, since we already know your skill set doesn't include actual mountain climbing, my lady."

"And I can't read the symbols," Thom said.

"Right, which leaves you to anchor me," he said to Thom, then pointed a finger at Bithia. "Stay well back in case the ledge crumbles any further under my weight."

"Can your knee take the pressure?" Thom asked as he got into position.

Nate shrugged. "It'll have to."

Once he'd linked by a safety rope to the sergeant, Nate climbed sideways across the mountain, going along a promising crevice in the rocks below the door and then managing to locate enough handholds and footholds to bring himself up the cliff to a point where he could steady himself beside the personnel entrance. Clinging with his right hand, toes of his boots dug firmly into the cracks in the cliff face, Nate activated the symbols left-handed.

For once on Talonque, an alien device responded promptly. The door unsealed with an audible hiss of escaping air and swung open with surprising force. Nate leaned over to peer inside.

"No lights," he said, raising his voice to be heard over the wind. "All clear in the passageway. No blockages as far as I can see. Time to get the lady on the safety line and transfer her over here."

The maneuver was delicate work, and as she'd told him several times, Bithia lacked even basic mountain-climbing skills. Sheer desire to reach her goal drove her to make the transition from the ledge to where Nate waited, hand extended to catch her when she'd gotten close enough. Once she was safely inside, Nate and Thom managed to get themselves and their gear transported across the small gap and into the unlit access tunnel.

Nate and Thom keyed the hand lamps they'd brought along from the *Murphy*, drew their Mark 27s, and the three proceeded cautiously through the echoing talmere-lined tunnel into the mountain.

"Odd that the lights aren't working for us," Bithia remarked at least twice as she proceeded.

"Probably not a good sign," Nate said. "Remember what we agreed about not having expectations."

Another door loomed at the opposite end of the tunnel. Bithia keyed the symbols with a happy exclamation, and this portal opened as easily as the outer one had. The trio stepped into the huge expanse of a flyer hangar, larger than the one at Nochen. Flashing his hand lamp from side to side, Nate saw one sizable vehicle parked crookedly at the far end of the space.

"They left a flyer," Bithia said excitedly as the beams of the lamps played over the shiny skin of the object.

"Probably for some compelling reason." Thom, as usual, refused to be too optimistic. "In for repairs maybe."

"Why aren't the lights coming on the way they did at the Nochen facility? I'm more concerned about illumination at the moment," Nate said. "This place is the same age as the Nochen facility, give or take a few months, right?"

Bithia nodded, barely visible in the beam of the lamp.

"We'd better check the pleikn chamber first," Nate said. "If the expedition shut the power source down, then we aren't going to be able to do much here beyond spending a night or two. I'd like to know now. Save the issue of the flyer's viability for later. If we can't depend on this place for a long-term home, then we'll want to expend our own resources differently."

"I agree." Taking his hand lamp, she led them unhesitatingly out of the flyer bay into another unlit corridor. The distance wasn't far to walk, but in the eerie gloom, breathing the stagnant air, it felt like forever to Nate before Bithia opened the next door, admitting them to a pleikn observation chamber. It was similar to the room at Nochen in design, but constructed on a bigger scale.

No blue power globe rotated on the other side of the crystal talmere shield.

Bithia stared in disbelief, flashing her lamp in all the corners. "Completely deactivated? I can't believe this. We had three pleikn to run this place, with three spares. Why would someone take away all six? And yet leave the one in Nochen?"

Nate wondered if her people left the one in Nochen because whoever was in charge knew it was unbalanced and would self-destruct, given enough time. It didn't square too well with what Bithia had said of her people, but then neither did their abandonment of her or the two corpses in the warehouse.

Thom's considerations appeared to be in a more practical vein. "Spares, ma'am? Where would extras have been kept? Did you have any kind of auxiliary power source?"

"Auxiliary?"

"For emergencies, for backup," he elaborated.

"There's a system to provide power for the setup team, from their first day of landing and establishment until the pleikn were brought in and placed into service, but then the initial system was no longer needed."

"Thom's asking if the original system is still available." Nate tried to bridge the momentary communication gap between his companions. "Or did your setup contractors take it with them when they completed their part of the job?"

"I imagine it must be here. Such things are not portable." Dubious, Bithia apparently clung to the idea of having full, glorious power supplied by the pleikn. "The spare pleikn would have been here." She flashed her hand lamp at the far corner, double-checking again that no containers of any type, much less power-generator shields, had escaped her first search.

"Show us the auxiliary?" Nate asked. He was patient with her, knowing this trip to the main base was more stressful for her than anything else since escaping from Nochen.

She exited the useless pleikn chamber, slamming the door angrily after Nate and Thom exited. She headed to the flyer bay. Crossing the broad expanse with rapid strides, almost reckless in the gloom, she stopped at a large panel of jeweled switches and symbols, inert and colorless. "This is the original system, or backup as you call it. Shall I try the activation sequence?"

"Nothing to lose—go ahead."

She handed Nate the lamp. "Point the light on the wall panel for me, please." She began the activation process. Gradually, as she played her graceful fingers across the gems, switches and symbols, the board came to colorful life. An encouraging hum emanated from the display.

Suddenly, there was a fat sparking snap, and many of the lights came on in the flyer bay. Not with the full brilliance Nate preferred, but at least bright enough to see without the hand lamps, which Nate and Thom snapped off.

"This is progress," Thom said.

"If you say so." Bithia clearly wasn't impressed. "I've no idea how long the power will last. We mustn't try to activate too many things, because the system was never designed to run the entire base."

"All right, you tell us, since this is your place, where to next?" Nate kept his tone amiable. He had no great expectations for this excursion, but he was interested in seeing whatever she wanted to show them.

"There are the storerooms. A spare pleikn might have been left there—"

Nate shook his head. "I doubt it. Any other priority choices? Your personal quarters maybe?"

Bithia gave him a reproachful look. "Remembering how my quarters at Nochen were handled, sealed with no attempt at preservation, I'm not eager to investigate the corridor here."

"Ma'am, the place we ought to be going is wherever you think your father might have left you a message," Thom said with a gentleness that was unusual for him. "Ain't that what you want to see, bottom line?"

She hung her head for a moment, toying with her gilintrae, rolling it around her wrist, then nodded. "Yes, you're right. I admit it."

"But?" Nate prompted. "You're afraid there may not be a message. Want us to go first, check his quarters or wherever we need to go, see what the conditions are?"

Bithia stood straighter. "No, but thank you. As you said about your trip to the warehouse, even if there was a message, you might not recognize it for what it is. I need to stop being foolish. If he left me a message, or anything at all, it'll be in the central control room where he had his workspace, where he loved to sit and direct all activities, talk to the researchers and the students about new finds and discoveries. That place was the hub of his existence on an expedition. The others—the ones who'd served with him in the field before—used to joke he could go for days at a time without leaving his chair in the central room, except for brief moments. He had to be in the middle of the activity, eating and sleeping there oftentimes. New discoveries were his passion."

"Lead the way." Nate stepped aside to let her pass. *I know this is hard for you.*

I appreciate your understanding. She sent him a warm flood of affection. *I'm scared of what we may find.*

Not moving as rapidly, she took them to the corridor outside the flyer bay and went to the left. A few yards down the hall, Bithia easily activated a door that opened onto a dark stairwell extending up as far as the beams of the lamps reached.

"More climbing." Thom stretched to unkink his back and grimaced.

"My aching knee," Nate said. "Getting a workout."

"Not all the way to the top." Bithia was already close to the first landing. "If the base power was on, we'd have a different way to go, antigravity assisted, but as things stand, stairs are the only option."

Trailing Bithia, Nate and Thom ascended three levels of darkened stairs, the backup lighting providing only sparse illumination in certain areas.

"Kinda warm in here, ain't it, for a place with no power?" Thom asked as he climbed the third set of stairs. He took off his big, fur-lined jacket and stuffed it sloppily into his pack.

"My father assigned one of the student teams to engineer a heating system using the volcano's magma chambers. The students were also to stabilize it, so the Sleeping Goddess couldn't erupt again. My father worried about the villages. So he had the team redirect the magma to another peak farther on into the range. There were no people at risk there, because the area is totally uninhabited. At least in my time." She chuckled. "Probably still is. The farther you go across the mountains, the more desolate the terrain becomes. I'll never understand how Sarbordon's people made it across."

"Probably something worse drove them," Nate said. "That's usually the case in a mass migration."

"My father was quite pleased with the results of the students' work."

Nate found it interesting how casually she discussed this achievement the Sectors technologists and engineers couldn't have duplicated. Drawing heat from the volcano's energy, perhaps, but not stabilizing the whole volcanic system to ensure eruptions would occur only where you wanted them to. Obviously, there was a lot to learn from this vanished civilization. "Would a report of relevant data be somewhere in the files here?"

"Of course. I told you my father's most precious possession on any expedition was the data he gathered. I hoped to find some extra data chips sized for my gilintrae while we were here, so I could try to preserve more of the expedition's records. Of course, I planned to recharge it too with the pleikn that unfortunately isn't here anymore." She laughed somewhat bitterly and stopped on the landing, although the stairs continued to wind as far as the eye could see in the gloom.

"The stairs take you to the crater," she said, pointing upward. "We used to go there sometimes to enjoy the crater lake, especially after the students heated it."

"The whole lake?"

"Yes. Something to do with geothermal exchanges. Not my area of expertise, sorry." She laughed. "Light over here, please. We need to open this door to access the central areas of the base."

Thom leaned over, pondering the gloom they'd climbed from. He stared upward next. "Gives me an uneasy feeling, all this darkness and empty, abandoned space."

Nate raised his eyebrows. "Getting sensitive in your old age?"

Thom didn't appear bothered by the good-natured teasing. "Don't seem right, such a big base, all deserted."

Nate had to admit he instinctively became more relaxed when he left the stairwell and heard the access door close snugly behind them. Bithia chose the left corridor again and headed off, her pace slowing as the corridor curved.

"After this curve the hall opens into the central area," she said, whispering as she paused.

Nate took her hand, giving it a reassuring squeeze. They strolled on, hand in hand, Thom following at their heels, until the area came into view.

There were two men standing in the middle of the alien control center.

Bithia gasped. Nate shoved her behind him with one hand, blaster in his other. Thom flattened against the opposite wall, his blaster at the ready.

With Thom guarding his six, Nate inched forward to peer around the curve. The two men stood in the exact same spot, staring at the corridor. *Both men have their eyes shut.*

"Holograms," Nate said. "I think we've found your message."

Her eyes widened, and she whispered something under her breath Nate couldn't catch. The next second, she darted past him, raced the last few yards to the edge of the nerve center and hopped down the three stairs into the well of the central area. She stopped a yard or so in front of the two holograms.

"My father," she murmured, voice choking on a sob as she stared at the person on the left. "I don't believe it. It truly is him." She reached out with one hand, then let it fall to her side before her touch could break the illusion that the real man stood waiting for her.

Nate followed more slowly, Thom at his back. Now he studied the representation of Fr'taray, who was taller than Bithia and had the same basic facial features, only he was the masculine version, heavier and older. The family relationship was glaringly obvious. His bearded face was peaceful, calm. His hair was the same dark blue and purple as hers, brushing the gemmed collar of his dark blue one-piece garment. He appeared poised to walk away but looked like he wanted to tell them something first, as if he'd waited to impart vital information that only he could reveal. Nate hoped for Bithia's sake that the subliminal impression was true.

"Who's the other guy?"

Bithia shook her head, reluctantly taking her gaze from her father's face to focus on the companion hologram. "I never met him. He wasn't on our expedition—oh!" She glanced at her wrist, where the heavy gold identification bracelet set with red and purple gemstones rode loosely. "See? It's his. He's M'negel." She held her arm close to the arm of the hologram, and Nate realized the bracelets were identical.

It bothered him to be viewing a lifelike hologram of a man who'd ended up a dead, burnt corpse in Nochen sometime after leaving this message, whatever it might contain. And it bothered Nate to be bothered. Excess imagination wasn't one of his standard problems on a mission. *This isn't exactly a mission anymore, and we've never been sent to explore a millennia-old, abandoned alien facility either.* He took a deep breath and studied the second hologram's face, trying to suppress the image of the man as an ashy corpse clutching the red box.

"You never heard of him? No one ever mentioned his name?"

Bithia shook her head again. Tiring of the subject of the unknown M'negel, she walked to the nearest console and started flipping gemmed levers, pushing symbols in a deliberate sequence.

"Do you want us to step outside so you can hear the message in private?" Nate asked.

She shook her head emphatically and stopped what she was doing to respond. "It can only be played once and will be gone. I want the two of you to hear it with me."

"Only once? An inefficient idea," Thom said. "What if the contents got played by accident somehow?"

"Originally, it would have been set for infinite replay. But once those in charge took the pleikn out, then this device also has a finite auxiliary power, as you call it. We're seeing the images because the power's drained to the last level. The device displays the image of what is contained as a warning to take action or lose the data. Or so I've been told. I never heard of it actually occurring before. It would take eons for the power to drain away." She stopped and grimaced at what she'd just said. "I guess I must be glad enough power remains to display the image and play the message once."

Thumbnail lecture on holographic-messaging technology over, she turned to the controls. "Here we go. Listen carefully."

Nate stopped her. "Wait. We aren't going to understand it, are we? I mean, neither of these guys speaks Basic."

"Neither do I, you know." She seemed amused at the idea. "You didn't realize? You and Thom hear me in your own language because of the way I speak and project to you mind to mind simultaneously. I'll project to you what I hear my father say, translated to a format your minds can understand."

"Even me?" Eyes wide and mouth gaping in astonishment, Thom rubbed his head. "I tested negative on any test for latent psionic abilities."

"I guess the lady has more than enough for the three of us," Nate said. He flipped a mental switch, activating a top-secret, special data-recording implant of his own. There might never be a way to play it, if he didn't make it home, but at least there'd be a chance. She'd tried to save the course home for him, and he was going to try to save her father's last message for her. "Whenever you're ready."

"Now."

She flipped over a sapphire triangle on the far left corner of the board.

Her father took a breath and opened his eyes, gazing straight ahead. For the space of a few heartbeats, he said nothing, apparently mulling over what he wanted to say. Nate could hear subdued noises, as if other people were talking, coming and going in the same space where they now stood. It was eerie and unsettling. He caught himself checking the perimeter for the people making the sounds. The deep voice of Fr'taray brought his attention sharply to the hologram.

"Bithia, I'm leaving this message for you just in case. I'm not actually sure why, but something odd is going on back home, and I don't like the feel of it. We've been urgently recalled. All the expeditions in this quadrant have been summoned, the research canceled. I believe it may be a total recall, everywhere. I don't know." He ran a hand over his face, his expression more tired than serene now. "Definitely one of the things I intend to find out. Whatever it is, it's totally unprecedented in my career."

And he doesn't much like it. Used to giving orders, not taking them.

"I requested a three-day delay so you could come with us and was refused in no uncertain terms, even when I sent more detail. I sent a private message to the representative of our expedition's sponsor, which went unanswered. An affront which has never happened, not to *me*."

Now Nate could tell he was annoyed. Maybe even a little worried.

Fr'taray went on, "There isn't time to try again or to contact anyone else. We're leaving within moments. Two of the transport flyers have lifted off already—" He glanced to the side of the room. Involuntarily, Nate looked the same direction. "The official in charge will be in here again any moment, glaring at me for delaying the departure schedule, so I must be brief. I've given Hialar strict instructions not to let you out of the healing chamber under any circumstances until I can oversee your release personally. I'm sorry, daughter, but whatever is going on, at least I know you'll be perfectly safe and protected within the chamber for however long it takes me to straighten them out at home and return here." He rubbed his forehead and forced a smile. "You won't even miss me, being asleep of course. Anyway, beloved child, hopefully we can celebrate your day of birth and the Festival of the Red Moons together as we'd planned, with Hialar and Frantlia and her famous six-spice cakes. I should be back by then. This message is…is—I don't know—ridiculously unnecessary. I should erase it." The figure leaned forward impatiently, as if to toggle the same switch Bithia had been manipulating. She moved, eyes locked on the face of the hologram. "But, on the other hand, it's for you only. You won't laugh too much at the foolishness of your fond old father, will you? It's just, this is all so odd."

And with that, the figure of Fr'taray winked out.

Bithia screamed from the bottom of her heart, as if the real man had perished in front of her eyes, instead of his last message erasing itself. "No!" She collapsed in a heap to the floor.

Cursing himself for not anticipating the depth of her distress, Nate rushed to her, kneeling to enfold her in his arms. She'd come apart, weeping hysterical tears as if she'd never be able to stop. He murmured soothing things in her ear, stroked her hair, tried everything he knew to be gentle and calming.

Thom, ever practical, removed his pack and dug through the contents for the medkit in case a tranquilizer inject became necessary.

Nate picked Bithia up and took her to an oversized, heavily cushioned gray and blue chair pushed back at an angle from the console. *Wonder if this was the chair she said her father favored on these expeditions?* Dismissing the fleeting thought as a distraction he didn't need and she wouldn't appreciate, Nate sat with her in his lap, curled against his chest, sobbing. Her whole body shook and convulsed with the force of her grief. It tore at the heart to hear, even for such a hardened veteran as he was. Nate frowned over her head at Thom and shook his head at the inject. He felt he should endure her storm of emotion, let her express the anguish and sorrow, not try to dull it with medication. She'd waited thousands of years for this moment. He could offer a few moments of silent comfort.

Eventually, to Nate's relief, her weeping became less wild, the sobs softer.

"Sweetheart, at least you got to see him, to hear he was thinking of you, he loved you. And now you know the Hialar didn't play a cruel trick on you all these centuries. The clan was obeying your father's last request to keep you safe. He must have loved you very much."

"Yeah, you could tell," Thom said gruffly. "Listening to how many times he questioned his orders and tried to get a break on going without you tells you the truth."

"But I'll never know—"

"Until five minutes ago, you were sure you'd never see him again, never hear his voice, never know why he left you behind, okay? I think you have to take what the Lords of Space gave and not ask for more." Nate ruthlessly cut off her beginning protest, sad for her pain but firm in his belief. There was silence for a moment or two, other than Bithia's occasional sobs diminishing in intensity, mixed with hiccups. Thom put away the inject and got out his canteen instead, offering it to Nate.

He handed it to Bithia. "Here, sweetheart, try a little water. We have one last piece of the story to uncover when you're ready to deal with it."

"What do you mean?" she asked, choking slightly on a residual hiccup as she sipped the water. She handed the canteen directly to Thom. Nate wiped a drop of water off her chin with one gentle fingertip, smiling. "That other guy is waiting to tell us something, isn't he? And he obviously came after your father left, so he might shed more light on events."

"Or he might not," Bithia said. "But you're right, we may as well hear all there is to know."

She unfolded herself from his lap, straightened her tunic and walked to the console. She hesitated. "My hands are shaking. Will you help me with this?"

"Of course." He came to her swiftly, kissing her cheek and taking one trembling hand firmly in his own warm grasp. "Tell me what to do."

A mental picture, three levers in a row, ending with the sapphire one. Nate reached out and executed the required sequence.

M'negel opened his eyes, studying the room curiously. "So strange to be here after all this time, after hearing Great-Great-Great-Uncle Tedesk's stories."

"Tedesk was my father's number one assistant," Bithia whispered.

In the next breath, M'negel turned his head in their direction as if he'd heard her whispering. "Ridiculous as it may sound, the uncles said that if I ever came here, I had to leave her a message. Excuse me, leave *you* a message, Bithia, daughter of Fr'taray." He executed a formal kind of bow, making a hand gesture almost like a salute. "As if you'll ever hear this message." His high-pitched and abrupt laugh was jarring. "Maybe I ought to start over, you think?"

He was asking some impatient companion there in his own time. The hairs on the back of Nate's neck rose. Was M'negel talking to the person who murdered him later in the warehouse? "All right, I know we have to hurry. It's just every time I heard the story, the uncles emphasized over and over the necessity of leaving her a message in case the extraction attempt fails. Bithia, we're going to Nochen to get you out, to take you home, even though you're not going to recognize it, or us!" He laughed again, an odd laugh, mocking rather than amused.

Nate was suddenly glad these people had failed in their attempt to rescue his lady. Something about this M'negel's attitude bothered him, completely separate from the knowledge of how the man had died.

"If you ever get this message, it probably means I failed somehow, or else the authorities came and stopped us. Some people don't think the daughter of Fr'taray should be brought back, into the mess things have become. You're a symbol of what was, our better days. So if you're hearing this because I got caught, I have to tell you I left my ship on the second of those pretty red moons. You can take my flyer to find it, if they don't take the flyer with them or disable it. I bequeath you my flyer and my ship," he said grandiosely, making a sweeping gesture with both hands. "But they won't find my ship, I can promise you. And as a precaution, I didn't leave the coordinates on the flyer. I'm too good at games after all these years of hide-and-seek with the enemy. The coordinates are—"

Suddenly, a vivid, burning flash of pain struck deep inside Nate's head, seeming to brand onto his optic nerves a string of numbers he simultaneously perceived as visible points in space. He groaned, putting both hands to his aching forehead, blinking back involuntary tears of pain.

He could hear M'negel concluding his remarks, "We're going now. I hope you never see this ridiculous message, because I hope to take you home in triumph. But I did what the uncle and his wrinkled cronies told me to. All right, all right, I'm coming!"

And he winked out of existence.

The three were silent for a moment.

"Odd from beginning to end," Bithia commented at last, tilting her head to the side and considering what she'd heard. "I can't say it explained much."

"He sounded drunk," Thom said. "Or high."

"Nate, are you okay?" Bithia asked with sudden concern, seeing him rubbing his temples, eyes screwed tightly shut. "What happened?"

"When he gave the coordinates for his ship, he sent them mentally too, the way you transmit instructions. Only you're about a thousand times more subtle, I'm glad to say. Didn't you get them?" Nate was amazed. He tried opening his eyes and promptly clamped them shut again, unable to handle the electric whorls and jagged lines obscuring his sight.

"What coordinates?" She stared at him. "The holo was interrupted, nothing but ripples and static. He didn't say anything for a moment."

"Well, he sure as hell thought it."

"May I look? If he left a ship, and if it's still there—"

Gesturing for her to come closer, Nate kept his eyes closed. "Be my guest. Read my mind. And if you can make it stop hurting so damn much and interfering with my vision, I'll be grateful."

Bithia moved his hands aside and rested her fingertips gently on his temples where he'd been rubbing. Nate kept his eyes closed. He had trouble keeping his balance and swayed a little, Bithia moving in time with him but keeping her eyes shut in deep concentration. Thom came to them, spreading his arms like wings to embrace their shoulders and hold them steady.

"Whatever you're doing helps," Nate said. "My head doesn't hurt so much. But the numbers, or coordinates, or whatever the data is, are fading. I can't see them anymore. And I don't remember them. He didn't manage to get them into my memory, just screwed up in my visual circuits."

"It's all right, I've got them," she announced with suppressed excitement in her voice. She took her hands away from Nate's face, opened her eyes and did a dance step. "M'negel left us the coordinates to his ship! To his interstellar ship!"

"But is it still there? Does it have room for three people? Would the ship be functional after all these centuries? And how do we get there from here?" Thom asked rapid-fire questions, ending with his final concern: "Can you pilot it?"

"The flyer in the hangar bay must be his," Nate said, trying to deal with the issues. He gingerly opened and closed his eyes a few times, much relieved to have his normal vision restored. "Step one is to check the vessel out, see if it has power. This is definitely a time to go slow and not get our hopes too high. After all, someone not from Talonque murdered M'negel and another person in the warehouse. The killers may have sabotaged his flyer or his ship or both. He seemed apprehensive, didn't he?"

"Yeah, kept talking as if his being here searching for you violated the rules," Thom said to Bithia.

"I wonder why Tedesk of all people would make his descendants promise anything to do with rescuing me? Perhaps there was a reward?" Bithia pondered, sinking into the chair she and Nate occupied earlier. "Of all the people on the expedition, he and I didn't get along."

"I remember you telling me the first time or so we dreamed together," Nate agreed. "I'm sorry we didn't find out anything else about your father."

She stared at the floor. When she spoke, her voice was so quiet he had to lean close to hear her. "I think I prefer this outcome. I think you're right, your—what do you call them? The Lords of Space? Granted me enough grace to hear my last message from my father, but not to know the rest." Then she did look at him. "Did you hear M'negel talk about years of dealing with some enemy?"

"I'm sorry he, and his companions, whoever they were, died in the attempt, but I have to tell you I'm glad he failed to rescue you." Nate shared with her what he had been thinking as M'negel talked. "Not only because I wouldn't have met you, but there was something off about him, about the whole deal—"

She nodded her agreement. "He reminded me of Tedesk, who wasn't a pleasant person. The longer he talked, the more I detected a family relationship. Clearly, M'negel had something to gain from this rescue attempt, a reward perhaps."

Thom, who'd been leaning against the hologram console, straightened decisively. "Ready for the flyer?"

"Let's check it out," Nate said. "Unless you want to rest a bit longer? Or did you want to check the personal quarters first? You said the area was off this level, right? See if your stuff is here, or if your father left anything you want to take with us?"

"No, let's get on with it. As you say, the flyer is the next step, and it may lead us to escaping this planet." She held up a hand to forestall the warning Nate was about to utter. "Yes, I know, one step at a time, your favorite approach."

"What about searching your quarters?"

"I don't want anything from the old life. Even if my father put the whole thing under stasis lock and it's there perfectly preserved and waiting, I don't want it."

"No jewelry, clothes, books, pictures of your parents? Nothing?"

She shook her head again, even more definitively. "We've been all through the discussion. I appreciate what you're doing, presenting the counterarguments, but I've thought my decision through. Now, can we go?"

Nate stood aside and made a sweeping gesture. "After you, my lady. No more arguments from me."

Nate realized the lighting wasn't as strong as they descended the endless stairs and made their way as rapidly as possible to the hangar.

"Auxiliary running down fast, you think?" Thom speculated as they crossed the vast expanse of the hangar floor to investigate the flyer.

"Yeah. I don't want to stay here in the dark, do you?"

Thom shook his head emphatically. "I'd prefer the snowstorm brewing outside if I didn't know we'd freeze to death inside of five minutes."

Nate studied the flyer for a few moments, walking around it. It had been parked haphazardly, one winglike projection nearly touching the wall.

"As if it was shoved out of the way of something bigger," Nate said. "How do we get inside? I don't think my Special Forces override code is going to be much help here."

Bithia smiled absently. "No, this is my job. This craft is similar to the ones we had on the expedition, but larger." She tried one combination of symbols on the single small, jeweled panel she located on the flyer's smooth exterior. Nothing happened.

Bithia frowned. "He didn't say anything about it being locked, or ID sealed—" She broke off, her eyes growing wide. "That's it—the ID bracelet! Thank goodness you brought it with you from the warehouse, because it has to be the key."

"How'd he expect you to get in without it?" Nate said. "He obviously didn't think things through too well."

"Or he truly didn't believe he'd fail," Thom added.

She tried the control panel again, this time holding her arm to the symbols, laying the red and purple gemstones across them as tightly as she could make it fit. There was a chiming noise from inside the flyer. Nate drew her out of the way as a portion of the hull unfolded into a ramp. Bright light shone from inside, inviting them to proceed.

Bithia exchanged looks with her companions. "A good sign certainly. Almost as if this flyer has a pleikn."

"I remember you telling me pleikn don't come this small?" Nate said.

"Scientists were working on a smaller version in my day. M'negel apparently came from somewhere in the future as it relates to my personal life, but in the long-ago past now." She smiled, shaking her head. "These concepts of time! I think I'll just be one of you, speaking in your present tense and refer to my people as the Ancient Observers from now on—it's easier for me to adopt your frame of reference for galactic history. Anyway, let's go find out if the AO of M'negel's day had miniaturized pleikn, shall we?"

Nate stopped her gently. "I'll go first." He drew his Mark 27. "Any likelihood of booby traps? Self-defense weapons?"

"I hope not. But after all his talk about the enemy and the mysterious 'they' who wouldn't like him being here on Talonque, I can't promise."

"Not to mention the fact he was murdered," Thom said. "A little caution is a good thing."

Despite their concerns, the flyer was perfectly harmless, even welcoming. Nate stepped into a uniformly open space. Four seats were located around the rim of the flyer's oval interior, a fifth in the center. A control console bearing the ubiquitous symbols was set into the arm of the central chair. A closed hatch with one large symbol surrounded by a ring of smaller ones was located at the flyer's "tail" end.

Bithia was tremendously excited. "See?" she said, pointing at the hatch door. Walking over to touch the symbols, she told them, "It's a warning, a do-not-open instruction. This ship is pleikn-powered, which means I can recharge my gilintrae, we can get the coordinates of your Sectors from its memory—"

"One step at a time, lady," Nate reminded her. "I know I sound like a broken message, but we can't get our hopes too high yet. M'negel's spaceship may not be where he said he left it, you know."

"Let's find out." She sat in the control chair, beginning to flip gemmed switches even before she'd fully settled into the seat. The flyer hummed, and a display holo appeared in midair in front of each chair. The view was curiously obscured, as if by blowing snow.

Nate realized it truly was snow, not interference nor a malfunction. The flyer's screens were showing the blizzard currently raging outside the shelter of the mountain base. *Weather patterns must have changed somewhat in the thousands of years since she was here, since she wasn't expecting storm season so early.*

Bithia hummed, in tune with the ship, working the console. On the viewscreens, the snowstorm cleared away, changing to a dizzying series of images taking them off the planet and out into space. Nate saw the three moons, orbiting in their tight formation. Even before he could fully register the moons' presence on the screens, the device homed in on the second of the celestial satellites. Suddenly, the view converted from reality to a contoured grid map outlining the moon's terrain in blazing purple and red. A green dot winked insistently in the center.

"It's there, and it's talking to the flyer." Bithia pointed at a small stream of symbols scrolling rapid-fire across the bottom of the contour map. "See? This is the data feed from the spaceship and our responses, our commands. It's powering up now. By the time we get there, atmosphere and life-support functions will be fully engaged."

"Power?" Nate liked the sound of that. "Will it have the power to go into hyperspace?" Now he too began to have trouble reining in his excitement. He wanted to get off Talonque and go home to his own civilization. The desire to be free and clear, and done with this mission, was too strong to hold back now that it finally appeared there might actually be a way to accomplish the journey.

Bithia watched the symbol stream for a long moment, the two men watching her with bated breath. She finally nodded. "According to this, the power plant is intact and balanced. We won't be exploring your Sectors with an unbalanced pleikn under our feet."

She poised her hand above the controls. "Shall we go? Are you as ready to be done with Talonque as I am?"

Nate didn't answer immediately. "I think we need to make some preparations first."

"Like?" Bithia's tone was challenging.

"Recharge your gilintrae, for one thing. Test the hangar doors. They may not open under just the auxiliary power available. We may have to blast them open."

"Good point." Thom nodded. "I'm not real excited about spending any more time here in the facility than necessary, since there's a chance we can make a good attempt at going home, courtesy of M'negel."

"Let me recharge the gilintrae," she said. "What you said about the hangar doors makes sense."

"You know what? Let's eat," Thom proposed. "You recharge the fancy bracelet, and we'll have some of these sandwich things Hatur's youngest daughter fixed for us while I was in the village getting our gear. A little wine maybe, to celebrate finding this flyer?"

"Excellent idea," Nate said. "Break out the provisions."

Bithia unclasped her device and set it straight up in a receptacle on the side of the control console she had been operating. Immediately, the entire length of the heavy bracelet glowed, sparks of light sizzling from the round bezel.

The three of them enjoyed a quiet picnic, sitting in the flyer, not talking much, certainly not lingering over the food, good though it was. After savoring a last swallow of wine, Nate asked Thom, "You ready to check out the tunnel doors?" He turned to Bithia. "Flying through a blizzard won't bother this ship, I'm assuming?"

"It should be fine. I used to fly ours through the worst storms with no problem, and we were running on charges, not the direct pleikn. Let me fasten the gilintrae on my wrist where it belongs, so I can activate the tunnel doors. I hope the facility's auxiliary power will be enough to work the mechanism."

"We can blow them out if we have to," Nate said as he walked out of the flyer and started across the hangar. "We brought along a few other nasty surprises from the *Murphy* besides the blasters."

"If we wanted to spend the time, we might be able to reroute all the auxiliary power to the doors," Thom commented. "Less drastic than blowing them. Don't want to leave this place open to the elements, do we? Might want to come back someday."

"Not in my worst nightmares," Bithia vowed. "I never want to visit Talonque under any circumstances."

"We haven't left yet, so let's don't get ahead of ourselves." Nate studied the huge, heavy round door before narrowing his eyes and staring across the hangar at the flyer. He whistled. "M'negel must have been some pilot. There's barely room for his big flyer to get through this hatch. Probably only a few feet of clearance altogether."

"If he could do it, I can do it," Bithia said. "You're blessed to have the number one pilot in her class at your disposal. Everyone on the expedition, even my father, wanted me to be their pilot when they needed to get someplace. I have hundreds of hours of flight time on Talonque, at home—"

"I believe you." Nate held up his hand to forestall her semi-indignant recitation of her flying credentials. "I'm glad to hear it, since neither Thom nor I have any flight time on this type of ship. You'll teach us, won't you?"

"Of course." She nodded. "But I have to warn you, I'm not a patient instructor. I like to get in and fly."

"Duly noted. Let's do the doors and go, then."

She raised her gilintrae and flicked the proper gems and disks into action with tiny taps from her nails. Obligingly, if slowly, the massive portal in front of them began ratcheting into the open position. Nate held his breath, remembering how stubborn the one at the Nochen tunnel had been, as it ground its way from fully closed to fully open. But this door was fully functional, and the locking mechanism thudded into place with a loud, satisfying click.

"I guess I'm not going to worry about this baby falling on us in midflight." Nate sighed with relief after watching the now motionless door stay securely in the open position for another moment. "Shall we?"

A few moments later, they were back inside the now sealed flyer. Bithia sat confidently at the controls, vehicle hovering at her command a yard off the talmere floor of the hangar and slowly edging toward the tunnel entrance.

"What about the door at the other end?" Thom asked.

"Triggered automatically by the approaching flyer," Bithia said. "I'll take it slow so if the expected doesn't occur, we won't crash. I can set down in the tunnel if need be, and we can get out and assess the best way to open the outer door should it not open on its own."

"Let the lady concentrate," Nate said. "She hasn't done this in a while."

"My reflexes are good. The healing device had protocols to maintain flexibility and viability of muscle and tendon tissues." Bithia flew the flyer into the tunnel as neatly as she'd boasted she could, not even brushing the sides. In one viewer Nate watched the tunnel door closing behind them, while ahead the other opened with pleasing synchronicity. Bithia increased their speed and fairly burst out of the tunnel into the blizzard, going vertical the instant she cleared the mountain overhang. Rejoicing in the freedom of the skies, and the responsive power of the flyer, Bithia flew them free of Talonque's atmosphere at the best speed the flyer could attain.

Shortly thereafter, they arrived in orbit around the second red moon. Bithia set the flyer for cruising speed and slowly skimmed the pockmarked terrain, following the beacon on the contour map.

"There it is," she cried, pointing at the viewscreen on the left side of the cabin. Nate and Thom rose from their chairs to watch intently as she flew a course to dock with M'negel's spacer. As the flyer homed in, a circular hatch opened in the side of the ship. In the next breath, Bithia brought their craft to a smooth landing inside the tight confines of a hangar deck.

"Well?" Eyebrows raised, one arm looped over the back of the pilot's chair, she was brash and challenging.

"You're one hell of a flyer pilot," Nate said. "Can you fly a spaceship?"

"Never satisfied, are you?" she teased. "With the help of the ship itself. We have something similar to your AI."

"We really are going home," Thom said as if this was the first time he had actually permitted himself to believe it.

Leaving the flyer in its bay, Nate and the others ascended one short flight of lightweight steps to the combination passenger area and flight deck. This ship had room for six people, judging by the number of seats. Bithia ran a quick check of the systems, informing Nate and Thom the ship had plenty of air, facilities for water and food stocks. "Although you may not like our space rations, the nutrients will keep you alive."

"No problem, believe me. If I could eat red mush in the Nochen prison day in and day out for breakfast, I can stomach your space rations," Nate said.

"I'll feed in the coordinates and information I got from your AI now." She turned a suddenly serious face to her companions. "This is the make-or-break moment, I must tell you. My gilintrae could take in the data from your AI, but I'm not sure it can do the translation to a format this ship requires."

"Well, let's try it," Nate said. "Nothing to lose now."

"Ma'am, does this ship carry weapons?" Thom asked. "Can you tell?"

Bithia frowned and ran a diagnostic inquiry separate from the operation ongoing between the ship and her gilintrae's memory. "It possesses a weapon system. I don't know about such things. But yes, there is definitely an offensive capability."

"We can figure weaponry out later," Nate told the sergeant. "It's good to know, though. When we left the vicinity of the blue giant star, there was a whole armada of Mawreg client warships passing through. I'm hoping the enemy ships will be long gone by now, but reassuring to know we could shoot back with something."

"Yeah," Thom said. "But if the ship's weapons are like the Mark Ones we acquired in the warehouse, I'm not sure how much good the ordnance'll do against Mawreg artillery."

"Better than nothing." Nate was charitable. "Those Mark Ones saved us a few times over."

A musical note signified the end of the data transfer between gilintrae and ship, ending their debate about armament.

"Indications are the ship's memory accepted all the information." Bithia leaned closely over the main viewscreen and scrutinized the symbol stream. "Are you ready? Shall we take to deep space and go find your blue giant star?"

"Take us home." Nate savored the sound of the command, knowing she could carry it out and they'd be in the Sectors, no longer condemned to life on the savage planet Talonque.

She maneuvered the spaceship away from the second red moon's surface, swinging easily past the third moon as it orbited into range. Increasing speed, Bithia directed their new ship out of the Talonque solar system. The large, hot star grew smaller and more insignificant in the aft viewer with each passing moment.

Bithia issued a cautionary statement, keeping her eyes on the viewscreen and the controls. "Hang on. I don't know how our hyperspace will affect you, but it makes me dizzy for the space of three breaths, then there's a flash of hot light, followed by a breath of bone cold, and then we'll be there. We'll know if the directions took or not."

No one spoke as the ship powered up, increasing its speed through space and gathering resources to make the programmed jump through the set of hyperspace nexi. There was a sudden overpowering pressure, the flash of light and heat, as Bithia had promised, followed by an instant of bone-chilling cold. Then silence and an end to motion.

The ship floated in space, the viewscreens indicating they'd tucked neatly into orbit at a safe distance from a big blue star. The star where the journey had begun so many months ago for Nate and Thom and their less-fortunate companions.

"No other ships of any kind in the vicinity," Bithia said, concentrating on her duties as pilot.

Elated, Nate swung Bithia out of the command chair and into a giant hug, kissing her soundly, Thom hugging both of them in his excitement.

"Welcome to the Sectors! Welcome to your new home." Nate felt drunk with relief and happiness.

"I'd be at home wherever you are," she said simply. "Do you want me to instruct the ship to make the next jump in the journey your own ship would have taken?"

"No, let me see the star maps you got from the *Murphy*. I don't want to go to Starbase Twelve. Not with you, not with this ship. There's a certain old friend I have to hunt down by the name of D'Aloun." Nate grinned at Thom over Bithia's shoulder. "I think you'll like him. He'll be somewhere in the Seventh Sector, I imagine. He holds the key to our future, and your expertise is something he'll want access to very much. I'll explain as we go."

And, shortly, they went.

***

Thank you for reading *Trapped on Talonque*! I hope you enjoyed it. If you did, please help other readers find this book:

1. This book is lendable, so send it to a friend who you think might like it so he or she can discover me, too.
2. Help other people find this book by writing a review.
3. Sign up for my new releases e-mail http://wordpress.us7.list-manage1. com/subscribe?u=2a337b96e2ee1ee1250004b9d&id=7462393c9eso you can find out about the next book as soon as it's available.
4. Follow me on twitter @vscottheauthor
5. Come like my Facebook page: https://www.facebook.com/pages/ Veronica-Scott/177217415659637?ref=hl

ABOUT THE AUTHOR

Best Selling Science Fiction & Paranormal Romance author and "SciFi Encounters" columnist for the USA Today Happily Ever After blog, Veronica Scott grew up in a house with a library as its heart. Dad loved science fiction, Mom loved ancient history and Veronica thought there needed to be more romance in everything. When she ran out of books to read, she started writing her own stories.

Veronica's life has taken many twists and turns, but she always makes time to keep reading and writing. Everything is good source material for the next novel or the one after that, right? She's been through earthquakes, tornadoes and near death experiences…Always more stories to tell, new adventures to experience—Veronica's personal motto is, "Never boring."

Veronica is a three time winner of the SFR Galaxy Award and a National Excellence in Romance Fiction Award.

Played Star Trek Enterprise Crew Member in the audiobook of Harlan Ellison's "City On the Edge of Forever" (2016)

She's the proud recipient of a NASA Exceptional Service Medal but must hasten to add the honor was not for her romantic fiction!

Blog: http://veronicascott.wordpress.com/
Email: veronica.scott.author@gmail.com

VERONICA'S OTHER TITLES

www.ingramcontent.com/pod-product-compliance
Lightning Source LLC
Chambersburg PA
CBHW070220260626
47160CB00002B/610